If anyone had asked me that morning how my life was going, I would have told them I was doing good. I'd had a five-million-dollar year in real estate sales, I'd just finished remodeling our impressive five-bedroom Italianate home in the exclusive Cambridge Heights neighborhood and my bright and beautiful daughter, Brynn, was in her second year at college back east.

Of course, things were not perfect.

David, my husband, was having his little "affair" with that tacky, blond, twentysomething hairstylist. It was so typical and such a cliché.

And Brynn was seeing a highly reputable and expensive therapist twice a week. Dr. Reiser felt it would be counterproductive for her to take time away from school and her sessions with him to visit her parents. I missed her.

So it wasn't as if I was living in a fairy tale, but I thought I was doing good.

"Her books capture a certain sweetness grounded in human fallibility that is utterly charming."
—*Miami Herald*

*Watch for Pamela Morsi's newest novel*

COURTING WISDOM

*Coming February 2003*
*Only from MIRA Books*

# PAMELA MORSI

## Doing Good

**MIRA®**

**MIRA**

ISBN 1-55166-884-X

DOING GOOD

Copyright © 2002 by Pamela Morsi.

All rights reserved. Except for use in any review, the reproduction or
utilization of this work in whole or in part in any form by any electronic,
mechanical or other means, now known or hereafter invented, including
xerography, photocopying and recording, or in any information storage or
retrieval system, is forbidden without the written permission of the publisher,
MIRA Books, 225 Duncan Mill Road, Don Mills, Ontario, Canada M3B 3K9.

All characters in this book have no existence outside the imagination of the
author and have no relation whatsoever to anyone bearing the same name
or names. They are not even distantly inspired by any individual known or
unknown to the author, and all incidents are pure invention.

MIRA and the Star Colophon are trademarks used under license and registered
in Australia, New Zealand, Philippines, United States Patent and Trademark
Office and in other countries.

Visit us at www.mirabooks.com

**Printed in U.S.A.**

For Tamer Morsi
who, despite my years of parenting,
has turned out well.

An honorable man, exceptional father
and a fine lawyer.
I am so proud to call you my son.

# 1

If anyone had asked me that morning how my life was going, I would have told them that I was doing good. I'd had a five-million-dollar year in real estate sales, much to the chagrin of some of my less ambitious colleagues. I'd just finished remodeling our impressive five-bedroom Italianate in the exclusive Cambridge Heights neighborhood. I chaired the Corporate Development Committee for the Junior League. And my bright and beautiful daughter, Brynn, was in her second year at college back East.

Of course, things were not perfect.

David, my husband, was having his little "affair" with that tacky, blond, twenty-something hairstylist. It was so typical and such a cliché.

I, though still dealing with that dead-skin feeling from my recent tuck and lift, was trying to schedule some free time to get my thighs sucked. Plastic surgery is like painting the baseboards. It makes you notice how bad the walls look.

Brynn was seeing a highly reputable and expensive therapist twice a week. He felt that it would be counterproductive for her to take time away from school and her sessions with him to visit her parents. I missed her.

So it wasn't as if I was living in a fairy tale, but I thought that I was doing good.

That same afternoon I took a couple with midlevel salaries and a Ford Expedition to look at a renovated ranch house in Stoney Hills. It was pretty lackluster, but the neighborhood was prime.

"It's a big house for just two people," the husband pointed out. His wife raised her head immediately. Whether they had opted for a childless marriage or it had been a medical issue, she was obviously defensive about it. I was on her side.

"The size of a house shouldn't be determined solely by the number of people who are going to live there," I told him. "A pair of successful, goal-focused individuals certainly deserve as roomy and as comfortable a living space as some Brady Bunch horde."

The description of the latter was voiced with deliberate disdain.

"A fine home," I continued, "like a luxurious car, is a reflection of the owner's personal worth and value in the community. I don't think *that* can ever be too large."

They offered a full-price contract on the house.

To celebrate this coup, I dropped by the Yesteryear Emporium on Broadway at San Jose near the edge of downtown. It was a dark, cavernous building that had housed a big department store that had gone bankrupt in the thirties. It was my favorite antique store in the city, and I had been to all of them. It wasn't just that they had some nice things from time to time, which they certainly did, but it was crammed full of every imaginable glass or chair or unimaginable farm implement. Three floors and a back lot to the alley—open for wandering among the superfluous and the sublime. Only the mezzanine level, where the owner lived, was off limits. Although for all that fellow noticed, I probably could have rifled though his apartment and bought his own door lock, and he would have neither known what it was nor recognized its value.

He was a big, burly, good-looking guy who didn't

know squat about antiques. No matter how unreasonably low the price might be on a treasured item, I could always intimidate him into letting me have it for less.

He rarely ventured from beyond the counter. Partly because he had a pronounced limp that frequently required the use of a cane. But more often, I think, because he was busily typing on a greasy old Underwood. I assumed he was either writing pornographic novels or editing an outlaw-biker magazine. Whatever his preoccupation, it was my pleasure to talk him out of his best inventory at a tenth of its value. I didn't feel bad about it. If the guy doesn't know what his merchandise is worth, he deserves to have it stolen.

That particular day I got away with a star-cut crystal jardiniere for forty-five dollars. I was smiling all the way home.

I fixed a light dinner. David's eighteen holes ran long, and he came straight from the shower to the table dressed in Dockers and a polo shirt.

"You should have seen me on the seventh green," he said. "I was perfectly aligned. If I hadn't seen it myself, I would have thought I'd put the ball down by hand. Dolph bogied and I cleaned it up. I tell you, when that happens I just feel like I can do anything."

I do not play golf. I never have. I never will. None of that mattered to David, of course. It was beyond his imagining that anyone might not be interested in a shot-by-shot replay of his game.

I didn't bother to interrupt him. I tuned out what he was saying and waited, rather patiently, I thought, for him to finish. Eventually, he did.

"You remember that we have that party at the club tonight," I said.

Clearly he didn't remember, but he nodded as if he did.

"You'll have to make my apologies," he said. "I can't make it tonight, I'm due back at the office."

David's work as a partner in the law practice started by his grandfather barely required a thirty-hour work week. Anything more than that would have conflicted drastically with his golfing schedule. The phrase *due back at the office* was David's private unspoken euphemism for his having made plans with Mikki, the aforementioned blond, twenty-something hairstylist.

I was furious, not because he was going to be with her, but because he was not going to be with me. I didn't really care where, or with whom, he slept, but when facing the lions of country club society it was always easier to go at it as a team, with someone beside you to watch your back.

"This is the most important get-together of the season," I pointed out. "Next year's membership applications are all in. There'll be plenty of discussion about who is to fill the vacancies."

The country club was as exclusive an old guard as can be imagined. It dated back to 1914, and most of the original family names were still on the roster. The annual fees were exorbitant—sufficient deterrent to keep out the vast majority of the populace. But there were plenty of other restrictions. Only a current member in good standing could put a name up for consideration. And new people were added reluctantly. Neither money nor politics nor social position could ensure acceptance. Inclusion was entirely at the whim of those already ensconced. The voting was done at the Christmas party, by secret ballot. And it had to be unanimous. Private pettiness was disguised as conservative concern. In the twenty years that I'd been a part of it, fewer than a dozen new families had been accepted for invitation. The only long-term way to sell exclusivity was to not sell too much of it.

"You just go without me and tell me later what I need to know," David said. "I always vote the way you want anyway."

That was certainly true. David could not have cared less about the club or the politics swirling within it—even though it had figured prominently in his childhood as the site of every birthday party, Easter-egg hunt and Fourth of July fireworks display. It was where he'd first learned to dance, where we'd had our wedding reception, where he'd introduced Brynn at her debutante ball. Close association with the club had made David less in awe of it. For him, it was just another golf course. And not even one of his favorites.

For me, who would have never been allowed through those gates without him, the club was the symbol of all I had attained in my life. I'd grown up as a west-side nobody. Now I was *Someone*, with a capital *S*, in the city. I was not likely to take that for granted.

"I talked to Brynn today," David said, deftly changing the subject.

I stopped in midbite and held myself completely still for an instant.

"She called you?"

It was not like her *to disturb Daddy at work*. Me, of course, she would call up on my mobile at any time of the day or night.

"She said she was working through her primary relationships with Dr. Reiser," David said. "She didn't want to confuse the situation with any input from you."

I nodded. Hopeful. Accepting. Dr. Reiser was not her first therapist. The previous half dozen had nodded a lot and appeared thoughtful, but none had ever been able to hone in on Brynn's problem.

It was a mystery to me as well. But is that surprising? I didn't know anything about raising children. I'd never even seen one up close until Brynn was born. I knew I didn't want to be like my own mother. Beyond that, I had no clue.

Having a child was David's idea. No, *idea* is not a strong enough word. David *insisted* that we have a child. It was the only time he'd truly demanded anything. And I acquiesced. How could I not? The need to reproduce, to ensure the survival of your genetic material, is primal. It's not like any rational arguments can counter it. In the human-fulfillment category, I wanted a baby as much as he did. So, I succumbed to marital pressure and Mother Nature. Brynn was the result.

I'm not sorry. Who could be sorry about having Brynn? And I thought I could handle it. Like every other goal in my life, I studied thoroughly, worked hard and met the challenge with determination.

I took so many parenting courses that I should have been a candidate for a postdoctoral studies program. There was not a *Mommy & Me* class in the whole city that Brynn and I hadn't attended.

I read all the parenting books. Not just the middle-of-the-road accepted ones. I checked out the fringe viewpoints as well. Everything from *Your Infant's Right to Bear Arms* to *Welcome to Reincarnation, Babygirl.* I weighed conflicting behavioral observation techniques. I even set up an Excel spreadsheet reflecting the varied opinions for handling typical problems. It was a proven formula, guaranteed to succeed.

Somehow it hadn't. From adolescence on, Brynn had been in almost continual conflict with me. And nothing I could say or do seemed to make it better. Honestly, I was relieved to give her adolescence issues to the care of knowledgeable mental-health professionals.

"Is she coming home at Christmas?" I asked.

David shrugged. "I didn't think to ask her."

"What did she have to say?"

He was thoughtful for a moment.

"She agreed that my slice was improving and that the pro at the Quarry was completely wrong about the titaniums being too sensitive."

"You talked about golf?"

"Well, yeah."

"Your daughter calls you at work for maybe the first time in her whole life and you talk to her about golf?"

"She's interested in golf."

"She is not interested in golf. She plays tennis. She chose it deliberately to avoid having to play golf."

David threw his napkin on the table in disgust as he rose to his feet. "There aren't any rules about what a father can talk about with his daughter," he said. "And what we do talk about it is really none of your business."

He was right in his own way, I guess. Anyway, that was how we left it. He headed out for his rendezvous with Mikki and I went to the club.

It was an evening much like others I had spent. I made my way through the familiar crowd, eating canapés and uttering clever witticisms.

Once, from across the room, I caught the eye of my mother-in-law. We both nodded cordially. Edith didn't dislike me. She wanted to. She wanted to hate me, but it would have run counter to her religion.

Although Edith was a home-run hitter who got a walk from third base, she was very certain about the unlimited opportunity available to the best and brightest on any rung of the economic ladder. She knew this because of the evidence for the truth in the life of her spiritual leader.

My mother-in-law was a devoted follower of Oprah Winfrey. She taped every program, so that whenever it wasn't being broadcast, she could watch it anyway. With the Oprah cable channel continually on in the kitchen and VCRs playing in the family room, Edith's home was in a constant state of Oprahization.

Edith tried to emulate the talk show host's life view as faithfully as if she were the Dalai Lama. Those little quotes cut out of *O Magazine* were all over her house. The selections from her booklist were on Edith's bedside table. And Rosie's recipes were always in her kitchen.

"Oprah came from a harsh, tragic, impoverished background," Edith would say. "And now she's graciously welcomed at any home in the country."

If Oprah can do it, so can you. That sounds good in premise. But naturally, the converse side of that theory is also true—those who stay in poverty and ignorance, or even the immobile middle class, deserve their fate.

It was social Darwinism. Or maybe in Edith's case, socialite Darwinism.

Her husband, W. D. Lofton Sr. was also a believer in the ideal of pulling yourself up by your bootstraps. If someone had questioned him about the truest character in American literature, he would not have mentioned Jay Gatsby or Willy Loman. Horatio Alger would have been his choice. I suppose it is very comforting for him to think that wealth and privilege are not the exclusive preserve of the wealthy and privileged.

"The cream of any society always rises to the top," W.D. would say. And also, "You can't keep a good man down."

Mr. Lofton was far from being a self-made man, though you wouldn't know it to hear him talk. He had scraped and clawed his way from prep school to Harvard with only his dividend portfolio and oil lease royalties to get by on.

As far as in-laws were concerned, I couldn't really complain that mine were overly difficult. W.D. had forgotten all his objections to me years ago. And Edith, well, I was not Oprah, of course. But, like her, I had been smart, determined and ambitious. I had risen above my humble beginnings in life. I was, at least, peripherally Oprahlike, and therefore to be lauded.

In truth, my mother-in-law and I had only one mutual interest. Brynn. And we disagreed about what was best for her on almost every occasion.

Still, we both waved a cheery little hello as if delightfully surprised to see each other, and then we deliberately headed in different directions.

I continued to work through the crowd. I spoke to my plastic surgeon. Exchanged rumors with a developer who was looking to buy up some property that he'd heard was soon to be rezoned as multifamily. And shared a couple of chatty comments with the tennis pro.

As always I ended in a huddle with my three closest girlfriends. *Girlfriends* might not be the best choice of words. None of us were girls and we were hardly friends. We were three women who shared some mutual goals and were not too circumspect about what happened to those unfortunate enough to get in our way.

Tookie, Teddy and Lexi, however, were born into this avocation. Like David, they'd grown up in the club. Unlike him, it had become the center of their world. I was, I suppose, their outside contact. I not only had my antecedents from the world of the average American, I actually went out there every day and worked. It was undoubtedly mind-boggling.

Also, I had utterly missed out in the name department. Tookie's birth certificate listed her as Portia Hlynn. Teddy was the nickname for Theodora. And Lexi was short for Alexandria. Still, they treated me as if I were one of them.

"Jane!" Lexi called out as soon as she saw me.

The other two waved me over as well.

"That is a great dress, " Teddy said. "Goldblum's?"

"Saks," I answered "It's a Louis Feraud, I think."

They all cooed appreciatively.

"David's not with you tonight?" Tookie asked.

"No, he was otherwise engaged," I said, rolling my eyes meaningfully.

The three nodded their understanding.

"Boffing the bleached blonde again?" Teddy said, sighing.

I didn't bother to answer.

Lexi shook her head, indignant. "You really don't need to put up with that, you know."

She spoke from experience. The former love of her life had lifted more skirts than a strong west wind. She finally caught him with his pants down, literally. At a dinner party in her own home she'd walked in to find him getting a blow job from the wife of one of his junior partners. These days Lexi was the third wife to an older man. She may not have loved him as much, but she was definitely a lot happier.

"I don't really care," I told them, which was mostly true. After a while you can develop a callus on nearly any muscle, including the heart. "The thing with David," I said, "is that no matter where his penis might be, his heart is on the golf course."

The absolute truth of that statement brought a round of distinctly unladylike guffaws. I used the humor as an uneasy segue.

"So who looks probable among the candidates," I asked.

"Mr. and Mrs. DigiTool are the favorites," Teddy said.

We all laughed again. It was a joke.

DigiTool was a local software company that had made its college-geek founder wealthy beyond his wildest dreams. He contributed heavily to local causes, but nobody would ever seriously consider him "country club."

"I saw them at the symphony," Tookie said. "Birkenstock sandals with hairy feet. What was he thinking?"

"Oh, you meant him," Lexi chimed in. "For a second I thought you meant his wife."

That snide remark evoked more snickers.

"Seriously," I said, "who may have a chance for membership?"

"Dr. and Mrs. Rubenstein look good this year," Teddy said. "She's been so visible at the art museum and they've given him a chair at the medical school."

Tookie tutted and shook her head. "They are very Jewish," she said.

"You're Jewish," Teddy pointed out.

Tookie gave a huff of incredulity and rolled her eyes. "We're only bar-mitzvah-and-sitting-shivah Jewish," she stated. "The Rubensteins actually go to temple."

"Well, that's all right with me," Lexi said. "Less crowding at the juice bar on Saturday morning."

We all giggled naughtily.

"Daisy and Thorn Whittingham are back on the board," Tookie said.

I was surprised. "I thought that after the last time they were blackballed they had huffed off and said they'd never try again."

"Never say never when it comes to the country club," Lexi philosophized.

"I suppose you're putting the Brandts' name in again," Teddy said.

I nodded. "Millie and Frank are adorable people," I told them. "And I'm not saying that just because I'm an associate in their real estate brokerage. They are just a darling couple."

"They are," Tookie agreed. "Everyone loves them. I

thought they'd get in two years ago. I can't believe they were rejected again last year."

I shook my head sadly.

"I wonder who it is that keeps voting against them?" Lexi asked, looking around the room as if hoping to spot the offending person.

"I haven't any idea," I said.

Of course, I knew exactly who kept voting against them. I did. As long as I was the person trying to get them into the country club, I was in a great position in the company. The last thing I wanted was for them to not need me anymore.

The evening dragged on in this manner. The four of us chatted together, gossiping about friends and assassinating the reputations of enemies. It was still early when I made my exit.

"The Beemer convertible?" the young, good-looking parking attendant said to me as I stepped out on the porch.

I nodded, not bothering to correct him. True aficionados know that the nickname *Beemer* actually refers to the BMW motorcycle. *Bimmer* is the correct nickname for the automobile. But *Beemer* just sounded so much better, I used it myself. Ignoring what you know is not the same thing as ignorance.

"You headed home already, Jane? The party's just getting started."

I turned to see Gil Mullins in the shadows of the patio. The middle-aged ne'er-do-well son of a recently deceased trucking company boss, Gil was always flirting with me, and when he was sloshed he tended to get obnoxious.

"That husband of yours ought to be worried, a sexy fox like you out among the wolves on her own."

*Sexy fox?* The man was still living in the seventies.

I gave him a dismissive half smile and focused my attention in the direction from which my car would arrive.

To my displeasure, Gil didn't pick up on my hint, but instead slithered up beside me and wound a sweaty arm around my waist. Gil was not an unattractive man. He had the tall, lean frame of an athlete. But the years, getting close to sixty, I'd guess, were beginning to collect around his belt, and his once-handsome face now had the perpetually florid hue of a daily drinker.

"Jane, baby," he said, his gin-and-tonic breath much too close to my face, "I've been hot for you for a while now."

"I'm not interested," I stated flatly, peeling his hand off my body.

"Ah, come on, honey," he tried again. "We're all interested. Life is short, we've got to grab for the gusto while we can."

I rolled my eyes and stepped away from him. My car, a red BMW 328i convertible, was coming up the driveway. I felt safe and confident enough to fling insults.

"It seems pretty pathetic, Gil," I said, "that your pickup lines are so stale you have to resort to beer commercials."

The Beemer stopped and I walked around the back of it to the driver's side. The parking attendant got out and handed me the keys.

"Bitch!" Gil cursed at me.

The parking attendant was immediately alert.

"Is he bothering you?"

"Not enough to make it worth your while," I told him.

"Whoring slut!" Gil shouted out. "Frigid lesbo!"

The young man's eyes widened.

I smiled reassuringly at him. "Is it possible to be all those things at the same time?" I asked, and gave the kid a teasing wink.

He opened the car door for me and I handed him his tip. I seated myself behind the steering wheel and reached for the handle just as the parking attendant closed the door. In the resulting collision I broke a fingernail.

I cursed under my breath, but he didn't hear it. Gil was screaming for his own car.

The young man leaned over my door to speak to me privately.

"Don't worry," he said. "I'll stall him long enough so he can't follow you."

I thanked the guy. It was nice of him to try to protect me, but the truth was that Gil knew exactly where I lived. If he was intent upon continuing this confrontation, he could easily do so.

"Better put up the top, ma'am," he said. "It's started sprinkling."

I nodded. As I headed down the drive and out of the gates, I pressed the button for the roof. It rose slowly, leisurely, like a protective cover keeping out the night sky and drops of rain. I slid the latch at the stop sign. There was just enough drizzle to be a nuisance. I switched the wipers on to intermittent.

Going straight home didn't seem like a good idea. I wasn't afraid of Gil Mullins showing up, I just didn't want the hassle of dealing with him if he did. And I wasn't ready to face the empty house yet. David would undoubtedly spend the night at Mikki's apartment and come sneaking in at breakfast. We'd both pretend that he'd been in his bedroom all night.

I drove down Highland Boulevard and got on the freeway. I wasn't headed anywhere specific, just driving in the night air. Driving and thinking.

Lexi was right, I probably shouldn't put up with David's infidelity. But I couldn't imagine what I could do about it. Of course I could ask him for a divorce. He'd probably love that. Our marriage had been over for years. Brynn was the only common interest we had. If we divorced I'd lose everything. Financially, I'd probably do all right. I didn't even need his cash, and I'm sure the court would see that I got plenty of it anyway. But it was David's lineage that was old money. His family had the rank and the prominence. Without him as my husband, I'd lose everything that I'd worked most of my life to gain. I'd be persona non grata at the club, a nobody in the community, a cautionary tale for younger women at the Junior League, and a regular scrapper and toiler at my job. No way was I going to go back to that. I wondered idly if a good lawyer could get me custody of our social position.

I took the outer loop, away from the lights and traffic of the city. Suburban housing developments glittered like constellations of earthbound stars in the darkness at the sides of the roads.

If I did divorce David, what would Brynn say? Or I guess, more importantly, what would Dr. Reiser say? How much permanent damage could a broken home do? Practically every girl she knew had been through at least one family breakup. They all seemed to manage. But Brynn was somehow so fragile, so easily wounded. Had I made her that way? She'd had the best of everything. I'd seen that she had everything that I had ever wanted.

I'd seen that *I* had everything I'd ever wanted. But I wasn't any happier than she was.

I didn't blame all the ills of my marriage on David. The infidelity, yes. But that was just a small example of a lot of things that were wrong. We hadn't shared our lives, really shared our lives, for a very long time. Maybe we never had. It might have been different if Brynn had been a boy. David had wanted a boy. If we'd had a son maybe he would have taken more responsibility for raising him. Perhaps I wouldn't have been so overwhelmed with it. Things could have worked out differently if our baby had been male.

David loved Brynn, there was no doubt of that. But he'd started pleading for another child when she was just a toddler. By then I knew that I was in over my head. I flatly refused. David didn't acquiesce gracefully. He hounded me about it for years. I'm not sure he ever really got over the idea. We just quit talking about it. I'm sad for Brynn that she didn't have siblings, but I was never sorry that I didn't have more children. I would have made two children twice as screwed up as one. And as for my career, no way. I'd have been too busy shuttling kids back and forth to therapy appointments.

I glanced down at my broken fingernail. I didn't have a manicure scheduled until Tuesday. My purse was sitting on the seat beside me and I began rifling through it, looking for an emery board.

I looked up again. The hairs on the back of my neck stood on end. I knew that something was wrong. I didn't know what. There was an alertness in me that was primordial, the kind of caution that saved my ancestors from saber-toothed tigers stalking from downwind. It zizzed adrenaline into my brain. I didn't know why. I didn't know what. I didn't quite see it. Then I realized what I was looking at.

An eighteen-wheeler coming from the opposite direction, maybe a quarter mile of empty freeway away from me, was haphazardly listing across three lanes of the interstate. It was a huge tanker truck. Not going particularly fast, but moving steadily and irrevocably toward the passing lane.

I watched it, detached. The driver must be asleep, I thought. It was a good thing there was no traffic, I thought. Somebody could get killed.

When the truck jumped the median, my reflexes went off like an alarm clock. It was coming across the road at me, the tanker load it hauled slithering to the left in front of me like a tail on a giant T. Rex.

I swerved into the far right lane. It kept coming. I leaned down hard on my horn.

"Wake up! Damnit!" I screamed.

If I sped up and went off on the shoulder I might be able to get around it. But if the tanker did hit me, my going faster wouldn't help. I didn't have time to think it through. I stomped the gas pedal all the way to the floorboard and fled toward the very edge of the pavement.

It was going to be close.

It was going to be too close.

I saw the clear freedom of three empty lanes ahead for just an instant. Then the back of the tanker jackknifed in front of me. I turned sharply and heard the scream of metal as the passenger side of the Beemer skidded along the guardrail. Friction sparks lit up the darkness. I hit the brakes.

The impact was surprisingly sudden, sharp, loud. For a half an instant I was held taut by the seat belt. Then the air bags deployed and I was completely immersed in a world of beige.

Propelled back into my seat, I gasped for breath. I don't know if I had been holding it or had it knocked out of me.

It was quiet. Amazingly quiet. The only sound was oxygen rushing into my lungs and the pounding of my pulse through my veins.

The air bags began their slow deflate and the faint whistle brought with it the first sense of reality.

"I'm all right," I whispered gently, not completely sure that it was true.

I quickly checked myself over. No blood, no protruding bones, no car parts sticking through my internal organs.

"I'm all right," I said again, this time more hopeful.

My wrists were sore, but I didn't see any injuries. I ran a trembling hand along my neck and the back of my head. I was shaking, but I was not hurt. I sat there for a couple of moments, just getting my shattered composure back together.

The interior of my car was a strange and unfamiliar place. The deflating air bags hung like a shroud over the dashboard, hiding from view the instrument panel, the clock, the CD player. Against the windshield I could see one bent and truncated wiper quivering spasmodically as if having some sort of electrical seizure. The Beemer didn't seem to have suffered much damage. The front end was squeezed up tight and the hood was partially buckled, but considering the size of the tanker beside me, I felt fortunate not to have been squashed like a bug.

In the narrow beam from my right headlight I saw that I had almost made it. The tanker had rolled to its side I was wedged between its rear bumper and the guardrail. No harm, no foul, I thought.

My hands were a little shaky as I began looking for my cell phone. The contents of my open purse had scattered on impact. The only thing that was still on the seat beside me was a tube of lipstick and a scattering of business cards.

The rain was sloshing down heavily on the trunk of the car. I looked at the spasming wiper blade once more. Strange. It didn't seem to be raining at all on the windshield.

It was at that moment that I became aware of the odor. The common, everyday, unmistakable odor. Gasoline. The eighteen-wheel tanker truck, tilted upon its side, was pouring gasoline like a river down the back of my car.

"Jesus!" I screamed.

I tried my door. Of course it wouldn't budge. There was a truck bumper wedged up against it.

I started to the passenger door, momentarily snarled up by my seat belt. I found the red button, released myself and hurriedly crawled over the console and gearshift to the other side of the car.

The door was locked.

I hit the unlock button.

Nothing happened.

I manually unlocked it.

The handle released, but the door opened only a couple of inches.

I pushed harder on it.

There was no give. The car was right up against the guardrail.

I began banging the door on the metal. The opening did not widen.

I would have to climb out the window.

I pressed the down button for the automatic window.

No response.

A glance at the windshield wiper revealed that it had stopped its tremulous dance. Beyond it I saw smoke rising from beneath the hood of my car.

Where there is smoke there is fire.

The gasoline rain continued to pour down upon the trunk. The smell of fumes was becoming intense.

"Turn off the ignition!" I ordered myself.

I could hardly recognize my own voice.

Frantically I searched beneath the heavy beige remnants of the air bags for the key that dangled from the steering column.

When I found it, I turned off the ignition. I even pulled out the key.

The smoke continued to billow from the engine.

I unhooked the manual latch on the soft-top. It was jammed. I pushed the automatic button, then twice, again, a half-dozen times. The car key was still in my hand. I tried to use it like a screwdriver to disengage the mechanism.

It didn't work. I opened the glove compartment and rifled through it for a tool, a hammer, a crowbar, a penknife, anything.

There was nothing but a plastic ice scraper, my insurance and registration and the owners manual.

I grabbed the ice scraper and banged it impotently against the window glass for half a minute.

I began scraping it across the soft-top to no effect. I tried to find a weak spot, a worn seam, a loose edge. There was none. I gripped the plastic scraper like an ice pick and tried to stab a hole through the canvas. It wasn't sharp enough.

Smoke rising from the hood had now completely obscured my view from the windshield. It had begun to seep inside the car.

It was as if I were the only person in all the world. I was too scared to be panicked. Too horrified to be afraid. I was alone in my car, helpless.

"You're never alone," I reminded myself, and began rummaging through the spilled contents of my purse on the floorboards looking for my cell phone.

Fire had to be the worst kind of death, I thought. Choking, hot, painful. It was not a good way to die. And I didn't want to die.

Why was the phone black? You could never see anything black in the dark. I'll never have another black phone, I declared to myself.

It began to look as if I might never need one.

I gave up trying to phone for help and lay down on the passenger's seat, my shoulders braced against the console. I began trying to kick a hole in the window with my high heels. In all the wrecks I could remember seeing, the windows were always broken. Why weren't my windows broken? Why couldn't I break them? I pounded and pounded on them with every bit of strength I had.

The smoke thickened, making me cough. I could hear the gasoline rain pouring unabated. The smell was so strong it burned.

"Please don't let me die," I pleaded, hoping someone, somewhere would hear. "Please get me out of here."

I felt the tears coursing down my cheeks. I thought of Brynn, my sweet, my precious baby Brynn. I saw her in memory as a little toddler, giggling as she chased the bubbles I blew for her on the patio. I saw her all dressed up for her debutante ball, looking so serene and mature. And I saw her looking at me, silently accusing from behind her reading glasses. How would she get over this? Would the guilt from the loss of her mother blight her life forever?

I hurt for her. And I hurt for me. I would never get to hold her again. I would never get to tell her how much I loved her. How glad I was that she was my daughter. How sorry I was that we hadn't had more time.

"Please God, get me out of here," I prayed. "I don't want to die. Please get me out of here."

I muttered my miserable prayer through tears.

"Get me out of here. Let me live," I pleaded. "I'll be a better person. I'll change my life. If you get me out of here, I'll…I'll do good. I promise. Give me another chance and I'll do good. Please get me out of here. I'll do good. I'll do good all my life."

Silence was the resulting answer. Silence amid the

deluge of gasoline pouring down upon the back of the car and the billowing smoke that now seared my lungs.

"Please," I said more quietly. "Please."

I lay upon my back. Directly above me, like the pivotal scene in a B-movie thriller, a huge butcher knife ripped through the soft-top.

I screamed.

It was an instant of terror before I recognized my deliverance.

The knife cut through a jagged line. It was my freedom. It was the chance that I had prayed for. With the strength of desperation, I reached up and began to part the material behind the knife cuts. It was tough and stubborn, but I persisted. It was my chance, my only chance. I was going to take it.

I fought to make an opening in the top. A firm hand grabbed my wrist.

"Come on," the man said. "This thing is going to blow."

I stood on the car seat, then one foot on the dash, one knee on the frame. Strong, forceful arms pulled me out onto the windshield on my stomach.

I was free.

We slid down onto the hood, through the smoke and heat of the engine. He pulled me onward. We were standing on the pavement.

"Run!" he told me as he pulled at my arm.

We did.

We ran thirty, maybe forty yards. He dropped to his knees and I went down beside him.

I glanced at my rescuer and saw beside me a withered old man, barefoot, wild-haired, dressed in stripped pajamas.

Behind us the wreckage exploded in a giant fireball that knocked us to the concrete.

# 2

My mother worked as a practical nurse most of her life, so hospitals hold very little interest or drama for me. But that night, lying on a gurney in a curtained alcove of the emergency room for what seemed like a lifetime, I concentrated intently on what was going on around me. It was not that the comings and goings of the noisy, coffee-drinking staff were of any importance—I was just trying not to think.

I couldn't do it, of course. Like the don't-imagine-an-elephant exercise from junior high, it's impossible to empty your mind on purpose. It can happen by accident. You can be sitting somewhere and suddenly realize that your brain has been on dead air for an indeterminate period of time. But it's simply impossible to try to think of nothing, so I tried to think of something else. Something else besides the frightening moments I'd experienced.

Getting help at the scene had not been a problem. The explosion worked significantly better than a 911 call. In no time we were surrounded by fire trucks, ambulances and police cars.

I just wanted to get away. To get in one of those vehicles that wasn't burning and just drive into the night. The EMS personnel would have none of that.

"Lie still," I was told a half-dozen times.

It hadn't been easy. It was a lot worse in the hospital. I suppose I was numb there on the pavement. Too overwhelmed with being alive to be concerned with how close I had come to death. With a little distance, I found myself almost hysterical with fear. No matter how carefully I listened to the mundane conversations around me, I couldn't quite control the mania that was just underneath my flesh. Lying there in deliberate repose, while bouncing around inside me was a crazy person shrieking in terror.

Deliberately I held on to the here and now. That included an apparatus resembling a giant plastic clothespin attached to my finger and a blood pressure cuff wrapped around my arm that automatically inflated every few minutes. Both were connected to a dazzling array of brightly lit monitors that undoubtedly revealed, to the knowing eye, just what was going on underneath my calm exterior.

Beyond my little claustrophobic cubicle I could hear the intimate details of problems and people hidden behind endless rows of pastel curtains.

There was a small child whining and crying. His mother sounded tired and robotic as she repeatedly told the little one to keep the ice bag on his hand.

Farther down there was someone, drunk or crazy, singing "Lucille Has Messed My Mind Up" in a rendition that Frank Zappa would have been proud to own up to.

Right next to my own space, an old woman tried for at least ten minutes to get the attention of anyone passing by. Finally a doctor stopped and she told him, her voice almost pleading, that she needed to go to the bathroom.

"I'll get someone," he assured her.

He must have gone to Australia to do so, because nobody ever showed up.

Across the corridor a man told the attending physician that he didn't want any X rays, just a shot of cortisone in his knee would be fine.

I listened and listened.

Somewhere down there was my rescuer. He'd come ahead of me in the first ambulance.

There had been some confusion initially. EMS had thought that he was the accident victim and that I'd pulled *him* out. The fellow had done very little to dispel that notion. When the attendant asked him if he was okay he'd nodded.

"I'm going to be fine," he said. "Thanks to her."

I figured that the explosion must have rattled him. I'd certainly felt rattled. I still did.

Abruptly the curtain jerked open and I startled. My nurse, in a uniform that was more tie-dyed hippie than starchy and efficient RN, entered. A good-looking young policeman was beside her.

"Doctor is going to let you go home soon," she said to me in that slightly too loud and inherently condescending tone professional people often use toward those within their control. "Officer Norton needs to ask you about the accident."

He was writing something in a small notepad.

"It happened so fast," I explained before he'd even asked one question.

The policeman looked at me, then at the nurse, and chuckled as he responded, his words clearly for her entertainment rather than my enlightenment.

"It couldn't have happened too fast," he said. "From the road evidence, the tanker was only traveling about thirty-five when it jumped the median. By the time it hit you, it must have been closer to thirty."

"The driver was asleep, I suppose."

"Dead as a doornail before he ever veered out of his lane," Officer Norton replied, his matter-of-fact tone seemed almost jovial. "We'll have to wait for the full report, but the ME on the scene says it was most likely a stroke."

I nodded. He had been dead already. Somehow that terrified me even more. I had been the only person on that highway. I would have died all alone.

"The man who saved me," I asked them. "Who is he? Is he all right? Is he still here in the emergency room?"

The policeman flicked back a page in his notepad.

"Chester W. Durbin," he read. "Seventy-eight years old. Widowed. Resident of Bluebonnet Manor Assisted Living Center, 177th East Loop and Toronto."

"He'll be fine," the nurse said. "We're getting ready to transfer him upstairs. We'll keep him a couple of days."

"He's hurt?"

"Not as bad as you'd think," she said. "He's got some cuts on his feet, a few bruises and skinned knees. Other than that, he's fine."

"Then why are you keeping him?"

The nurse was looking at me as if I was an idiot.

I am not an idiot. I was fine and therefore going home soon. If Chester Durbin was fine, why wasn't he going home as well?

"He's an old man," she answered.

Of course, I recalled how he looked sitting beside me on the pavement, ancient, barefoot, striped pajamas. But a flash of memory had me feeling once again the firm strength of his hand as he grasped my wrist and the sturdy arms that pulled me through the ripped opening of the soft-top.

"He's in pretty good shape," I told her. "He must be one of those seniors who pump iron or do tai chi."

The policeman looked at me incredulously. The hippie RN actually cackled.

"I don't think so," she said. "The gentleman is very frail."

"It's pretty amazing that he managed to help you out of that car," the policeman commented. "It must be five hundred yards from the nursing home to the site of the accident."

The nurse was shaking her head disbelievingly. "It's hard to believe the old guy could even walk that far, let alone be of any help when he got there."

The policeman obviously agreed. "What blows me away," he said, "is the image of him racing down the hill with that big butcher knife."

"He had the foresight to bring a knife, but not the good sense to put his shoes on," the nurse pointed out, chuckling.

I lay there trying to reconcile the person they were talking about with my rescuer.

"I have to see him," I stated suddenly, adamantly, surprising myself. The hippie nurse looked doubtful. "No, I don't think—"

"Now!" I interrupted her, already scrambling off the gurney.

I was never the type of woman who could easily follow orders. And I was inexplicably desperate to see this man again before he slipped out of my life.

I jerked the high-tech clothespin off my finger and tossed it on the gurney. Getting out of the blood pressure cuff was more dramatic as the Velcro noisily pulled apart.

"Wait!" The nurse's voice was almost desperate.

"Are you going to try to stop me?" I asked the woman, almost daring her to do so. "Or are you going to help me?"

She hesitated, as if considering her choices. "Let me get you a wheelchair," she said.

"I don't need a wheelchair."

"It's hospital policy," she said. "You get in a wheelchair and I'll take you to see him."

By the time she wheeled me around to the other side of the E.R., the staff was already in the process of moving Chester Durbin upstairs to a room. My hippie nurse stopped them abruptly and spoke to one of the orderlies privately. I don't know what she said, but I was given a dirty look before they pushed the bed back into its curtain alcove and told me, "Five minutes!"

I thanked them dismissively. The man in the bed was quiet and appeared tired and sleepy. I felt uncharacteristically timid as I approached him, rising from my chair to stand at his bedside.

"Hello," I said.

He squinted at me through rheumy eyes.

"Are you the endocrinologist?" he asked.

"No, I'm the woman from the car," I told him.

"Oh." He nodded, offering the slightest smile.

"I...I just wanted to thank you."

"You're welcome," he replied. His gnarled, brown-blotched hand slid out from beneath the white sheets and patted my own at the bedrail. "You're all right now?"

"Oh yeah, sure," I answered. "I'm fine."

That was not how I felt. I was edgy, nervous, ill at ease. The nurse and the policeman had been right about this guy. He did look very old and unreasonably frail. But I could still clearly recall the strength in the arm that had grasped my hand and pulled me to safety. I couldn't get things straight in my mind. I wanted to talk about it, get the details, resurrect the chain of events.

"How did you do it?" I asked him.

The man gave a shoulder wiggle that passed for a supine shrug. "I don't really know," he admitted with a light chuckle. "I guess it was one of those curiosities where in an emergency folks discover strength they didn't know they had."

I had heard about that sort of thing. Tabloid tales of a man who lifts a truck off a trapped victim, or a child who can't swim miraculously managing to drag his unconscious father to shore after a boating mishap. "Did you see the accident?"

"No, no, I was asleep," the man said. "But I guess I must have heard it."

"You heard it?"

"I must have," he said. "I woke with a start, like when you have a bad dream. I looked out my window and I could see the truck on the wrong side of the road. I just knew I had to get down there."

"Where did you get the knife?" I asked.

"The kitchen."

"Why did you get it?"

He looked as puzzled as I was myself. "I don't know," he answered. "I can't even remember thinking about needing it. I do recall running into the kitchen and grabbing it out of one of the drawers." He chuckled. "I'd never even been in that room. It's off limits to the residents."

His words left me with more questions than answers. I wanted the events of my rescue tied up neatly, rationally, in a context that I was familiar dealing with. I was not interested in contemplating any mysterious, inexplicable happening. And I staunchly resisted doing so.

From beyond the confines of the curtains I heard a familiar voice.

"I was three strokes off the fourteenth hole at La Cantera last Thursday…"

David.

The confusion in my thoughts immediately eased. David was here. And with him came the sounds of my own life, my real life. The ordinary safe and comfortable life to which I was so accustomed.

"My husband is here," I told my rescuer, as if all baffling enigmas had become scrutable. "He's come to take me home."

I couldn't remember being more excited to see David. He was his usual calm, pleasant self. I introduced him to my rescuer. He gave the old man a sort of bedside high-five.

"We need to take Mr. Durbin upstairs," one of the nurses said.

"Of course," David told him. "Nice to meet you, Chester, and thanks."

I watched them roll the bed toward the elevator. I was overwhelmed with a queasy sense of unreality. Deliberately I turned my back on the sight.

"David, I want to go home."

My husband was grinning at me as if everything was fine.

"Sure," he said. "If it's okay with Pete."

The *Pete* in question was emergency room physician, Pete Murfey, M.D., with whom David, apparently, had a golfing acquaintance.

"I think we can let her go. If she promises to get plenty of rest and not blow up any more cars."

They both had a good laugh. I smiled along with them, but I was faking it. I just wanted to get home. To get back to the way things were before. To forget everything that happened that night.

It wasn't all that easy.

Over the next few days I convalesced around the house. I had no lingering injuries, a few bruises and some sore muscles, but in general I was all right.

Surprisingly, I wasn't all that eager to get back to work. I had several things pending. I got Millie Brandt to handle a closing for me. Everything else I just let ride. Millie and the people at work were floored. Even

David seemed curious. But no one was more surprised at this than me.

I liked being on top of things—at home, and on the job. I liked to get down to the minutiae, to personally make sure that all the *i's* were dotted and all the *t's* were crossed. Controlling was the word Brynn's shrink used. What an ugly word. It just seemed to me that when I took care of everything, there were no unexpected complications. I had such a problem with delegating that I couldn't even keep a cleaning lady. I hate housework, but I couldn't stand opening the silverware drawer and finding spoons in the knife slot. Or walking into the guest bathroom and finding the liner for the shower curtain hanging on the outside of the tub. People couldn't do things to suit me, so I simply preferred to do them myself.

But in the days after the accident, I was different. I watered the plants on my deck, stared off into the distance and ducked phone calls from the office.

It was almost as if I couldn't bring myself to resume my life. I wanted things to be just as they had been, but I couldn't pretend that nothing had happened.

Friends were in and out. David's mother came by to see me twice. There were flowers and cards and well wishes from associates and competitors.

We called Brynn together. David did most of the talking. She was pretty quiet, as if she didn't quite know what to say. She called back an hour later, after discussing it with her therapist. Then she didn't have any trouble speaking her mind.

"Dr. Reiser says that there are no accidents, Mother," she told me. "We don't know if this is an attempt at manipulation, or merely a cry for help."

I should have been stung by the accusation, but I was too dispassionate to even be insulted.

I handed the phone to David.

Tookie and her husband, Joel, came to see me. She brought over a broccoli casserole that her maid had cooked.

"It's a Southern thing," she told me. "Taking food to the sick."

It was not hard to imagine Tookie as the great lady from the big house. Even casual and dressed down, as she was that night, she looked so perfectly put together, so unpretentiously expensive.

"I'm not sick," I assured her. "I'm just sort of stunned."

She nodded as if she understood, but I was pretty sure she didn't.

"Losing your car like that," she said. "Who could imagine that they could just blow up?"

Joel laughed at her. "Tookie, if you pour enough gasoline on it, anything will explode."

"I know," she said. "But it must have been very scary."

I nodded, but didn't go into what it had been like. I was trying not to think about it. I was trying not to remember the fear on a level never before imagined.

"Well, I guess David will have to buy you a new car," Tookie said. She directed these words to him. "I've been telling her for months now that she should trade in that silly little convertible for a Range Rover. You would have been a lot safer than in that Beemer."

"If she hadn't been in the convertible," David pointed out, "she would have been trapped inside."

Just hearing him say the words made the bottom fall out of my stomach, as if I'd just topped out on the highest point of a roller coaster. I thought I might throw up.

"I liked my little Beemer," I managed to get out, forcing a smile across my face.

"BMW makes an SUV," Tookie informed me.

"David, don't you go buying Jane anything too

fancy," Joel warned. "If you do, all the women at the club will be blowing up their cars to see what their husbands will get for them."

We all laughed as if it were funny.

It was an interminable social evening. I finally pleaded exhaustion about ten-thirty. David gave me a worried look. After they'd left, he voiced it. "You probably wouldn't be so tired," he said, "if you didn't walk the floor all night long."

"I can't sleep," I answered.

"Maybe you should get the doctor to give you something," he said. "Or maybe you should not sleep so much during the day."

I resented his words. He only wanted me to get back to normal so that *he* could get back to normal. He'd been at home every night since the accident. Mikki must miss him. In the evenings he spent hours in his den on the phone.

Friday, a full week after the wreck, his parents showed up, ostensibly to take us out to dinner. I didn't want to go, but David absolutely insisted, and his mother never took no for an answer. I dressed and put on makeup as they whispered together in the living room.

I leaned close to the mirror and applied a thin streak of ripe plum liner at the edge of my collagen-enhanced lips. I pulled back and surveyed the result, then was caught up short by my reflection. I looked just exactly as I had looked before. There was no line or mark on my face as lingering evidence of what had occurred on that night on the highway.

"Because nothing happened to you," I reminded myself.

But something had happened.

Determinedly I put that thought behind me and hurried to join David, Edith and W.D.

"Here she is," David announced at my entrance.

They were all looking at me hopefully. I smiled.

"I'm ready when you are," I assured them.

"We'd better take two cars," W.D. said. "Then Mommy and I can go home directly from the restaurant."

I could never understand how David's father could call Edith, Mommy. She was not at all the type for it. Even her only son called her by her first name. And it was my impression that she didn't really care for the appellation herself. Why she never said so is open to question.

"Sure," David agreed as we walked toward the front door. "You two go in your car, and Jane and I will take her car."

"My car?"

He opened the door. Parked in the circular driveway, directly in front of our house, was a brand-new blue BMW convertible. The new Roadster Z3 model was a luxury two-seater that looked more like a 1960s race car than new-millennium town transportation.

I glanced at the people around me. David was looking puffed up and proud. W.D. and Edith were both grinning like fools.

"Now, if you don't like it," David said in a tone that could hardly hazard the possibility, "we can take it back and get you whatever you want."

It was a great car. It was sporty and expensive and a real attention getter. It was exactly the kind of car that I had always admired. I was sure that I still did. But I couldn't quite dredge up the proper enthusiasm. I did try.

"Thank you, David," I said, giving him a quick kiss. "It's a great car."

"It is absolutely you," Edith said.

"Yes," I agreed, feeling vaguely uneasy with the comparison.

"Come on, let's get a look at you behind the wheel," David said.

I hadn't driven since the accident and I was hesitant to do so, but once I started, I realized I wasn't really afraid. With David in the passenger seat, I drove the quick and powerful Z3. It handled beautifully.

We went to my most favorite eating establishment in the city, Le Parapluie. The veal they prepared was inevitably perfect. The bread was to die for. And once, I'd spotted Tommy Lee Jones there having lunch. But, of course, the real reason for my preference had always been the chic and trendy clientele that frequented the place.

As soon as we walked in, the maître d' hurried to the kitchen to announce that we were there. Frederic, the owner and head chef, came out to the front and kissed my hand, welcoming me in lovely round tones. "It is wonderful to see you looking just the same." His accent was more likely the French of Cambodia or Vietnam than Paris, but his customers were all provincial enough to be dazzled anyway.

"This terrible automobile accident has been the talk for days," he assured me in a whisper.

It was a snippet meant to please me. Being the object of gossip and speculation is only unpleasant when it's negative. Becoming the talk of the town was better than having your picture in the society column. If you were in the paper, everybody knew the details and nobody bothered to talk about them anymore.

Amazingly, I was not as buoyed by the knowledge as I should have been. I thanked him anyway. He'd been a loyal and well-positioned ally for years. We had a kind of unspoken kinship—we were both outsiders who had managed to make a place for ourselves in this

social stratum. He had created an in-demand business.
I had married into the right family.

Single file, with Frederic leading the way, we made
sporadic progress toward our table. My in-laws, my
husband and I all have different circles of friends and
associates. As we moved through the eclectically decorated restaurant, crowded with cloth-covered tables,
somebody would hail W.D. And then Edith would
greet one of her friends. David would acknowledge one
of his golfing buddies.

And every person that I had ever been introduced to
in my life took the opportunity to quiz me about the accident. Their interest was only transitory. The concerned questions were barely voiced before the subject
was turned to more salacious topics. I listened. I
smiled. I quipped. In short, I put on a perfect imitation
of my usual self, but my heart was not in it. It was as
though I was standing beside myself, watching my
own interaction, and found the show to be dismally
boring.

By the time we were seated, I felt as if I had run a social gauntlet, and I made the mistake of saying so out
loud.

"What on earth is wrong with you?" Edith demanded. "You're annoyed by the concern of your
friends? David says you're not working. You just hang
around the house, all moody and listless. Are you
menopausal? Oprah had Dr. Phil on this week talking
about the symptoms."

I was saved from answering by the arrival of the
waiter, who came for our drink orders. For the brief
moments he was present at the table, Edith was charming, David was amenable and W.D. carried off just the
right balance of congeniality and condescension.

As soon as he left, all three faces were turned in my
direction. Edith repeated her question.

"What *is* wrong with you?"

They were expecting some kind of explanation. I didn't have one to give.

"I don't know," I said. "When I was trapped in the car, I thought I was going to die."

"So?" W.D. said. "You've had a little scare. You're fine now."

"Yes," I admitted. "I'm fine now, but…" I hesitated.

"Don't worry," David assured his parents. "Jane will be back to her usual self in no time."

The three of them smiled at me, soothed.

Hours later, as I lay alone in my bed, I wondered if getting back to my usual self was really such a worthwhile goal.

The house was empty. David had left when we got home, making a lame excuse about running an errand. I knew he was going to be with Mikki. I couldn't really fault him, I suppose. I didn't need him to be in the house with me. Life was back to normal. I was back to normal, or mostly so.

Sleeping was still a problem. I had taken two little blue aspirin before going to bed. As on previous nights, I'd slept for about three hours and then awakened in a cold sweat. I didn't dream specifically about the accident. My brain did the more usual kind of mental ramblings. But throughout the normal strangeness of nocturnal wandering, fear pervaded everything. Now I was wide awake and the memories of those frightening few moments returned with total clarity.

I walked through my darkened house, my footsteps nearly soundless on the floor. I was purposefully quiet, as much by habit as any need for peace. The night lured me outside. It was cool and crisp and had the faint scent of fall rain in the air. I went through the French doors to the comfortably decorated seating area of the deck. It was vibrant, blooming with flowers and lush with potted plants. This was my favorite retreat, but tonight it wasn't welcoming. The eight-foot distressed-brick walls around the backyard enclosed more than the pool, the patios and the gardens. They enclosed me. Shuddering, I went back inside and to the front of the house.

I stepped out onto the long, Italianate porch with its faux Doric columns and skirting steps. There was no chair or swing or bench. It would not have been consistent with the design. And David and I were not the kind of people to spend time sitting in open view on a public street. Or I wasn't anyway. I don't suppose I'd ever asked David one way or the other.

I seated myself on the steps. I just sat there. Staring, in turn, at each direction of the wide suburban street. My shiny new car, casually left in the circular driveway, was brilliant in the moonlight. I could hear the click of crickets and the noise of traffic in the distance. I allowed the night to seep inside of me, into that emptiness. But the peace that I craved was elusive. In memory I heard my own voice pleading.

"I don't want to die. Get me out of here. Get me out of here and I'll be a better person. I'll change my life. I'll do good. I promise I'll do good."

I shivered. It must be post-traumatic stress or something.

I tried to laugh at my own desperation. It's a good thing that I hadn't told anyone about it. I could only imagine what Tookie or Teddy or Lexi would think about my ravings. Brynn would have offered me a seat beside her on the therapist's couch. David would have insisted I get medication.

People always talk like that when they are scared. They always try to make deals with God. What was that old wartime adage? There are no atheists in foxholes. That's all my "prayer" had been. Some kind of mid-brain survival superstition. It was a normal human stress reaction to a life-and-death situation. Anyone in the same place would have said pretty much the same thing.

And my words certainly had nothing to do with my being rescued. If all it took to get out of trouble were some heavenward mutterings, nobody would ever get hurt or die.

I had been saved by sheer chance and dumb luck. A man, awakened by the sound of the wreck, had acted spontaneously to help a stranger. I was fortunate that he'd come to my aid. That he'd happened to grab a knife first was coincidence.

No higher power had intervened. That idea was silly.

I believed in God, of course. David and I were members of one of the oldest, most influential churches in the city. But I would never be one of those over-made-up, fanatic women crying on TV-preacher talk shows about a miracle that had happened in their life.

Still, it wouldn't hurt me to do something good.

I approached the idea almost as if I were sticking a pin in a voodoo doll. It felt strange, superstitious, out of my control. I didn't like those kinds of feelings. I wasn't comfortable with them.

But I was glad to be alive. There was no harm in making a gesture of appreciation for that. The man from the retirement home had helped me. It wasn't a bad idea to pass that on, to help somebody else.

I got up and walked back into the house.

In my office, I flipped on the light and sat down at my desk. From the top left-hand drawer I took out my checkbook. Using a four-hundred-dollar Mont Blanc pen, I filled in the date. I stared for a long moment at the *Pay to the order of.*

When David came in the next morning, he found me

still sitting there, tired, sleepless but somehow rejuvenated.

"What are you doing?" he asked me.

"Writing checks."

He raised a startled eyebrow, looking puzzled. "The bills are all paid up."

"I'm not paying bills," I told him. "I'm making donations."

That surprised him even more.

"The Westin Gala or the Republican National Committee?" he asked.

"Neither."

Truthfully I didn't want to talk about it. I didn't even want to examine my feelings. But David was my husband. We kept our finances jointly, so I owed him some sort of justification.

"I just feel so lucky to be alive," I said, "I guess I just want to sort of celebrate that. I'm giving some money to…to some worthy causes."

David was looking through the stack of sealed, stamped envelopes lined up neatly along the edge of in my out box.

He read the addressees aloud. "American Cancer Society, American Heart Association, American Kidney Foundation…"

"They're alphabetical," I said.

He looked at me quizzically.

"Your favorite charities?"

"I'm not sure I really have any favorites."

His brow furrowed.

"I got them out of the Yellow Pages."

"What are you down to now?" He was glancing at my checkbook.

"Special Olympics," I answered.

David and I never argued. It wasn't that we agreed about things, it was simply that we didn't disagree enough to make it worth the confrontation. I wasn't concerned about his disapproval, I just honestly didn't quite know how to explain.

"I want to do something good," I said. "I...I just want to do something good."

# 3

I went back to work that very day, even without having had any sleep. It was as if a burden had been lifted off my shoulders. I had promised to "do good" and I'd fulfilled my end of the deal. I'd given money to forty-seven of the two hundred and four charitable organizations listed in the Yellow Pages—all of the ones that I was familiar with. I'd given ten times the amount of money we'd spent on contributions the year before, and had pretty much blown my clothes and entertainment budget for the rest of the season. But I felt good about it.

Millie and Frank were especially glad to see me. And I think it wasn't just because I was their heavy hitter. Which, of course, I was. My first day back on the job I got a major deal brewing. I remembered Lexi saying at the club that Barbara Jarman had hired a full-time nurse for her mother-in-law. I called Barb and convinced her that that big old house—a two-story Victorian with double wraparound porches on four lots at the edge of Park Square—was just too much for an infirm old lady, and that the nurse was probably walking off with every antique that wasn't bolted to the floor.

The Victorian would have to go. The piece of ground it sat on was prime. With the help of my friends at the club, I knew I could get it rezoned as multifamily. There were at least a hundred developers who would be thrilled to turn that edge of the park into half-million-dollar condos. That would net me a small fortune. And I'd get my little commission for finding the old lady a nice two-bedroom garden home in a complex managed by a trendy seniors living center as well.

That was a pretty good day's work for my first morning back. I returned phone calls, caught up on paperwork, and I even managed to leave a little early for a quick trip to Yesteryear Emporium. The narrow, thirties-style revolving door creaked and complained as I made my way through it.

The owner was behind the sales counter, as usual, typing away on his pingy Underwood.

"Look around all you want," he said without even bothering to glance up.

"I will," I assured him.

As I passed the mezzanine stairway with its oak steps and rails guarded only by a flimsy piece of cord bearing a sign that read Private Keep Out, I was secretly thinking it would serve the guy right if I went rifling through his apartment. I resisted the temptation only because I figured that as little as the man seemed to know about antiques, there wouldn't be anything up there even remotely interesting to me.

I wandered happily through the building for the better part of an hour. The store acquired new stock rather haphazardly and it was jumbled together in such a way that you simply had to happen upon things. It wasn't a very good way to run a business, but it certainly did add a treasure-hunt aspect to shopping. I found a beautiful one-piece dry-sink cabinet. I absolutely loved it, but I'd have to renovate my kitchen to use it. If I hadn't spent so much money on those charities, I would have done exactly that. But I *had* written those checks, so I rolled up my sleeves and moved a half-dozen scratched twenties-era machine-made bed frames in front of it, hoping that no one would unearth the cabinet until my new condo deal panned out.

I spend a lot of money buying antiques. But owning them is not a big thing for me. The fact that my house is stuffed to the seams appears to belie that statement. The truth is, I had always been drawn to them. They are like some attachment with history. Maybe because I had no family history I could speculate about, I transferred that curiosity to objects that people from the past held or touched or used.

Whatever the reason, antiques were very special to me. And an afternoon just wandering among them could lift my spirits when they were low, soothe me when I was anxious and entertain me when things were going fine.

In a big wooden bin full of miscellaneous metalwork, I found a very handsome set of silver casters, the three pieces wrapped together with a couple of rounds of masking tape. The price, written in black marker on the tape, was about what they were worth. I figured I could talk the owner down a few dollars and still get them at a bargain. Then I spotted a pair of modern silver-plate salt and pepper shakers. They were wrapped in the same tape and the price on them was less than half of what was on the casters.

The masking tape came off fairly easily. I wadded the casters' tape into a ball and stuck it into my pocket. I put the cheaper silver-plate price around the silver casters and went to the counter.

The owner was still pounding determinedly upon his typewriter.

"Excuse me!" I said in a high, haughty tone that was meant to convey the idea that *I'm too important to be ignored.*

"One second," the guy said without looking up. "Just let me finish this thought."

I was annoyed. It was just more evidence of the failings of the service economy when an owner couldn't be hurried to take a customer's money.

Impatiently I began to tap my fingernails upon the counter. It was calculatedly rude, but I was not a woman accustomed to waiting.

Then it suddenly struck me as funny that I was put out because this fellow wasn't quicker to let me rob him.

As unexpected as the arrival of such a thought was the truth in it. I had grown accustomed to talking this man out of his inventory. Getting a better deal than I deserved. But changing prices was not a negotiation— it was a fraud or shoplifting or…well, it was something and it wasn't something good. I had promised to "do good."

Right there, in my favorite store, in the middle of the afternoon, I had an acute attack of conscience.

"Okay," the owner said, rising from his little desk behind the counter. He didn't bother with his cane. His gait was awkward, the right leg was scraggly somehow, he moved it keeping his knee stiff, and it was not as well muscled as the left. "Did you want to buy these?"

The question was mostly rhetorical as he picked up the casters. He glanced at the price on the masking tape and reached over to punch it in on the ancient cash register.

"I don't want to buy them," I blurted out.

He looked up, surprised.

I don't think I'd ever looked at him eye to eye before. His were a surprising vivid blue. I'd always thought the man to be about my age, but the depths behind his gaze were like aeons of time. He'd seen a lot. Maybe he'd seen too much.

"I don't want to buy them," I repeated. "I…I brought

them up because I think they are mismarked. These are eighteenth-century silver. I don't recognize the mark, but they are obviously American. You've got them priced here as if they were ordinary silver plate."

"Really?"

He examined the three little containers more closely.

I told him what I thought a reasonable price would be for the set. The amount I suggested was a little higher than the one that had been on the original masking tape, but it was what I thought he could get.

"I'd pay that much for them myself," I said, "but I'm just looking today."

His eyes narrowed and he glared at me intently. Slowly he nodded as if he understood.

"So," he said, "you don't want to *buy* anything. You're just coming up here to point out what an idiot I am."

"Ah...no, of course not," I stammered.

"I'm really busy today," he told me, his words rife with deliberate patience. "If you want these you can have them at the price marked on them."

"No, I don't want them," I assured him. "I just wanted you to know that the price is wrong."

"Okay," he said, though he continued to look at me unpleasantly.

"I'm just trying to help you," I told him.

"Right."

"You could say thank you."

"Look," he snarled firmly, "I don't have time for this little song-and-dance number you always do. I'm not sure what you're up to, but I'm not haggling over this crap today."

"I'm not haggling," I assured him a little sharply. "And this is excellent artisan silverwork not crap."

His mouth thinned into one disapproving line.

"What ever," he said as if it were two distinct words. He laid the casters in my hands. "Take them."

"What?"

"They're all yours."

He turned away as if that was the end of it.

"Wait! No, I couldn't do that."

"Of course you can."

"Then I have to pay you."

"That would involve coming to an agreement on a price," he said. "And I just don't have the stomach for it."

I stood there staring at him, speechless, dumbfounded.

He relented slightly, his tone more conciliatory. "Just accept them as a gift, Janey," he said. "They're yours."

The sound of my name on his lips was a surprise.

"You know me?"

The man folded his arms across his chest, and in a singsong voice, like a brattish pubescent, said, "Janey Domschke is no dumb-ski, she's the smartest girl in school. If you don't believe it, ask her."

The little taunt was so far in my past, yet so familiar.

"Lofton," I corrected. "Janey…Jane Lofton." But…

"Jane Lofton," he said. "Just take the silver. Think of it as a gift from someone from the old neighborhood."

"We knew each other in Sunnyside?"

"Middle school," he answered. "I'm Scott. Your project partner in seventh-grade science. Sedimentary-rock strata."

I'm sure my jaw dropped open. I stood there looking at his face, remembering him from another lifetime.

"Scott? The junkman's son?"

That designation would have been an insult back in Sunnyside. Scott held out his arms, indicating our surroundings.

"Of course, we don't call it junk anymore, Janey," he

told me with more than a hint of condescension in his tone. "Now we say 'antiques and collectibles.'"

I was too disconcerted to even comment. Fortunately, it wasn't necessary.

"If you don't mind," he said, "I'm very busy. Take your gift and run along. Next week, I promise to bargain like a fishwife."

He turned back to his grimy typewriter and I walked out, reluctantly carrying the silver casters.

All the time I'd been getting bargains off the junkman's son from Sunnyside. I shook my head with disbelief.

Sunnyside was an area of town that now existed only in the memories of those who had lived there. The final leg of the interstates that brought suburban dwellers into downtown had its three-level interchange built right over the neighborhood. The junior high, directly underneath one of the massive cloverleafs, was the first thing to go. Our class of impressionable thirteen-year-olds had been scattered by buses to distant schools. I'd gotten a scholarship to St. Agnes. When the house we lived in was slated for demolition, my mother moved us to an apartment closer to the hospital. I never saw any of my fellow classmates again.

As far as I was concerned, that was just as well. The last thing in the world that I would ever want to do is to wax nostalgic about my working-class origins.

My mother was a smart, attractive, ambitious young woman. I think perhaps she only made one mistake in her life. That was marrying my dad. Leon Domschke had been suave and handsome, a German Frank Sinatra, my mother had said. A difficult type to imagine. And imagine was all I could ever do. Mom left him when I was just a toddler and there was not a photograph of him in her possession. As a teenager I conjured up the idea that he was like Allison MacKenzie's father in *Peyton Place,* just a name made up to hide my out-of-wedlock birth. But after Mom died, I found her divorce decree among her papers. There had, indeed, been a Leon Wilbur Domschke. Where he came from or went to, I never knew.

I put the silver casters, still wrapped together in the wrong masking tape, in the cup holder of the Z3.

I should have gone ahead and cheated him, I thought to myself. The junkman's son at least would have gotten half the money he deserved and I wouldn't feel as though I owed the man anything. But no, I had to try doing something good, get my motives questioned and end up with an unwelcome obligation.

Annoyed, I started up the car, slipped it into gear and laid rubber as I drove away. Back at the office, I'd just walked in the door when Kelli, the receptionist, said I had a call. It was from the Shelter for Displaced Wild Creatures asking for a donation. It was the first ripple in what turned out to be a tidal wave.

The next few weeks were some of the strangest I had ever lived.

The response to my night of check writing was immediate and overwhelming. Never underestimate the scope and range of a donors list. It was as if my phone number had appeared out of thin air on the speed dial of every solicitation organization in the world. There were reputable, well-known philanthropic organizations, obscure, esoteric charities, and there were scams of every form and function.

I became very adept at saying no. I'd given what I had given and that was all I intended to give. I was forceful and certain. Disabusing any and all about my willingness to make further contributions.

David was more irate than I was. Not as much at the unwelcome callers as at me for the chaos that had been brought into our lives. The charities, solicitors and con artists were just doing what they do, but I had brought this on us. And I had never really been able to explain my motives to him. Now we had strangers, often unpleasant strangers, intruding on our privacy day and night.

With his parents beside him, David finally confronted me. We were having a cocktail together beside their pool before going for an evening at the club.

"This whole business is some kind of craziness," he said. "You are just not acting like yourself."

"I am myself," I insisted. "I just feel differently about some things."

The three original members of the Lofton family shared a look confirming my suspicion that I had already been the subject of a long and involved discussion.

"I think you ought to see a therapist," Edith said. "Oprah is always telling us not to be afraid to reach out for help."

David and W.D. nodded in agreement.

"That's a great idea," David said. "It will give you an opportunity to talk about what happened."

"I'm surprised that you don't have a psychiatrist already," W.D. said. "Edith, don't most of those women friends of yours go to shrinks?"

"They are artists," she answered. "Of course they're in therapy."

"Jane, do you know someone who you can make an appointment with?" David asked.

"What about that doctor of Brynn's you liked so well?" Edith asked.

David was shaking his head. "He turned out to be way too obsequious and permissive."

"That won't be a problem for Jane," W.D. pointed out. "It's not as if she's easily influenced."

"Wait a minute!" I interrupted them finally. "I haven't said that I will see a therapist. I haven't even thought about it."

"Well you certainly *should* think about it," Edith said.

"Really, Jane," David agreed. "We just want you to get back to being yourself. We want our lives to be the way they always were."

I didn't know anymore if that was even possible.

My thoughts eventually drove me to the library. The library had always been my rescue, my haven, my source. It was at the library that I first realized that there was a life beyond the tacky ordinariness of Sunnyside. And it was the library that showed me how to purchase my ticket out. Whenever I'd faced something unfamiliar, whether it was the Graduate Record Exam or the flatware layout at the Junior League Tea, it was there that I'd found my answers.

Truthfully, I don't believe I would have been able to manage motherhood otherwise. Not only had the library furnished every possible type of reading material on child rearing, it was the clearinghouse for hundreds of short courses, workshops and children's activities that had filled Brynn's early years.

So, with my thoughts in a whirl and my curiosity as strong as my determination, I made my way through the flocks of noisy children and chairs full of homeless people toward the reference desk at the public library. And before you could say altruism, I was up to my eyeballs in Comte and Aquinas, Locke and Hegel. Is there such a thing as a truly altruistic act? Is it the nature of man to do good or to be self-serving?

I read and read and read some more, but the answers just didn't come. The more knowledge I accumulated the less clear my understanding. The whole thing just gave me a headache. I'm not a philosopher, I'm a Realtor. I just needed to sell someone a great house that would keep their family safe and comfortable for a decade, that's all the good I knew how to do.

I threw myself into my work. I had made some contributions. I had done some good. That was all I had promised. I'd delivered. Anyone in town could tell you, Jane Lofton doesn't make deals that she can't deliver. If the nagging thought that I could still do even more lingered, I didn't pay it much attention.

The fall afternoons at the library had me missing Brynn and the time we used to spend together. It's one of those crazy truths about parent bonding that you can love your child desperately, totally. Understand her only superficially. And get along with her abysmally.

I had just finished examining an Excel spreadsheet on last quarter's sale prices and checked my watch. On the East Coast it was late afternoon already and she'd be out of class. I picked up the phone and pressed her name on my speed dial.

She answered on the second ring.

"Hello, Mother."

Her words were punctuated with a sigh, but she'd obviously checked the caller ID before answering. If she knew it was me and picked up anyway, it was a good sign.

"Hi, sweetie," I said. "How was your day?"

There was a long moment of silence before her reply. "Fine."

She didn't return the inquiry, but I filled her in on my life anyway.

"I was at the public library today and I was thinking about you and all the hours we spent there," I said.

"Yeah?"

"They were actually having a Bookworms meeting," I said. "Do you remember Bookworms?"

"No," she answered.

"Oh sure you do," I coaxed. "It's a third- and fourth-grade reading group."

"Fourth and fifth," Brynn corrected.

"Was it?" I asked, pleased that she did recall those days even if she wouldn't admit it. "They all look so young. Carrying their Louisa May Alcotts and Judy Blumes."

"Were they all skinny, gangly girls with braces?" she asked.

Of course they hadn't been. Some were all pretty and precious, nymphlike perfection. Everything that Brynn had not been at that age. She got her looks from the Loftons—patrician lean, long-necked and graceful. But age nine to eleven, she was not at her best. I had wanted to help her, to give her confidence. But everything I did and said made it worse. Even now I tried lying to protect her.

"It's an awkward age for every girl," I said.

"Yeah," Brynn agreed. "But I guess some of us just never get past it."

In a way, she was right about that. That was the beginning of Brynn's years in counseling. She'd suddenly been so unhappy. And her timing couldn't have been worse. I'd just gotten to the place where I wanted to go on with my own life, pursue my own goals. I wanted her to need me less. It seemed as if she deliberately needed me more.

A child psychologist was a perfect solution. Why not delegate unfathomable teenage crises to someone with the knowledge and experience to deal with them? And it was certainly easier to pay for therapy than to figure out what was going on in my daughter's head.

Now, eight years later, she was still in twice-weekly sessions with no end in sight. The therapist knew her hopes, her dreams, her ambitions. I knew what the therapist wrote about her in one-paragraph reports.

Deliberately I changed the subject.

"You know that lady with the braids rolled up on either side of her head," I told her. "She is still at the circulation desk."

"I don't remember any lady at the circulation desk," Brynn replied.

"Of course you do," I insisted. "You were always fascinated by her. You asked me if she was wearing hair earmuffs."

"You make this stuff up, Mother," she answered. "Anyway, nobody goes to libraries anymore. You're supposed to do your research on the Internet."

"Not everything is on the Internet," I said.

"Everything that matters is," she answered.

"Well, maybe I just like going there," I said. "And I'm sure there are plenty of people who go to the library on your campus."

"Sure, plenty," Brynn replied. "They go there to make dope deals, though, not to study."

The last was said for the specific purpose of unnerving me. It was my greatest dread that Brynn would get involved in drugs or alcohol. There was so much recreational use of marijuana and cocaine around her. And getting drunk was considered an innocent fixture of college life, like football games and panty raids. For a young woman with the insecurities and self-image problems of Brynn, getting high might be a leaven that would keep her from ever fixing what was actually wrong in her life.

"Well, if there were any dope deals done in front of me today, I didn't see them," I said, deliberately making light of my fears. "Do you think the lady with the hair earmuffs is in a smuggling ring?"

She giggled then. It was the same giggle that she's had at age five, and I let the sound wash over me wonderfully for a moment. She had not been a carefree child, but she'd been happy.

"Or maybe she's a cop," I suggested. "Working under hair-muff cover."

We had never had that closeness I envied among mothers and daughters. She had never told me her secrets. I had never offered words of wisdom. But we had shared some fun times in our rocky parent-child relationship.

"You're making me laugh, Mom," she said. "That must mean you are softening me up for something."

I loved it when she called me *Mom*.

"No," I assured her. "I'm not softening you up."

"If you're thinking I'll attend that disgusting Christmas gala at the club," she said, "I won't."

"Your father doesn't like going either," I said. "Maybe we'll just skip it."

"As if!" Brynn said facetiously. "Anyway, I'm not coming home."

"You're not coming home for Christmas?"

"That's what I just said." Her tone was defensive. "I'm a grown woman. I can make my own decisions. Dr. Reiser said I don't have to go home if I don't want to."

I felt bereft, as if she'd punched me in the stomach. I tried not to reveal it in my words or tone.

"No, no, of course you don't have to come home," I said.

"I'd rather be with my friends," she said. "You understand that. I'm sure you feel the same way."

I didn't, but I did understand how it felt to be young. I had never wanted to spend time with my own mother.

"Brynn, we'll really miss you," I said.

"Sorry." She threw the word out with a casualness

the belied its meaning. "So why did you call?" she asked.

"No reason, I just wanted to talk to you."

"If you want to talk, make an appointment with a therapist," she said. "Edith told me you really need one."

"You've spoken with your grandmother?"

"She said you're going through 'the change' or something," Brynn answered.

"I'm not going through 'the change,'" I told her. "That's just Oprah's latest topic. I'm just a little confused right now. I went through a very scary, life-threatening experience."

"Mother," Brynn retorted with a long suffering sigh. "It was a car wreck and you weren't even injured." She chided me as if she were the adult. "You are always so dramatic. Dr. Reiser says that your life is just so comfortable that you have to exaggerate your little day-to-day challenges."

"Dr. Reiser doesn't know me," I pointed out.

"Oh puh-lease, Mother," she said. "Everybody knows you. You're practically a *type*—shallow, egocentric narcissist."

"That isn't who I am," I insisted.

"Isn't it?"

There was more truth to her observation than I wanted to acknowledge.

# 4

Sunday is the busiest day in real estate. Business properties are big on Wednesday. New homes and developments hit the top of the radar on Saturday. But existing family homes, the bread and butter of American real estate, makes its biggest splash on the last day of the weekend. That's when house hunters are out in force, and brokers are frantically competing for their attention.

The housing section of the newspaper hits front porches about 5:00 a.m. By seven-thirty my phone is already ringing. For most of the week, it's a waste of money to even buy space in the classifieds. On Sunday, I think reading them must be more popular than the sports page. I always have a couple of my current listings highlighted, and more often than not, I have an open house scheduled.

So I have always considered it particularly admirable on my part that on this most crazy and hectic of days I almost always attend church.

Not that it is easy. Inevitably, as the service begins, I will be standing out on the front steps. All around me smokers frantically suck down that last bit of tar and nicotine to get them through the hour service. Unhappy babies scream at the top of their lungs as frazzled young mommies or daddies juggle them up and down ineffectually. Teenagers, momentarily safe from parental supervision, neck and grope in the parking lot.

And real estate brokers, like myself, take care of some inevitable last-minute crisis on our respective cell phones.

I don't think I've seen the processional in at least ten years. But I usually make it to my seat before the opening prayer.

With lots of limestone, dark woods and neo-gothic flourishes, St. Jude's is one of the oldest and most architecturally beautiful churches in the city. It is also the prominent religious institution of wealthy and powerful Protestants. The Loftons have been parishioners there for generations. They actually have their own pew. As do most of the "better-known families" in town. Which may not be the only reason that the congregation is always back heavy. The pews in front, with their little brass plates upon the side, are often empty. Still, the nameless attendees who must sit where they can, all crowd in the back, as if unwilling to risk the possible humiliation of being ousted from a seat that was spoken for.

The Loftons sit sixth row, center section. Both David and his parents are faithful members. W.D. seems to attend out of a sense of personal duty; Edith, because Oprah has repeatedly stressed the importance of faith in a balanced life. David goes, I think, because it fits into his schedule. He has a regular foursome dawn-patrol tee-off. They are done in time to dress for services. Beyond that, my husband's religious motivation is a mystery to me.

Though I have attended with David for twenty years and raised my daughter here, I am not actually a member of the congregation. Not that I am in any way opposed to that. It is simply that joining requires attending workshops and courses, participating in rituals, that sort of thing. I never really saw any advantage in it.

I have all the privileges of being a part of St. Jude's without any of the burdens or obligations.

I slipped in at the last moment and took my place at David's side as inconspicuously as possible. I nodded to my mother-in-law, who gave me a warm smile that seemed strictly for public consumption.

David, who was in deep discussion with his father, didn't even glance in my direction.

"I was completely off on my irons," he was whispering. "My drivers were good and my putting was above par, but I could have just stayed home for all that the irons did for me."

I picked up the prayer book and feigned glancing at it as I scanned the front of the room. I spotted Lexi sitting with her slightly slump-shouldered and gray, older husband. In a vivid red suit, she sparkled like a beam of sunshine in the dark, somber interior.

I saw Teddy, too. She didn't have Lexi's style or chic. She was as drab and conservative as I was myself. I have always been a little unsure of my fashion sense. I think Teddy dressed that way because she wanted to be taken more seriously. I'm not sure how well that was working.

What definitely was not working was the little fur-puff hat that Beverly Mullins had on. Gil's wife sat two rows up from me and across the aisle. The hat was probably mink and undoubtedly expensive. Her recently deceased father-in-law had left Gil and Beverly very well off. And the fact that the old man's will had forced Gil to sell controlling interest of the family business to Gil's cousin, Henry, had put even more money in their pockets. But even mink could be worn miserably. It might have been all right if she'd put her hair up. But, as usual, she'd simply pulled it all together with a clip at the nape of her neck. Her hair was almost the exact color of the hat, giving her a Davy Crockett appear-

ance. Lexi caught my eye. She indicated with a glance
that she too had noticed the would-be coonskin cap,
and we shared a catty grin at Beverly's expense as the
music ended.

We stood up. We sat down. We stood up. We knelt.
We stood. We sat. It was over and we filed out.

The sermon touched me virtually not at all. I'm not
faulting the quality of the teaching or the delivery of
the message. Honestly, I was rather in the habit of not
listening. Sunday church was an extension of my social
world. I'm not saying that I went there only to see and
be seen. But I do admit to attending more out of routine
than moral obligation.

The promise that I'd made in those frightening moments in the car felt more like an obligation than any religious injunction I'd ever encountered.

As David and I took leave of his parents and made
our way through the parking lot, I considered that. My
words, when I was trapped inside the car, indicated a
belief in *something* that could make things change, in
*someone* who could intervene. But I was not really
aware, on a rational level, of any belief in that someone
or something at all.

"Do you want me to take you to lunch?" David
asked.

I shook my head.

The Loftons always went out for a meal after church.
I was never interested, and my work was paramount
on the biggest real estate day of the week.

"I'll just drop you off then and grab a bite at the
club," he said.

I didn't bother to answer. David had just come from
the club. He'd already played eighteen holes that
morning. I knew he wasn't headed back there, but I'd
grown accustomed to letting him get by with those little lies.

He unlocked the passenger's side of his Volvo and opened it for me. It was an achingly sweet and deferential gesture. David might be carrying on a tacky affair with a bleached blonde twenty-something, but it was still in his nature to be attentive to his wife. I was grateful and I let him do it. Though when he shut the door behind me, I held my breath, claustrophobic, as he walked around the car to let himself in.

The minute he turned the key, I hit the button to open the sunroof.

He glanced in my direction.

"You're not quite over it yet, huh."

"It's stuffy in here," I lied. "Smells like golf shoes."

He shrugged with apology.

The rush of traffic trying to get out of the church parking lot was horrendous, as usual. At least in the Volvo I felt relatively safe. In the Z3 I would have felt like a bug about to be squashed by a hundred, three-ton SUVs.

Of course none of these Suburbans or Expeditions were even close competition to the eighteen-wheel tanker that had squeezed me up against that guardrail and made my little BMW into a fiery coffin. A chill went through me. I was still afraid, I was still very afraid. And I couldn't quite comprehend my survival. After all these years of not thinking much about my life, I now saw it as if it were over, and I wanted more.

I gazed out at the gray, overcast autumn day and the neighborhood lawns passing beyond my window.

"David," I asked, "do you believe in God?"

"Sure," he answered quickly and with complete confidence.

I looked over at him. It was strange, I suppose, that having been married to the man for twenty years this was the first time I'd thought to ask that.

"Do you ever…well…pray?"

He looked at me, puzzled. "Didn't we just do that?" he asked rhetorically.

"No, I don't mean in church," I said. "I mean, do you ever ask God for things?"

"Like what things?"

"I don't know, not *things* really. Do you ask God to help you?"

"Well, yeah," he admitted.

"Really?"

"Sure," he said. "All the time."

"Does he answer?"

"He doesn't speak to me from a burning bush," David said, sounding a little defensive.

"Of course not," I agreed. "But still, you ask him and you feel like he answers."

He nodded. "If I've got something that I have to make a decision on and I'm not sure which way to go, I put it to him."

"What do you say?"

"What do you mean?"

"What do you say when you ask God to help you?"

"Well…it's not so much that I *say* anything," he explained.

David appeared increasingly uncomfortable with the conversation.

"Do you just assume that he knows and then assume that he answers?"

"I don't assume anything," he said. "I let God give me a sign."

"A sign."

"Yeah, it's like this, if I need to decide whether to enter the Pro-Am this year, I say, 'Okay, if I make this hole in three strokes or less then the answer is yes. If it's four, then it's no.'"

I stared at him for a moment, disbelieving.

"You think that is the same thing as praying?"

"Well, maybe it's not exactly praying. But golf is not completely a game of skill," he assured me. "Luck plays a big part."

"And luck is God?"

He nodded. "Well, sure," then added, "if I think it's not luck I do two out of three."

So much for the omnipotent golf gods.

"Have you thought any more about therapy?" David asked me.

"I'm fine," I assured him. "I lived through a frightening experience. But it's over now and I'm almost completely back to normal."

He chuckled. There was a skeptical sound to it.

"Well, if this is normal, it must be a new kind," he said. "I don't ever remember having such a deep conversation with you."

The truth made me a little defensive.

"We've talked about serious stuff before," I insisted. "Maybe not often, but sometimes we do. Anyway, we don't have all that many serious things to discuss."

"No, I guess not," he agreed. "And we usually don't talk at all on the way home from church. You're always on the phone."

"Oh my God!" I said suddenly, digging my cellular out of the bottom of my purse. "I forgot to turn it back on."

It rang as soon as I did.

In the days that followed, I forced my life back into a more normal mode. I resumed working with a renewed enthusiasm that was only partly feigned. I clearly remembered my promise to do good. But I hadn't gotten specific. Selling real estate is good. It's honest, much-needed work, and it requires significant amounts of energy and creativity. Much more so than simply writing checks.

However, there was one more check that I wanted to write. I wanted to write it and simply put everything behind me. The man who had rescued me deserved a reward. Yet I hesitated to take that final step to closure.

Finally, on a Saturday morning, not too early, not too close to lunch, I drove out to the area of town where it had all happened. I hadn't been out that way since that awful night. The very idea of being there again gave me an eerie feeling. I slowed down as I passed by, expecting to see something, but except for some scarring on the guardrail, there was no evidence that a man had died here, or that I had lived through the most frightening moments of my life.

I took the exit and backtracked to the Bluebonnet Manor Assisted Living Center. The parking lot was about half filled and I pulled the Z3 into a space that faced the freeway. As I got out of the car, I gazed down toward the site of the accident. It was a very long way. My vision was better than twenty-twenty with my contacts, but I couldn't distinguish anything at that distance. I might have been able to see a wreck, but I wouldn't have seen anybody trapped inside a car.

No one could have seen me. No one could have heard me.

I made my way to the wide, glassed-in entryway. Inside, the foyer was wide and nicely furnished with wood floors and expensive area rugs. A massive dark wood desk that was grand enough to be a dining table was the predominant feature of the reception area. Unfortunately, no one was seated there. A sign read Check in at Nursing Station, so I wandered on past and into the living-room area, which was rather heavily occupied.

A row of wheelchairs were parked in front of a television set that was turned up unpleasantly loud. The occupants didn't seem to be paying much attention to the blaring game show with its flashing lights and excited, screaming participants. On the numerous couches, other aged people sat quietly, some watching, some not. One woman was talking nonstop to nobody in particular. Her conversation sounded as if she were recounting a bridge game. She was dressed to the nines, sported gigantic hair and makeup heavy enough for the stage.

I spotted a high counter at the juncture of two wide hallways. I took that to be the nurses' station, though no one was there either. I walked over and stood for several minutes just waiting.

I had assumed that an assisted living center was somehow different from a nursing home, that the patients would be younger, healthier, and that the atmosphere would be more upbeat. I saw absolutely none of that at Bluebonnet Manor.

"May I help you?"

I was startled out of my thoughts by a heavyset woman in a pink uniform pantsuit. Her words were polite, but her tone was not. She sounded annoyed. As if my presence was unwelcome.

"I'm here to see Chester Durbin," I said.

She gave me a long, assessing look. "Are you a member of the family?"

I probably should have told her that I was the woman Chester saved in the car accident, but somehow I couldn't bring myself to confide anything to the woman.

"No, I'm...I'm a friend," I answered.

She immediately seemed to lose interest.

"Twenty-two," she said, pointing down one of the hallways. "He should be up in a chair."

I made my way in the direction she indicated. Like the main room, this area was heavily populated with patients, some in wheelchairs or pushing walkers, others on their own, but still hanging close to the wooden handrails on either side of the corridor.

Room twenty-two was near the far end of the vinyl-tiled passage. The door was half-open. More than a little hesitantly, I peeked inside. I thought I had the wrong room. I double-checked the number beside the door, then looked again.

In the yellow glow of a gaudy table lamp, a very little old man, emaciatedly thin, sat in a faded recliner. His plaid sport shirt hung upon his frame as if a couple of sizes too large. His legs were crossed in front of him and looked like there was more trouser fabric than flesh and bone. His feet were bound up in some kind of strange bandage material and he wore little slippers that had a high-tech look, quite incongruent with the rest of his fashion statement.

"Mr. Durbin?" I asked.

"Yes."

I was disconcerted by the sight of him, familiar, yet so unlike what I remembered.

"Yes, come in," he encouraged after a moment. "You're looking for me?"

"Ah…ah, yes, sir," I answered, stumbling a little over the words. "I'm Jane Lofton, remember me?"

He laughed. "At my age, I'm lucky to remember myself," he joked.

"I'm the woman from the car," I said.

His brow furrowed, puzzled. "The car?"

"The car in the accident," I said. "Down on the freeway. You saved me."

"Of course, you're the young lady in the convertible," he said.

I never bicker with the word *young* when used to describe me, and I certainly didn't in this case. My rescuer seemed infinitely older than I recalled, and surprisingly frail.

"Have a seat, have a seat," he coaxed, patting the threadbare armchair beside him. "Let me have a look at you."

With hesitance, I seated myself, wishing I hadn't come. I should have just put a check in the mail.

He leaned forward slightly, a grimace distorting his face as he peered at me through rheumy eyes and thick glasses.

"You're looking real good this morning," he said.

I nodded. "I'm sure I look a lot better than I did that night. I'm feeling a lot better, too."

"Good, good," he said. "Wasn't that something? I can tell you that night was the most excitement we've seen around this place in a month of Sundays. Your life must be a lot more interesting."

Clearly he wanted to steer the discussion in some other direction, but I silently encouraged myself to stay on point. This was an obligation that I wanted to get behind me.

"I came here to thank you for what you did..." I began.

He shook his head, snorting.

"You already thanked me," he said. "And I don't even remember what I did. The whole dang night is just a blur to me. That's the way it is sometimes. If I'd been *trying* to get out there and help you, I'd never have made it in a million years."

"Well, you did get out there and help me, Mr. Durbin," I told him. "I wouldn't be here otherwise."

"Lord help us, you'd better call me Chester," he said. "When you say that *Mr. Durbin*, I'm looking over my shoulder for my daddy. And that bad-tempered old drunk has been dead since 1934."

He laughed wholeheartedly, as if what he'd said was funny. I was far too uncomfortable to find any humor in it at all.

"I want to thank you, Mr. Dur...ah, Chester. You saved my life."

"Why, you're welcome, you're welcome," he said. "If it hadn't been me, it would have been someone else. The important thing is that you were saved, weren't ya?"

"Well, yes...uh..."

"Enough said."

I felt a tug of annoyance. He seemed to be trying to wave away my gratitude. I couldn't let him do that.

"It's not enough said," I insisted. "I'm here to thank you and to...and to offer you a reward."

I fished through my purse hurriedly, coming up with a pen and my checkbook. I flipped it open and immediately began writing. When I got to the amount, I hesitated. The thought of how much my life was worth stopped me cold. A thousand dollars? Ten thousand? A million? Or much more? Infinitely more.

"What are you doing?" he asked.

"I'm writing you a check."

"What would I do with that?"

The question surprised me. Was the fellow not all there, mentally? "You can take the check to the bank and get money," I explained.

He chuckled.

"I know that," he assured me. "My question is, what can I do with money?"

I looked at him quizzically, still not sure if he was getting it.

"You could buy yourself something."

He held up his hands, gesturing to the little crowded room that surrounded him.

"Why would I want to buy myself anything," he said with a tone that indicated wry humor. "I've already had to give up nearly everything I've ever had to fit myself into this little room."

He had a point. The place was cozy to the point of crowded with bookshelves, chairs, lamps, a writing desk, chest of drawers. Fine wood carvings sat next to cheesy ceramic knickknacks and see-through plastic boxes crammed with fading papers. I didn't know if he meant his words philosophically or literally. But the place where he lived was tiny and filled.

"I don't even cash my social security. They just send it directly to my keepers here, who dole the excess out to me in new undershorts, tooth powder and little bottles of shampoo."

His goofy grin was somehow contagious. I was feeling more upbeat about the meeting, yet it obviously was not going at all the way I'd planned.

"I need to repay you somehow for what you did for me," I said.

"Why?" he asked.

"Because I promised."

"You didn't promise me," he pointed out. "Who did you promise?"

I wasn't sure exactly how I wanted to answer that.

"When I was out in the car," I said, "when I was trapped…"

I hadn't yet spoken of it. I hadn't told anyone. I hadn't said a word out loud. It sounded too strange, too crazy, too otherworldly. People like me didn't make bargains with God. We didn't plead for miracles. I didn't know if I *could* even say what I meant.

Surprisingly, I didn't have to.

Chester's rheumy eyes suddenly brightened with mischief and understanding. "Oh, I see," he said. "You, Miss Jane Lofton, you're one of us, aren't you."

"I don't know what you mean."

"You're one of us," he said. "You got in a jam that you couldn't get out of and you made him a deal."

"Yes," I whispered with a guilty glance toward the door.

"You made a deal with God," he said. "No need to be ashamed of that with me. I've got one going myself."

"You made a deal, too?" I was surprised.

"Years ago," he answered. "And it's not just the two of us. It happens every day of the week. Things get bad and people start making promises. I'll go straight. Or I'll quit drinking, we say. We tell him we're going to take up a vocation or go back to our family. We've vowed never to cheat again or to limit our conversation to truth and silence."

"I...I just promised to do good," I admitted.

He whistled appreciatively. "Well, that certainly covers it," he said. "I bet it's not as easy as it sounds. How is it going?"

"Not that great so far."

The story came pouring out of me. I told him about my Yellow Pages charity checks and the unpleasant inundating response. I told him everything.

"So that's why you came here," he said. "You were trying to do something good for me."

I nodded.

"Well, there's not much left that can be done for me," Chester told me. "I'm not getting well or getting younger. I'm in here for the duration. And I've got no way of knowing how long that might be."

"I'm...I'm sorry," I said, not knowing what other response to make.

Chester chuckled. "No use apologizing," he said. "I've had a good long life, happy mostly, and I tried to do what I said I would."

"What was your deal with God?" I asked him.

"Me?" He chuckled again. "I made promises that I spent a lifetime trying to keep."

"What kind of promises?" I asked.

"Oh, kind of like yours. I said I'd be a help to folks in need," he told me. "And I vowed to live decently and upright, to be truthful, principled and honorable. But hardest of all, I promised never to ask for anything else again."

He spoke the words with a quiet dignity that was familiar, yet strangely unsettling. Words like *decency* and *honor* were only spoken in political campaigns, when everyone knew they were lies. Chester Durbin spoke them with absolute conviction, like some Gary Cooper hero. It was disconcerting. I lived in a world where the most violent, grisly murder is portrayed in graphic detail for the delight of an audience. And where the most heinous sexual perversions are admitted and rationalized on afternoon TV talk shows. The old man's integrity was out of the ordinary, and made me ill at ease.

Deliberately, I tried joking us out of the seriousness of the discussion.

"You must have been really scared to promise all that."

He did laugh at my words. But then, he was not the one who was bothered by our conversation.

"Probably not any more than you were, trapped in that car," he said.

"I didn't promise nearly as much," I pointed out.

"That's because you didn't have nearly as much time," he said. "You only had five or ten minutes to make the deal."

"It seemed like a lot longer," I said.

He nodded. "I'm sure it did," he said. "I had all night, and that night fills a bigger block in my memory than whole decades of my life."

Chester was gazing off into space as if seeing it all again. Surprisingly, he was smiling. He turned his gaze to me.

"Vera and I had only been married about a year," he began. "Though it had been a very busy time—1942. My eighteenth birthday I left high school and volunteered for service. I couldn't wait to go to war. I was full of vinegar. I wanted to wear a uniform and to fight Japs and Germans. Heck, I would have been happy to fight redheaded drunks at the local bar."

Chester chuckled aloud at the memory of his youth.

"Things didn't work out that way," he went on. "I thought I was fit as a fiddle, but the army didn't see it that way. They bounced me out of boot camp on a medical excuse. I was back home in thirty days."

He leaned toward me slightly and raised a collusive eyebrow. "Marrying Vera was my consolation prize," he told me.

"Oh." I nodded.

"Don't mistake me, now," Chester said. "I was in love with that girl. I'd been in love with her since the first moment I ever saw her. But in no time, I was working long hours and we had a baby on the way. It seemed to me that all the other men my age were off to far places, doing exciting, important things. I was jealous of them. And I guess I was resentful of the quiet little life I led."

"You were young," I offered as an extenuation.

He shrugged, but didn't take the truth up as an excuse.

"The foreman came out to get me, saying Vera was in the hospital. For a second, I was excited, thrilled. I thought she'd gone into labor. But there was something on the boss's face that stopped me short. I knew it was bad before he'd even got the words out. Vera had been in an accident.

"The baby had been born dead before I even got there, but the doctor hardly gave me time to take that in when he hit me with the rest of it. There would never be any more children. And Vera had lost a lot of blood. The doctor didn't think she would live. And Vera didn't appear to be trying very much to do so."

Even after all these years, Chester's aged, lined hand trembled as he stroked his temple.

"I'd never been much of a praying man," he admitted. "I figured that if there was a God and he's all-knowing like they say, then what I'm thinking and wanting should be no big mystery to him. But for once in my life, I prayed.

"I was beside her bed that long, long night, pleading, begging, deal making."

"And she lived?"

He nodded. "It didn't feel like a miracle exactly," he said. "She didn't open her eyes, give me a big smile and the two of us get up and walk home. The doctor was surprised that she'd lived through the night. As the minute hand had crept around the clock, it was just one hour at a time that she didn't die. After a day or so, she gradually began to get stronger. She was in the hospital more than a month, but finally I was able to take her home."

"And you kept your promises."

A wry grin crossed his face.

"At first I did, because she seemed so fragile," he admitted. "I thought that if I didn't keep my part of the bargain, God might not keep his either."

"And later?" I asked.

"Well, I guess I just came to the understanding that a deal is a deal," he said. "Vera got well and strong and we were happy together. Fifty-four years we'd been married when she passed on. I never regretted my choice."

"Then you think it was a choice," I said. "Do you think she might have lived anyway, even if you hadn't made the deal?"

Chester shrugged. "Maybe," he said. He looked at me questioningly. "Do you think you would have got out of that car?"

I didn't want to think about it.

I left Bluebonnet Manor Assisted Living Center an hour later, convinced that Chester was right. A deal was a deal. I wanted to keep my promise. I wanted to do good. I still didn't quite know how to go about it, but I was willing to give it a try.

"Just let the opportunities come to you," he suggested. "But no more thinking that this is something where you can just write a check."

"Are you sure I can't at least write one for you? Or maybe donate to your favorite charity?"

He made a tutting noise and shook a finger at me, brooking no further discussion.

"I'll tell you what you can do, Jane Lofton," he said. "You can come visit me from time to time."

"I'd like that," I said, surprising myself with the truth of the statement. "And maybe I could bring you…a fruit basket or gourmet cookies."

A strange look came into his eyes, one that I couldn't quite interpret. A moment passed, then he smiled.

"You know what you could bring me," he said. "I haven't had one of those Snickers bars in…Lord, I don't know how long. They were always my favorite. If every time you come visit me you could bring me a Snickers bar, that would be real good. That would be doing real good."

It seemed like a very small thing to ask.

# 5

The next few days were not any easier than those that had gone before. I thought often of my afternoon with Chester. He had said I should wait for opportunities to do good. He'd assured me that they would come my way. I didn't see anything like that on my horizon. But I kept my eye out anyway.

I was in the mall when a mother and daughter squeezed by me on the escalator. The woman side-swiped me with her shopping bag and then raised a disapproving eyebrow at me, as if the collision were my fault. I probably wouldn't even have noticed the two, but the mom was half dragging the little girl along. The child was pouty and reluctant, digging her heels in at every opportunity. I remembered a million shopping trips with Brynn that were just that way.

About ten or fifteen minutes later I was looking through some blouses and I saw the little girl. She was wandering through the clothes racks, crying and calling for her mother.

I looked around, and being a lot taller, I could see her mother across the room rifling through some Anne Klein sportswear. Apparently, she hadn't even noticed that her daughter was missing.

"Are you lost?" I asked the child.

She wiped her tears and sniveled out, "Yes."

I took her hand and told her that I'd take her to her mother. Ordinarily, I would never get involved in any-

thing with strangers, but as I *was* trying to turn over
this new leaf, it seemed like a perfect opportunity to
help. And the girl did remind me of Brynn when she
was that age.

We wove our way through the maze of clothes racks
and counters, and were just within sight of the mother,
when the woman finally realized her daughter wasn't
with her.

She looked around frantically, and spotted us.

I don't know what I expected. I suppose I thought
there would be a polite thank-you and a happy reunion
between the two of them. Nothing could have been further from the truth.

At the sight of us, her expression changed from anxious parent to rage-crazed she-wolf.

"Get your hands off my daughter!" she screamed.

Every person in the store went immediately still and
then turned to look accusingly at me.

"I was just bringing her back to you," I stammered
stupidly.

The mother paid no attention. She raced over to us
and grabbed the girl by the arm.

Instead of hugging her, she shook her by the shoulders and yelled, "What have I told you about talking to
strangers!"

Feeling inexplicably guilty, I slunk away as inconspicuously as possible.

Days later when I repeated the story to Chester, he
laughed out loud.

"I was thinking I was such a hero, saving the day," I
admitted derisively. "And then a whole store full of
strangers assume I'm a kidnapper or a pedophile."

"I'm so sorry," Chester said.

"I guess it's like they say. No good deed goes unpun-
ished." I quoted.

"Now, don't start thinking that way," he told me.

"It's important to try to do the right thing, even if it turns out differently than you thought it would."

"So motive is more important than outcome?" I asked.

He was thoughtful for a moment and then shook his head. "Motive is not more important than outcome. But the truth is, you don't know the outcome. You only see what happens today. A month from now maybe that mother and daughter are in another store and there is a real predator there. Because of what happened with you, the mother keeps a better eye on the little girl, or the child is less receptive to a person she doesn't know. Or maybe nothing like that happens, but somewhere deep in the mind of that child is a vague memory of a person who helped her when she needed it. And so she helps someone herself. We can't know the kind of effect we have tomorrow or next week or next year or ten years from now."

"So," I said, "we're supposed to keep doing what we think are the right things and just assume that life somehow works out better because of it."

Chester smiled, his eyes bright with humor. "I believe we call that faith."

I wasn't sure that Chester had the right of it, but I felt better after going to see him. Just talking with him made me feel less crazy about what I was trying to do. Chester had been there. Just like me, he knew what it felt like to make a promise. And he knew how important it was for me to keep it.

"Oh, I almost forgot," I said, pulling a Snickers out of my purse. "As per your request, sir."

Chester held the candy bar in his hands almost reverently. Then he got up and shuffled to the chest next to his bed. I watched him carefully hide his treasure under a pile of papers, like a kid who feared that his treat would be stolen.

"I'll save this for later," he told me.

A couple of days later I got an e-mail from the Metro Realtors Alliance about a special low-income housing seminar that was being held downtown. They needed real estate professionals to offer individualized counseling to potential first-time home buyers. I checked my Day-Timer, rearranged a couple of things and replied that I was interested. Five minutes later my phone rang.

"This is a joke, right?"

The question came from Ann Rhoder Hines, chair of the Metro Realtors Outreach Commission. I had shared a passing acquaintance with Ann over the years, but we certainly moved in different circles. She was exactly the kind of woman I had worked very hard not to be. Like me, she'd grown up working-class; smart, motivated and ambitious. But she'd married young and wrong. Her husband drank cheap beer and puttered around at low-paying jobs, her children were hopelessly mediocre. No matter how much real estate the woman sold, no matter how many committees she served on, it was doubtful she could ever overcome those handicaps.

"It's no joke," I assured her in my most egalitarian-colleague voice. "I've cleared my calendar and I'm available to help that Saturday."

There was a long pause at the end of the line. So long, in fact, that I became a little bit desperate to fill it.

"I've always intended to help, Ann," I lied. "But I just couldn't work it into my schedule before."

I don't think she believed me. But she was hardly in a position to turn me down.

"Do you even know anything about affordable housing?"

"Well, no, not specifically," I admitted, then added on an optimistic note, "but it's an area of the market that I'm very interested in learning about."

Ann clearly didn't believe that either, but she did say I could help.

I showed up promptly on Saturday morning at the Downtown Motor Lodge. It was an old and now infrequently utilized conference hotel on the interstate end of the business district. Graffiti-laden and grimy, it had all the decor ambience of a bus station. I was hesitant to even put my ungloved hand on the dirty doorknob. But I whispered a pep talk under my breath, promised myself a half hour of bath beads with whirlpool bubbles and ventured inside.

It wasn't quite as bad as the exterior led me to believe. There was an old, musty smell about the place, the furnishings were out of date and faded, but the lobby appeared to be relatively clean.

A misspelled letter-board sign directed me to the appropriate room, where a dozen rows of straight-back chairs in the middle of the room faced a podium. Tables were set up around the perimeter bearing literature, some of it government issue, but mostly just advertising material from the various local Realtors. No one was bothering to look at any of it. The only area that seemed to have attracted any people was the refreshment table, which bore a coffeemaker, stacks of disposable cups, a big box of doughnuts and a pile of institutional paper towels in lieu of napkins.

Ann Rhoder Hines spotted me and immediately hurried in my direction. With every frosted-blond hair in place, she was dressed in a very nice-looking Dior that had been the height of fashion a couple of years earlier. Undoubtedly, she was buying her designers at the outlet mall. They carry all the leftover merchandise at bargain prices. A lot of women in real estate feel as if they can get away with pretending that yesterday's fashions are merely old favorites. Besides, in her end of the business, the clients didn't know a Dana from a dog biscuit.

I, on the other hand, was wearing an outrageously expensive young designer called Q.T. The suit was gray and functional enough to be sold at Restoration Hardware. I picked it because I thought it might be best to look a little dowdy among the poor people.

"Good morning!" I called out cheerfully.

"You're late," was her rather cranky response.

I glanced down at my watch. It was barely fifteen minutes past the time I was supposed to be there. It hardly seemed worth mentioning, but I gave an explanation anyway.

"I had trouble finding a place to park," I told her.

Ann's expression was still disgruntled. "Didn't you get my e-mail? I told you to park here in the back."

Her suggestion was laughable. And I admit I did come out with a little chuckle as I shook my head. "Surely you don't think that I should leave my new BMW in an open lot in this neighborhood."

Apparently, she didn't appreciate my humor. She certainly didn't crack a smile.

"Did you at least read the material that I faxed to you?"

"Oh yes, of course," I assured her, and it was absolutely true. I didn't sell five million dollars' worth of real estate the previous year by ignoring my homework. I would never attempt to do business being unprepared. I think Ann wanted to believe that I was an airhead who was successful because of my connections. Admittedly, I married for money and position, but I worked at my career. And everything that I had achieved, I had reason to be proud of.

"Are you clear on how the government programs operate?" she asked. "Most of your clients don't even employ gardeners who could qualify."

That was stretching it.

"I guess I don't see much of Fannie Mae at the club,"

I joked, referring to the nickname of the well-known affordable-housing foundation. "But I have a passing acquaintance with the old gal."

My attempt at humor failed to lighten Ms. Hines's mood, and I decided that she was simply the same cranky, dour, frustrated person I always believed her to be. A characterization that seemed to ring absolutely true as I met the other Realtor/volunteers and we were given our orders and assigned our tables.

Once the participants had taken their seats, Ann stepped up to the podium. Immediately, the persona presented was entirely different.

Ann Rhoder Hines had probably been a benchwarmer on the girls' field hockey team at her high school. But in front of the audience seeking affordable housing, she became a cheerleader. I watched and listened with growing fascination as she made her presentation. She was a true believer. She spoke of the value and opportunity of owning a home with all the certainty and zeal of a faith healer in a revival tent.

Even I, who had been a joint owner of several homes in the twenty years of my marriage, found my heart pounding, my blood racing, my thoughts soaring with expectation.

I glanced around the room at the people assembled, feeling hopeful and optimistic that they would feel exactly the same. They were not regulars at the juice bar, but they were not panhandlers either. It was a room full of working-class citizens, much like those I'd grown up with in Sunnyside. I took some comfort in that. They were basically just like me, I supposed. They put in their days, drew their pay and raised their children. My mother might have called them clean and well-mended. The men were in shirtsleeves. The women were wearing discount. They were mostly white, but people of color made up a third of the numbers.

These folks, according to Ann Rhoder Hines, were the salt of the earth, rock of the community, the foundation of American society. They deserved to live their lives and raise their children in a single-family, three-bedroom, one-bath that they could call their own.

I suddenly saw with great clarity what an opportunity for doing good this was. I should give up selling real estate to the people in my neighborhood and see that each and every person in this room, and all their friends and neighbors, had their own little pieces of the American dream.

When Ann finished speaking, there was a spattering of applause. I clapped louder than anyone, rising to my feet. I was so excited. I was amazed that I had avoided these seminars for so many years. I couldn't wait to be a helping hand to the downtrodden in this honorable undertaking.

I sat eager and anxious at the table Ann had assigned to me, ready to sort through intake papers, tax records and qualifying sheets to determine lending possibilities.

To my dismay, most of the people who sat down at my table were very hard to help.

A very attractive thirty-four-year-old single mother certainly looked the part of the deserving home owner. But she'd had eleven different jobs in the last five years. She was twice divorced and had credit problems under three different names. Armed with a brand-new MasterCard, her plan was to get a big cash advance to use as a down payment.

An even more problematic situation was the four able-bodied adults, none of whom were related to each other by blood or marriage. Their thinking was that it would be cheaper to pool their rent money and buy a house in common. The legal complexities of such an arrangement had not even occurred to them.

Over and over I told people that they needed to get jobs or get out of debt or accumulate some savings. Sometimes I had to suggest they do all three!

Most listened to what I said, took an information packet and left, disappointed. I was beginning to lose heart.

Finally, Mr. and Mrs. Guerra and Mr. Guerra's mother took seats at my table. I greeted them with as much warmth and enthusiasm as any potential client I'd ever dealt with. In truth, it was probably more. I often kept myself at an intensely polite but cool distance that gave me a psychological advantage, an advantage much needed in selling. Giving, I realized, didn't require any such power.

"Good morning, I'm so glad to meet you," I told them.

Mr. Guerra was short and stocky, in his mid-forties, with a full head of black hair, just beginning to gray around the edges of his face. Both he and his mother bore the distinctive semblance of locally indigenous people. The wife was more European in both facial features and manner. It was she who handed me their papers.

"So you're wanting to buy a house," I said to her by way of conversation.

She glanced toward her husband and he answered.

"We want to stay in our neighborhood," Guerra said firmly. "We are not interested in developments on the north side."

Obviously this had not been this family's initial introduction to *affordable housing* seminars. Often, as tax breaks or eligibility for special programs, builders would throw in a few low-income housing units, usually at gate fronts or backing against the thoroughfares of their developments—the least desirable spots that were the most difficult to sell. It is a perfectly good idea.

However Mr. Guerra, like a lot of other people, preferred to buy a home in an area he knew and cared about, rather than one developed completely from scratch.

I looked at the zip code on his address and didn't think there would be much of a problem. There would be some single-family homes in that area that would qualify for low-income financing.

"How many in your household, Mr. Guerra?"

He glanced toward his wife. She counted it out on her fingers.

"Eight," he answered. "Our three children, two of my nephews and my mother, of course."

I kept smiling, but I wasn't pleased. Eight people required a pretty big house.

I looked through their income information.

"You and your wife are both employed?"

He nodded. "Mama keeps the children," he answered.

According to his tax forms, he was something called a *table braider* at Weigan Industrial. I knew Les Weigan. He was a member of the club and a friend of David's father.

Mrs. Guerra worked at a local pizza place. I was surprised. I suppose I thought those minimum-wage jobs were part-time work done exclusively by students.

I frowned at the total that Mr. Guerra had written down on his application form. It was more than what was indicated on his 1040.

"Your annual household income is higher than your taxable earnings would suggest," I said.

"I added in Mama's social security," Mr. Guerra told me. "The other woman said that we could." He indicated Ann Rhoder Hines who was filling out forms at another table.

"Yes, of course," I agreed, glancing at the older

woman. "If Mrs. Guerra lives with you, her income can be included.

The older woman raised her chin and announced proudly, "Three hundred twenty-three dollars a month."

I felt a thrill of hope rush through me. These were fine people, hardworking people. And I was going to help them buy a home. That was really something good.

I perused their expense reports and was less heartened. Food, clothing, utilities, none of these things came cheap.

"This six-thousand-dollar debt?" I asked. "Is this automobile or credit cards?"

There was a silent stillness so abrupt, I looked up.

The Guerra family was extremely ill at ease, not so much as casting a glance at each other.

"It's Papa's funeral expenses," Mr. Guerra finally told me quietly. "We're paying it off directly to the funeral home."

"What kind of interest are you paying?"

The man shrugged and shook his head. "I didn't ask," he told me. I stared at him in disbelief.

"The paper is in there," he said.

I shuffled through until I found it. I almost moaned out loud. The interest on it was twenty-four percent, the highest allowed by law. They'd already made payments for two years and had yet to touch the principal.

"You could have gotten a better rate at the bank," I pointed out.

Mr. Guerra looked at me, puzzled. "A bank? A bank wants…what was it?" he asked his wife.

"Collateral," she answered.

He nodded. "The bank wants collateral for their loans," he said.

That's right, of course. The bank wouldn't loan

money for a funeral. What could they do if the money wasn't paid back? Dig up the corpse? You had to own something in order to borrow. The Guerras didn't have anything but a strong work ethic and a handful of kids.

I continued to look through their forms and records, worry superseding hope.

Finally I smiled brightly at them.

"Would you excuse me for just a minute," I said. "I need to ask a couple of questions." I smiled even harder. "Just one minute."

I grabbed up my notepad as if I was going to use it and hurried over to where Ann Rhoder Hines was orchestrating the movement of families to different tables. I signaled that I needed a word with her and then waited patiently as she made no attempt to hurry.

Finally she was free and she turned to me.

"I've got a problem here," I said.

She raised a condescending eyebrow. "I thought you were supposed to be such a hotshot real estate person," she said. "You find something you can't handle?"

I refused to let the poisonous drip of her tongue deter me. We were both trying to do good here, I was just worried about how we were going to do it.

"I'm having trouble with the Guerras' finances," I told her. "Their credit score barely meets requirements and they've got a commercial service debt that could really impact their ability to pay."

"So do they qualify or not?" she asked me.

"Well, yes, they do," I admitted. "But they'll have to borrow the down payment and closing costs from the affordable housing consortium. Then there will be the real estate loan and this outstanding obligation, I don't think they'll be able to make it."

She folded her arms across her chest and glared at me, annoyed.

"It's not for you to make that judgment," she said.

"It's your job to get them through the paperwork to buy a home."

"But what if something, anything happens?" I said. "One little unexpected expense and they won't be able to make their payments. They'll lose the house."

Ann shrugged. "You know, 35.6 percent of affordables get foreclosed," she said. "What we're giving these people is a chance. What they make of it is up to them. Don't tell me you've never sold a house where you thought the buyers were in over their heads."

She was right about that, of course. I sold houses every week to high rollers whose financial house of cards could come tumbling down any second. But I'd never made those deals as an altruistic act.

"If they try now and fail, they'll never get another chance."

That was the grim, awful truth that stared me in the face, as sure and stoic as Mr. Guerra's mother.

"So what did you do?" Chester asked me on my next visit to the assisted living center.

"I went ahead with the deal," I told him. "The Guerras were happy. Ann Rhoder Hines was happy. I'm sure the sponsors of the seminar were happy. But I don't feel happy about it at all. I'm nervous. I gave Mr. Guerra my card, and I am personally handling everything. I don't want any slipups or unexpected glitches. These people will be walking a financial tightrope for at least the next five years."

Chester nodded sympathetically. "They probably already have been," he pointed out. "They might very well be used to it."

I agreed with him, but it didn't make me feel one bit better.

"I thought about just paying off that loan," I said. "David would probably have me committed. I've been giving away money faster than I'm taking it in. But I'd do it anyway if I thought the Guerras would accept it. I'm sure they won't."

"And they shouldn't," Chester said. "It was their loved one who died. Having a stranger pick up the tab as charity does nothing to honor his memory."

"But I want to do something to help," I complained.

"You are and you will," he assured me. "You can't just rush in like a fairy godmother and wave a wand, making everything perfect. You've got to wait for your opportunities. They'll come."

"You're sure?" I asked him.

He nodded.

Chester was looking very thin in the morning sunshine that striped the room through the window blinds. His bony frame was covered by a shirt and pants that looked two sizes too big, giving him a thin, shrunken appearance. His feet, which were swathed heavily in bandages and covered by huge paper slippers, seemed to dwarf the rest of him.

His thinness reminded me of what I'd brought. I dug down into my purse and retrieved a giant, king-size Snickers. I handed it to him.

"My do-good deed of the day," I said, teasing.

To my surprise, he didn't laugh at my little joke. He looked down at the candy bar as if it represented a lot more than chocolate, sugar and empty calories.

"Thank you," he said softly. "I'm just going to save this for later."

He secreted it in the chest next to his bed. When he returned to his chair, he patted my hand gratefully.

"You are doing good," he assured me. "Sometimes when you don't even know."

I laughed with a lot of self-derision.

"In all honesty," I admitted, "this whole promise thing just terrifies me."

"Why is that?"

"In that car, when I said I'd do good, I really meant it."

"And now you don't?"

"I do," I assured him. "But I'm scared of what it might require. I'm scared that maybe I promised to take in motherless crack babies or nurse AIDS patients in Africa or counsel rape victims on a hot line."

"And you don't want to do those things."

"I don't know how to do those things," I said. "They take a really special kind of person. I'm not a special person. I'm a very ordinary person."

Chester shook his head. "I think you are an extraordinary person," he told me. "You just haven't figured out the difference between the volunteers and the draftees."

"What?"

"During the war," he said, "a lot of men, including myself, knew exactly what we wanted to do. We wanted to drop bombs on the Germans or do jungle combat with the Japanese. We had it in our minds to storm a beach or shoot down a plane. So we hurried down to the recruitment office and signed up."

He gave a slight smile as if the memory of his short-lived military career was still bittersweet.

"But, Jane, there were lots of other men, fine men, who didn't know what to do," he continued. "All they really wanted was for the war to be over so they could stay home with their sweethearts and families. When their country called them, they took whatever job they were given, big or small. And those fellows did as well with it as the volunteers."

I nodded. That was absolutely true.

"It's a fine thing to have folks in the world who set out to make it a better place," Chester said. "Those are the volunteers, we admire them and we should. But us draftees are needed too. We're just waiting to be called, and we will be—to do those good things, big or small, that need to be done."

"Well, that's a comfort," I said. "I'll try to be a ready draftee, although so far my efforts aren't working all that well."

"Sometimes that's the way it is," he said.

There was one place where I was not a draftee. In the life of my daughter, Brynn, I was meant to be a force for good. I had volunteered for motherhood, albeit reluctantly, and doing good is what mothering is all about. From the memory of those frightening moments in the car, it was perfectly clear that the most important thing in my life was my daughter. I'd forgotten that, somehow, in the last few years. I wanted to make up for that lapse. I wanted to be the kind of mother she needed. I wanted to do some good just for her.

Brynn was not impressed with the idea.

"Dr. Reiser thinks you're probably having a breakdown," she told me when I tried to express my feelings to her. "He says that you're a histrionic empty nest seeking a cloak of worthiness."

"I don't think Dr. Reiser can possibly diagnose me from twelve hundred miles away," I countered. "And the man hardly knows me."

"Oh, we've talked about you, plenty," Brynn answered. "How you try to live your life through me, virtually negating everything about me that is unique and personal. How you've tried to make *me* the person that you could never be yourself. Everything."

"Brynn, I'm sorry if I've done that," I told her. "I really love you and I really want you to be happy."

"I am happy, Mother," she said. "I'm happy in *my own life.*"

She made the statement calmly, rationally, as if her

words were a reasonable exchange of ideas. But they hurt me anyway.

"I do have some good news for you, Mother," she said. "I'm coming home for Christmas after all."

"Oh, that's wonderful!" I said, feeling exactly that way. That news completely washed away the sting of what she'd said before.

"Daddy sent me a ticket," she said.

"David sent you a ticket?"

I was surprised. Brynn's comings and goings were virtually always done by my arrangements. He never got involved in such mundane details.

"He says he has something he wants us to discuss as a family," Brynn replied. "Undoubtedly it's your craziness. You should get into therapy and save all the emotional wear and tear on Daddy."

David hadn't mentioned anything to me about a family discussion. And even his suggestions that I seek professional help had dwindled to no discussion at all. I had assumed that he was no longer concerned. However, contacting Brynn on his own was unusual.

"Maybe I should see someone," I admitted.

I had been quick to get a doctor for Brynn when things weren't going well. Perhaps it would please her to see that I was willing to do the same for myself. At the very least, it would give us something in common.

# 6

I picked Milton Feinstein, III, M.D., FAADEP, at random from the preferred provider list of my insurance company. I didn't want to go to any of the therapists that had seen Brynn, and I wasn't ready to get a list of suggestions from my friends and associates. It was curious, really. I'd been in family counseling several times, most often to try to work out problems with Brynn, but also earlier in my marriage, the first time I'd discovered David was unfaithful. I'd not actually been very embarrassed about those things. Everybody I knew had trouble with their kids, and almost everybody had an affair, either their own or their spouse's, that threatened their marriage. Those seemed to be perfectly acceptable and legitimate reasons for seeking help. But to ask a doctor how to help me to be a better person, well, I admit I felt uncomfortable about that.

Dr. Feinstein's office was located in a big medical office building way out in the suburban sprawl. It was conveniently located near the new hospital, though inconveniently located for any sick person who might be in need of a doctor. The parking lot was expansive and could have easily served an NFL-franchise stadium. Each and every car was charged a dollar for the first hour and fifty cents more for every additional thirty minutes. I buttoned my suede jacket as I walked across it, the wintry day was cold and the wind had become unpleasantly chilly.

I took the elevator from the lobby level. I got off on the correct floor, only to discover myself surrounded by an overflowing crowd of metal-mouthed preadolescents. The dental practice that took up the south half of the building had apparently removed the walls to the waiting room and had expanded into the hallway. Their obvious success may have been based, at least partially, upon their name, Budget Braces.

I skirted my way through strewn backpacks, math books and boom boxes toward the direction indicated by the arrows for Suite 902.

An electronic buzzer went off as I walked inside. There was no one at the reception window. I glanced at my watch a little uncertainly. I was actually two minutes early.

Within the office a door opened and a young guy, about Brynn's age, I thought, stepped up to the other side of the counter and gave me a big smile.

"Hi! You must be…" He glanced down at the appointment book on the desk. "Jane Lofton?"

"Yes, I have an appointment with Dr. Feinstein."

"Buddy."

"I beg your pardon?"

"Everybody just calls me Buddy," he explained, clumsily offering his hand to me through the opening.

He was dressed in Dockers and a brown sweater. I took his hand and managed, with some difficulty, not to say one word about how unexpectedly young he looked.

"My receptionist isn't here today," he said. "She's home with a sick baby. She's my wife, actually. She works here for me, part-time. I do most of my own paperwork."

This was far more than I wanted to know.

Fumbling around, he found a clipboard with a pen attached and gave me a form to fill out.

I thanked him and seated myself just on the edge of one of the narrow uncomfortable chairs provided. I quickly filled in my pertinent information: name, address, birth date, insurance provider. It took me a good deal longer to answer the long list of questions on the back of the form about night sweats, panic attacks, hormone replacement and family mental health history.

I was trying to fit all of Brynn's issues into two lines when Dr. Feinstein—Buddy—opened the door to the room.

"You about ready?" he asked.

"I haven't quite got it all filled out."

He shrugged dismissingly. "That stuff really doesn't matter that much," he said.

Somewhat deflated, I looked down at the questions I'd already taken the time to answer.

I handed him the clipboard and he led me directly into his office. It was unspectacularly furnished with somebody's cast-off, family-room rejects. I was certain the green plaid Early American sofa that I sat down on was older than he was.

He took a seat on a beat-up slat-wood rocker with faded, buff-colored cushions. I watched him speed-reading my written responses on the clipboard.

"How did you hear about me?" he asked.

I'd left the *referred by* question blank.

"I didn't," I admitted. "I just picked your name at random."

His forehead creased as he read further on the sheet.

"Who did your daughter see for counseling?" he asked.

"Jacob Trendall," I answered.

His eyes widened. Trendall was the most successful and certainly the wealthiest psychiatrist in the city.

"Brynn was only with him about a year," I explained. "Then we tried Esther Ashley, Daniel Welch,

Howard Boyle." I hesitated, thinking I'd left someone out. I couldn't remember who, so I just continued. "After Boyle, I decided they were all too dependent upon either Freud or pharmacology, so I switched her to Gestalt and we saw Clifford Sheldon for about three months, then Paul Zaharoff. Now she's seeing an Adlerian near where she goes to college."

Buddy Feinstein was staring at me, eyebrows furrowed.

"You're familiar with all the most prominent therapists in town," he said. "What do you think you'll get from me that you couldn't get from them?"

I tried to be really honest. It was my impression that honesty was the basic tenet of the doctor/patient relationship.

"I don't know if I really want to get anything," I admitted. "My daughter and my husband see that I'm acting differently and think that's a problem."

Briefly I related the events of the accident. He listened intently. Nothing in his expression betrayed in any way what he might have been thinking. When I finished, he hesitated a long moment before posing a question.

"Do you believe that God actually intervened to save your life?" he asked.

I shrugged and shook my head.

"I don't know what to believe," I admitted. "But I feel obligated to fulfill my commitment. I said I would change my life. I said I would be a better person. I said I would do good. So now…so now, I'm trying to do what I said."

He nodded slowly, thoughtfully.

"My family thinks I'm depressed or suffering from post-traumatic stress or having a breakdown," I said.

"And what do you think?" he asked.

"Does it matter what I think?"

"What you think is all that matters," he answered.

I feigned shock. "What branch of psychoanalysis is that from?" I asked him.

He raised his eyebrows and made a silly face like an unruly schoolboy before replying, "The Buddy Feinstein School of Minds?"

"Ah..."

We both laughed. It felt good.

"You keep this sort of thing up, Buddy," I teased, "and you'll never make membership in Cambridge Heights Country Club."

"*As if* I would even know what to say to one of those people," he retorted, laughing.

I just gave him a long look and smiled.

He recognized his own gaffe.

"You're in Cambridge Heights Country Club."

It was a statement more than I question, but I nodded affirmatively.

He moaned aloud.

"It's okay," I assured him, genuinely amused. "Truthfully, I didn't always know what I was going to say to them myself."

"You weren't born to the purple?"

"Mmm, no," I answered. "It was more like rusty orange."

He nodded. "So, with a good education and hard work you managed to climb the social ladder."

I shook my head. "Not me, I just married well. I did make good grades and go to college. But I married my way into money and social position."

He leaned back into the rocker, observing me, elbow on the armrest, his face cradled in his hand.

"Oh?"

It was an implied question loaded with significance. But I wasn't there to talk about my loving relationship with David's wealth and family name.

"I'm not sorry about any of the decisions I made," I stated flatly. "I'm not sure if terms like gold digger even exist anymore. But if I were called something like that, I don't think I would be insulted."

He reached over and picked up the clipboard that had the form I'd filled out.

"You sell real estate," he said, looking more closely at what I'd written there.

"Yes."

"Just occasionally, to give yourself a job description?"

"No," I answered. "I suppose it might have started out that way. But I've actually been very successful."

"Perhaps that's why you don't feel like a gold digger."

I shrugged.

"Maybe," I admitted. "Although I think the career had more to do with Brynn than David."

"How so?"

"I think I needed to accomplish something," I told him. "I devoted so much time and effort to Brynn, and the more I tried to do, the less competent I felt. I needed some way to be successful. So I went to work. Having a career kind of took me off the hook."

"What do you mean?"

"Girls with workaholic career mothers are supposed to be screwed up," I told him, not completely joking.

He didn't laugh at all.

"What do you mean by screwed up?" he asked. "Is she self-destructive? Suicidal? Drugs and alcohol? Lost weekends?"

"Oh no, nothing like that. She has a really poor self-image and never fit in well with the other children at the club. She could be a really pretty, popular girl if she would just make the effort."

He made no comment on that.

"I put her in therapy when she was eleven," I said. "And she hates me for it."

"I doubt if she hates you," he said.

"Well, she's got a pretty good imitation going," I answered.

"She actually sounds like a normal, ordinary teenager," Buddy told me. "Rejecting your mother and all she stands for is a typical way of establishing your own identity."

Surprised, I couldn't resist teasing him.

"Let me give you a clue, Buddy," I said. "You're not going to make a lot of money in this business if you tell people their disagreeable teenagers are just being normal."

He chuckled in a very boyish, unprofessional fashion.

"Making a lot of money," he said, "was never my primary objective going into this *business*."

I nodded. I could appreciate that.

"So," I asked him, "what was your primary motivation for becoming a therapist?"

Buddy hesitated a long moment, considering his answer or perhaps considering a reply that would be a polite version of *mind your own business*.

"I guess I became interested in psychiatry because of my brother," he said finally. "He's schizophrenic."

My smile faded.

"Oh," I said, feeling extremely uncomfortable.

Buddy warmed up to the subject immediately, apparently having missed the class explaining that the therapist shouldn't discuss the mental health of those in his own family.

"Jake's illness was the single most defining factor of my childhood," he said. "It changed my parents. And it changed me."

"I'm so sorry," I said.

He nodded, accepting my sympathy graciously.

"It changes one's perspective on problem children," he pointed out.

"Yes, I guess so."

"Jake's on medication," he said. "He has been for years. And he does pretty well. He's very charming and smart, a real math whiz."

He spoke with genuine affection.

"It sounds like a real success story," I said.

"Yes, he is," Buddy answered. "He does just fine for months, sometimes even years. Then he'll just disappear and my parents will be calling missing persons, hiring private detectives, sending out pictures to shelters. A month or so will go by and then they'll get a call from Boston or Sarasota or Seattle and Jake will be in a hospital and back on his medication."

I swallowed hard imagining myself in his mother's place, imagining my Brynn lost and alone in the world.

"It's like, all the time when Jake's doing well and things are going fine, they are always waiting for the other shoe to drop."

"So you went into psychiatry to help your brother," I said.

"Yes, of course," Buddy answered. "And to help my parents and myself and other people who are suffering."

I nodded, thinking about myself, thinking about Brynn, thinking about Buddy and his mom and dad.

"Your brother was kind of like my car accident," I said to him. "He led you to a decision to do good."

Buddy looked at me, hesitating a moment, and then he grinned. "Yeah, I guess so."

"So you've chosen a career that simply lets you do good every day," I said. "That's terrific. In real estate it's not quite so cut-and-dried. Sometimes it's hard to tell if what I'm doing actually helps or hurts the people I'm working for."

He laughed out loud at that.

"Honestly, Jane," he said. "Psychiatry is exactly the same way. Half the time when people leave my office, I worry that I've done as much harm as good."

"I'm sure that's not true."

"Well, let's hope it's not, anyway," he said.

"So?" I asked, bringing the discussion back to the reason for my visit. "Do you think I need therapy? Do you think I'm crazy to try to keep the promise I made in the car?"

"Do you?" he asked.

"No."

"Then if you think you can do some good in the world," he said, "if you think that's what you're supposed to do. Then I say, go for it!"

His enthusiasm felt wonderful.

"I've been trying," I told him. "But it hasn't been easy."

"I doubt if it's supposed to be."

He looked thoughtful for a moment.

"Have you ever heard of Maimonides?" he asked.

The name sounded familiar, as if I'd seen it mentioned in a book somewhere, but I couldn't place it. I shook my head.

"He was a Spanish philosopher and physician," Buddy told me. "He was the leader of a twelfth-century Jewish community in Cairo, big on indexes and lists. One you might be interested in is called the Eight Levels of Tzedakah."

"Tzedakah?"

"It translates as charity, but I think it means a lot more than that," he said. "The list is sort of the eight tiers of do-gooding."

I was sitting up straighter in my chair.

"Let me write this down," I said. "So I can look it up at the library."

"I can do better than that," Buddy said, reaching for the phone. "I'll call my dad, he'll be able to put his hand right on it."

"Your dad?"

"He's a rabbi," Buddy said.

The phone conversation was short but productive, and within a few minutes we could hear the ring of the telephone in the outer office and the distinctive buzz, beep and growl of fax communication.

I wrote Buddy a check for the office visit and he gave me his home phone and offered to talk to me anytime.

"You just do what you feel you need to," he said. "And don't let anyone tell you that it's less sane than the shortsighted selfishness that surrounds you."

"Thanks."

He handed me the fax. I said goodbye and walked out of the office. I skirted through the throngs of teenage tooth-straightenees and waited for the elevator. It was not until I was enclosed inside, completely alone, that I read through the list for the first time.

Levels of charity, from least meritorious to most:

1. Giving begrudgingly
2. Giving less than you should, but giving it cheerfully
3. Giving after being asked
4. Giving before being asked
5. Giving when you do not know the recipient's identity, but the recipient knows your identity
6. Giving when you know the recipient's identity, but the recipient doesn't know your identity
7. Giving when neither party knows the other's identity
8. Enabling the recipient to become self-reliant

I stepped out of the elevator, walked through the lobby and out into the parking lot. At least now I had a basic framework to go by.

That very afternoon I started keeping a journal of my do-good efforts in my Day-Timer. Truthfully, I kept it in a kind of code. It all seemed silly but I was just a little bit afraid that someone would see it and expect an explanation.

*Red Toy Rite-O-Way 1* was my way of recording my slowing down to let a burgundy Camry enter the freeway. The numeral 1, of course, referred to the rating on the rankings list. It was a good thing and I did it, but begrudgingly.

*JL Trash Cash* got a four, because I called up and volunteered to run the Junior League rummage sale prior to the organizational meeting.

*Fridge Free 2/6*, defrosting the refrigerator at the office, was less quantifiable. It was a two because I got rid of the ice buildup cheerfully, but could have bought the staff a new no-frost model. It was a six because I know everyone who works in the office, but no one would have ever suspected that it was me who broke down and did the cleanup.

On my next visit to Chester, I took both the rankings list and my journal to show him.

He was seated in his chair with his feet up on some new, high-tech footstool.

"It's like a hot seat," he told me, laughing. "Fortunately it's not for my backside. It gets mighty chilly around here with these linoleum floors."

I nodded. It was undoubtedly true. The heated ottoman was a weird cushiony thing that his feet and ankles sank into completely. He was swathed in a strange, netlike bandage up to his knees.

"Why don't they just get you some wool socks and a pair of house slippers?" I asked.

Chester shrugged. "They couldn't charge that off to Medicare," he speculated. "Anyway it's a pretty neat idea for keeping warm."

I told him about my visit to Buddy Feinstein and he looked over my Day-Timer.

"It does seem like you've been a busy lady," he said.

"I don't know," I told him. "Buying Girl Scout cookies and getting a lost cat back to its owner doesn't seem like world-changing altruism."

He laughed and reassured me.

"Everybody wants to do the big things," he said. "Everybody wants to make peace in the world or cure terrible diseases or end racism. But there are plenty of little things that need to be done just as badly. When you take care of the little things, you make a difference."

He made me feel good just by saying that.

"What is *Brynn Tongue Bite 1*?" he asked.

"Oh, I talked to Brynn after my visit to Dr. Feinstein," I said. "She wanted to know how it went."

He nodded.

"I could have told her the truth, that he didn't seem to think I was crazy, and that I should keep on trying to keep my promise. I actually wanted to tell her that," I admitted.

"But you lied instead?"

"Not really, but I hedged."

"Why?"

"It would be as if I were saying, 'Brynn, you've got problems and I don't,'" I told him. "That would make me feel better, but it wouldn't do much for her self-image."

"I suppose not."

"I just said I didn't want to discuss it," I told him.

"And she accepted that?"

"She loved it," I said. "Brynn always believes the worst of me. So I'm sure she thinks I would never hold back anything good about myself."

Chester thought about that for a long moment and then agreed that that was probably the best way to handle it.

"What about what the doctor said about Brynn's behavior?" he asked. "Maybe it would help her to know that he thinks she's being pretty typical for a teenager."

"I did think about saying that," I said. "But it's been years since going to therapy was something I made her do. She is very involved in her own care. And she picked Dr. Reiser herself. She's very confident in him."

Chester looked skeptical.

"I don't ever put more confidence in a doctor than he does in me," he said. "And if what I've heard from you is any indication, this Reiser fellow is giving that girl of yours far too little credit."

"You think so?"

"Absolutely," he said. "Brynn is your daughter. She's bound to have a great deal of the same spunk and drive that you have. You saw a life you wanted and thought you needed, so you went after it. Brynn doesn't know yet what she wants, and you and your husband have made sure there isn't anything that she needs."

That was certainly true.

"It's hard to take aim at the world when you haven't got an obvious target to shoot for."

"I guess that's true," I said. "I just wish I'd been a better mother. I tried everything. I was lenient and flexible. That didn't work. So I got to be exacting and disciplinary. That was even worse. So I became inconsistent and conflicted. And I've been paying ten thousand dollars a year for therapists ever since."

Chester chuckled.

"Your mistake was thinking that youngsters are supposed to be happy," he said. "Some are, I guess. Those who are just naturally good-natured. But the bulk of them aren't. And that's nature's way. If they were pleased with their lives and satisfied, they would never get out on their own, they would never seek their separate lives. The mother bird has to push the chicks out of the nest. Jane, not being the perfect mother was maybe the good Lord's way of getting little Brynn out into the big world."

"You talk like you've had a lot of experience with children," I said.

Chester lowered his chin and eyed me over his glasses. "Not one dang bit," he said.

I laughed.

"Vera and I never had any of our own," he said. "She had a niece and nephew, but we didn't see them much."

"So how did you get so wise about parents and children?" I asked.

"Oh, just watching around the neighborhood, I suppose," he said. "We were lucky, where we lived. There were always young people moving in. A young couple would move in down the street with a baby or two. By the time they were grown, we knew all about them."

I smiled a little uncertainly. I had no idea how many young couples lived down the street from me. And I wouldn't know any of their children if they showed up at my door.

"Growing up is hard," Chester said. "Even in the best of times and with the best of parents. Sometimes another adult can get to the heart of a child the way his own parents can't."

"I suppose so."

"We had this one young boy…" He hesitated. "Now,

what was his name? It was Joe, no Jim—no, that's not it either—it was James, oh yes, it was Jamie. I remember now. Jamie liked to take things apart. He nearly drove his mother out of her mind. He'd open up the back of the television and try to figure out how it worked. While she wasn't looking, he'd take apart the motor on the refrigerator. Or his father would come outside and find the transmission on his company van strung all over the driveway."

"Oh no."

"Oh yes." He was chuckling. "I'll never forget that night. We could hear both his parents yelling at the boy for hours. It was like a tag-team match."

"I'm laughing, but it's not funny."

"No, it wasn't funny at all," Chester said. "Things that were said to that boy could never be taken back. And they had to take the van into the shop to get it running again."

I shook my head, able to visualize exactly what that scene was like.

"Vera said to me, 'Chester, you've got to do something for those folks. They are at their wit's end with that boy.'"

"So what did you do?" I asked.

"Well, I had this old lawn mower I'd bought second-hand," he said. "It hadn't worked in five years at least. I invited Jamie over and we were sitting around in my garage and I asked him if he'd take a look at it."

"What a great idea," I said. "That kept him occupied for a while."

"About two weeks," Chester answered. "He got that old beat-up thing running like a sewing machine."

"You're kidding."

"Nope. He did such a good job, I went down to the junkyard and found an old washing machine that somebody'd thrown out. That took him about a month, but he had to make up some of the broken parts from scraps."

"Oh my gosh."

"From then on, we went to the dump together," Chester said. "He got to where he could fix any kind of motor or machinery. He began scavenging junk to fix up and sell. He sent himself to college on the money he made."

"Chester that's wonderful," I said. *"Enabling the recipient to become self-reliant, that's an eight!"*

He chuckled like a venerable old sage.

"How long did it take you to get this smart?" I asked him.

"You live, you watch, you eventually learn," he said. "Although truth to tell, most people don't even start till they're about thirty-five."

"Thirty-five?"

"Believe so," he said. "It takes that long just to find out what's going on in the world. Then it takes thirty-five more years to figure out what you're supposed to be doing about it."

"Ah…" I said. "So you've had thirty-five years to find out what's going on and thirty-five to figure out what you're supposed to do. What have you been doing the last eight?"

"Good question," he answered. "I guess I'm been trying to figure how to get out."

I didn't quite get the joke, but he obviously thought it was one, so I laughed with him.

"Did you bring me my treat?" he asked quietly.

"Oh yes, of course," I said. "I'm glad you didn't let me forget."

I pulled the Snickers bar out of my purse and gave it to him.

"Thank you, Jane," he said to me. "I'm going to save it for later, when I can really enjoy it."

Chester glanced down at his feet, which were still on the heated ottoman, and then looked over at the drawer where he always hid the candy. He stretched as far as he could, trying to reach the drawer. I guess he was so comfortable he didn't want to move his feet off the warming footstool.

"You want me to put it up for you?" I asked.

"No!" he answered a little sharply.

I didn't take offense. I decided he must be getting tired and therefore a little cranky. I was willing to cut him some slack. He was a very old man and he'd saved my life.

I said goodbye and got up to leave.

"Jane," he said, "just scoot that bedside table over this way. It's on rollers."

It was the chest where he hid his candy. I easily moved it over within arm's length of him.

"Thank you," he said with deeper sincerity than was honestly warranted.

"You're welcome."

I went to the door, and, glancing back, I saw him put away the Snickers bar. He wanted to do that himself. Then he gave the chest a good strong push and it was back in place beside the bed.

He was a curious fellow, there was no doubt about that. But I felt better by going to see him. I was sure that he was doing me a lot of good.

# 7

Although Thanksgiving had never been a big holiday for me, and this one was to be especially noneventful since Brynn was not coming home, I began to look forward to that Thursday as a built-in doing-good opportunity.

It was a tradition in David's family to spend that day volunteering at the interfaith meal for needy families that was held annually in the exposition hall downtown. I had participated, in my own way, for several years. Teddy's family also did the citywide service dinner and the two of us typically spent the day watching coats in the volunteers room. Somebody had to keep those coats from walking off on the backs of the guests. But I figured coat watching was probably only a two.

This year, however, I was determined to actually get out there among the less fortunate. That might even be considered a seven. So with benevolence in my heart, I visualized a day of shoveling congealed mashed potatoes onto metal trays for dirty, street-crazed homeless people.

David and I went in separate cars. He had a tee-time at two o'clock and I didn't want to be forced to leave just when the good work was getting started. He, however, was the first person I saw. He was standing in the doorway of the volunteers room, chatting with two other guys in polo shirts. I didn't know the men, so I stopped to say hi.

David introduced me a little reluctantly, I thought.

The big blond guy, who was introduced as Earl, an Automotive Center franchisee, shook my hand enthusiastically.

"It's so great to finally meet you," he said. "Dave talks about you all the time."

I couldn't imagine that. But then I couldn't imagine that anyone called my husband Dave.

I smiled warmly and made my getaway. Teddy hadn't arrived yet and it was just as well. I didn't want to get stuck sipping champagne from disposable cups and watching the coats. The area was already crowded with people I knew from the club or Junior League, friends of David's family or those I'd met through my work. I was smiling and waving continuously, and exchanged little hugs and overenthusiastic greetings of delight with numerous acquaintances.

But I didn't stop and chat. I headed for the heat of the kitchen.

The huge industrial area, with its white-tiled walls and gleaming metal equipment was buzzing with activity. The volunteer area, where the coats were kept, had been equally crowded. But those men and women were well dressed, affluent and mostly white. The kitchen was peopled by folks of different races and ethnic roots, dressed in clean work clothes covered by aprons. There was a lot going on, lots of rushing, lots of questions and answers flying back and forth. But I got no sense of panic, worry or disorganization. Everyone seemed to be familiar with their task and competent to do it.

For me, it was a roomful of strangers. I didn't know anyone and had no idea who to approach about finding a job to do.

"Who's in charge back here?" I asked one young black woman who was using a two-foot-long pair of tongs to put dinner rolls in a bread basket big enough to be used for laundry.

"Back there," she answered, pointing beyond the long rows of counters thick with little white bowls of salad.

I headed that way, trying to stay out of the paths of those busily engaged in the preparation activity.

Around the corner the first person I saw was the chef from Le Parapluie. He was working alongside a square-built middle-aged cook in a thick hair net.

"Good morning, Frederic," I called out, capturing his attention as I hurried in his direction. "I didn't realize that you supervised this meal."

He seemed as surprised to see me as I was him.

"Oh, I don't," he assured me quickly. "I just help out. Mrs. Owens is in charge here."

The unattractive woman in the hair net turned to look at me. Immediately her mouth curved into a big smile.

"Hello there," she said, and then glanced toward Frederic. "Who is your pretty friend, Fred?"

The name was so ill-fitting on the elegant man, that I covered my giggle by offering my hand.

"I'm Jane Lofton."

Mrs. Owens didn't take it, but held up her own, which were covered with gloves.

"Nice to meet you," she said.

"I've come to volunteer," I told her. "Who do I talk to about finding something that I can do to help."

"Mrs. Owens is the woman to see," Frederic said. "She is the head cook at Roosevelt High School, and she's been in charge of this meal preparation since it started."

"Oh really?" I said, puzzled. "I can't believe I haven't met you before. My husband's family is on the

Founders' Committee. I've been coming down here for years."

The woman's expression changed immediately. In an instant she went from warm and welcoming to annoyed and imposed upon.

"Excuse me," she said. "I've got two hundred and fifty turkeys to carve and three thousand gallons of gravy to make."

Mrs. Owens turned her back on me as if I were the golf pro's new wife asking for an application to join the Junior League.

Stunned. Helpless. I glanced over at Frederic. He looked uncomfortable, covering the awkwardness of the moment with a shrug and a self-conscious chuckle.

"What's that about?" I asked him.

For a moment he hesitated, then answered honestly.

"There is kind of a…well, I guess you'd call it a rivalry or maybe…well, a differentiation of volunteers," he said. "We call you, the people who spend the day talking to each other in the volunteers room…we call you the *No-Mess Oblige.* You come down here every year to see and be seen. But you don't get your hands dirty."

I felt embarrassed. More than that, I felt caught. I had always thought that nobody noticed that I never actually did anything. Now I found out that not only was it known, there was even a disparaging name for me and my kind.

I was tempted to just walk away. I wanted to find Teddy, pop open some midpriced bubbly and spend the afternoon sharing gossip. But the memory of those moments in the car were still amazingly fresh. Chester thought I was someone like him now. And Buddy Feinstein thought that adding any part of good to the world was valuable. More than those things, however, was the knowledge that I had promised.

"I really want to help, Frederic," I said. "Can't you just give me a job?"

"Okay," he said. "What can you do?"

The answer, unfortunately, was, "Not much."

Although this was one place where my working-class upbringing was not really a detriment, the truth was that even as a girl I hadn't learned a great deal about cooking. My mother had considered TV dinners to be innovative, and convenient that vegetables came in cans. It would have been a lark for many of my friends to take a course at the Cordon Bleu—I had always felt that it was more fun to eat a beautiful meal than prepare one.

"I can wash dishes," I assured him.

Very shortly I found myself in the scullery room assisting an aging black man named Cecil who was about twice my size. The whole room was wet and steamy, and my Eileen Fisher linen began to droop sadly as soon as I walked through the door.

Dishwashing was nothing like I had imagined. For one thing, there weren't any dishes. The plates, cups, bowls and dessert dishes were all disposable, though dirty flatware arrived in bus carts. All the giant metal cooking pots and serving trays had to be washed out and put in the huge industrial scrubber. The whole operation was more akin to a visit to the car wash than any ancient memories I had of my mother's kitchen.

A flexible spray hose hung down from the ceiling over the deep stainless-steel sinks. All the leftover food and grease was washed out with a quick rinse of hot, high-pressured water. Then the pot, pan or lid was laid on a conveyor that slowly moved it through the washer for a sequence of soap, water and hot air that cleaned, sanitized and dried each piece.

Cecil, the man running this high-tech operation, appeared genuinely grateful to see me, obviously not knowing that I was virtually inept and a *No-Mess Oblige* as well. He had me taking the clean stuff off the back end of the machine. The metal was so hot, I had to wear big white oven mitts to unload it.

At first I felt a little like Lucy Ricardo at the candy factory. The conveyor moved a lot faster than I did. Cecil had to shut it down a couple of times and help me catch up. But eventually I got the rhythm right, and he and I were working like a well-oiled machine, or maybe a very soapy dishwasher.

The work arrived in spurts. Sometimes there were so many bus carts that they were spilling out the doors. At other times we would be able to take a breather and chat.

"This your first time to work the dinner?" he asked me.

I avoided outright confession of my lazy past.

"It's my first time to ever see a dishwasher like this," I answered.

"It's a beauty, isn't it," he said. "Although I guess it must be a little intimidating the first time you see it. I've been working around them for twenty years."

"So that's why you're so good at this," I said. "You do this for a living?"

He looked a little surprised.

"Dishwashing? No, I just do that on special occasions," he answered. "I work in custom sheet-metal fabrication. Among other things, we build restaurant equipment. This is one of ours."

He ran his hand over the nameplate almost reverently.

Any further discussion was forestalled by the arrival of another swarm of bus carts.

About two o'clock, Cecil made me stop.

"Take a break and get something to eat," he said. "My wife is going to bring me a plate in about half an hour. I don't want to be eating in front of a hungry helper."

I laughed. I liked the man. I liked him and I liked the work. The hours had just flown. But I was hungry. Famished even. In my experience at the interfaith dinner, I could never recall actually eating the food. There was always plenty of wine, celebratory champagne and choice little hors d'oeuvres among my friends. But I could not remember any Thanksgiving when I was actually handed a plate with turkey, dressing, cranberries and sweet potatoes.

Today I was, however, and was waved toward the back door. Outside, in the alley behind the kitchen, I found two crowded picnic tables and a score of cheerful but hungry volunteers. The sun was shining brightly, though the day was chilly. After the muggy warmth of the scullery, the cold felt good. A place on the corner was made for me at one of the tables. And, at the urging of one of the women, a young kid, maybe fourteen or fifteen, went to get me a glass of iced tea.

I listened with interest to the discussions around me. I learned that the servers, those who actually saw the people, were chosen specifically for the job from among people who regularly worked in local shelters. Because many of the homeless had emotional problems, it was thought best not to frighten them away with new faces. And for those who were not from the street, the working poor, it was concluded that they would feel more welcome if no one from their jobs, their church, their children's school saw them accepting this free meal. That was also the reason why, for media coverage, they always had one of the *No-Mess Oblige* volunteers in front of the camera.

"You have to admit," one of the women said with a delighted chuckle, "that old lady with the Christmas tree on her chest puts on quite a show."

Everybody laughed.

The woman with the Christmas tree was, of course, my mother-in-law. That brooch she always wore was jade set with garnets, and a diamond star at the top. Edith spoke often, and with enthusiasm, about her annual television experience. It was one of the many things she had in common with Oprah.

"So what's your name, honey?" I was asked by a very obese woman with a mole on her cheek and a half bale of hair confined to a sparkly net.

"I'm Jane," I answered simply.

"Do you have children?" she asked.

I was a little surprised at the question. Not that it wasn't a perfectly ordinary one, but in my experience, after getting a person's name, it was typical to inquire, *What do you do?*

But perhaps that wasn't of prime importance to everyone.

"Yes," I told her, and most of the rest of my table, who looked on politely. "I have a daughter, Brynn, she's nineteen."

"You don't look much past nineteen yourself," a very thin and bowed older man assured me.

I laughed, delighted, and thanked him.

"I know what you're going through," the woman with the mole assured me, shaking her head. "I remember when my twins were just that age."

I smiled without comment.

"I hope you're planning a big holiday feast. Do you make pies? I have a special pumpkin pie recipe. I made it for years. The twins always loved it."

"Brynn's away at college," I said.

It was a flat statement, factual. Not meant to convey any of how I felt about her staying away.

"For me and my husband, I suppose this is our big

holiday meal," I told her, indicating the food on the paper plate in front of me.

She nodded.

"Me too," she said.

"The twins always came home for holiday dinners. Of course, they went to the university here in town. Scholarships, both of them," she said proudly. "Nicki in art and Ricki in mathematics. But, honestly, Ricki painted as well as Nicki and often went to her for help with math problems."

The woman laughed infectiously and it was hard not to smile.

She continued as gushing mom, telling me in great detail of all the myriad accomplishments of her two daughters. I didn't reciprocate. Brynn had never been especially accomplished in anything. I'd made her try art, music, dance, pottery, poetry, horseback riding, baton twirling. She did moderately well at everything, but never excelled. And she never seemed to take any special interest in any of it. Even now, in her second year of college, her grades were fine, but they were all the same. B's in everything. There was not one subject that she was better in than any other. She'd yet to even choose a major.

The twin daughters of the woman with the mole, however, could do everything. They both played piano, sang in the church choir and played soccer.

I dodged all questions directed my way. It was easier than trying to explain how proud I was of my Brynn, who'd never really done anything. I didn't understand it myself. But it was true. I was proud of her. Just for being my daughter.

I finished my surprisingly tasty meal and took the opportunity of throwing my plate away to sneak out of the kitchen and check on my friends in the volunteers room.

Even before I reached the door, I could hear the merriment going on inside. I put a hand to smooth my hair from my face and felt the dampness at the nape of my neck. I must look hideous! I made a quick detour to the ladies' room to confirm my suspicions. I was absolutely right. The oomph had gone out of my hair, leaving my professional look limp and draggy, held together only by the stiff magic of superhold hair spray. My face was no better. My foundation had melted and disappeared, leaving the rough, slight ruddiness of my complexion visible. My dyed eyebrows and tattooed eyeliner looked good, at least, though the crow's-feet around my eyes were no longer completely disguised. I made a mental note to give the plastic surgeon a call. After forty, life was just patch, patch, patch.

Oculoplasty, of course, would not help me today. My hairbrush and makeup were in the volunteers room. There was no way to repair the damage done. Briefly, I considered sneaking out of the building, driving to the mall and throwing myself upon the mercy of the cosmetics counter at Macy's. I might have actually done it, but it was Thanksgiving and the stores at the mall were closed.

I stared at myself under the fluorescent glow in the rest-room mirror. Just staring, not really knowing what to do. I hadn't realized how much I had begun to resemble my mother. People had always thought that my mother was attractive. She was, in sort of a rough way. Style for her was the moderate-dress section at JCPenney. But she had a good figure and always managed to carry it off. Mom had raised herself out of poverty, and somehow that always showed.

I had raised myself out of working class and was determined that no one should ever suspect.

I tried fluffing my hair with my hands. It worked a little bit. I still didn't look great. I decided it would have to do. I couldn't comfort myself with the knowledge that no one would notice. Among my crowd, noticing was a sacred calling. I had the option of not seeing anyone and heading back to Cecil and the folks in the kitchen, but I had family and acquaintances among the *No-Mess Oblige* and they would wonder about me if I didn't show my face.

Besides, I reminded myself a bit smugly, I had nothing to be ashamed of. While they had been frittering away the day with gossip and champagne, I had been engaged in actually doing good.

As I entered the room, I heard Teddy before I saw her. She was seated next to my mother-in-law, who was talking with excited animation. Edith was wearing a two-thousand-dollar St. John's silk pantsuit that made her look fat. She had accessorized with the jade and garnet Christmas-tree brooch that my comrades in the alleyway had found so amusing.

Teddy, on the other hand, looked especially chic in the institutional surroundings. She glanced up, spied me and grinned broadly.

"Jane Lofton, where have you been?" she demanded with good humor. "I talked to David an hour ago and he assured me that you were here somewhere."

Edith glanced up and took in my appearance with obvious dismay.

"Good heavens! Is it raining outside?"

"I don't think so," I replied, and moved to quickly change the subject. "Has David already left?"

I knew, of course, that he had. He was in the middle of the sixth hole by now, but it was a useful way to divert questions about my dishevelment.

"He's long gone," Will Hyfals told me. "On a sunny day like this, it's a crying shame to be stuck indoors."

I smiled. Stuck was definitely what these people were up to. Besides Will and Teddy and Edith, Bob and Mimi Parton were there, along with Fayrene Ancil and Laura Martin, Pete McNally and Sugar Van Veen. They were all crowded around one little table as if they had a wad of money riding on twenty-three red.

"Oh, Jane," Edith said. "We've just come up with the greatest idea for expanding this Thanksgiving to the entire city."

"And it was your mother-in-law's idea," Teddy piped in.

"Oh no," Edith said, shaking her head. "I'm sure it was yours, Teddy, or maybe Fayrene's," she suggested, glancing toward one of the woman across from her.

"Well, Bob first mentioned all the seniors who can't come," Fayrene pointed out.

"And then you brought up the Meals on Wheels program," Teddy said.

"Well, whoever," Edith said. "It's a wonderful idea and we've just got to go with it."

"It's an idea that ought to get Edith a nomination as one of Oprah's angels," Laura suggested.

My mother-in-law blushed to the roots of her hair, obviously pleased and hopeful that it would do just that.

"So what's the plan?" I asked.

They all began talking at once, obviously so excited. Teddy hushed everybody in that ever-so-polite and patrician manner she had, and personally began the chronology of events.

"We were talking about what a good thing the dinner is. And what a wonderful service to the community it is," she said.

"Yes, absolutely," Will agreed.

We all nodded.

"Then," Teddy continued, "the conversation drifted to those who don't participate."

"There are so many older folks and disabled people who just can't get here," Edith piped in. "Downtown is getting so empty."

"More and more of the less fortunate are living way out in the suburbs," Mimi said.

Everyone agreed with that as well.

"And a lot of those people simply don't have any transportation," Will said. "Even those with access to the bus lines find the schedule abbreviated on holidays."

"Edith thought it would be good if we could somehow go and get them," Fayrene said.

"Then Teddy got the idea that we could pay city-bus personnel and cabdrivers who would normally take Thanksgiving as vacation to pick people up and bring them here."

"It would be a good deal for them," Teddy said, "as well as a financial incentive. And we'd be asking the people most capable of doing the job to do it."

"So," Edith said, "Teddy called the city manager and asked how we'd go about getting that done. He thought it was a great idea."

"It *is* a great idea," I told them, more than a little surprised that Teddy could even care.

"Naturally, we'll need to raise the money," she said. "I was thinking maybe a more relaxed version of the Chrysanthemum Ball."

Sugar was nodding eagerly. "We're talking Latin rhythms," she told me. "A Cuban buffet, perhaps, and those slinky dresses like Brazilian Carnival."

With Sugar's short, pudgy figure, I didn't imagine that slinky Brazilian dresses would be quite her thing, but I was encouraging nonetheless.

"You know, we could even do it as a Mardi Gras celebration," Teddy pointed out.

"It could be masked!" Mimi almost squealed the suggestion.

The enthusiasm around the table was generous and genuine. There was nothing these ladies liked better than a party. And there was no better party than one that was for *a good cause*.

"So this is really great," I said, congratulating them. "I'm sure it's going to be a fabulous success."

"But you haven't even heard the half of it," Will said.

"Yeah," Pete McNally spoke up. "We were all sitting around basking in the potential of this new way to expand the program, when we started thinking about those people who can't ride the buses or taxis. They simply can't leave home."

Laura's tone was sympathetic. "It's really sad to just leave them out completely. And some of them have no family, no one to see that they get a nice dinner on Thanksgiving."

"I guess not," I replied.

"Fayrene started telling us about the Meals on Wheels program," Edith said. "Those people take dinner to the needy every day of the year. And we said, maybe we could furnish the food for this one day."

"And then we said, hey, maybe those people would like a day off."

"So then Pete mentioned his brother's pizza-delivery business, you know, Corleone's—The Pizza You Can't Refuse."

I did know the company. It was difficult not to. The local TV station was awash in commercials with Mike McNally dressed up like the Godfather.

"All the pizza locations are closed on Thanksgiving," Pete said. "And Mike's delivery fleet is just parked for the day."

"Pete called his brother and, sure enough, he's willing to donate the cars and drivers," Bob said.

"Picture it," Teddy said. "Thanksgiving dinner delivered as easily as pizza."

I did picture it. Dozens of PT Cruisers decorated like thirties mobster vehicles delivering dinner to old people who could probably still recall the days when the image of mobsters was not so benevolent.

"It's a great idea," I said honestly.

I continued to think about Edith and Teddy and what they'd come up with all afternoon. Even after rejoining Cecil and immersing myself once more in the "real work" of dishwashing, I thought more about what they had accomplished.

It was hard to say that what I'd spent the day doing was somehow better than what they had done. Certainly the dishes needed washing and Cecil needed help. But the money raised for transportation and the delivery to those who were homebound loomed large in comparison.

Chester had said that the little things were just as important as curing cancer or being a foster mother to crack babies. But, as I pulled the damp linen away from my skin and mopped my forehead, I didn't feel as if dishwashing was nearly as worthwhile as I'd originally hoped. Still, Cecil seemed grateful for the help and I hung in there, determined to complete a full day's work.

His wife, Emily, dropped by, and I really liked meeting her. She was tiny and delicate, but seemed to have no problem whatsoever keeping a big bruiser like Cecil in line.

Cecil lit up like a Christmas tree the minute she walked into the room. I watched the two of them together. Talking closely, teasing each other. They were definitely still in love. There was a part of me that envied them a little bit. David and I had never really had that. But we'd had a lot of other things. And of course, I reminded myself, that kind of romantic stuff never lasts.

"How long have you and Emily been married?" I asked Cecil after his bride left to return to her own duty of the day.

"Twenty-four years," he answered.

So much for the fleetingness of starry-eyed adoration.

Serving was scheduled to stop at six. They continued, however, to feed people until after seven, and it was close to nine o'clock at night before we had things cleaned up.

I was more exhausted than I could ever remember being in my whole life. And a trip to the ladies' room revealed that I looked exactly as bad as I felt. Fortunately, all of the *No-Mess Oblige* had left the building. In fact, most everybody was gone. I saw Frederic and Mrs. Owens; the former appeared genuinely surprised to see me still there. The latter seemed to have completely forgotten her earlier hostility. Either that, or she didn't recognize me in my current condition, and wished me a very happy Thanksgiving.

I said goodbye to Cecil and Emily, and then surprised myself by giving Emily my card and suggesting that we get together for lunch sometime.

She thanked me and said she would call. I wasn't sure she would, but in truth, I really wanted her to.

Determinedly putting one foot in front of the other, I went to the volunteers room to get my coat. It was one of the last still hanging there. The room was a mess. Unlike the kitchen, nobody had thought to sweep up or carry out the trash.

I tutted disapprovingly and then reminded myself

that there was nothing wrong with me cleaning the place. It was an easy four points.

I found a broom and dustpan and began cleaning up. It only took me a few minutes and made a big difference in how the room looked.

I put on my coat and carried the volunteers room trash, heavy with champagne bottles and bulky with disposable cups and plates, out to the Dumpster on my way to the parking lot.

"It is Jane, isn't it?" he said.

The heavyset Hispanic man was about my age and was one of the people I'd eaten lunch with. I certainly didn't recall his name and was very wary of his remembering mine.

"Yes, Jane Lofton," I answered.

"Are you on your way home?" he asked.

"Ah…yes."

"Let me walk you to your car," he said. "This is not the best neighborhood to be wandering around in at this time of night."

With his lead we headed in the direction of the parking lot.

The man seemed nervous, uncomfortable. Conversation obviously didn't come easily for him. But he had something he was determined to say.

"I wanted to thank you for what you did for Lula," he said.

"Lula?"

"Yeah, the woman you were talking with at lunch, Lula Alvarez. She's my sister."

I stared at him stupidly, trying to get my brain to function. Finally the memory of the big woman with all the hair and a mole on her cheek came to mind.

"You mean the woman with the twin daughters?" I asked.

He nodded, a little sadly, I thought.

"The girls were the light of Lula's life," he said. "The both of them bright and shiny as new copper pennies. They were killed by a drunk driver three years ago."

I was stunned momentarily speechless.

"It was so good of you to talk to her about them, to let her think about them again without having to think about how they died."

"I had no idea," I admitted.

He nodded. "That was what worked so well," he said. "Those of us who love Lula and who miss the girls, well, we have a hard time talking to her about them. But you, you just listened to everything and were happy and proud for her. It was more like the old Lula than our family has seen in a very long time. I just wanted to thank you."

"It was nothing to just listen to somebody," I assured him.

"It wasn't nothing to us, Jane," he said. "It was real important. You done something really good today for somebody really special."

# 8

The weeks between Thanksgiving and Christmas were jam-packed with doing-good opportunities. I began tallying up my scores at the end of the day, at first just trying to hit a daily minimum of fifteen points. As that got easier, I tried to hit my all-time high scores, besting my best. But even in the season of giving, giving was not without its complications.

I donated to a holiday toy drive. The money and gifts simply poured in. Everybody loves children. And Christmas and children were the perfect combination to touch the heart of the stingiest Scrooge. I was uplifted. That is, until I made the mistake of being on hand for the distribution.

Perhaps it was the fault of my own presumption. I envisioned humble and grateful adults choosing the one gift that they were not able to get for their child. Instead, I saw a near riot. The whole family came, everyone with their lists, yelling, pushing, demanding all the newest, hottest, most expensive items. And, in a hurry! These people didn't have all day to wait on a bunch of slack volunteers who couldn't get what they wanted fast enough.

The angelic underprivileged child I imagined, lovingly clutching the toy that they might never have had, was instead a screaming brat, stomping her foot and demanding, "I want the purple one!"

It was supposed to be Toys for the Needy. It didn't

take me long to suggest that they change the name to Toys for the Greedy.

"Don't let them get to you," a veteran volunteer said, trying to cheer me after a parent, to whom I'd handed a CD player that was not the most popular brand, had berated me for giving her "this fucking piece of junk!"

"Nobody likes to take charity," the veteran explained. "So they pretend that it's a right, not a gift."

I decided that giving to thankless people who despise you ought to have a place on my list, so I gave myself a 4.5. Though, by the end of the day, it didn't seem all that onerous. In fact, the attitudes and atmosphere were actually familiar.

I could recall many holiday seasons when Brynn's letter to Santa read more like a list of demands. The year she'd turned sixteen she'd announced that she wanted a red Humvee. David had tried to reason with her—how unhandy the vehicle was for passengers, how terrible the gas mileage, and how difficult to park—but Brynn was adamant.

"If you won't get me a Hummer, then just don't get me anything," she'd declared dramatically. "Because nothing else could make me happy."

We bought her a little red Jeep. It was just as impractical as the Humvee, but not as big. She never liked it, not even the first day. She traded it in within six months and chose a bright pink Mustang that looked like something Barbie would drive.

I decided that needy people were simply people. And some of them, like some in my own family, weren't particularly good at receiving.

The Respite Care Christmas party, held a couple of days later, was a stark contrast. The handicapped, from tiny babies to age-old crones, seemed delighted to even be having Christmas. They sat and watched with awed attention as a series of teenage beauty queens sang and danced and twirled batons onstage. Then they ate their Santa cookies and opened their presents.

Cries of thrilled delight were heard everywhere as each and every attendee got a red sweatshirt that said Merry Christmas from Mervin County Health and Welfare. It was a fashion faux pas that was unparalleled, but no one noticed. Within moments, half the sweatshirts had been excitedly donned. I watched the guests' happy faces and listened to their animated thanks, and secretly wished I had some of those generic CD players and toys in the wrong color.

It was later, as the crowd was thinning, that I first heard about the new battered families safe house. Apparently there were so many women and children seeking shelter that a new property had been purchased and had opened only weeks earlier.

"The foundation has been so busy furnishing the place and making sure all the children were going to be remembered at Christmas, that we forgot about decorating the place," a board member informed me.

"I'd be happy to do it," I piped in quickly.

The woman hesitated.

"The locations of safe houses are a closely guarded secret," she said.

"I would never tell anyone," I assured her.

"Well, you can't just hire someone to do the decorating," she said. "If you take on the work, you'll have to do it yourself. With no help from anyone but the residents."

She gave me the number for Loretta Campbell, the contact person, and by that afternoon I had permission, plus the date and time, to show up with a Christmas tree. I wanted to buy a twelve-foot Noble fir, like the one I'd had put up in my own living room. But I certainly couldn't manage a tree of that size by myself. And Loretta had stipulated the purchase of an artificial tree. It was not only a fire-safety issue, she'd said, but one of practicality as well. The house could use it year after year.

I was a little disappointed. Artificial trees were not my favorite, and there was not much creativity involved in selecting one. I got a fancy silk one, prelit with little candle-shaped lights. And consoled myself with the purchase of decorations.

Since the house was all women and children, I decided pink would be a great color. Not traditional, but definitely festive. I bought a dozen strands of bright pink beads and yards and yards of silver tinsel. That was quick and easy. But I selected each ornament individually and with great care.

It took me two whole days of scouring holiday displays to find everything I wanted. They all had to have some tie-in to the color scheme and the mother-and-children theme I'd decided upon.

The pièce de résistance was a huge but fragile stylized star of pink blown glass for the top of the tree. I'd seen it, dusty and unheralded on a second-floor shelf at Yesteryear Emporium. I was delighted to find it still there. It had a couple of hairline cracks, but they didn't detract from its beauty or character.

I had carried it to the counter a little less than enthusiastically, distinctly remembering my last encounter with the proprietor, my old school chum. He was cranky and self-involved, but his opinion of me was right on target. I had been less than fair with him and I wanted to change. He wasn't going to make it that easy.

The best course of action, I decided, was to quietly pay the marked price with no comment or discussion. Unfortunately, the pink glass tree topper was not priced at all.

He was whistling, a distinct difference from the last time I was in his store.

"Good morning," I said.

"Ah…" he said, smiling as he shuffled over toward me. "It's Janey Domschke, or I suppose I should say, Mrs.…ah, Mrs.…"

"Lofton."

"Mrs. Lofton," he repeated. "What amazing feat of shopping expertise are you up to this morning?"

His cheerful mood and teasing words were a sharp contrast to our last meeting, but I wasn't interested in resuming a tête-à-tête of any kind.

"I want to buy this, but it's not marked," I stated simply.

He picked up the ornament and eyed it critically for a couple of moments.

"What is it?" he asked.

"It's a Christmas-tree topper."

"Really?"

Holding up the decoration, he examined the hole in the bottom of it and frowned. "How much is a thing like this worth?" he asked.

I didn't really know. It was a 1960s piece, made for one of those campy silver-metallic trees, the first of the artificial species. It was not the kind of thing that would appeal to many people. I suspected its value wouldn't be more than fifty dollars. But it wasn't my responsibility to appraise his inventory.

"I just want to buy it," I told him. "It doesn't matter what it costs."

"Okay," he said, nodding slowly. "Twenty thousand dollars."

"What!"

"You said it didn't matter what it costs," he pointed out. "For all I know, it's a priceless piece of art deco."

"It's not," I assured him. "It's handblown, which is good, but it's not that old or particularly collectible."

"How do I know that?" he said.

"Because I told you so," I answered.

"And I can trust you, Janey?"

There was the rub. Truthfully, he couldn't trust me. At least he couldn't in the past. Now, however, things were different.

"Okay, it's confession time," I announced bravely. "I've been buying stuff from you here for years. I took great pride in getting great things for next to nothing."

He looked neither shocked nor angered. My secret intrigue apparently didn't come as a surprise.

"It can't have been that much of a challenge," he pointed out.

"Well, no, now that you mention it, I guess it wasn't," I said. "Half the time I probably could have shoplifted an anvil through the front door and you wouldn't have noticed."

He feigned a pained grimace. "Guilty as charged," he admitted.

"Anyway, I'm not interested in doing that anymore," I told him.

"Why not?" he asked. "Changed your philosophy of consumerism?"

"Not exactly."

I just stood there looking at him, wondering how to explain. The last thing in the world I wanted to do was admit to a stranger that I had been transformed by a brush with death and a desperate promise.

"You can trust me," I said, determined to make it true.

"Scott," he prompted.

"You can trust me, Scott."

"If you tell me that I can, Janey," he said, "then I will."

He held up the pink glass. "How much?"

"Fifty dollars."

I left the store pleased, and so proud of myself. And I

was thrilled about my plans for the tree. These women and their children had probably never in their lives seen a Christmas tree that was truly decorative art. I could still recall with disdain the tacky trees my mother and I had always had in our house. Tiny little shrubs of greenery perched on the table in front of the living-room window. They had been adorned each year, late and hastily, with the cheap multicolored offerings of the local five-and-dime. My mother had always seemed a little embarrassed about Christmas. As if it somehow made her lack of family and friends more obvious than usual.

I was going to see that these mothers and children, who undoubtedly felt their lack of family and friends this holiday, had more than a spindly three-foot fir to celebrate around.

I loaded the decorations, filling the Z3 roadster's trunk. At the last minute I included a box of big pink candy canes. I put the top down and loaded the long rectangular-boxed tree, sitting up in the passenger seat beside me, securing it with the seat belt and shoulder harness.

I arrived right on time. Loretta and a half-dozen eager little faces met me at the door.

"We're so excited!" she told me.

I could have easily guessed that from the noisy, boisterous reception I received.

"Not any more excited than me," I assured them. "And I have a big surprise."

"We've got a sap-pwise, too!" a little girl with a nose full of freckles and missing front teeth declared.

I was introduced all around. Children were of every color. The little girls varied in age from infants to preteens. The boys were all less than ten. Most of the women were young, but some were my age, one woman was old enough to be my mother. I think I'd expected them to be shy, cowering, even wimpy. That was not the impression I got. And when I thought about it, I supposed I should have known that running away from abuse, seeking shelter, took tremendous courage.

Loretta and I had to bring the tree from the car without any help from the residents. The women and children, I learned, were not encouraged to be seen in the front yard. What made the safe house safe was the fact that their spouses didn't know where they were. A high privacy fence around the back enclosed a patio for lounging and smoking, and a place for the children to play, keeping the anonymity of the residents secure.

"I thought you had more women here than this," I told her.

"We do," she said. "And we will. As Christmas approaches, the husbands and boyfriends are on their best behavior. The women begin hoping for a new start. They want their children to have a beautiful family Christmas full of happy tradition and Kodak moments."

"That's wonderful," I said.

Loretta shook her head. "The holidays invariably bring disappointment, drinking and ultimately more abuse. By the afternoon of the twenty-fifth we'll begin filling up. We'll be bursting at the seams and doubling up before New Year's."

"Oh, that's awful."

She shrugged. "We can't control any of that," she said. "All we can do is plan to give them the best Christmas we can manage."

I was determined to be a part of that.

When we got the clumsy rectangular box inside, everyone helped us open it, big kids, little kids, moms. Of course, I'd assumed we would save the cardboard to store the tree in January, but the eager and enthusiastic ripping and tearing quickly dissuaded me of that idea.

It was fun somehow just getting the tree out of the box. Once it was lying in pieces all over the living room, I began to read the instructions. That, however, wasn't really necessary. One of the mom's, Nedra, a young, very thin woman in her late twenties, had obviously never seen anything she couldn't put together. Without so much as a hesitation or misstep, she had the thing assembled, in place and plugged into the electrical outlet in ten minutes.

The kids started applauding and the rest of us joined in with them. She took an exaggerated bow, which the children loved even more.

"Now, do you want to show Miss Jane what you made for the tree?" Loretta asked the kids.

The little ones required no further encouragement as they hurried noisily out of the room and promptly returned, loaded down with Christmas booty.

"See what I made! See what I made!"

There were bells made out of foam cups and chains of red and green construction paper. They'd covered their round plastic Pokémon balls with glitter. And had cut out reindeer figures from Christmas cards to hang on ribbons. There were tiny snowmen made from cotton balls and stars formed from macaroni and Elmer's glue.

"We worked all day," the freckled, toothless girl told me.

"I did all the cutting myself," Jarone, a chubby-cheeked, little black boy told me.

The mothers were just as proud as the children.

"I think the decorations are cute as can be," the oldest woman in the group assured those younger. "It's every bit new and won't remind the kids of any Christmases before."

Her words hinted at ominous memories I didn't even want to think about.

"We talked about pooling our money to buy ornaments," one heavyset brunette, with a baby in her arms, explained quietly to me. "But we wanted to use that cash to buy something from Santa." The last was added in a surreptitious whisper.

"I understood that gifts were going to be provided," I said.

"Oh, yeah, sure," she replied.

Beside her someone else spoke up. "The agency sees that they all get something nice," she said. "But it wouldn't be like Christmas if we didn't get something for our kids ourselves."

The woman's hair was a bright red color, unavailable in nature, and she was as toothless as her freckle-faced daughter, but she spoke with a quiet dignity that belied her appearance.

The kids were having some problems with the tremendous lengths of popcorn they'd strung. The older preteens tried, without much success, to get some of it wrapped around the higher limbs of the tree. Eventually Loretta stepped in with a bit of authority and a stepladder to help get the decoration distributed evenly all the way to the top.

The popcorn looked surprisingly good. It stood out in a way that shiny, synthetic tinsel never could.

Shanekwa, the mother of the chubby-faced black boy, came in from the dining room carrying the premier production of the kids' Christmas crafts. Oohs and aahs emanated from every direction at the sight of an angel made of paper plates.

One plate, folded, created a flowing robe. Another was cut in two, with half utilized for silver, glitter-covered wings. The other half was bent forward like arms and stapled together with a miniature matchbook hymnal. Gold glitter adorned the pasteboard halo that fit snugly upon a plastic-spoon head festooned with long tresses of curled yellow ribbon. The taped-on face of the angel was less than serene, having been drawn with Crayola by someone from the Happy Face school of artistic portraiture. However, my opinion was not one that counted.

"She's beautiful," a little voice whispered, near awe-struck.

"She goes at the very top of the tree," Shanekwa announced, handing the treasure up to Loretta, who was still on the stepladder. "She'll watch over our Christmas like the real angels watch over us always."

With the help of some trashbag twist ties, Loretta managed to get the angel firmly fastened to the top of the tree.

She came down from the ladder and stepped back. We all took the opportunity to survey the decorations thoroughly.

"Didn't you say you had a surprise?" Loretta asked.

I was momentarily speechless. Not quite knowing what to say.

"Ah…yeah, yeah," I said finally. "It's just outside."

I gave one more long look at the tree before walking outside to the Z3, still not sure what to do. I fished my keys out of my jacket pocket, opened the trunk and stared inside. The beautiful pink strands of beads, the yards of fancy tinsel, the expensive themed ornaments and the incomparable handblown glass star stared back at me.

It would have made such a beautiful Christmas tree—in a layout for a decorating magazine.

In the corner of the trunk, almost forgotten, was the little last-minute purchase. I grabbed up the bag and hurried back inside.

"What's a Christmas tree," I announced to the eagerly waiting group, "without candy canes?"

There was a whoop of excitement from the children as I opened my offering and gave it to them.

"There is enough for everybody," I assured the small eager hands that reached out to me.

"They'll look so pretty on the tree," the mother with the red hair assured everyone.

"And they'll taste good, too," her little freckle-faced daughter piped in.

"So what did you do with your fancy pink Christmas frills?" Chester asked me when I relayed the story to him later that same week.

"I drove straight down to Toys for the Greedy and dropped them off," I told him. "I'm sure they will be exactly the wrong color for some unfortunate family."

He laughed.

"That's one of the things I like about you, Jane Lofton," he said. "You never let sentiment overcome cynicism."

"A lot of people wouldn't consider that a virtue," I pointed out.

He shrugged. "I think as long as you don't lose sight of sentiment completely, you'll be all right," he said.

I was seated in his chair that had been pulled over to the side of his bed. He was, by his own admission, just getting over a bout of flu. Though he wasn't coughing or sneezing or queasy, what I tend to think of as typical flu symptoms, he did look pale, and said he didn't feel like getting up.

He'd called me on the phone to warn me away with contagion, but I'd shown up anyway, unwilling to miss the opportunity to give him his Christmas present.

I'd made it myself, utilizing at least some of what I'd learned at the safe house. It was an eighteen-inch-high

artificial tree with tiny lights. In lieu of fancy ornaments, I had decorated it with the recipient's gift of
choice. I'd bought a sack of red- and green–wrapped
Snickers Miniatures and punched a hole in the edge of
each wrapper, tying them to the tree with ribbons.

Chester was delighted when he saw the tree. I set it
up on the table next to his bed and plugged it in. He
laughed, as pleased as any kid with his own special
gift.

"I wanted to get you something you really wanted,"
I told him. "And this is the only thing that you've ever
indicated wanting."

He reached out and patted my hand.

"You're good to me, Jane Lofton," he said. "And I
think you're good for me, as well."

It was a wonderful compliment. And I accepted it
with all the grace I could muster.

"It cuts both ways, Chester," I said. "I'm not such a
kind person that I would keep visiting if I didn't enjoy
it."

"Oh, I don't know about that," he said. "From what
I hear, you're becoming a regular do-gooder."

We both laughed at that.

His smile faded a moment later when the nurse
dropped by.

"Just need to make a quick prick," she said by way of
explanation.

She picked up Chester's hand, and without even a
word of warning, stabbed him in the finger with a little
needle.

He didn't make a face or say a word. The nurse
pinched his finger until a bead of blood formed, then
blotted it upon a small plastic slide.

"That's it," she said, as if poking people was a routine venture and she was in a hurry.

"Well, look at this," she said, hesitating as she noticed the little tree. She glanced in my direction. "What a cute idea!"

"Thank you," I said.

Chester seemed strangely nervous, almost guilty, not making eye contact with me or the nurse.

"It's just a little something that I put together to brighten up Chester's room," I said.

"And it does that," she said. "Though, I don't know if it's a good idea to have it right here next to his bed."

I was surprised at her words, then surmised that there must be some kind of safety regulation against having holiday decorations in the room. Before I had a chance to ask, Chester spoke up.

"Why don't you take it out into the TV room," he suggested to the nurse. "That way, everyone can share it."

"I'll do that," she said, and immediately leaned down to unplug it. "You two have a nice visit. And Merry Christmas."

This last was directed at me, but I wasn't feeling very merry at all as she carried the gift I'd brought for Chester out of his room.

"What's this 'everybody can share it' stuff?" I asked him. "You're stuck in this bed and won't get to get your share."

"Oh, I'm sure they'll wheel me out to the TV room for Christmas," he told me.

"It's not a fire hazard," I assured him. "Even if there were a short in the lights, the material the tree is made from is nonflammable."

Chester looked at me strangely and then nodded, but he still seemed a bit guarded. He put up a good front, laughing in a way that didn't seem wholly genuine.

"The nurse is probably right," he said. "I shouldn't hog all the sweets. I'm sure some of the people here don't get anything."

The answer didn't really satisfy me, but I let it go. Only because Chester clearly wanted me to.

"So tell me about your holiday plans," he said.

"Brynn is coming home, after all," I told him. "David and I are both so excited. She's been telling me for months that she wasn't going to come. But somehow David talked her into it."

"That's wonderful," he said. "When does she arrive?"

"Tomorrow," I told him. "We're supposed to go to the Christmas party at the club, but I talked with David and we're staying home for Brynn's first night."

He nodded. "You did tell me she doesn't enjoy the club very much."

"Not at all," I reiterated. "She despises it and complains about every moment she's forced to spend there."

"Then staying home is probably the best idea," he said.

"Oh, I know it is, though the party is the biggest event of the year. All our friends will be wondering where we are."

"Real friends will always understand that you want to be with your daughter," he said.

"Yes, I guess so," I said. "Brynn's only going to be home for four days."

"That's all the vacation she gets?"

"Oh no, the school is out for a month, but she went into Manhattan for a week to do some shopping. After Christmas she wants to go skiing in Colorado with her friends. Then they are all flying down to Belize for a big New Year's Eve party. She'll spend a few days and leave from there to go back to school."

"She sounds busy," Chester said. "And with lots of friends."

"I guess that's true," I admitted. "I'm just glad for

the opportunity to really give my daughter a wonderful Christmas experience. I want it to be the best holiday she's ever had."

Chester raised his eyebrows at that, but didn't comment.

"What kind of plans do you have?" he asked.

"Well," I began, "it seems like traditional is best. The tree will have all the decorations she remembers. I'm going to have a holly and mistletoe, and hang stockings from the chimney mantel. Of course, we'll have a big Christmas feast with all her favorites. And we'll mellow out the day with carols playing on the stereo."

"Oh, that sounds very nice," Chester told me with great sincerity.

"I hope she'll like it," I said. "She loves puzzles, so I bought this marvelous, three-dimensional one of Notre Dame Cathedral. I'm going to set it up in the family room where we can all work on it. I want to totally devote myself to being with her and doing the things she likes to do."

"You know, of course, that she loves you," he said.

I liked the sound of it, but I wasn't sure that it was true. I shrugged.

"I hate that you're not feeling well enough to come to our house for Christmas," I told him. "I was really looking forward to getting you out of here. And I wish Brynn could meet you."

"I'd like to meet her, too."

"Next year, you have to come," I said.

Chester didn't answer, he just smiled.

"I don't like the idea of you spending the holiday alone."

"I'm never all that alone," he answered, and then pointed to a shelf behind me. "Get those down for me, Jane," he said.

I walked over to where he indicated. Two Christmas

cards were propped up like trophies, hard-won and infinitely precious. One was glossy bright red with an embossed green Christmas tree being decorated by little birds. The other was a solemn and stylized manger scene all in white, except for the star in the sky and the halo around the baby's head.

I carried the cards to the bed, but when I held them out to Chester, he shook his head.

"Read them to me," he directed.

"All right," I answered as I seated myself in the chair once more.

I opened the white one first. The printing was as elegant and expensive as the outside suggested.

I read aloud, "'And his name shall be called Wonderful, Counsellor, the mighty God, the everlasting Father, the Prince of Peace.'" Beneath that in larger bold print I read, "The 'Statens'."

"That's my nephew, Ches Staten," Chester said.

"He was named for you," I said.

Chester nodded. "Yes, his father and I were real close. I keep trying to remember the names."

"The names?"

"He's got two sons and I can't for the life of me remember what either of them is called," Chester said with a sigh. "And his wife, she's either Eva or Ida or Ada, something like that." He shook his head. "I've been thinking about it all week and I just can't come up with the names. It's one of the things I hate about getting old."

I glanced down at the card. There was no hint of what the first names might be.

"Read the other one," he said.

I opened the red one.

Above the printed verse was a salutation in blue ink. "'For Uncle Chester,'" I read aloud, feeling better about this one already. "'Birds are singing, bells are ringing, songs are here of Christmas cheer.'"

Beneath it the greeter had written, "'Much love and Merry Christmas!'" Then in four different hands it was signed, "Molly, Mike, Megan and Maddy."

"Molly is Vera's niece," Chester told me. "She lives up in New Jersey, married a guy named Michael McGarrity."

"They seem very nice," I said, looking down at the card in my hands.

"I'm sure they are," Chester agreed. "I've never met her husband, of course, nor those girls. In fact, I haven't seen Molly since she was a teenager. She couldn't have been more than sixteen or seventeen, I suppose, but real pretty, like you."

I accepted the compliment with a smile.

"Now, Ches, I saw him just two years ago," he said. "When I got sick, there wasn't anyone else to call."

"So he came down," I said.

Chester nodded. "He took care of it all in less than a week," he said. "While I was in the hospital he sold my house and got me this room here, had my things moved in."

"That was…nice," I said a little uncertainly.

"It was for the best," Chester said with resignation. "I suppose I couldn't stay there by myself anymore."

I knew that was right. I could see the evidence before my own eyes. Chester was in no condition to take care of himself. His nephew had put him here at Bluebonnet because he was trying to do a good thing. At that moment, it didn't seem as if it was good. But what else could his nephew have done? What would I have done? I wasn't able to answer either question.

A half hour later, as I walked through the lobby on my way out, I saw the little tree with the Snickers Miniatures sitting up on the counter at the nurses' station.

From the number of empty ribbons clinging to its branches, I could tell that the candy was disappearing fast. It made me furious. It was my gift to Chester. The nurse had no right to appropriate it the way that she had.

I got in my car and drove to a service station near the freeway entrance. I walked inside and perused the candy aisle. It took me a couple of minutes, but I found what I was looking for—a huge Snickers bar. I bought it and carried it out to the car. I had several small festively trimmed gifts in the trunk that I'd planned on delivering that afternoon. I carefully removed the paper from one, utilizing it to rather inexpertly wrap the candy bar.

Feeling very determined and justified, I drove back to the nursing home. Chester might be spending Christmas alone with only two Christmas cards for company, but he was not giving up his only gift.

The door to his room was unexpectedly closed. Without thinking, I opened it and barged right in.

He was lying on the bed, turned away from me. The sheet was down, revealing the open back of a hospital gown and a thin, old body, naked except for bandages upon his legs. A nurse was giving him a shot in his bony-looking hip.

She turned and glanced at me, surprised at my abrupt entry.

"Excuse me," I said, immediately trying to retreat.

"Oh, come on in, honey," she called out. "I'm done here."

Between her half-interested efforts and Chester's, the man's modesty was hastily restored. But I was embarrassed for him. He was obviously embarrassed as well.

"They're giving you antibiotics?"

It was as much a statement as a question.

"Antibiotics? Oh, yes, it…it was a flu shot," he said.

I started to correct him. An antibiotic is a far cry from a flu shot, but I decided the explanation wasn't worth the effort.

"I got you another Christmas present," I told him. "Since Nurse Grabby decided to co-opt your Christmas tree."

I handed him the hastily wrapped candy and he opened it.

"This is the biggest Snickers bar I've ever seen!" he said.

"It's Christmas," I told him.

# 9

Brynn's plane was delayed. I waited over two hours in a crowded airport, but I did so very happily, anxious to see her. If there was anyone in my life for whom I wanted to do something good, it was my daughter, Brynn. I had not been *Mommy Dearest*, but I hadn't been all apple pie either. I was eager for a chance to do better for my only child.

It seemed like a lifetime since she'd left, and when I saw her walking through the gate, I hardly recognized her. In the fall her hair had been, for the most part, style-free. It was mouse brown, much like my own natural color, and she'd kept it long and pulled back in a ponytail most days. Except for her high-school uniform, she'd dressed only in baggy, shapeless clothing. Her face never bore any hint of makeup.

The young woman who stepped off the plane was a bleached blonde dressed in a short spandex skirt and a sweater that clung to her attractive nineteen-year-old figure faithfully. She had on enough mascara to be the wife of a television evangelist.

"Brynn?" It was, of course, impossible for me not to recognize my own daughter, but the question hinted at my total surprise.

"Hello, Mother." The words were said without any emotion at all. She seemed so grown-up, such a self-possessed, sophisticated young adult. I was startled to discover myself at a loss for words.

"Let me carry that," I said finally, offering to juggle her carry-on bag as she toted her laptop.

We began to walk up the concourse.

"Did you have a good flight?"

She gave me a long-suffering look. "The plane was packed for the holidays, Mother, and delayed two hours. What do you think?"

"I think you're probably exhausted," I answered. "When you get home you can have a nice long soak in the tub and maybe a little nap before dinner."

She nodded but didn't reply. The conversation lagged as we hiked through the hordes of holiday travelers and dodged handicapped-transport carts.

When we reached baggage claim, there was nothing for her to do but stop. Above the luggage conveyer her flight was listed, but it was not yet moving. She leaned up against a column.

Standing on one foot, she flexed her ankle as if attempting to relieve a cramp.

"Are the shoes new?" I asked.

Brynn looked over at me, her expression clearly conveying impatience.

"Of course they're new, Mother," she said. "I've just come from a shopping trip."

"Oh yes, right," I agreed.

She was tired, cranky, and I was the nearest available target. I was determined not to take it personally.

"I like your new look," I said, basing my opinion not upon the actual fashion statement itself, but more on the optimistic impression that she was developing her own style. Slut chic was all the rage with younger women these days. If Brynn wanted to venture in that direction, well, I was all for it.

"I suppose you think I'm going to become obsessed with my own grooming, the way you are," she said.

I let that remark stand unchallenged. It wasn't completely fair, but I do spend an inordinate amount of time and money being concerned about my appearance.

"I'm not anything like you," Brynn continued. "That threatens you, doesn't it?"

She didn't give me an opportunity to reply.

"Dr. Reiser told me that you would be threatened."

The statement was made in a tone so confrontational it could have been a gang member casting aspersions on a rival's parentage.

"I'm seeing my own therapist," I said in my defense.

"It's a first step, Mother," Brynn commented loftily.

I decided it was the better part of valor to change the subject.

"Dad and I are very excited to have you home," I told her.

"Well, it's good that somebody is," she said. "Right now I am way too fagged to even care where I am or who I'm with."

As if to illustrate her point, she leaned even more heavily against the pillar, her shoulders sagging in exhaustion.

"We will get you rested up while you're home," I assured her. "You won't have to think about anything but lounging around and relaxing."

"Brynn? Brynn Lofton? Is that you?"

The question came from a perky little blonde in low-cut leather pants and a sequined crop-T.

"Kasey!" Brynn screeched in delight as she sprang up to full height once more. "Oh, I hoped I would get to see you over the holidays."

I tried to keep my jaw from dropping to the floor as I watched Brynn hug her friend from high school. Kasey Carlisle was the dowdy, nose-stuck-in-a-book valedictorian of St. Mary's High.

"How is MIT?" Brynn asked her.

"Intellectually, it's extreme," she answered. "And for guy acquirement, it's positively pullalating."

"I am too jealous!" Brynn answered. "Simmons is so lesbo track, I spend half my waking hours scavenging for XYs. And most of what's available is baseline wretched."

"Classic," her friend agreed.

The two chatted eagerly.

Kasey's mother, whose banker husband was a little too boring for social life, nodded politely to me. We'd never had more than a passing acquaintance, but now for a rapt moment we shared the wonder of this strangely transformed pair.

Seeing Kasey had, at least, succeeded in getting Brynn out of her bad doldrums. But it also got her out of the house for the rest of the day. She had me drop her off at the Carlisles' where Kasey already had the SUV running.

I drove home alone and unloaded the car, none too happily. I had never been one of those martyr mothers. Even in the worst of my relationship with Brynn, I'd never allowed my life to be controlled by the whim of my child.

Today, however, it had simply happened and I had been unable or unwilling to stop it. I thought of my own mother, who was probably turning in her grave. Never in all the years of our life together had my preferences ever come first. Of course, Mom wanted what was best for me. And she made sure that I went after it.

At that moment I envied her certainty. I had no idea what might be best for my Brynn.

Alone, my house felt surprisingly big and empty. I was there by myself most of the time without even noticing that five thousand square feet was a lot of personal space. With Brynn in town but not at home, I felt lonely.

I'd taken the whole day off in honor of her arrival. Her favorite dinner, merluza del vasco, was being catered from Le Parapluie. I could refrigerate everything I assured myself, and it would be just as good tomorrow.

I called David to let him know that Brynn had gotten home okay.

"I guess this frees us up to go to the Christmas party at the club," I told him.

"You go ahead," David suggested eagerly. "I'm going to put together a foursome, I think."

"Fine," I answered, not bothering to point out to him that there are no lights on the golf course for night play. "But you *will* be home later."

The verb stress assured that he would know that it hadn't been meant as a question. The last thing I wanted was for Brynn to suspect that her father spent his nights elsewhere.

"Of course," he assured me. "I'll catch up with you before ten."

I had no choice but to take him at his word.

The party was like a hundred others I had attended. My trio of comrades d'chic and I laughed and drank champagne and picked apart our least favorite ladies in the crowd.

Teddy asked about Brynn and I made light of it.

"At this age," I told my friends, "the last thing a young woman wants to do is go to a party with Mother and Dad!"

My statement brought laughter. It seemed perfectly reasonable. And I felt a little better about not being with her for her first night home.

Unfortunately I couldn't spend the entire evening with Teddy, Tookie and Lexi. Such cliquishness was unacceptable at the club. Though there were dozens of tight little circles just like ours, the only image that was acceptable to portray was an egalitarian one, within the limits of the membership itself.

So we were forced to circulate a bit. Besides, if we stayed together too tightly, we wouldn't find out what else was going on.

I wandered from room to room. Talking to people. Chatting meaninglessly. I repeated my statement about Brynn several times. Everyone laughed. Everyone agreed.

Next to the bar, I spoke to my father-in-law briefly. He was in a deep political discussion about the future of public education.

"Tax dollars shouldn't be funding any of it," he told his buddies. "If those welfare parents had to pay out of their own pockets, they'd care more about how their kids do in school."

Those around were in full agreement. "Giveaways never foster initiative," Les Weigan stated flatly.

His statement struck me as rather ironic. Weigan, like the other men present, was born into a family of wealth and privilege. Literally everything that he had, had been given to him, including a first-rate education and a profitable business. If that hadn't fostered his own initiative, he would have been dragged into bankruptcy years ago.

"I haven't seen my little Brynn. Is she here tonight?" W.D. interrupted their discussion to pose the question to me.

"She's out with Kasey Carlisle," I answered. "They ran into each other at the airport and made girl-plans for the evening."

W.D. nodded, smiling, but somehow he didn't look pleased. I wasn't sure if he was simply disappointed that she wasn't here, disapproving of her spending time with Kasey Carlisle, or unhappy with me for not making things work out differently.

I extricated myself from his confab as quickly as possible.

Unfortunately for me, it was out of the frying pan and into the fire. I'd just made it to the doorway, when someone actually reached over and tugged at my sleeve.

I glanced up to see Beverly Mullins.

"I want a word with you," she said, and then ominously added, "In private."

"Of course," I replied, feigning a brightness I definitely did not feel.

"This way, I think," she said, leading me back through the room and out the side doorway. The deserted locker room was chilly and unwelcoming, the odor of sweaty golf shoes hung in the air.

Beverly faced me. Her demeanor was matter-of-fact, but her expression was serious. I didn't know what she was going to say. She'd undoubtedly become aware of her husband's fruitless pursuit of me. Or maybe worse, maybe she thought I was encouraging him. Perhaps she thought that I was actively trying to break up her marriage. Defending myself by saying what a worthless, pathetic jerk I thought Gil to be was insulting. I couldn't do that. But what could I do? No matter what was said, afterward, our relationship, tenuous and shallow as it had always been, would cease to exist.

All I could hope was that this would be quick.

"There is no way to say this but just to say it," Beverly began.

"All right," I agreed. "Say it."

"Gil let it slip that David's building a house for that woman."

"What?"

"That woman, Mikki," she explained. "David is buying a house for her out in Stone Oak. Richland Garza did the plans. Monck and Sons are the contractors. She's quit her job and just spends her days out there making sure they do everything to suit her."

I just stood there, stunned. I was so certain that she was going to accuse me of chasing Gil. I was completely unprepared for this revelation in my own marriage. He was building her a house? I was speechless.

"You did know about her," Beverly said, looking at me with grave concern. "I was sure that you already knew about her."

"Oh yes, sure," I admitted. "I knew about her."

"Good, that's good," she said. "Myself, I don't even bother to keep up anymore. Who's sleeping with Gil ceased to matter years ago, as long as it didn't have to be me. But if he were spending that kind of money on somebody else, I'd want to know about it."

"Yes," I said. "Thank you."

She accepted my gratitude a little uneasily. "I think your girlfriends know it, too," she said. "Probably everybody does, or will. I'm sure they just didn't want to have to tell you."

"Yes, you're probably right," I said. "It really was good of you to let me know."

"No problem," Beverly answered. "Those of us with husbands like this have to stick together. Maybe we should start a support group, Women Married to Assholes. We could call ourselves the WMA and people would think we were a bunch of female doctors."

Her joke wasn't all that funny and I disliked her characterization of David as an asshole. I also didn't appreciate having him lumped in with the Gil Mullinses of the world. I suppose there was enough love and loyalty left to make me want to defend him. I didn't, however. I just thanked her again and made my exit from the locker room as quickly as possible.

I went back to join the party, but deliberately kept myself upon the edge of things, lost in my own thoughts.

I considered what Beverly had said, but I couldn't really believe that it was true. Gil had told her about this. Gil was a man who definitely had an agenda of his own. Though how he might think a story like this could benefit him, I didn't know.

Richland Garza was the architect, she'd said. David loved the man's work. But it was much too slick and contemporary for me. I had put the kibosh on that suggestion for our house the minute David had proposed him.

Maybe Mikki hadn't.

Perhaps she was building the new house. She could have changed jobs. I was sure that David had nothing to do with it.

There had been a number of "other women" in the years of our marriage. I'm not sure when David first began to be unfaithful. I'd been aware of a dalliance or two in the last ten years. I was pretty sure that what I knew was only the tip of the iceberg. This little hairdresser was just another one of those. Someone cute and sexy who made him feel young and virile. These affairs were never serious. David was very married. At least in the sense that his commitment to Brynn, and the concept of our family, was total. No amount of happy good-time-girl would ever change that. Any of the people around me who felt differently obviously just wanted some soap opera scenario to gossip about.

I continued circulating from room to room. Eventually I found myself on the sun terrace, a satillo-tiled enclosed porch facing the gardens. It had floor-to-ceiling glass doors on three sides, and in the spring it was opened up like a patio. Tonight it was closed, and heated against the winter chill, and was being utilized as the voting gallery.

On tables set up all around were the profiles of prospective members, each person or couple had their photograph, résumé and letter of recommendation from the nominating member. Some also had evidence of their business successes, civic leadership or genealogy connections.

On the table with each profile was a beautiful handcrafted antique voting box. They were simple, rectangular, with open sections on either side. These held marbles, black on the left, white on the right. A lid with one small hole covered the center compartment.

The voting boxes were as old as the club itself. Every family in membership had at one time had their name written on a neat white card that fit in the front slot.

The room was nearly empty. Not everyone bothered to vote. No quorum was required. Any number of white marbles was enough to vote a member in. But just one lone black marble meant rejection. Election had to be unequivocally unanimous.

I walked through, dropping white marbles into slots without much consideration. The sight of my own letterhead caught my attention. This was the Brandts' third try at club membership. Last year Millie had called me three times the day of the party, worried, nervous, wondering if anything had been said about her. She hadn't mentioned a word this year. Perhaps she had given up. Or she'd gotten afraid to hope.

If Millie and Frank were accepted in the club, they wouldn't need me anymore. They wouldn't have to treat me with kid gloves. They wouldn't have to suck up to me like I was somebody.

It felt strange to me as I stood there looking at their picture and the carefully worded family histories and personal biographies. How hard they had tried to appease the esoteric tastes of the club membership. How brave they were to put themselves out again, after twice being rejected.

They wanted this pretty badly. More than I needed to have them under my thumb? Somehow in the new world of doing good, the joy of being indispensable to their social ambitions had lost a lot of its luster.

I picked up a white marble, slipped it through the little hole in the lid of the box and smiling, walked away.

It counts as a five-pointer easily, I assured myself.


The next few days were as carefully orchestrated and as skillfully staged as if we'd all memorized our scripts.

David was endlessly available. He spent hours talking with Brynn about school, working with her on the jigsaw puzzle, telling her tales about his misspent youth at Harvard.

In return she dutifully played a round of golf with him.

I devoted my time to being the new-millennium version of Donna Reed. I decorated, baked, cleaned up, cooked, cleaned up and baked some more. My lines in this sitcom were limited to things such as:

"Who wants hot popovers?"

By Christmas morning, the shimmer on this shining vision of family life was beginning to dull.

We opened gifts in our pajamas. We had each bought dozens of things, and the boxes and torn wrapping paper piled up around the room. When it was all opened and politely acknowledged, none of us was particularly pleased with what we got.

David had bought me a pair of jewel-encrusted earrings—the type that his mother loved. I had a half-dozen similar pair from other occasions and I never wore any of them.

I got him a little desktop humidor for his office. He

thanked me before admitting that he'd given up cigars. A change that I hadn't noticed.

Brynn's choices were far better than my own. She'd run up over two thousand dollars on department store credit cards during her shopping trip to New York. But it was well worth it when David tore through the red and green tissue to find his new gold club.

"This is exactly what I wanted," he told Brynn.

She rolled her eyes. "Like I couldn't catch a hint," she teased. "You've mentioned the Ray Cook putter in every conversation since October."

I realized that I'd heard about it several times myself, but I had never made the connection between what he wanted and what I could give him.

Brynn had visited Elizabeth Arden for my gift, a beautifully presented basket of expensive bath items. She knew what a fan I was of a long soak. The bubble beads were moisturizing, non-allergic and oil-free whirlpool friendly. There was a bath mitt, a bath pillow and a pair of tub safe champagne glasses. The pampered, self-indulgent Jane I had been in the past would have loved it.

We thanked each other profusely with hugs all around. Then I headed to the kitchen to put together a Christmas breakfast. To my surprise, Brynn followed me.

The pajamas she wore was actually an oversize gray T-shirt that bore the likeness of Monica Lewinsky wearing a white moustache. The caption beneath it read *Not Milk.*

With a welcoming warmth June Allyson would envy, I got her seated at the prep island to watch me chop ingredients for omelettes.

Her bleached-blond hair was pulled back into a messy wad held together with a giant turquoise plastic clip at the crown of her head. Strands escaped on either side of her fresh-washed face, giving her a young, vulnerable appearance.

"So, Mother," she began "are you still being Lady Bountiful all over town?"

I shrugged a little guiltily.

"I'm involved in a few activities," I admitted.

"I don't get it," she said. "This is not the way you are, Mother."

She was right, of course. She knew me. But she was wrong as well. She knew me as I'd always been.

"I want to become a better person," I told her. "I want to live my life differently."

Her expression was skeptical.

"And what do you get out of this?" she asked me.

"I'm not sure I get anything out of it," I said.

"Well, I read something at school that says practicing acts of altruism makes people healthier and happier," Brynn said.

"Really?" I was surprised.

"I guess there's got to be some kind of payoff," Brynn insisted. "Or people would never do it."

I thought about that for a long moment before I answered. "Maybe they would," I told her.

"Don't be naïve, Mother," she said. "Everybody's out for themselves."

"No, I don't think they are," I told her. "If a man runs into a burning building to save a child and he and the child both die, would it have been better for him to have stayed on the sidewalk."

"It would have been smarter," she said. "He would have been alive."

"But could he have lived with the memory of that child's screams in his ears?"

"Eww, you're getting morbid," Brynn complained.

"There is no guarantee the good things we do always turn out well for us," I told her. "And when we do good, the world around us doesn't suddenly become a visibly better place. But doing it anyway, I guess, is the real challenge."

Brynn leaned back in her chair and looked at me, puzzled.

"Is this for real, Mom?"

I laughed.

"Are you still visiting that old man every chance you get?"

"Chester? Yes, I try to see him every week," I said. "He's a very interesting man."

"He encourages your corybantic behavior."

"Corybantic?"

Brynn hesitated, debating whether or not she wished to elaborate on her statement. She decided to do so.

"Dr. Reiser says that your brush with death has manifested itself in changes reminiscent of a religious-conversion experience. It's positively manic and this man, Chester, simply exacerbates the whole unstable situation."

This analysis belittled what had become, for me, a very important aspect of my life. And she made Chester sound like some sort of wild-eyed cult-figure swami.

"I don't think there is anything wrong with my wanting to be a kinder person," I said. "I want to be a more caring citizen, an eager volunteer, a more understanding parent. Those are good things."

"Look, Mother," she said, her expression long-suffering. "I am not opposed to your newfound social conscience. I'm sure Dr. Reiser is right—at your time of life you undoubtedly need validation and purpose. But leave me out of it, okay? You've had eighteen years to play mommy to me. For the first half of that you wouldn't let me out of your sight, and in the second half, you could hardly bear the sight of me. I'm finally on my own now and I don't want any of your last minute largesse."

"I just love you and want to help you," I told her.

Brynn's jaw was set stubbornly. "Help, unsolicited, is intrusion," she said. "You've tried to see that I've had all the things that *you* always wanted. The problem is, those have never been the things that *I've* wanted. Now you want to be Claire Huxtable. Okay, but don't expect me to be an enabler. I have my own life and the less contact I have with you the better."

David walked through the door all smiles. "How are my two best girls coming with that breakfast?"

I'm not sure what the two of us looked like, but David's happy expression sobered up immediately.

"We're almost ready," I assured him with a smile deliberately bright. "If you and Brynn want to set the table…"

Breakfast was a mostly silent affair. David did most of the talking, presenting a long and complicated discourse on how the swing plane, an imaginary line from the base of your neck to the ground, is the least understood and appreciated of the five golf fundamentals.

He had the full attention of both myself and Brynn, as neither of us was willing to so much as glance in the other's direction.

I still had dishes in the sink when Edith and W.D. showed up. They were invited for a late holiday dinner at three o'clock, but apparently they couldn't stay away. They had seen even less of Brynn than we had and monopolized her time for the rest of the day.

That was all right with me. I knew that only time could lessen the sting of the words we'd spoken. And with Brynn involved with her grandparents, I could focus my attention on creating the perfect holiday meal. I'd had the goose and cranberry dressing catered, of course, but there were plenty of salads and vegetable dishes for me to spend the day on.

By three-thirty we were sitting at the dining table, festive with Christmas-tree Spode. David secured the camera on its tripod and set the timer so that we could all be happy and smiling around the table at the same time. The light from the flash had barely faded before the mood around the table darkened.

My father-in-law said grace, evoking a generalized thankfulness that seemed perfunctory, as if our blessings were not heaven-sent but personally acquired. Still, he asked for more in the coming year—good health, a safe home and the family together. My thoughts drifted to Chester; alone today, he had none of those things. If I was going to expend energies on doing good, that wonderful man should certainly be on the receiving end of those efforts.

W.D. finished his prayer with a hearty amen. David seconded it before rising to his feet. With good humor and exaggerated ceremony, he began carving the bird.

I was smiling when I glanced over at Edith and caught her surveying the napkins and place settings with a critical eye.

"Is something wrong?" I asked.

"Oh no, not wrong exactly," she said. "You know, on Oprah's holiday table, she chose to mix and match the colors and patterns."

"Really? Is she trying to be Martha Stewart now?"

"Of course not!" Edith sounded vaguely insulted. "Martha Stewart is so…well, she's not one of *us*—like Oprah."

It was truly astonishing that Edith would choose to identify with the populist rather than the patrician, but I smiled politely, unwilling to contradict her.

"By mixing the colors and patterns, the presentation

is so much more cozy and reflective of family," she continued, critiquing my table. "This is so…well, so cold."

"The ivory tablecloth was a wedding present," I pointed out. "From the Coburns. It's been on our table every Christmas for the last twenty years."

"Hettie Coburn, God rest her soul, never had a smidgen of good taste in her little finger," Edith said.

Brynn touched the tablecloth as if contact with it was distasteful. "It's older than I am," she said, voicing disbelief.

"Fine household goods become more valuable as they age," I told her.

Edith tutted and shook her head. "Things change," she said. "Styles change."

"Tradition is important."

"Not if it's boring," Edith countered.

"And this tablecloth is boring," Brynn said a little too pointedly. "I suppose I'm going to get it when you die. That's one of the downsides of being the only child, you inherit all your parents' crap."

Edith tutted lightly, but corrected her as well. "These are belongings, dear, not *crap*."

"Whatever," Brynn responded, unwilling to antagonize her grandmother. "Anyway, I promise to give this to the thrift store."

Edith giggled girlishly, obviously tickled with my daughter's cutting humor. I was not particularly amused.

David began the dinner conversation by giving us a shot-by-shot description of his golf game with Brynn. He had obviously enjoyed playing with her, though he clearly felt that she had much room for improvement. Just as he got about midway through the course, his father interrupted him.

"Did you see yesterday's editorial page?" W.D. asked abruptly.

David was momentarily taken aback. But recovered quickly enough to shrug and reply, "Not much news."

That was what David always answered. He rarely even looked at the newspaper. More often than not, I was the first to open the paper, quickly scanning the style section as I put it in the recycle bin.

W.D. apparently didn't require any feedback.

"It's bad enough that the media tilt every news story toward a liberal bias, but now, right at Christmastime, they play Scrooge to a federal tax cut."

"They came out against it?" David asked.

"Oh, they say they're neutral, not going to take a position on the issue," W.D. explained. "But then they go and give half a column on the editorial page to that damn empty-headed bleeding heart, Scott Robbins. He's mad because the top income brackets get the biggest part of the cut."

The man's name caught my attention. I looked up.

"We are the people who *pay* those taxes," W.D. continued. "And when we get money back, we invest it, do the country some good."

David nodded and forked himself another piece of cranberry goose.

"You give more money to some low wage worker, he's just going to spend it uselessly," W.D. went on. "Oh, I suppose it helps cheap discount chains and the local beer joint, but it doesn't do a thing for the economy as a whole."

"Scott Robbins?" I asked. "Where have I heard that name?"

W.D. looked over at me, obviously annoyed.

"You've seen his name a least once a week in the 'Letters to the Editor,'" W.D. complained. "The damn fool has some stupid opinion on practically everything."

Not having read the "Letters to the Editor" at any time in my memory, I was pretty sure that was not the source of this familiarity. I mentally scanned the list of people who worked in my office, current and former clients, people at church, the folks that I'd met in charities and service organizations. I couldn't come up with anyone. Still, I knew that name, but I just didn't know from where.

I shrugged and let it go.

# 10

The rest of Christmas Day was basically pleasant. I volunteered to do all the cleanup and nobody tried to talk me out of it. Having had the main dish and the desserts catered, the job didn't really take me all that long, but I lingered at it.

Occasionally I glanced into the family room where Brynn, David and his parents played Scattergories with more noise and enthusiasm than I could have ever brought to the game.

W.D. and Edith had been proud and doting with David. They were the same way with Brynn. They treated her as if she were the brightest, wittiest, most delightful human on the planet. And she responded by being exactly what they expected her to be.

They seemed so patrician. So comfortable and at ease with the advantages of their life. As I watched them from the kitchen, I realized that this was the world that I had wanted so very long ago back in that tacky little house in Sunnyside. I had been watching from a distance then. Now, in my own home, I was watching from a distance still.

Brynn was relaxed and charming. She laughed at all her grandfather's jokes. Though these occasionally covered such themes as politics and religion, they mostly concerned the personal lives of senior citizens. She gave as good as she got with punch lines of her own on subjects more pertinent to those of her age. But basically they were both finding humor in sex, drinking and bathroom habits.

Edith giggled ad infinitum. The Christmas cognac may have had something to do with that.

David rolled his eyes and accepted the part of reasonable person, condemned to spend the evening with three goofballs.

Occasionally one of them would call out to me.

"Jane! Jane! Did you hear that one?" David asked. "The reason why the chicken crossed the road? To prove to the armadillo that it could be done."

"Mom, do you know how many sorority girls it takes to change a lightbulb?" Brynn called out. "Two. One to call Daddy for help and the other to pour the Diet Pepsi."

I listened to them, laughed with them. But I didn't go in and join them. It wasn't as if I felt unwelcome. It was more that I didn't want to intrude on what was obviously a Kodak moment. I gave myself four points for staying alone in the kitchen.

W.D. and Edith left just after nightfall, looking happy but exhausted from their busy day. Edith made a date for shopping with Brynn the next morning. I would never have wanted to visit the mall the day after Christmas. But those two were serious consumers, relishing the challenge.

W.D. moaned, as if the idea of Edith and her granddaughter alone in the mall with credit cards was a fearful thing to contemplate. We laughed appropriately.

As they drove away, David, Brynn and I watched from the porch, arms around each other's shoulders until they were out of sight. Brynn stepped away from me rather deliberately, I thought, before walking silently back into the house.

David fabricated some urgent business and disappeared for a couple of hours.

Seating herself on the couch in the family room, one leg bent beneath her, Brynn booted up her laptop and was sharing Christmas disaster stories with a chat room from her dorm. Her own undoubtedly included the morning's confrontation with her overbearing and unpleasant mother.

With no one to talk to, nothing to do and the cleanest kitchen in Cambridge Heights, I retired to my room. I combed my hair out, brushed my teeth and dressed comfortably in my sleeping-sheep pajamas.

I lay down in bed and resigned myself to fanning listlessly through the stack of unread fashion magazines that had piled up on my night table. There were a lot of them. I was so far behind, I hadn't even seen the layout of sexy vampire costumes that promised to *score wild tricks and wicked treats for you and your honey on Halloween.*

With a disgusted grimace, I decided to just give up the end of the year as a loss. I found a January issue. It was devoted almost exclusively to diet and exercise. There were glossy photos of beautiful fit young starlets in evening gowns, martini in hand, declaring that they had *lost five pounds just by giving up pasta.*

A former Olympic athlete demonstrated her new body-contouring regimen. Just looking at the pictures made me tired, sweaty and out of breath. I pulled down the covers to get a look at my own thighs.

"Well, Jane," I admonished myself aloud, "it is definitely time for another visit to Dr. Plastic and his amazing lard-sucking machine."

I skipped through the rest of the weight-loss advice, the dozens of cigarette ads and the lovely scenic vistas touting freshness for *that* time of the month. There was a ten-question quiz on how to *recognize the clues when your man is cheating.* I glanced through casually.

"I see that building a house with his girlfriend is not mentioned anywhere."

My intrapersonal conversation was interrupted by a discreet tapping on my door.

"Come in," I called out eagerly.

I expected Brynn. Amazingly, it was David who opened the door.

He must have witnessed the surprise on my face.

"I saw the light," he explained.

"I didn't know you'd come home," I told him.

"I just got back," he admitted.

He walked in a little uncomfortably and closed the door behind him. There was a strangeness about his presence. It wasn't as if he hadn't been in my room. He just hadn't been in it lately, or when I was lying down.

When he reached the bedside he seemed awkward, as if not sure what to do or where to put his hands. He stuffed them in his pockets first and then pulled them out to wrap uneasily around his own waist.

I scooted over a bit.

"Sit down," I offered.

He visibly relaxed as he did.

"Is Brynn still up?" I asked him.

"I just said good-night to her in the hall."

That pleased me. I wanted her to see her father visiting my room. It made us seem more normal.

"I just wanted to talk to you…" David began and then sort of faded off.

"I wanted to talk to you, too," I admitted. "Brynn was lovely today. She seems very grown-up since summer."

He nodded. "Yes, she is. Did you two have words this morning?"

"Not much," I assured him. "I'm surprised you noticed."

"It's hard to miss. When you two are unhappy, I get to do all the talking."

"So I guess it's not all bad," I teased.

David chuckled. He was looking at me very intently. There was an earnestness about his expression that was a little bit intimidating.

"What is it?" I asked. "Do I have toothpaste on my nose?"

With a long index finger, he tapped the end of my nose, teasing.

"No, I guess not," he said. "I was thinking how very young you look when you laugh. It reminds me so much of when we were just kids."

"What a sweet thing to say."

"It's true, Jane. Absolutely true."

"Thank you."

He nodded. "I wanted to come in here and tell you that I had a really nice Christmas."

"Good," I told him.

"And I know that I have you to thank for that," he continued. "I know how much planning and effort you put into making this a very special holiday for Brynn and for me."

I was touched.

"You're welcome," I said. "And the earrings you got me were fabulous."

He shrugged. "Actually, Mom picked them out," he confessed.

"Oh, that was sweet of her," I said. I wasn't surprised. It was exactly the kind of thing that Edith liked. Me, I'd throw them in the back of the jewelry safe with the hope of never seeing them again.

A silence settled upon us. Not a comfortable silence that would be unexceptional between two people who'd been married twenty years, but an edgy, expectant silence. Both of us wondering what would happen next.

David continued to look at me in that strange, searching manner. It made me nervous. It made me curious. What was he feeling? What was he thinking?

He took my left hand in his own. At first, he just held it, lightly running his thumb over the bright cluster of diamonds on the third finger.

Then tentatively, hesitantly, he brought it up to his face. He pressed it a moment against his cheek and then kissed my palm.

The tenderness of the gesture sent a shiver of anticipation through me. It had been a very long time since David and I had touched.

I missed that. I missed him. If his infidelity made me hesitate, it was only for a minute.

"Oh, David." I breathed his name like a prayer.

I slid my arm around his neck and edged him closer to me. I raised my mouth up to his own.

"Stay with me tonight," I whispered one instant before our lips met.

Instantaneously it was foreplay. These were not the gentle, friendly pecks shared between Brynn's mother and daddy, This was open-mouth sensual exploration, deep, eager and greedy.

"Oh, baby," David started murmuring. "Oh, baby." It was his sex-act liturgy. I remembered it very well.

Beneath my palms, his shoulders and back were strong and muscular, more so now than in his youth. His kisses were better, too. And his touch more confident, more skillful, more seductive.

"This feels good," I told him.

He threw the covers back, scattering slick glossy magazines all over the room. With nimble fingers he began undoing the buttons on my flannel pj's.

I had never attempted to repress my sexual desire.

But for the last several years, I had mainly ignored it. I tried to channel that energy into my work, my social life. And I was not too prudish to ease my own frustrations, but there is nothing in the world quite as captivating and gratifying as another human body pressed up against your own.

I slid my hands underneath his shirt and lightly raked my nails against the softness of his skin.

"Oh, baby," he murmured as he bared my breasts. "You look good, you smell good."

"I am good," I assured him as I clicked off the bedside lamp, allowing the silvery shimmer through the skylight to illuminate us.

He chuckled lightly as he nuzzled against my bosom.

I threaded my fingers through his hair. My breath caught in my throat at the touch of his tongue.

"You always were good," he told me.

That was the truth. In bed, I had always been good. And he had been, too. That night was no different. We knew all the ways to caress each other, tease each other, tempt each other. And neither of us hesitated to make full use of that knowledge.

Fired up, laughing, kinky, we romped on the mattress like newlyweds. David stuffed a pillow behind the headboard to keep it from banging against the wall. I dragged off his briefs with my teeth.

We giggled. We panted. We moaned.

It took a while for me to get to the edge. I wrapped my legs around him tightly, urging him on. He stayed with me until my climax and then he came a half minute later.

We lay there in each other's arms, catching our breath as the sweat on our bodies gleamed in the moonlight. I felt wonderful. Totally exhausted, yet somehow brimming with energy as well.

I wanted to giggle, to kiss him, to hug him. I wanted

to relive the moments just past. To marvel together about how wonderful it felt and how well we understood each other, how intuitively we satisfied each other's need. I resisted the desire.

David was quiet, thoughtful, as he sometimes was after sex. I decided to let him slip into that place in his heart where he went without me.

I did plant one more kiss on his cheek.

"That was fantastic, darling," I told him. "I'm wrung out like a dishrag and never enjoyed it more. Let's not wait so long before we do it next time, okay?"

I don't know what he replied, if anything. The moment I lay my head against the pillow, I was asleep. I awakened late in the morning and he was already gone. He probably had an early tee-time.

Two days later we got Brynn on her plane to Colorado with hugs and kisses and admonitions to be careful. The holiday hadn't been a complete disappointment, but I was a little down anyway. I had tried so hard to make her time with us fun and special and pleasant. Not just because I wanted her to visit us more often, but because that was the kind of relationship I wanted to have with my daughter. I wanted to be a good mother. I wanted Brynn to have a good family life. I wanted our home to be a source of strength for her.

The simple things can sometimes be the hardest to attain.

David appeared as thoughtful as I was myself. We walked the long concourse and took the train to short-term parking without much discussion at all. When we reached the Volvo, I spoke for the first time.

"Just drop me off at home, I think I'm just going to hang around the house this afternoon."

That wasn't really such a good idea. I'd already taken

off all four days that Brynn was home. Since the accident my sales had gone way down. I really needed to get something closed before the year was out. Somehow my heart wasn't in it.

"Home is where I'm headed," David answered. "I think I'll play hooky this afternoon as well."

"You don't have a golf game?"

"No," he said. "I canceled."

His words surprised me. And worried me a bit as well. It was a cool crisp afternoon with sunshine and blue skies. David played golf almost every day and certainly every pretty day.

"Are you not feeling well?" I asked him.

"Oh no, I'm fine," he assured me.

He certainly looked fine. He seemed a lot happier than usual. It was the kind of inner cheerfulness and optimism that had attracted me to the man in the first place. Amazingly, I'd forgotten that. I'd forgotten how his upbeat, positive attitude had so intrigued me.

I'd thought that it was an outward manifestation of status and money. Over the years, however, I'd discovered that most of the wealthy and privileged, at least the ones I'd met in this city, were not nearly so pleased with life.

It was just David being David. Deliberately choosing to see the world at its best.

I attributed today's inner glow as residual joy at having Brynn at home.

"She really looks so grown-up in those new clothes," I said.

"Who?"

"Brynn."

"Oh, yeah," he agreed. "Can you believe that she's finally dating. She's been such a wallflower for so long. I was beginning to think she never would."

"It's pretty scary," I admitted.

"Scary? No, it's great," David assured me.

"It's usually the father who worries that his daughter will fall for the wrong guy," I pointed out.

"Not me," he answered. "I'm sure anybody Brynn chooses will be fine."

I shook my head. "How can you know that?" I asked him. "What if she gets involved with some terrible jerk."

"That's not going to happen."

"David, there are men out there who are absolutely vicious, cruel," I said.

"Of course there are," he agreed. "And there are zealots who pray to maharishi mud wrestlers, and weirdos who get healthy by eating pond slime on their granola. But I don't think we should automatically assume our Brynn would be attracted to them."

"But she might be," I told him.

He shook his head. "Brynn's a smart girl," he said.

"But she's emotionally fragile."

"I don't know," he said. "She's sure been standing up to you pretty well for the last ten years."

He was right, of course. Brynn's problems had never been that she wouldn't stand up for herself, it was that she always locked horns with me when she did so.

"All right," I said. "She probably wouldn't let somebody just walk all over her. But even if the man she loves is just irresponsible and selfish, he could make her life a hell on earth."

David looked at me and actually chuckled.

"Brynn would never fall for somebody like that," he said with a certainty that I envied.

"People do, David," I explained. "Every day people make bad choices about who to love. I just don't want her to do that."

"It's worth the risk," he answered.

"What?"

"It is absolutely worth the risk," he said. "We want her to be happy. The key to that is finding someone to share your life."

His words surprised me, but pleased me as well. And his absolute conviction about them gave me hope.

As we drove home, I thought about us. Daddy and Mommy and Brynn. Our little family unit. I had always assumed that the Mommy and Brynn part of that was somehow the biggest portion. It was certainly the part that had always required the most upkeep and maintenance. I hadn't really given much consideration to what David's role had been in our daughter's life. Maybe because there was no father figure in my own upbringing, I hadn't thought much about his input, his influence.

I'd always assumed Brynn was like me. That premise had obviously caused a good deal of conflict between my daughter and myself. Maybe Brynn was like her father.

That idea brought my whole thought process to a startling, grinding halt. I glanced over at David beside me. She had his coloring. She had his eyes. Sometimes I saw his smile on her lips. Was it possible that she had his disposition as well?

I considered that seriously for the first time.

No, she wasn't like him entirely, or she would have just let me run things and been content to devote herself to golf. But perhaps there was more of her father's nature in her than I'd considered.

Not being driven to succeed, not being socially ambitious, not particularly enjoying the privileges of her status in the world, I'd thought those behaviors were some kind of rebellion against me. And perhaps they were, but they could also have been a reflection of her father, who had never gone after any achievement greater than putting an eagle and didn't give a rat's ass about powerful people, important parties and sumptuous things.

When we arrived home I turned on the lights on the Christmas tree. The holiday was over, but the sight of those unlit decorations was depressing somehow.

I went into my office and checked my messages. There were several from work, including a personal one from Millie. She asked me to call her immediately. I chose to ignore it and instead called Loretta at the battered women's safe house to find out how their Christmas had been.

She was too busy to talk. The place was overrun with new clients, they were having to double up in some of the rooms.

"It's like this every year," Loretta told me. "It's as if all the talk about joy and peace just brings out the worst in some men."

I hung up feeling worse instead of better. I went online to get my e-mail and promised myself that if I got everything taken care of, I'd go see Chester in the afternoon. There wasn't quite enough incentive to get me digging into work immediately.

From my doorway I could see a sliver of the kitchen. David was on his knees. Beside him was his red plastic toolbox, neat, clean and nearly new from nonuse. To my complete amazement I watched him tightening the loose handle on the flatware drawer.

Incredulous, I got up and went into the kitchen.

"What are you doing?" I asked him.

"I noticed this handle was loose, it just takes a second to fix," he said.

I laughed and shook my head. "David, that handle has been loose for more than two years. What made you come in here to fix it today?"

I was still smiling when he looked up at me. There was an intensity in his gaze that was sobering. He looked oddly familiar kneeling there at my feet. He had knelt that way the day he'd proposed. It had been so old-fashioned and earnestly romantic. And so long ago.

His expression now was equally as sincere.

"What is it?" I asked.

He carefully placed the screwdriver back into the toolbox and closed the lid. He looked up at me. Nervously, he wiped his hands on his thighs.

"I'm leaving you, Jane," he said simply.

"What?"

"I'm leaving," he repeated. "I want a divorce."

I just stood there staring at him.

"I'm in love," he explained. "Real love. Maybe for the first time in my life. You and I have had a good marriage, I guess. But it's over. Now I want to be with her. I have to be with her."

"Her?"

"Mikki," he answered. "Mikki Conyers. I figured you knew."

I nodded.

"I never meant for this to happen, honestly," David said. "And she didn't either. But we fell in love, the everlasting, ever-faithful, eternal kind of love."

His voice was soft, almost soothing as he said the words.

"We want to be married, Jane," he said. "We want to build a life together."

Strangely relaxed, I just stood there, listening to him. I suppose he thought my silence was a signal that more explanation was necessary—that if he just presented everything honestly and openly, I'd say, *Yes, that sounds wonderful, David. Of course you should dump me and go off with her. Be happy. Congratulations!*

He continued to talk until he finally ran out of words. The stillness between us grew long. I was almost too stunned by this unexpected development to even speak. It wasn't like my thoughts were racing. It was more like I couldn't get my brain to function at all. I had no idea what I was going to say. David waited. The quiet lingered. Then, suddenly, the words came to me.

"Forget it."

My tone was not sharp, but it was adamant.

His expression immediately changed.

"What?"

"I said, forget it, David," I clarified. "I'm going to. I'm going to forget this conversation ever took place."

He rose to his feet. He was surprisingly puzzled at my reaction, but clearly determined to have his way.

"Jane. I want out."

I shook my head.

"David, that is not going to happen," I said. "I have always let you have somebody on the side. I've never stopped you, never even tried to slow you down. I won't be repaid for that by being thrown over for a slutty blond hairdresser with a high-school education."

"There is nothing slutty about Mikki," he defended. "She's a wonderful girl. I love her."

"A wonderful *girl*," I shot back with emphasis on the last word. "Does she make you feel like a boy, David? Newsflash! You're forty, you've got a daughter almost her age and your hair's thinning."

He had enough vanity to look stricken. He immediately rubbed the crown of his head to verify what I'd said.

"Look, I'm not saying you have to give her up," I told him. "Keep seeing her, take her on a vacation with you. Enjoy her. Get it out of your system, but don't throw away our marriage for nothing."

"Mikki is everything," he said. "It's our marriage that is nothing."

"How can you say that?"

"Because it's true. It's been true for years. Maybe it's always been true."

The words hurt. They hurt terribly.

"I don't want to discuss it," I said, trying to regain control. "The answer is no. That's it. Simple. No."

"You won't be able to stop it."

"Of course I will," I answered. "I have been one hundred percent faithful to you. I haven't so much as eaten dinner with another man who wasn't a client. You can't divorce me unless I let you. And I'm not about to let you."

"You have to."

"I do not have to and I don't intend to," I insisted. "I'm not the one who's been dropping his pants all over town for the last ten years. And speaking of that, if Mikki is everything and you are so damn in love, ever faithful and everlasting, then what in the hell was Christmas night?"

He blushed a vivid red. At least he had the decency to be embarrassed about it.

"That was a mistake," he said.

"I'm sure it was," I said. "Mistakes are pretty common to you. Is that what you told Mikki? Or did you bother to tell her about making it with me?"

I could see in his expression that he hadn't.

"Well," I said, "I guess you could say that it really doesn't count as being 'unfaithful' if the person you're screwing happens to be your spouse of record at the time."

"Jane," he began, and reached out to me.

I slapped at him and yelled.

"Don't touch me!"

He caught my hand before it found his cheek. He held both my wrists. I struggled in his grasp. I tried to kick him.

He wrapped me in a constricting embrace, holding

me tightly against his chest. He wasn't hurting me, but I could hardly move.

"Let me go! Let me go!"

"Don't do this, Jane," he whispered against my hair. "Don't do this to us. Don't make it end like this. I love you, Jane. I love you as a friend, as my best friend. Don't make it end with us tearing each other apart."

I can't say if David released me, or if I broke away, but I was suddenly free. I raced to my office. Slammed the door and locked it. I stood with my back braced against the door. He did not pursue me.

I heard him moving about in the house. I tried to sort my thoughts, to ready myself for the next onslaught. David hated confrontation. He always had. That would work in my favor. Divorce was the poster child for confrontation. If I made it hard enough for him, he'd give up the whole idea. And he had to give up the whole idea.

I heard the side door slam. It wasn't an angry noise, merely imbued in finality.

I ran over to the window. David carried two suitcases, his golf bag slung over his shoulder. He opened the trunk of the Volvo and stowed them inside. As he headed for the driver's door, he glanced up directly at me as if he knew exactly where I would be. He raised his hand and waved goodbye.

I hurried away from the window. I felt as if my insides had been ripped out. I was hollow, empty. I sat down in my chair, rubbed my temples.

He'd be back, I assured myself. Marriages don't end in a day. Even if things go sour, couples keep trying. The process goes on for years and years. And I was stronger than David. I could outlast him. I could always have whatever I wanted.

I burst into tears. Once I started crying, I found I couldn't stop.

# 11

---

The road from "Forget it. No divorce!" to *Ms. Jane Lofton, former wife of* was not nearly as long or rigorous a distance as I would have imagined.

After David left, I had my cry. It was cathartic at the very least. Every few minutes the telephone would ring. I'd eagerly check the caller ID to see if it was David's cell or the number at the club or any golf course in America. He had to phone me. He had to say he was sorry. He had to say he was coming home. But instead the tiny LED display revealed my office, Edith, Teddy or one of my clients. I couldn't talk to any of them.

It was barely 8:00 p.m. when I crawled into bed, exhausted from the emotional effort. I turned the phone off and welcomed sleep. But, of course, it didn't come. I couldn't stop thinking. And the more I thought, the more frightened I became. I got so scared, I started shaking. Then I was shaking so much, I got cold.

Shaky, shivering, I finally went to the kitchen and poured myself a glass of shiraz. I thought about calling Dr. Feinstein, but then I'd have to talk about it. The last thing I wanted to do was talk about it.

I climbed into a hot bath. With water pouring from the faucet and the whirlpool jets running on high, there was a cocoon of noise around me, surprisingly pleasant.

I sipped my wine and tried to get a grip on myself. Denial seemed like the way to go. If I just insisted that nothing had happened, that nothing had changed, then I could really wait this out and it would all be fine. The memory of David's face, however, made denial especially difficult.

I, of course, had thought about divorce before. Maybe more times than I would have liked to admit. Any person in a less than totally satisfactory marriage undoubtedly would. But in all those imaginary instances, I had been the person who decided to get out. I had been the instigator, not the victim.

This divorce was not because I'd grown tired of his infidelities and had decided I was better off without him. David wanted to leave me for another woman. Call it ego, pride or just a sense of competition, but I did not relish that scenario. And it was more than just losing David. I would lose everything I had ever wanted. It would mean losing everything that I'd worked for in my entire life.

I don't know how late I stayed up, how long I stayed in the bath or how many glasses of wine I downed. But eventually I did get to sleep. I awoke in my bathrobe on the family-room couch. I was easily as tired as when I went to bed.

I squinted at the sun pouring in from the patio French doors. My head was pounding. The cottony taste in my mouth was rank enough for a camel to have died there.

The doorbell was ringing. I realized that it had been ringing for some time.

I jumped up too quickly. The dregs of a glass of wine, which had been sitting on the edge of the couch, spilled down my bathrobe.

I cursed, but didn't even attempt to clean up the mess. The ringing was insistent. I couldn't ignore it.

"Coming!" I hollered, hoping to shut up the stupid bell.

It didn't work. I continued through the house. When I got to the front door I jerked it open angrily. The annoyance of the doorbell was just too much.

"What!"

Millie Brandt was obviously startled, but she recovered quickly.

"Thank God you're all right!" she said. "I've been calling and calling—your home, your cell. I've left half a dozen messages. I saw your car here, I knew you had to be inside. I was just minutes away from dialing 911 and getting the police to break down the door."

I just stood there in front of her, not knowing exactly what to say. There was a part of me that wanted to throw my arms around this woman and say, "Millie, David has left me. What will I do?" Fortunately, that part was held in check by the real Jane Lofton, who knew not to divulge too much information to anyone who might be able to use it against her.

"Oh, sorry," I said. "I've had a terrible migraine and I turned the phones off."

It was not much of an explanation, but it hung there between us. I took a deep breath, and mustered every bit of strength and self-control I'd ever been able to manage.

"I didn't know you got migraines," she said.

"Oh, it's very rare," I assured her. "I get maybe one a decade or something."

She glanced down at the wine stain on my robe.

"They say you shouldn't drink alcohol when you have them," she said. "It just makes them worse."

"Really? Well, that's good to know."

Millie looked as she always did. Her hair was a little bit bigger than was stylish and she wore her reading glasses on a chain around her neck. But Millie was small, tidy and conservatively fashionable. Easily ten years my senior, with careful makeup and frequent nips, tucks and peels, she maintained the appearance of a woman trying to hang on to thirty-five.

"I didn't mean to intrude," she assured me. "I just wanted to make sure that you were all right."

Smiling brightly, I opened the door all the way and invited her in. This was mainly to show that my house was not a wreck, no evidence of a lost weekend or a wild toga party.

I caught a vague reflection of myself in the hall mirror. My hair was completely flattened on one side of my head. My day-old mascara had melted, run and reformed itself into that familiar makeup mask unpleasantly known as raccoon eyes.

I fought the desire to run shrieking from the room and instead put on my very best formal manners, hoping such aplomb would distract any notice from my stained robe, flat-headed, black-eyed appearance.

"Come on into the kitchen and I'll fix us some coffee," I said.

"Can you drink coffee with migraines?" she asked.

"Oh sure," I said. "It actually helps."

I don't know what she thought about that, but she didn't argue with me.

As the coffee dripped, we talked about clients, listings, properties we thought we'd get to contract. It hadn't been a great year for real estate overall, but the high-end market was always pretty stable.

Having her there in the familiar surroundings of my home, discussing things that we always discussed, made the nightmare of the previous evening much less frightening.

She filled me in on what I'd missed when she'd covered for me during Brynn's visit. She voiced concern that I had not really gotten back to full speed since my car accident. My sales looked as if they were going to be unusually low overall.

"I can't be top seller every year," I said, giving her my most dazzling smile. "I'm happy to give someone else a chance."

She didn't believe it for a minute, of course, but she didn't say any more about it either.

"Actually, the reason I first called you was to give you some good news," she said.

"Oh?"

She looked very pleased, but a little self-conscious. "Frank and I have been voted into the country club at last."

For an instant I just stared at her mutely. For me this was not a revelation. If I wasn't going to blackball her, I was pretty sure that nobody else would. I didn't think I was up to faking surprise, so I didn't.

"This is not news to me, Millie," I said. "You should have gotten in two years ago. Everybody likes you."

"Oh, thanks for your confidence," she said. "We so appreciate it, Jane. We know that from the very first, you did all you could to make this possible. I can't tell you how much it means to us."

"It was nothing," I assured her. I didn't feel up to accepting unearned praise.

"It was very much something," she said. "And we know it. We've both worked so hard all our lives, sacrificed, but money doesn't mean anything if you don't have friends."

"Yes, that's true," I said, thinking her words were only a cliché. Everybody said that, but people didn't mean it. Most everybody I knew would toss off every friend they had if it paid cold hard cash. I assumed that tough businesspeople like Frank and Millie were the same way. So what Millie said next was unexpected.

"Frank and I both grew up...we grew up in unfortunate circumstances." She hesitated. "We met as teenagers at Methodist Home. You've heard of it, I'm sure."

I nodded. I was vaguely aware of the facility for troubled teens who were abandoned or neglected and were hard to place in foster care.

"Frank ended up there when his mother went to prison," Millie said. "I was taken in after...after I lost my parents in a murder/suicide."

"My God, Millie!" I said, stunned. "I'm so sorry."

"It's not the kind of family history that you bring up for discussion over lunch," she said with a rare flash of wry humor.

"No, of course not," I said.

"We've worked hard to beat the odds," she said. "We wanted to live a better life than we were raised into and we wanted our children never to know anything about what that world was like."

"Well, you've certainly succeeded," I said.

"Yes, in a lot of ways," Millie told me. "The kids go to great schools and have wonderful friends. They fit in. Frank and I...ah, not so well. We moved into this neighborhood ten years ago. No one has ever welcomed us."

"You're kidding!"

"We haven't been snubbed," she clarified. "Everyone has been perfectly nice. But we've been excluded."

"Oh, Millie, I had no idea."

"For me it's not too bad," she said. "I have the women at the office. And there are the girls in my bridge club. But Frank doesn't have any men friends, really. He's active in Rotary and Metro Realtors Alliance, but I think he still feels like he doesn't belong."

"It's harder for men to make friends."

She agreed.

"Anyway, this acceptance has been a real shot in the arm to him, Jane. I just can't tell you..." Her voiced faded off. "And I can't thank you enough."

"Millie, really, no thanks are required," I said. "I'm

just so happy that you and Frank are now a part of the club. You're going to be wonderful members. Just the kind of people we need."

"You're sweet," she said. "But then, I guess you know where we're coming from. I heard that you grew up in Sunnyside."

I was surprised.

"I didn't know you knew that," I said.

Millie shrugged. "People talk," she said.

I have heard it said, and now I believe it to be true, that the quickest way to forget your own troubles is to listen to somebody else's.

As soon as Millie left, I plugged in my phone and began making calls. Tookie was first. My life might be out of control, but the rest of the world wasn't.

"Do you remember years ago we talked about having a mentor program at the club?"

"Sure," she answered. "We decided we didn't need it because the new people are always sponsored by someone in the membership."

"Well," I said, "I'm not going to officially propose a change, but as a favor to me, could you and Joel take on Frank and Millie Brandt."

There was only an instant of hesitation.

"Well, sure we can," she said. "But we wouldn't want to get in the way of you and David."

"You won't, I'm sure of that," I told her. "David's so uninvolved with the club, it would really help if Joel introduced Frank around and you got them invited to parties."

"Sure, Jane," she said. "I'd be happy to do that."

"Great!" I said.

"Uh, Jane…"

I heard uncertainty in her tone.

"What?" I asked.

"We've heard…I mean, Joel got wind of this rumor…well…some people are saying that David…that David has left you."

"What?" I feigned incredulity. "Who would start a rumor like that?"

The words were hardly out of my mouth before I regretted them. Tookie was supposed to be one of my best friends. If I couldn't at least be honest with her, I couldn't be honest with anyone.

"Listen," I said, "things are really up in the air right now. Could you do what you can to squelch the rumor. That could give us some time to work things out."

"Of course," she said. "I'm sure he'll come around, Jane. You can ride this one out. You always have. I know she's really young and perky and he's built this house with her, but she isn't one-tenth as smart or interesting as you are."

Something in her words made the hair stand up on the back of my neck.

"You've met her?"

There was a long pause in the conversation.

"They play golf together all the time," she said. "It's impossible to be on the course and not run into them eventually."

"Oh."

In some ways I felt more betrayed by Tookie than by David. When I hung up the phone, I thought of Buddy Feinstein once more. But I didn't think I needed a therapist. I needed a friend. And in the days that followed I knew where to find one.

Chester was sitting up in his chair again. He was in his pajamas and bathrobe and those high-tech house shoes, but he was in very good spirits. At least he was until I told him my news.

He patted my hand.

"David has always cheated on me," I explained. "But I convinced myself that it was all meaningless."

Chester nodded sympathetically. "That kind of thing always means something," he said.

"I never imagined that he could love her," I told him. "I guess I never imagined that David could love."

"You don't think he ever loved you?"

I shook my head.

He didn't believe me. "I think you're looking at yesterday through today's glasses," he said.

"I made him marry me," I admitted. "I went after him, lured him in and wouldn't let go."

Chester chuckled at that. "I'd say that describes about half the marriages in the world. The other half, it's the fellow who's guilty of the luring. Either way, somebody got the idea first. But the other person had to go along with it."

"It was easier to marry me than to stand up for himself," I said.

Chester found that amusing as well. "It's never easier to marry than not," he said. "Besides, the man you've been talking about doesn't sound like a spineless worm letting you call the shots for twenty years."

"But he has," I insisted. "I always did everything I wanted."

"And he always did everything he wanted."

"Yes, except for things that involved me," I said. "Then I had to have my way."

"Such as?"

"Children," I said. "David loves children. He wanted to have a whole houseful. I didn't want any. After Brynn was born, I just flatly refused to have any more."

"But you did have the one," Chester pointed out. "I don't think that's having your own way, I think that's compromising."

"He begged me at least to try for a boy," I told Chester. "I said no and wouldn't even discuss it."

"Would that have made a difference in what has happened now?"

"It might have," I said. "He might have been happier and more fulfilled. He might never have started playing around, and then he would never have met this Mikki."

"What about you?" he asked. "Would having another child have been better for you?"

"Well, of course not," I said with certainty. "I could barely manage Brynn."

"Then don't start trying to second-guess your past," Chester said. "It's like wrestling a pig, it doesn't do any good and it annoys the pig."

I laughed, which was exactly what he wanted.

"Don't waste your time worrying about what you can't change," he said. "You need to be focusing on the future."

"You're right," I said. "I need to figure out what to do. I've got to keep my marriage together."

"If that's what you want," Chester said.

The question in his voice surprised me. Chester was a man who'd lived most of his life in another era, with old-fashioned rules. He'd married his Vera for life and lived happily with her until death did them part. I couldn't believe that he wasn't for keeping a marriage together at all costs. "I've got to fight for my family," I said. "It's what a woman is supposed to do."

"Of course it is," he answered. "Except when it's not."

"What are you saying? I should let David go?"

"Oh no," he assured me hurriedly. "I'm not saying that at all. What I think is that sometimes we react to things on impulse. Someone hits us, we hit back. Someone tries to get away, we hang on to them. We move too quickly, and fall back on instinct. But we are not just creatures of instinct. There is the spiritual side of us as well."

I eyed him skeptically.

"The spiritual side can push through and beyond our initial tendency and give us a whole different view of how the world might go."

"I don't know if I believe that," I admitted.

"Okay," Chester said. "Let's try looking at it this way. If you'd been killed in that car, David wouldn't have to be asking you for a divorce."

That suggestion brought a thousand possibilities tumbling through my thoughts all at once. They took my breath away.

"You think that I was supposed to die in that car and David was supposed to be free to marry Mikki? And because I asked to live, I messed all that up for him?"

"Whoa! Slow that old caboose down," Chester said, chuckling. "I'm not saying anything of the sort. I'm just saying that I believe there is a distinct possibility that the world is all tied together in a humongous pattern. And it might do you some good to take a deep breath, think things through slowly, calmly. You'll see what is the right thing to do."

"Are you sure?" I asked.

He shrugged. "Pretty much so," he answered.

I went home, sat in my darkened office. The place made me feel more in control. The darkness suited my mood.

I thought about Chester's words. I thought about those moments in the car. Had my pleas somehow altered fate? Not just my fate, but David's and Mikki's and everybody's.

Did that mean I should just pretend that I had died? Or more correctly stated, just roll over and play dead? Should I let David walk off into the sunset with his young, blond person? I didn't want that. But why didn't I?

Did I love David?

I examined that question, trying to hold back on my rush to pessimism. We'd shared a lot of our lives together. We'd just been kids when I maneuvered him into marrying me. And he had made all my dreams come true. The wedding at the club had been a Cinderella fairy tale come to life. The whole extravaganza in daffodil and cream had been provided by him and his family. Our little three-bedroom "starter home" had been the nicest place that I'd ever lived. And a pile of student loans that would have taken a decade to get out from under were wiped away with the stroke of a pen.

But there was more than money to our marriage. Even in my most cynical frame of mind, I couldn't discount the quiet times we'd spent together, the warmth and tenderness that we'd shared. I could remember the look in his eyes the first time he'd held Brynn in his arms. I could remember the comfort of his hand in mine at the funeral of a dear friend. I could almost hear the way my name sounded on his lips. And I enjoyed the noise of his boisterous, baritone laughter.

I loved David. I cared about him. I wanted him to be happy.

Could I make him happy?

This was a question that deserved consideration. David wanted Mikki because he thought he was in love. He wanted more in his relationship than he was getting from me. Did I want more in a relationship with him? If I got him back, was I willing to try harder, to build a stronger marriage, to grow and change with him?

Of that, I wasn't so sure. What I really wanted was for things to go on as they had been. I wanted the relationship that we had. Sort of a no-frills marriage. He did his thing. I did mine. If he wanted to see other women, all right, that was fine, as long as he was discreet. And if he didn't want to show up with me at the club, okay, I was comfortable going without him. Why was it necessary to break up a partnership that was, from my point of view, working very nicely?

The doorbell rang, interrupting the direction of my thoughts. I went to the window, but the car in the driveway, a white Lexus SUV, was unfamiliar. I considered not answering at all, but when the bell rang a second time, I headed in that direction. I wasn't really anxious for visitors. But sometimes a distraction can be welcome. Even cleaning-products salesmen or Mormon missionaries would be a break from difficult considerations.

I looked through the security peephole to see a familiar young woman. I couldn't immediately put a name with her face, but I knew I recognized her. Undoubtedly she was one of the younger brokers or a new member of the Junior League. I opened the door.

"Hi! How are you?" I said pleasantly.

The woman responded to my warm greeting with a stunned look—an instant later I realized why.

"Mikki, I hardly recognized you," I said. "Is that jacket a Sharagano? I thought your taste ran more to the Kathie Lee Collection."

She glanced down at her coat as if unsure of what she was wearing. The catty little jab that I'd leveled at her went over her head completely.

"It…it was a present for my birthday," she said.

I knew immediately that David had bought it for her. He cared very little for fashion or designers, but he had impeccable taste, and when he bought clothes they were always perfect.

"Happy birthday," I said. "You're twenty-one?"

"Oh no, I'm twenty-six," she assured me, as if that were a lifetime of difference. "May I come in?"

I thought about refusing her. Even Miss Manners would agree that I wouldn't be required to offer the hospitality of my home to the woman my husband wants to marry.

Still, Mikki obviously had something to say. I decided I didn't particularly want to hear it on the porch. I opened the door and invited her inside.

I tried not to really look at her. I didn't want to see how cute and perky she was. I didn't want to remember how much closer she was to my daughter's age than my own. But I couldn't not look at her. She was the woman who was ruining my life and she was standing in the middle of my living room. Like rubberneckers at the site of a grizzly crash, I just couldn't draw my eyes away.

In truth, it wasn't a satisfying experience. When your husband wants to leave you for another woman, you would hope, at least, that she would be gorgeous, if not witty, wealthy and famous. If he leaves for Tyra Banks or Mena Suvari, then you can throw up your hands and say, "What could I do?" But on close examination, this young woman was absolutely nothing special.

Her hair was bright blond, but it had that dry, over-treated look. Her makeup was too heavy and too contrasting. The eyeliner and mascara was thick and black. The lipstick too red and glossy. She was not long, lean and lissome. She was short. And although in the past when I'd seen her I'd thought she was thin, today that expensive designer coat couldn't disguise the fact that the young woman was downright pudgy.

"May I take your coat?"

She grabbed hold of the lapels as if she thought I might rip it from her back. "Oh no," she said.

The girl had probably never owned anything so nice in her whole life and was afraid to let it out of her sight.

I sat down. Mikki sat as well. She was ill at ease and

uncomfortable, but that didn't stop her from gazing around curiously as if she were in a museum or a gallery.

"You like the room?" I asked.

"Oh yes, it's great," she answered. "And it's so…kind of foreign, like Europe or something. It's…it's nice. I never thought David's place would look like this."

I had never really thought of my home as *David's place* and I wondered about the Richland Garza house in Stone Oak.

"Are you hoping to try to take over my house as well as my husband?"

My words were deliberately cutting.

"Oh!" she said. "Please don't worry about your house, Mrs. Lofton. I could never live here."

Her tone was conciliatory. I chose to take offense.

"That's a comfort to know," I said sarcastically.

She looked at me, wide-eyed. She wasn't sure, but she obviously thought that remark might have been insulting. But she decided to give me the benefit of the doubt.

"I'm really excited to meet you at last," she told me. "David talks about you a lot. He says I remind him of you. I never liked hearing that, but now I see what a compliment that is."

There was nothing disingenuous about her words. In fact, there was so much sincerity, I felt a rush to protect her. Someone was going to eat this little naive girl alive. And it could easily be her boyfriend's wife.

"David thinks you and I are alike?" I said. "I can't imagine that."

"Me neither," she said. "Especially now that I see you. I mean, I knew you were, like, smart and educated and everything. But I didn't know how sort of sophisticated you are. I know you know about antiques and architecture and stuff, and I'm really an idiot about those things. I think Mr. Garza, the man who designed our house, would just get exhausted having to explain everything to me. Where I grew up there were only two kinds of houses, singlewides and doublewides."

Mikki laughed at her own little joke. The self-effacing humor was charming, but it was the kind of thing that would put her at a distinct disadvantage at the club. I quickly reminded myself that she was never getting into the club. She was only getting David over my dead body. Unbidden, the memory of the car crash came back to vividly taunt me. Chester had been right. If I had been killed in that accident, David and Mikki would not have had to worry about me.

And vice versa, I would not have had to worry about them. I had wanted to live. I had begged to live. I had bargained to live. And I hadn't made any stipulations that life be easy, painless and without complications.

"Okay, Mikki," I said. "I'm fairly certain that David didn't send you here to talk to me. So, I think I can assume this was your idea."

She nodded.

"David told me that you'd come around," she explained.

"Oh?"

"I'm sure he's right," she said. "David knows you so well and he is very savvy about people."

I was astounded. That my husband of twenty years might presume to understand me was reasonable, of course. But beyond that, I didn't believe David was particularly savvy about anything. Or perhaps I had simply never trusted his opinion.

Either way, I clearly needed to dissuade both David and young Mikki from any idea that I would give up my marriage without a fight.

"I have absolutely no reason to divorce David," I explained to her. "I know all about you and the women that came before you. His little flings are no reason to give up a very satisfactory marriage."

Mikki looked momentarily puzzled.

"But it's not a satisfactory marriage," she told me. "David says that you never really loved him and that the two of you have nothing in common."

"Of course I love David," I insisted quickly. "Perhaps I am not the most demonstrative woman in the world and I could never be a clinging-vine type, but I do care about him. And as for having nothing in common, it's not my fault that he has no interest besides golf."

Mikki's tone was soft yet some how accusatory. "If you loved him," she said, "you'd learn to play golf."

It was all I could do not to groan and roll my eyes.

"David and I have our own interests," I said. "That is a plus in a long-term marriage. It is how we've stayed together so many years."

Mikki shook her head in disagreement.

"I think you've stayed together all this time because David doesn't like to fight, and divorces almost always mean a lot of fighting."

The accuracy of her statement was intimidating. I was counting on David's aversion to conflict as an advantage to me. If Mikki was already aware of it, then she'd undoubtedly already figured out how to compensate for it.

"Then you're ready to do battle?" I asked.

"I don't think we need to fight," she said. "David and I are willing to give you whatever you want, the house, your car, half of the investments. David's even willing to fund a trust for you so that you'll not have to worry about the future. And of course, he will pay for all the expenses involving Brynn."

"This is not about money," I stated honestly. "I have

been making a very good living for the last few years all on my own. I don't need David's money to keep me afloat."

Mikki shrugged. "Then put it away for Brynn," she said. "You've been David's wife most of your life, you've earned a share in what he has. Nobody is saying that you need it, just that it's yours."

"I don't want any shares," I reiterated. "David is my husband. I want my marriage. I'm not about to let you take it away from me."

She shook her head. "Your marriage has been over for years," she said. "There is not anything you or I or even David can do about that. I'm not taking anything away from you. David was gone before he ever even met me."

Her calmness, her certainty, genuinely surprised me. She was just a kid, absolutely no match for me, but somehow she wasn't the least bit afraid, or even intimidated.

"If you know so much about David," I said, "then you must realize that he never left me for another woman. He left me for golf."

She dodged the jab easily. "We play together," she said a little too smugly. "I love the game."

I smiled. "Good for you," I said. "But David doesn't love golf, he's addicted to it."

"That's a pretty strong statement," she said.

I shrugged. "It's the truth," I said. "David has had a very easy life. Everything he ever wanted was either handed to him outright, or the brass ring was pulled so close there was hardly a chance that he could miss it."

Her back stiffened. Clearly she wanted to disagree with me, but she knew him well enough not to.

"Golf was really the first challenge he ever faced," I told her. "It was just him, doing what he was doing."

"And he plays very well," Mikki pointed out.

I nodded. "On some days he does play well, on some days he's great and sometimes he stinks," I said. "That's the deal with golf. It's called random gratification. If he played every day and he was terrible, he'd give up. If he played every day and he was fabulous, he'd get bored. But because he never knows how the day is going to go, he can't get enough of it."

"I won't let golf take him away from me," she said with certainty. "Not golf, not other women, not anything. I love David and I intend to make him happy. Happier than he's ever been in his life."

"You seem very sure that you're going to win," I said.

"There is no winning or losing here," she answered. "We're just three people, you and me and David. And we're all only trying to get on with our lives in the best way possible."

"And what you think is best is for me to just step aside?"

"I know it is," she said.

"Why would I do that?"

"Because it's time for you to get a new life, too."

We just sat there in my living room, two women looking at each other. Strangely I felt no anger, no animosity. David had said she reminded him of me. I now knew why. I would have done what she was doing. I would have done anything to marry him.

When she spoke, her tone was firm and sure. "David said that sooner or later you'd see that divorce is inevitable," she said. Mikki let that sink in for a long moment then added. "I came to ask you to make it sooner."

She rose to her feet. For an instant I thought she was going to leave. Instead, she shrugged off her coat. The casual slacks outfit she had on looked like a Kenneth Cole, but there was something distinctly wrong with it.

It fit very badly, the belt raised up above her natural waist.

My first thought was that if this woman wanted to hang on to David, she was either going to have to make more visits to the gym or get the number of that wonderful Dr. Plastic.

Mikki laid a hand upon her pooching tummy. Immediately, I knew.

"When are you due?" I asked.

"May fifth," she said.

# 12

We got a Dominican divorce. Very fashionable in some circles, I've heard. It certainly worked for us, anyway. I had to sign a power of attorney to a Dominican lawyer. David and Mikki went off with their beach clothes packed. Within two weeks, twenty years of marriage was over. I was divorced one day, they were married the next. It was easy. Everything was agreed. It's always easy when everything is agreed.

I'd spent two hours in Dr. Feinstein's office coming to that conclusion. Voicing all my doubts and hopes as he nodded benignly.

When I'd told Chester, he patted my hand and said he was proud.

Of course, there were people who thought I was wrong. Tookie, Teddy and Lexi were amazed that I just gave in without a fight. Even the women at the office were openly disapproving of my behavior.

"You don't just let them out of the deal," Kelli the receptionist told me. "It sets a bad precedent for every cheating son of a bitch in town."

The two people who were most upset by my actions were Edith and Brynn. The former was just going to have to get over it. But I felt very badly about the latter.

"Oh, this is great!" Brynn screeched at me facetiously. "Just throw my father out, tear up my home, don't even give a thought to me and what I want."

We were in the bar at the airport. We were perched

atop high, uncomfortable bar stools on either side of a table the size of a large postage stamp. People came and went through the place in droves. The light was glaring and the noise level horrendous. Not exactly the perfect spot for an important family moment.

Brynn was en route, stopping in for two hours on the last leg of her Christmas vacation trip. She was in town, basically, to pick up the rest of her luggage, which I had dutifully carted out to the terminal for her. The other *baggage* I brought to her was definitely the emotional kind.

"I didn't throw your father out," I said. "He left me of his own accord."

"Of course he did," she said a little too loudly for a public discussion. "No wonder, after years of putting up with your pushing, your constant criticism, your inability to love him and accept him for who he was."

I was more puzzled by her words than hurt. Pushing, criticizing and being unaccepting were sins of which I was undoubtedly guilty. But not with David, only with Brynn. If *she* had wanted to divorce me, I suppose she had grounds.

"I'm sorry that this happened, but…"

She gave me a hard look, unwilling to listen to my apologies as she fumbled around in her backpack.

"Where's my cell?" she cried out in frustration.

Losing patience with her fruitless search, she dumped the contents of her pack onto the tiny table. Her stuff spilled out everywhere. Brynn spotted the phone and grabbed it up immediately. I picked up the less essential items, such as her wallet, passport and plane ticket.

She flipped open the silver metallic lid. I could hear the dial tone.

"Dr. Reiser at his office," she said distinctly into the mouthpiece.

She looked up at me, her eyes were narrowed with anger but they were also swimming with tears.

"Mother, this is the worst thing you've ever done to me," she told me. "It is totally unforgivable."

I wanted to tell her that I hadn't done anything. It was David who had hurt her. But it wasn't true of course. Divorces always concern two people and nobody comes out completely innocent.

Brynn's attention turned to her phone call.

"Is he in the office?" she asked. She bit down on her index fingernail. "I've got to talk to him right away."

I couldn't hear the other side of the conversation, but there was a long pause while my daughter was listening.

"How long will he be?"

She actually moaned as if the answer caused her physical pain.

"Okay, this is Brynn, tell him that my mother has thrown Dad out. He's run off to the Dominican Republic to marry his trampy pregnant girlfriend and I'm about to get on a plane to fly back to Boston."

She snapped the phone closed and sat there, not looking at me.

I just wanted to finish my iced tea, shake hands and walk away. But I was her mother, lousy at the job as I had always been. I had no other choice but to sit and watch her suffer.

"Brynn, you have every right to be upset," I told her. "But I know that somehow all of this is going to work out fine."

"Why would you think that, Mother?" she asked, steely-voiced. "Why would you think that anything, let alone *everything*, is going to 'work out fine'?"

"Because I'm sure that what we're doing is a good thing," I told her. "Your father, Mikki and I, we're all really trying to do what's best for everybody."

She rolled her eyes at that.

"What would have been best would have been for you and Dad to continue to do what you're supposed to do," she said. "To be my parents like you're supposed to be. Not start changing the rules on me and making everything different."

"Different can be better," I pointed out. "Sometimes it can actually be the best."

She really didn't like that statement. Her eyes narrowed furiously.

"How can my parents' divorce be best for me?" she asked.

It was a damn difficult question to answer, so I didn't even try.

"Think of that little baby," I said instead. "It's going to be your little brother or sister. That little person should have a chance to come into the world with a mommy and a daddy."

Her mouth came open. She stared a me incredulously.

"Think of the baby!" she said. "You want me to think of the baby?"

Brynn threw up a hand dismissingly. She was shaking her head.

"I can't believe this. I can't believe this, even of you, Mother," she said. "I'm supposed to consider the feelings of an unborn fetus that was conceived in an adulterous affair by my dad. And you sound like you care more about that fucking baby than the emotional well-being of your own daughter!"

Brynn's voice had slowly risen until the last was actually yelled. Everyone in the room was looking at us.

"Don't use that kind of language, Brynn," I said quietly. "It's very offensive."

"I fucking want to be offensive!" she screamed.

She grabbed up her backpack, her computer and her carry-on.

"Goodbye, Mother," she said. "I am totally done with you. I don't want to see you. I don't want to hear from you. I don't want to know anything about you ever. And I mean EVER!"

"Brynn, no, wait," I said.

She brushed past.

"Don't follow me!" she demanded.

I just stood there for a moment, not knowing what to do. In all honesty, I was tempted just to let it go. I couldn't help Brynn with this. I could hardly help myself. I felt as betrayed, confused and rootless as she did. It was all I could do to simply drag myself out of bed in the mornings. I was in no position to offer comfort to anyone else.

The waitress came over with the check. I dug around in my purse for the right amount of cash. I didn't want to wait for her to process my credit card so I gave her a twenty. I just wanted out of there.

"Keep the change," I said.

It was a big tip, much better than she deserved, but she didn't even offer thanks.

"Sure," she said.

As I reached the exit, she called out to me.

"Hey, lady! Are these your keys?"

I kept mine in a special compartment in the side of my purse. I touched it and felt them still there, but I turned back anyway. They were Brynn's. They provided a valid excuse, a good reason, and a motherly necessity for me to go after my daughter.

"Thanks," I said, clutching the collection of chinking metal in my hand. I headed down to the gate.

My daughter was furious with me. She blamed me. But that was to be expected. Even if we didn't have our history, if she loved and trusted and respected me, bringing such news would still have evoked a reaction of anger. I knew that as well as if I were reading it from a text on parent-child relations.

It probably would have been better if David and I had talked to her together. If he had been there to reassure her that their relationship would not change. But he and Mikki had already gone to the Dominican Republic. And we certainly couldn't wait until he came back to tell her. There was too much risk that she would have heard it from somebody else.

It was me or nobody. Of course, it wasn't the first time that I was all that Brynn had. That was strange in itself. With a loving and involved father and two grandparents, she should have had tons of outside support. But so many times it had really been no different than me and my own mother. Life was just the two of us. A bilateral universe.

The airport was bustling and crowded with weekend travelers. But I spotted Brynn the moment I arrived at the gate. Next to the window, she was sitting elbows on knees, head in hands. Her expression was lost, forlorn. She was so young. Decked out all sexy in tight jeans, clunky heels and a blue clingy sweater, I was reminded of finding her in my closet playing dress-up in my glamorous after-fives.

I walked over to her.

The moment she saw me, she sat up, back ramrod straight, defenses fully engaged.

"I told you not to follow me," she hissed between clenched teeth.

I held up the keys. "You left these," I said.

At the sight she visibly deflated. Resuming her disillusioned-thinker position, she looked close to tears.

"I can't do anything right," she said in a sad, tiny voice. "I can't even manage a dramatic exit."

I sat down in the chair beside her. "I was never any good at them either," I said.

She snorted, disbelieving.

"You're good at everything," she said. "You always know what to do and how to do it. You get along with everybody and don't take crap from anyone. You even make getting dumped by your husband look like some sort of personal triumph."

I listened and thought about what she was saying. After a minute or two the irony of the situation got to me and I gave a little chuckle.

"What's so funny?" she asked unhappily.

"I guess it's knowing how much you despise me," I answered. "While still giving me a lot more credit than I deserve."

"I don't get it."

"I'm not the woman that you think I am," I told her. "I'd really like to be that woman. I've worked at it all my life. But when you get right down to it, I'm not her."

Brynn didn't bother to argue. She looked so pitiful, so deflated. I almost wished that she would growl at me again. I put my arm around her shoulders. She didn't even shrug it off.

"When is it going to happen?" she asked.

"I don't know for sure," I told her. "The legal proceedings might already be over or it may be tomorrow. After the decree is granted they have to wait twenty-four hours before they can get married."

"Not much time for Dad to play the field," she said, attempting sarcasm.

"It's all been so quick because of the baby," I explained. "I'm trying to look at it like ripping off a bandage. Maybe it hurts more, but it's over sooner."

She nodded.

"I am truly sorry, sweetie," I said.

"I just feel like I'm lost," she said. "I was having such

a great time with my friends. I met a guy and he seemed to really like me. I was so psyched up for going back to school. It's like I looked away for a minute, and when I looked back...when I looked back, my life was just gone."

Her words struck a surprisingly familiar note with me. Feelings that I hadn't thought about in years suddenly weighed down on me. I knew what Brynn was feeling. I knew it exactly.

"I've talked to you about how my mother died."

It was as much a question as a statement. Of course, I had told my daughter about her grandmother. Of course, she knew that I was alone in the world, but I honestly didn't remember any in-depth discussion on the subject.

"She had, like, breast cancer or something," Brynn answered.

"Yes," I answered. "But I didn't know it. I was away at school living with a roommate, working part-time, studying." I hesitated a moment and then continued frankly, "I was hanging with my friends, partying, dating this really cute guy in a fraternity."

"Eeeww, Mother, please, I don't want to know."

I nodded, but continued.

"My mom didn't tell me she was sick. She had a mastectomy and radiation treatments and she never let me know. When she'd call, she'd talk about her work or ask me about school. She never said she was sick. The hospital called me when she was too unresponsive to make her own decisions. Even after I got there, seeing how awful she looked, I was sure she was going to be fine."

"Did she explain why she didn't tell you?" Brynn asked.

I shook my head. "She was getting so much pain

medication, I'm not sure if she even knew who I was," I answered. "She died six days later."

I glanced over at Brynn. She looked as though she might cry. There was an empathetic aspect of her that I was very aware of, but I rarely saw it focused in my direction.

"Oh, Mom, that's so awful," she said with genuine sincerity.

I felt as though I might cry as well. Not just from the story of my loss, but from the sound of *Mom* on her lips. She so rarely called me that.

"Brynn," I said, "I don't know what you're feeling, what you're going through. But I do know the feeling that a familiar world has just disappeared without warning. I can't make it be different, but I am sorry."

She nodded.

We just sat there in the middle of the noisy hustle and bustle, the gray sky beyond the windows, unwelcoming, the smell of jet fuel and stale air around us. We were a mother and daughter. My arm around her shoulder, the warmth of her body close to mine. United for a precious moment by more than interactive history and shared genetic material. It was a sweet space of time that I treasure.

It ended abruptly with the sound of her cell phone beeping out the tune to "Girls Just Wanna Have Fun."

Brynn fished it out of her backpack and glanced quickly at the caller ID before answering.

"Thank God you called me back," she said without prelude. "My parents are getting a divorce. Everything is just totally screwed."

I waited for a moment while she listened to the other end of the line. "No, it's not like that at all," she said. "It's worse."

She glanced in my direction.

"Dr. Reiser, could you hold on for a minute," she said.

Taking the phone from her ear, she spoke to me.

"Thanks Mom," she said dismissively. "If you don't mind, I am talking to my therapist."

We were back to our relationship as usual.

"Okay," I said, rising to my feet. "Be safe and call me when you can."

Brynn was noncommittal. I walked away.

It was two nights later when I finally got the news from David. We were divorced. They were married. It was all nice and neat and very, very final.

These facts filled David with optimism and enthusiasm. My own bag of emotions was stuffed with emptiness.

"The weather here is great," he told me. "Mikki's feeling wonderful. The morning sickness hasn't bothered her a bit here. We're so happy."

I tried to talk to him about Brynn. I give him credit, he did his best to give me his full attention on that. But his heart just wasn't in it. He was brimming with excitement and exuberance. Who could blame him for wanting to keep the cares of his past in the past?

"She feels so lost right now," I said. "We've turned her world upside down and she needs some reassurance."

"Brynn'll be fine," David insisted. "She's a strong girl, lots of grit and depth. She gets that from you, I guess."

I wasn't sure that grit and depth were ever in sufficient supply in either of us.

"You should call her," I suggested. "Tell her yourself what's happening and how much you still love her."

"Yeah, I do need to call her," he agreed. "When I get back I'll do that."

There was a pause. I suppose in our married life I

would have filled it with an insistence that he call her *now*. But he wasn't my husband anymore. I couldn't really tell him to do anything. So I didn't.

The silence lingered and he was obliged to say something.

"I shot a five under today," he told me. "And Mikki is at the top of her game. Her putting still needs work, but she's been playing some great golf here."

"That's wonderful, David," I said. "Listen, I need to hang up now. But I appreciate your call. Best wishes to you both."

"Thanks, Jane," he said. "We…well, I'm sure all of us are going to be happier now."

"Yeah," I agreed with as much hopefulness as I could muster. I hung up the phone and allowed myself a good old-fashioned cry. I felt as if I had earned the luxury. But I didn't linger in self-pity. Within an hour I was past the moment. I washed my face and went on.

Before I gave myself a chance to chicken out, I called Brynn at her dorm. Hailey, her roommate, said she was out. Of course, she said it in a way that sounded as if Brynn just didn't want to talk to me.

Hailey connected me with her voice mail and I didn't tell her anything, I just asked her to call. Maybe I should have just said, "Okay, it's over. Your dad is now married to somebody else." But somehow it didn't seem like the kind of words that should be left on a message machine.

David thought that we were all going to be happier. I wasn't so sure. He knew nothing about being a faithful, devoted husband. That wouldn't be easy to learn. Mikki would have a name for her baby, but she was going to have to work at making a marriage. Brynn was going to find her position as David's daughter a secondary one to the new baby. And me, well, I wasn't sure what was going to happen to me.

The next few days did give me some ideas.

News of our divorce must have been posted in a flash box on the Internet. I didn't have to tell a soul. Everyone I knew was already informed. The dinner invitations dried up immediately. Even my calls at the office dwindled to nothingness. I couldn't tell whether people no longer wanted to talk to me, or just didn't want to bother me while the wound was still fresh. But it seemed that none of my friends or long-term associates had any interest in commiserating with me.

A lot of people I didn't know got the details of my social downsizing as well.

Thursday morning I received a call from a woman I'd never even heard of, Nancy, who introduced herself as executive assistant to the general manager at the club. She had been given the unenviable task of calling to tell me that my membership in the club existed as Mrs. David Lofton. Since someone else now held that title, I was…I was basically nobody.

I kept myself deliberately calm, although I was almost nauseated by the finality of it. The club had been the symbol of everything that I'd gone after in life, everything that I'd achieved. I watched it slip away, unable, or maybe just unwilling, to stop it.

"Of course," Nancy assured me in a tone almost syrupy with sympathy, "we would be happy to write you a reference to any of the other country clubs in town. They say the tennis at Western Hollow is to die for."

"Thank you," I answered. "I really don't play much these days."

My reasonable behavior relaxed the woman tremendously. She began to chatter. She gave me several interesting tales of her confrontations with other women in my position. Women who were not nearly as cognizant of the fact that she merely had a job to do and was doing it.

She also admitted that she'd admired my car.

"Are you going to get to keep it?" she asked me. "If you're going to have to convert it to cash or anything like that, I really might be interested, if you don't want too much for it."

Her words seemed genuine, although it did occur to me that she might be fishing for gossip about the financial arrangements of my divorce.

"I'll let you know if I decide to sell it," I told her. "I've only had the car a couple of months. It's practically new, hardly any mileage at all."

"I'm really sorry about having to call you like this," she admitted. "It's the policy of the club. But the people who make the policy don't have to be the ones to call up and enforce it."

"I understand," I said honestly.

"I heard some talk about *her*," Nancy said, lowering her voice conspiratorially.

At first I didn't know what *her* she meant, then realized she was talking about Mikki. I probably should have refused to listen to anything the woman said. Fortunately, I'm not that nice a person.

"She's woefully ignorant and completely gauche," Nancy assured me. "They say she picked her china pattern at Nordstrom's instead of Scrivener's."

For a moment I was stunned into silence. Then I laughed out loud. Encouraged by my response, Nancy kept talking.

"Can you believe it?" she said. "It is so new-money. And the way she dresses! I heard that Mimi Parton described her fashion style as 'drug-dealer's girlfriend.'"

I continued to laugh. Not really at Mikki's expense. Unbeknownst to Nancy, I was not all that interested in the trials and tribulations of my *Mrs. Lofton replacement*.

I was actually laughing with the delightful realization that after twenty years of toeing the line, I was now free to select my china pattern anywhere I wanted.

I felt so good after I got off of the phone, that when I went to fill up the Roadster Z3, I bought a gigantic Snickers bar and headed out to Bluebonnet Manor Assisted Living. I'd been to see Chester twice in the last week. I'd discovered the man had a strong shoulder to lean on.

I had to walk around an ambulance-like vehicle called a Handi-cab that was blocking the doorway. A white-garbed attendant was loading up an empty gurney. He gave me such a thorough once-over that I wondered if somehow I now *looked* like a divorced woman.

Inside the lobby area the usual suspects were bunched with their wheelchairs facing the booming voice of Bob Barker cajoling them to "Come on down!"

The sight was a familiar one to me now, these people, this place, had become as much a part of my life as the office. I comfortably and confidently walked down the hallway.

As I approached Chester's room, a nurse stopped me.

"You're here to see Mr. Durbin?"

"Yes."

"Give the aides a minute or two," she said. "He's just come back from his treatment and they're getting him settled."

"His treatment? What kind of treatment?" I questioned her.

"HBO," she answered.

A woman down the hall called out to her and she hastily excused herself before I could ask more.

HBO? I was pretty sure they weren't taking Chester anywhere for cable-movie therapy. I waited outside his room for a few more minutes before two middle-aged women in white slacks and pink uniform shirts emerged.

I brushed past them, worried, eager to see Chester.

Sitting up in his chair in clean pajamas and robe, he looking bright-eyed and healthy. Immediately I was reassured. Why had I worried?

"What's HBO?" I asked immediately.

He glanced up and smiled.

"And hello to you too, Jane Lofton," he said.

I smiled, apologized, greeted him more politely, seated myself in the chair beside him and then rephrased my question.

"What kind of treatments are you having?"

"It's some nonsense my doctor is trying," he said. "Hyperbaric oxygen. You know, like Michael Jackson."

From somewhere in the dim recesses of my mind I could recall a doctored photograph on the front of a grocery-store tabloid. It showed the gloved one lying in a big glass compartment with a shocker headline like Pop Star Discovers Secret to Eternal Life.

"You're getting hyperbaric oxygen treatments?"

"Yeah, they're taking me down to Memorial Ambulatory twice a week now," he said. "I guess it's a pretty good outing. I told the fellow today that it would be perfect if we could schedule in a picnic lunch."

"What is this therapy for?" I asked.

"It's something covered by Medicare," he said. It wasn't so much an answer as a reason.

"Is it helping?"

He shrugged. "I breathe better," he replied. "What about you? Are you breathing any easier these days?"

It was a deft ability of his, to steer the conversation away from anything he didn't want to discuss. And I had long since learned that his health was something he never liked to discuss.

I recognized it for what it was, but figured he had a

right not to talk about himself. The nursing home didn't offer a whole lot of privacy of any kind. I was more than willing to give him as much as I personally could.

"Are you getting along all right?" he asked.

"Yes, I think so," I said. "If I'm not, I guess I just don't realize it yet."

"Are you afraid that you might accidentally break down in public?" he asked.

"I think I'm more likely to start screaming, tearing my hair out and go running through the room," I said.

"Well, that would certainly be interesting to watch," he teased.

"And I wouldn't mind you watching," I told him, chuckling. "It's just the rest of the world that would probably take offense."

"If you can laugh," he said, "then you're beginning to accept it.

"I suppose so," I said. "Although at times it's almost more change than I can really take in."

"Ahh…" He was thoughtful, considering, as he gazed at me through rheumy eyes.

"Everything has happened so quickly," I told him. "Twenty years of marriage just disappearing before my eyes."

"It didn't disappear," he corrected. "It finished. Now it exists forever. It just exists in the past."

I nodded, agreeing with his words, but somehow not very comforted by them.

"Maybe I should have insisted that we move slower," I said. "Legally, I probably could have dragged it out for years."

"You didn't have years," he said. "That baby will be here in months."

"Being born out of wedlock is not the big deal that it

used to be," I reminded him. "Half the little kids in his kindergarten class will probably end up the same."

"But you would know the difference," he said. "It was best for the child, it was best for his parents. And it will be best for you."

"You think so?"

"I know so."

He took my hand in his own. His tone was solemn, almost sad.

"It is my duly considered opinion, Jane Lofton, and I think I can speak about this with some authority, that it's better to do things quickly, face the unknown defiantly and take control. Otherwise the shilly-shallying just chip, chip, chips away at you, tainting all the good that went before."

There was such emotion in this declaration, I wondered at the depth of it. I found myself reassuring him.

"I know I did the right thing," I said.

"Not only the right thing, you did a good thing," Chester said. "How many points did you give yourself for that one?"

# 13

They say that in the months after divorce you are numb. I suppose on some level that was true. But it was just as true that I felt everything with an intensity that I'd never really experienced before.

I went on about my days, putting one foot in front of another and somehow life went on. I spoke with Brynn briefly on the phone, but she asked me not to call her again. According to Dr. Reiser's latest pronouncement, she needed to face her father's new marriage without the distraction of her mother's undoubtedly irrational point of view.

I missed her terribly, but gave her the space she requested. I figured that was probably some help. Perhaps that was a kind of true motherhood, willingness to be the lightning rod in the midst of the storms of young adulthood.

I saw David from time to time, often enough to keep up with how his golf game was going. He always volunteered that information. If I wanted to know about Mikki's pregnancy, I had to politely inquire. He seemed a little disconnected from the process and more than a little embarrassed by it.

"Do you want a boy or a girl?" I asked him.

He seemed surprised by the question.

"I don't know," he said. "I guess I haven't really thought about it."

"What about Mikki? Does she have a preference?"

He shrugged. "I don't guess so," he answered. "I don't think she's said anything about it."

That didn't seem very likely to me.

"What has she said?" I asked him.

David hesitated, pondering. "Oh, she said something about classes," he admitted. "But I told her that I'd already been through this."

I frowned at him. "David, I had an emergency C-section, that isn't the same as natural childbirth. And you weren't even there."

"I wasn't?" He was genuinely surprised.

"You and your father were out on some boat in the gulf, fishing for marlin."

"Oh yeah," he agreed, nodding. "I remember now. That was really before I got into golf."

"David," I said firmly, "take the classes with Mikki. You always wanted more children. This is your chance. I don't want to see you throw it away."

"Sure, Jane, sure," he answered a little uneasily. "I'm…well, I'm surprised that you are really into this."

Honestly, I was a little surprised, myself, but I didn't tell him that.

"You and I have spent the biggest part of our lives together," I said. "We share a daughter and a lot of memories. I will always care about what happens to you. I will always want you to be happy."

It felt good to say it. It felt good to feel it.

I tried for the same sort of magnanimous sentiment with W.D. and Edith. W.D. wasn't that interested in maintaining friendly relations. He did engage me for a few moments one evening about how sorry he was that things had not worked out between David and I.

"Of course," he explained in a tone that was boastfully oracular, "I said from the beginning that the marriage was doomed to failure."

He didn't elaborate as to whom he had said this. It no

longer mattered to me to even know. Although I did wonder if all those years when I was trying so desperately to fit in at the club he had been quietly undermining my efforts with suggestions about the temporary nature of my relationship with his son.

Edith was more interested in my mental health and ongoing role as Brynn's mother. She called regularly to keep me updated on every program that Oprah did on divorce, blended families, troubled adolescents or women starting over. She raptured at length on the wisdom of Oprah's Dr. Phil. And she sent me postcards with the authors and titles of all the books mentioned. Edith had never really liked me that much, but clearly she was working hard to transcend that reality.

"Don't allow yourself to lapse into despair, Jane," she cautioned me over the phone one evening. "Light some candles around the house and focus on your inner joy."

I didn't do any candles, but then I never felt in any danger of despair. I was not housebound, depressed or unable to concentrate. Quite the opposite, actually, I was very, very busy. I went to my job every day. I was working cleanup crew at the homeless mission one evening a week. Reading to toddlers at the library while their preschool siblings attended storytime. And I was working with Ann Rhoder Hines and the Metro Realtors Alliance on a regular basis, trying to evaluate non-qualifying households and prepare them for home ownership.

If that wasn't enough, Loretta called me and asked if I would give a talk to the women in the safe house about reinventing yourself as a career woman.

I don't know what Loretta thought I would have to say, but once I got started talking about my own experiences and the things I had to learn to get from Sunnyside to Cambridge Heights, the women were completely engaged. I took questions for three hours. A week later Loretta called again and asked if I would talk to a larger audience, with other clients of Domestic Violence Alternatives. I showed up at the basement of First Presbyterian to a crowd of over a hundred. I was still no formal speaker, but that wasn't what anyone wanted. They were ordinary women who wanted to hear from an ordinary woman. Being ordinary was something that heretofore had never appealed to me.

The event had been so successful, the DVA decided to begin a program series. They asked me for suggestions. I had a few contacts with knowledgeable people in town, which I passed on to them. My personal suggestion was to have Cecil and Emily, from the Interfaith Thanksgiving Dinner.

"I just think it would be good for these women to see a truly happily married couple," I told them. "Two ordinary people who are facing life together, neither one of them abusing or dominating the other. If you've never seen that, you might not believe it really exists unless you see it with your own eyes."

The board was wary at first, and Cecil and Emily were unsure about what they had to offer. But it turned out spectacularly and was acknowledged to be the most helpful of all the presentations.

As the weeks and months passed I was on my own, and I began to feel a whole lot better. Strangely it reminded me of something that had happened in a long-ago summer when we'd been out at the lake for a month. Arriving home during Labor Day weekend, I realized I'd forgotten to clean out the refrigerator before we left. I nearly wore out my touch tone trying to get a maid service to come take care of the job. No one would. I simply had to deal with the foul, disgusting ickiness myself. I'd hated that. But when it was done I had felt a tremendous high, as if I'd scaled Mount Everest or swum the English Channel.

My marriage had been an unpleasant mess that I should have taken care of years ago. Now that it was over and done, I felt unencumbered enough to almost free-float up to the ceiling.

Lexi called to accuse me of becoming a hermit.

"We've looked for you at every trunk show in town," she said. "We are all wondering what you're planning? Are you going to New York? Paris? Where are you going to buy clothes this season?"

I was momentarily at a loss for words. For the first time in twenty years, I had completely forgotten both the after-Christmas sales and the new spring fashions. Shocked at myself, I suffered an instant of uncertainty at what I would do for something to wear. Then I actually laughed out loud. The women from Loretta's safe houses probably wouldn't know last year's wardrobe from last decade's. And Chester's vision seemed to be getting so bad that I was doubtful if he could tell whether I was dressed at all.

"I think I have enough to get by," I assured Lexi. "I've just been too busy lately to shop."

Such a suggestion stunned Lexi into silence.

When she finally found her voice again she utilized it to haltingly ask what I am sure seemed to her to be the obvious question.

"Did David not do right by you in the divorce settlement? Because if he didn't my divorce lawyer can renegotiate the whole thing," she assured me. "Building that house for her, flaunting his affair among your friends, it doesn't matter how *old family* he is, in court they'd easily crucify him."

"No, Lexi, please don't worry," I told her. "David was very generous and I am completely satisfied with the arrangement."

She hesitated as if trying to decide whether to believe me.

"Okay," she said finally. "Then why aren't you buying clothes?"

In the end I agreed to meet her, along with Tookie and Teddy, for lunch at Le Parapluie. It was not as fun a time as it should have been. I wanted to talk about all the things I was doing, all the interesting people I was meeting. They wanted to badmouth Mikki behind her back and assumed that I would be an eager participant in that game. I wasn't. It wasn't that I wanted to protect the woman, or defend her. I just found the whole pre-occupation with her pretty boring. I tried changing the subject. But I discovered that having lost interest in shopping, decorating and social climbing, there were no longer any interests that I shared with them.

We parted with hugs and kisses, promising to stay in touch, but I knew that we wouldn't. I regretted the loss.

Other than that, my life was great. Until the morning that Brynn called me.

"Dad invited me to stay with them, but I'm not coming home at all this summer," Brynn announced rather casually. "I'm spending three months in Tuscany."

"Tuscany? You mean as in Italy?" I was surprised, to say the least, but also pleased. Brynn had never shown any interest in traveling to Europe.

"Yes, Mother, where else could I mean?"

"For all I know there is a Tuscany, Missouri, out there," I said, chuckling. "Are you going by yourself?"

"Of course not," she answered.

"Who are you going with?"

There was a moment's hesitation on the other end of the line.

"I don't believe that is any of your business, Mother," she said.

"What do you mean it's not my business?"

"I mean exactly that," Brynn answered. "I'm calling as a courtesy. I do not require your permission or approval for anything I do."

"I'm your mother," I pointed out. "You at least owe me an explanation."

"Dr. Reiser told me you'd say that."

"Dr. Reiser?"

"He said I should be prepared for your interference and guard against it," she said.

"You're to guard against me," I said, "but he can interfere all he wants."

"Dr. Reiser isn't interfering, he's directly involved."

"What do you mean he's directly involved?"

"He's my therapist."

"Well, he's not going with you to Europe."

There was another moment's hesitation and then a heavy sigh.

"Whether he is or not is really none of your business, Mother."

I was standing in the kitchen putting soup in the microwave. Brynn's matter-of-fact comment caught me off guard. I spilled soup all over the cabinet.

"What do you mean by that?" I asked her.

"I mean that Dr. Reiser and I are none of your business."

*Dr. Reiser and I.* Somehow the link of their names together created an irrational fear in my gut.

"Brynn, are you involved intimately with Dr. Reiser?" I asked with deliberate calm.

"Is that what you think?" she asked.

"No, no, of course not," I backtracked quickly.

"Dr. Reiser is helping me," she said. "He understands that I don't want to stay with Dad, and seeing you would be counter to my personal growth. So he's helping me make plans for a wonderful summer on my own."

"Just so he isn't personally included in these plans," I said.

"My plans, Mother," she answered, "are my own, and are none of your business."

Even after she hung up on me, the worry nagged me. I couldn't protect Brynn if I wasn't sure what to protect her from. There were awful men in the world; powerful, manipulating, unethical men. I couldn't stand the idea of one of them taking advantage of my beautiful Brynn.

I sat down at the breakfast nook and tried to get my bearings. My first thought was to call Dr. Reiser directly and find out the truth. If he and Brynn were going to Europe together, I could threaten him. I could almost hear myself saying, "If you have so much as touched my daughter, your license to practice is something you'd better kiss goodbye. And that's the easy part. If you've hurt her, I'm coming to find you. When I do, I'll castrate you with a rusty garden tool!"

I managed not to call and say that. Coming up with an alternative course of action was far more difficult.

What had I decided about Brynn?

I dug through my purse until I found my journal. Flipping through the pages to where I'd written her words down.

"Help, unrequested, is intrusion," it read.

That sounded really good, really right. When I put that idea down on paper, I'd thought it was a mantra to live by. But did it mean that when my own daughter was perhaps being taken advantage of by an older and more sophisticated man, I should just let it happen? No, I was sure that I shouldn't. I was sure that as a mother I couldn't.

I called David to ask his advice.

"Oh, I'm sure she's not going anywhere with her therapist," he responded.

He was on his cell phone at the golf course. In the background I could hear Mikki chatting with someone.

"How can we know that?" I asked him. "If she doesn't tell us what's going on, we can't really know. David, we can't let her go to Europe if we don't know who she's going with."

"Jane," he said, "we've got to let this one go by."

"What do you mean?"

"I don't have the time or energy for another crisis with Brynn," he told me. "She's almost twenty years old. And she's right. We can't tell her where she can go, who she can see. We can't and we shouldn't."

"Well, we can certainly tell him that we'll drag him into court if he's pursuing a relationship with her outside the office," I said.

"She wouldn't like that," David said. "If we go against her on this, it might encourage her to cut ties with us completely. We might never see her again."

"Have you been watching Oprah with your mother?" I asked facetiously. "She can't cut ties with us. She's never had a job in her life. We pay for everything."

Behind him someone called out, "David, it's your shot."

"Look, Jane, do what you have to do, but leave me out of it," he said. "She's already mad at me about Mikki and the baby. I don't want to rock the boat anymore."

"David, this is important," I told him. "For all we know, she could be doing this just to see if you still are interested in her. To make sure that your new family isn't going to take up all your attention."

"Well, honestly," he said, "they *are* taking all my attention. I can't really talk now. I've got to get off the phone. You just do what you want to do, Jane. That always works out best anyway."

With David's hasty goodbye, the phone went dead. I had no better idea of what I should do than before I called him.

I might have fretted over the problem even more than I did, but other life dilemmas began to take over. I was having some genuine trouble with my career.

A rising interest rate didn't help the mortgage market, of course. And my contacts among the people of the club having been curtailed, I found myself suddenly off the realty fast track. I probably could have weathered the upheaval—I'd seen tough times in my career before. But somehow I no longer cared all that much about it.

My colleagues probably said that I'd lost my edge. I think a better description is to say that I had lost my killer instinct. I realized that what had really made me so successful was pushing the margin. Getting the buyer to go for just a little bit more, getting the seller to offer that minuscule extra. It was that small percentage that set me above the rest. And I had loved doing it. I had loved how it made me feel.

I just didn't feel that way anymore. I got no thrill out of the push. Now I worried about the buyer's finances. I worried about the seller's equity. I was up front and honest with both. I was sure I was doing good. Such frankness, however, made me the least liked agent at my brokerage. My old clients didn't want me and new clients thought they could do better.

Real estate agents don't get fired. At least they don't in independent agencies like the one the Brandts owned. But if you don't generate sales, you don't make money for the agency. And if you don't make money for the agency, why should they waste their office space on you when someone else could make them money? Millie and Frank were very patient, I think.

They were grateful to me for their entrance into the club, but since Tookie and Joel had taken them under their wing, socially, they didn't really need me at all. Still, they were loyal. They believed the change in my sales performance was only temporary, having to do with a post-divorce malaise.

Still, as weeks turned into months, winter turned into spring, and I was still not selling, listing or even showing, they became concerned. But there was that big Victorian on a prime piece of property on the edge of Park Square. Before Christmas I'd convinced Barb Jarman to sell the place and relocate her ancient mother-in-law into assisted living.

I called upon old friends to facilitate the paperwork to get the old place rezoned as multifamily. And I'd lined up a developer to turn the corner into twenty high-end condos to be listed for seven hundred thousand per.

Such a sweet sale, lucrative with a capital L.

The commission would have been close to two million dollars to the brokerage. Most of that would have been mine, but nearly a million would go to Frank and Millie. That's a lot more than coffee cash. And the deal was as secure as money in the bank.

That is until I went to talk to old Mrs. Jarman. The faded widow was eighty-one, wheelchair-bound, and suffered occasional bouts of dementia. Part of my agreement with Barb was that I find her a nice little place where she'd have round-the-clock care and a little garden to sit in and enjoy the sunshine.

As a four–point score on my doing good tally, I took this part of the deal as seriously as the more profitable end. I did my homework, which wasn't that difficult. I talked to some of the professionals at Bluebonnet Assisted Living when I went to visit Chester. They gave me names and phone numbers of people in the industry, and ultimately an introduction to a wonderful new community being built for seniors. I checked the place out completely and was very excited when I discussed it with Barb, who became completely sold on the idea.

Enthusiastically, I went to see Mrs. Jarman. Barb had told me that, as far as the condo project was concerned, the fewer details her mother-in-law had to understand the better. That made sense. The picturesque old house had been her home for a long time. Families no longer wanted that kind of floorplan, but that didn't mean she wouldn't be fond of the place and sad to see it go.

So I loaded up my portfolio with big glossy photographs of the little garden home, complete with shady bench and bright pink bougainvillea, and went to see her.

She met with me in her drawing room, both were pristine and quaint. As an antique lover I was practically sighing aloud over the beautiful old chairs, the fainting couch, the beaded lampshades. The portrait over the mantel was of a portly gentleman with a thick, curling mustache, who could have been Grover Cleveland, but I wasn't positive.

We sat at a little parlor table as the tiny woman served me English tea from a set of Belleek porcelain decorated with little yellow butterflies. She listened intently as I told her all about the place I'd found, and she even *oohed* and *aahed* appropriately when I brought out the photos. I thought she might take some convincing. I was wrong about that. She may have lived a lot of years, but she was the kind of person open to change and new experiences.

"Oh, it all sounds lovely, lovely, dear," she assured me.

"I do think you'll like it, Mrs. Jarman," I said.

"Oh, call me Miss Heloise, everybody does."

She was a tiny, sprightly little lady with features worn enough to be ancient yet small enough to be a child's. Her bright eyes looked out on the world with an excitement and anticipation that belied her ill health and dependent situation.

I suppose my relationship with Chester had made me more accustomed to older people. I was genuinely enjoying my afternoon with her and had to stop and remind myself a couple of times that this was not a coffee klatch. I was here on business.

Still, Miss Heloise elicited from me a genuine regard and concern for her ultimate welfare.

"I hope you are not anxious about the move," I said.

"Oh, not at all," she assured me. "How exciting at my age to be going into a new home."

Her attitude was delightful, hopeful, refreshing.

"I suppose you've lived here in this house a long time," I said.

She giggled like a girl. "I've always lived here," she said. "I was born in the front bedroom."

"Really?"

"Oh yes," she said. "My grandfather built this house." She indicated the Grover Cleveland guy in the portrait. "He was the last governor, you know."

I frowned. I couldn't imagine what she meant. The last governor, as in the governor before the current one, was half this woman's age and had left office to take a seat in the U.S. Senate. I thought perhaps that this was an example of old-age confusion.

"What do you mean, the *last* governor?" I asked.

"Oh," she answered. "He was the last of the Hattenbachers to go into politics."

"Hattenbacher?"

The name was well-known, synonymous with state history. The family had been one of the first to settle in the territory. A Hattenbacher had written the state constitution, and a half-dozen members of the family had pursued elected office.

"You're related to *those* Hattenbachers?"

"Oh yes," she said. "I'm one of the last. We used to be thick upon the ground in this state, but now there are not enough of us to make a table of bridge. My father was the rector at Saint Michael's and later head of the college. I was his only daughter, the former Heloise Hattenbacher."

Her bright eyes widened and she giggled delightedly.

"My goodness! I haven't said that name in a very long time." She shook her head. "I always thought it was a very big name for a rather little person. Don't you think so?"

Her humor was infectious. I couldn't help smiling at her.

"It's long, but has very nice alliteration."

"Yes, I suppose it does."

"So, this man was governor," I said.

She nodded. "He served one term and wasn't reelected. He was a fair and honest fellow, they tell me. Which made him an enemy to both the railroad barons and the Grangers."

Miss Heloise gave me a brief explanation of the local political intrigues of the late nineteenth century.

"So, he left political circles and came to the city to start his life over," she said. "He donated the family home near the Capitol to be the Governor's Mansion. Times were hard back then and he thought it was a great location for the chief executive to live." She leaned forward and lowered her tone slightly as if revealing a secret. "My father once said that the governor knew there were men who could have afforded to buy that house, but he didn't want a one of them living that close to the seat of power."

I laughed.

"Either way, it was a fine, good thing our family did for the state," she said.

"It certainly was," I agreed.

"I don't think he ever regretted it," Miss Heloise said. "But he surely did miss the place. This house is an exact replica of that one. Built with the same materials from the same plans."

"Really?" I glanced around, surprised.

She nodded. "Of course, you couldn't tell it now," she said. "They've done so many updates and renovations on the Governor's Mansion, it's hardly recognizable."

She was right. David and I had been there to a campaign dinner. It resembled nothing more than an elaborately furnished brick box. It had none of the grace and charm of Miss Heloise's old Victorian.

"The Governor's Mansion originally looked like this?"

She nodded. "He had it duplicated to the last detail and we've always kept it just that way."

I looked around the room with the strange sense of viewing history.

"And you loved it so much you never left?"

Miss Heloise shook her head. "It was no grand decision," she assured me. "Circumstances just turned out that way. I stayed home until I married. The war was on and my husband shipped out two weeks after the wedding. So I simply stayed with my parents. When he returned, there was such a housing shortage that he just moved in here as well, and we never left."

"But you're leaving now."

She shrugged, unconcerned. "It's the kind of house that should be shared," she said. "I've had a glorious stint of living here. Now it's someone else's turn."

I looked into that old woman's bright blue eyes and

swallowed hard. I couldn't lie to her. But how could I tell Miss Heloise that I was having the place leveled?

I didn't even wait to get back to the office to start making calls. I contacted the historical society, the State Parks Department, the National Registry. It wasn't that hard to make a case for protecting the property. Bureaucrats seemed a good deal more in tune with the concept of protecting heritage sites than they had ever been in my previous dealings when trying to make old properties marketable.

Stumbling blocks, of course, occurred. Barb was one. Though the property was technically that of her mother-in-law, she'd more or less already planned where the money was going to go. None of my assurances about the advantages of an ongoing, continuous tax write-off sounded nearly as appealing as the cold hard cash she'd hope to make. These difficulties were compounded when I explained to Miss Heloise the full story of what was going on. The old lady immediately protested the sale and decided to change her will—to create a foundation to care for the house.

The influential Jarman family went on a public attack. Barb's brother was publisher of the daily newspaper. Though the press was typically in favor of conservation and restoration, in this particular instance personal property apparently trumped public preservation.

Attempts at compromise were not particularly substantial. The Jarmans' lawyer proposed naming the condo development Hattenbacher Hall. Miss Heloise clearly was not as concerned about the prominence of her family name as she was of the survival of the heritage the house represented.

News articles portrayed the aged woman as a wealthy, out-of-touch elitist. On kinder days it was slyly suggested that somehow I had deceived and manipulated a mentally frail old lady. A local columnist, whom I had met numerous times during my years with the Junior League, went even further, playing up my former gold-digger status. Openly questioning the motives of a woman who clawed her way to the top of the heap by way of other people's money. She never pointed out that I was losing big on the deal. And any assumption of altruism on my part was too far-fetched to even mention.

Dear little Miss Heloise, fragile and disappointed in her offspring, had to stand alone against her children. At one point, a competency hearing for her was threatened, but withdrawn. The Hattenbachers might not be plentiful enough to make up a bridge table, but they were still formidable enemies to anyone who crossed them. And the tiny little lady had apparently inherited a good measure of the determination and backbone that had helped her family forge a state.

I spent a lot of hours making contacts and shoring up the details with the appropriate government agencies. But then, I had plenty of time to do so after I'd lost my job.

Millie and Frank were beside themselves, furious at what they saw as a stab in the back from a trusted friend. After a couple of attempts to "reason with me" I was formally given notice to vacate my office. A personal note was attached from Millie suggesting that she was certain that the events of the last year had "unhinged" me, and that it would be thoughtless of her not to urge me to continue therapy.

Chester chuckled when I read the note to him.

"One thing I've learned," he told me. "If people think you're crazy, then you're usually on the right track."

He was in his bed cranked up on both ends, keeping both his head and his feet high. He'd had some kind of surgery on his leg, he didn't elaborate much, but it bothered me that I so rarely saw him dressed and seated among his treasures.

"Read me some more of that newspaper," he said.

I was happy to comply.

"What else do you want to hear?" I asked.

"Letters to the editor, those are sometimes good."

I found the section and scanned through the small bold-print headlines about trash recycling, national politics, potholes and police patrols.

"Oh my gosh," I said, surprised. "There is one here about the Hattenbacher house."

"For or against?"

"The headline reads Hattenbacher Backers."

Chester groaned good-naturedly. "Let's hear it," he said.

I complied.

"'In her recent commentary, Sandra Blake-Bunting suggests that the people of the city come up losers in the bid for preservation of the Heloise Hattenbacher House. She describes the establishment of the foundation as a precedent that sets families at war among themselves. And she calls the donation of the building to the State Parks Department an insult to private-property rights. Her contention has the surprising suggestion that the term *owner* should be expanded to include any and all family members who might have an interest in profiting from an investment. This concept will undoubtedly receive strong support from ne'er-do-well brothers-in-law statewide.'"

Chester laughed delightedly. It was pretty funny.

"'Ms. Blake-Bunting points to the loss of valuation revenues that would have been generated by the proposed development complex, the expense to taxpayers of the upkeep and maintenance of the hundred-fifteen year-old building, and the loss of a completely residential area, now to be burdened with the traffic and tourism of a state museum site.

"'I find none of these arguments convincing.

"'I have often driven by this majestic mansion with its fine proportions, Victorian detail and wraparound porches. I have sighed with pleasure at the grace and beauty of a time gone by. And wondered idly how the inside of such a lovely house must look. Like most people in this city, I was not even aware of the historical significance of the building, or of the heritage it represents.

"'Destroying such a treasure for the sake of enriching a few already wealthy developers, and providing more high-rent housing for city dwellers who can afford to live anywhere is worse than a bad idea. It is an obscene one.

"'Those involved in the campaign to save the house, including the city's own Jane Lofton, should be commended as the heroes they are. At considerable expense to themselves, they are offering us a gift for future generations that can never be duplicated. The cost of which can never be too much.'"

"Oh, I like that," Chester said.

I laughed. "At least somebody thinks I'm a hero."

"And at 'considerable expense to' yourself," Chester pointed out. "That's what? A three-pointer? A four?"

"I'm not sure how it scores," I said, "but I'll take whatever I can get."

"Who wrote it?"

I glanced back down at the newspaper.

"It's signed Scott Robbins." The name sounded familiar, but I didn't know from where.

"Ah yes," Chester said. "Good man."

"You know him?"

"Oh no," he answered. "But I've read a lot of things he's written. He's in 'Letters to the Editor' all the time."

"Really? That's strange."

"Actually, it's not," Chester corrected me. "The majority of the letter writers are repeaters. Most of us have one good letter to the editor in us," Chester said. "For these folks it's a hobby or a calling. They are in there every week or so, commenting on anything and everything. If you read regularly, you kind of get to know them."

Never having been a regular newspaper reader, I had to take Chester's word for it. In the past several weeks, since I realized the severity of his vision loss, I'd read the paper more often than I'd read it in the last ten years.

"Did you bring my Snickers?" he asked me.

"Of course!" I assured him, standing up to dig into my purse. "Would I forget?"

He smiled at me. It was a strange smile, almost melancholy somehow.

"No, Jane," he said in a low voice barely above a whisper. "I can depend upon you completely."

It was such a strange moment, I was somewhat taken aback. Then, as he took the candy from me, the indecipherable expression melted away.

"I'll just save this for later," he said as he secreted it in the chest beside him as he always did. "Later, when I can really enjoy it."

The nurse walked in right at that moment. He slammed the drawer shut abruptly.

"Sorry to barge in on your visit, honey," she said to me, "but it's almost the end of my shift and I need to change Mr. Durbin's surgical dressing before I leave."

"All right, let me say goodbye then," I said, rising to stand beside Chester's bed.

He had a right to his privacy and I had no need to invade it. My concern for him was no excuse for prying. I leaned forward and placed a kiss on his forehead. It was a familial gesture that surprised us both.

"I hope that you recover from this surgery very quickly," I said. Our relationship had been as friends. Somewhere I'd crossed the line, and I realized in that moment that he was as dear to me as any member of my family. He must have sensed the change as well.

"It's not anything too serious, Jane," he told me quietly. "I'm doing fine. I just had my foot amputated."

I was shocked. I glanced down at the long length of legs hidden by blankets. It looked to me as if his *foot* had been cut off right below the knee.

"What—" I began, but he cut me off.

"It's nothing for you to worry about, Jane," he assured me, patting my hand in a loving, fatherlike manner. "Just an old war wound acting up."

I nodded and left the room, almost in a daze, allowing the nurse to do her job.

I was in the car and on to the expressway before I remembered that Chester had not been in the war.

# 14

For the next two weeks, I came to the Assisted Living Center every day. Chester seemed to be recovering from the surgery very well and appeared to be rather nonchalant about the loss of his limb.

"It's a circulation problem," he told me.

That was hardly what could be called a satisfying answer. The more I grilled Chester as to the state of his health and the need for the operation, the less talkative he became.

I took my questions to the nursing staff with no more success. My status as friend of the resident did not entitle me to patient-care information.

"His medical condition is a protected right of privacy," the facility director told me without even bothering to glance at his chart. "If he doesn't want to discuss it, then I'm afraid I can't."

I didn't argue or insist. There was no use antagonizing the people whom I was counting on to take care of him.

I did catch a casual comment that seemed to explain a lot.

"At least we know he won't be running down to the highway getting his feet all cut up again," the nurse's aide cackled, as if it were a fine joke.

I blanched. Is that what had happened? Was the loss of his leg a long-term result of my rescue? That seemed to explain his reticence to talk about it. So I quit asking questions and just concentrated on being Chester's frequent visitor, dependable friend and entertaining conversationalist.

My other pressing concern was Brynn, who continued to avoid my calls. If I could only talk to her, I was sure I could convince her to confide her plans. How could I be a good mother to her if I wasn't sure what she was up to?

"There are some decisions in our lives that are ours alone to make," Chester told me. "What other folks think or want can just be distracting."

"But what if she is planning to go to Europe with her therapist?" I said. "I can't let her do that."

He shook his head. "Nothing you've told me about your Brynn leads me to think that the young woman is stupid or self-destructive," he said.

"It comes down to trust, Jane Lofton. No matter how it looks to you, you've got to trust that she'll know what's the right thing for her."

I took comfort in Chester's advice. Under the circumstances there was really nothing else I could do, on that front or any other.

Jobless and with no opportunity for mom-related duties, I now had more time to devote to volunteer work. That was great. Of course, my financial future looked a little bit scary.

Although David and I had divided our assets, a large part of my share was the house. I had wanted the place, I'd specifically asked for it. But I found that it now seemed too large for one person. And the taxes and utilities alone could have paid for a very nice condo for me.

Still, I couldn't really rent the place. No one who could afford a house of that size would want to forgo the tax advantages of owning. While I will always believe that good real estate is a commodity to hold, a residence, by its nature, doesn't make money. I considered selling the place and investing the profits. But with the value of the stock market these days, I worried that I'd be buying high.

So I just put off making a decision. Things would work out, I supposed, somehow.

I wasn't completely without career opportunities. There was no reason why I couldn't continue to sell houses. I wouldn't have the advantage of being in a large, well-respected brokerage, but my license was still perfectly valid. However, I was no longer very interested in the real estate market. And it's not really the kind of business concern that one can care about halfway.

My final closing was on a darling little west-side home for the Guerras, the family I'd met at the low-income-housing seminar. The place they wanted was barely fifteen hundred square feet. It had four tiny bedrooms, but the kitchen was very livable and structurally it was sound. I got a high appraisal value and a fair price for the seller. The house was what they wanted, where they wanted, and not more than they could afford. In real estate they'd say you couldn't do any better than that. But I did.

The high-interest debt that they were paying for his father's funeral put the Guerras in a vulnerable position. It kept them from qualifying for a mortgage at most banks, and even if I managed to get a home loan through the special low-income incentive programs, they would have a difficult time, financially, for a very long time. I wanted those funeral expenses paid off, and I wanted their home loan to do it.

Fortunately, you don't have to be a commercial lending institution to finance a mortgage. I got their money from a very unlikely source.

Gil Mullins was no one's favorite lender. I wasn't

sure there was an altruistic bone in the man's body. But I decided to find out.

I approached him with dread. Gil could be so obnoxious. He was, however, a likely candidate for the deal. Flush with the money his cousin, Henry, had paid him for the 51 percent share of the family business, Gil would need a good place to invest the cash. I was counting on his ability to see that making a personal decision about any part of that windfall would be a victory.

To get to that place, I knew I was going to need the confidence of high heels.

I rifled through the shoe racks in my closet until I found exactly the right pair. They were sandals, strappy, red and with five-inch stilettos. I put them on and I could hardly stand up. Walking was agony. But neither standing nor walking were going to be particularly necessary. I needed to be tall. I needed to be formidable. I needed to be Jane Lofton, at her loftiest.

My business suit was a very traditional gray, conservatively cut and almost mannish, with a little red handkerchief in the breast pocket, just to tie in with the shoes. The straight skirt had a modest hemline at midcalf. I wore no rings, no bracelets, not even my watch. My only jewelry was a delicate strand of pearls around my neck and even smaller ones at my ears.

I glanced at myself one last time in the mirror before heading out. I was absolute decorum…with killer shoes.

Gil's office, in the Mullins Trucking Company building was a fancy penthouse corner. The inscription on the door indicated that he was Executive Vice President for General Administration. It even sounded like a sham title. If I were him I would have preferred a more honest description like Founder's Son on the Payroll for Family Relations Purposes.

My appointment was at eleven o'clock. I wanted to talk to him in the morning, before he had a fortifying lunch of a couple of martinis. I was there at a quarter till, sitting in the outer office. Not reading, not checking my PalmPilot, not talking on the cell phone. I was sitting, obviously, purposely waiting.

I could see it unnerved his secretary, who called him twice without any prompting. Gil didn't hurry. He came to his door to invite me in at ten after. It was just the kind of power trip I knew he'd be into.

"Jane, it's good to see you. You haven't been at the club lately."

He was, of course, perfectly aware that I was no longer a member. I just smiled. Allowing him to have his little victory.

The minute I stood up in those five-inch heels, I could look him right in the eye. Which is just what I did as I brushed past him on the threshold. Twenty years of living among the hostile natives of Cambridge Heights had taught me a thing or two about engaging the enemy.

The chairs in Gil's office were plush and attractive. But they were a little bit low. I had no intention of allowing this man to look down on me. Before he could even offer a seat, I perched myself upon the wide, overstuffed arm of the chair and opened my briefcase on the edge of his personal desk.

He seated himself behind the wide expanse of expensive mahogany and looked up at me. His expression was still snide and superior.

"I was so sorry to hear about you and David," he said.

"Thank you."

"It's no surprise that guys go for something younger," he told me. "But most of us, certainly me personally—I wouldn't marry one."

If this line of conversation was meant to endear me to him, it wasn't working particularly well.

"I mean, what's the point?" Gil continued. "As soon as you marry her she starts to get old, and in ten years you're stuck with another woman on the decline."

I almost laughed out load. His comment was so over-the-top, it was practically a parody of the jerk he appeared to be.

"I'm sure David and Mikki will be very happy together," I told him. "And I intend to be happy myself."

It was a deliberately innocuous statement. Just the sort of thing to send a guy like Gil into mental overdrive. Utterly clueless about women, he searched for code, meaning, intent that he couldn't quite grasp. His eyes widened eagerly.

"So now that we're not going to run into each other at the club," he said with a self-congratulatory chuckle, "you've made an appointment to see me."

His attitude, rife with insinuation, suggested he thought my presence at his office to be one of a romantic nature.

"I'm here to make you a business proposal," I told him.

"Is that what they call it today?" he asked.

I resisted the desire to groan and roll my eyes. "I am not looking for a sugar daddy, Gil," I assured him. "I'm looking for an investor."

"An investor?"

"I know that your cousin, Henry, bought part of your business," I told him, making what was undoubtedly a vote of no confidence from his father's will sound more like an ordinary sales agreement. The elder Mr. Mullins, recently deceased, had stipulated that in order for Gil to inherit, he had to sell his 51 percent share of the family's trucking company to his cousin, Henry, whom the old man believed was more capable than Gil of keeping the business afloat. It was the kind of unforgivable family faux pas that would engender generations of squabbling and incivility.

"You're going to want to diversify," I told him. "Put that money in a lot of areas. I've got an excellent real estate opportunity for you."

"A real estate opportunity?" He gave a disdainful huff and shook his head. "Barbara Jarman's been telling everybody who'll listen about the great deal you made for her."

I couldn't quite control the blush that arose naturally from his facetious statement, but I insulated myself from it as well as I could, shrugging with feigned humor.

"Well, you know Barbara," I said, fairly certain that the two had never had a great deal of use for each other.

Gil grabbed the bait. "Yeah, that stupid bitch," he said. "Always thinks she's just a damn bit better."

I deftly changed the direction of the conversation, grateful that Gil's personal venom of self-loathing and insecurity spewed out on most of the people he encountered in the world. I hoped it might work in my favor.

"This is the deal I wanted you to take a look at," I told him, spreading the Guerras' file open on the desk in front of him.

It was all there in a very readable order. Gil glanced through the document casually. Not bothering to read very much or even make much attempt to understand what it was.

"You want me to buy a house on the west side?" he asked, puzzled.

"No, I don't want you to buy it," I told him. "I want you to lend the money."

"What?"

"The Guerras are going to buy the house," I told him. "They just need a mortgage lender."

Gil snorted and, gesturing toward his elegant surroundings, said, "Do I look like a west-side savings and loan?"

"Anyone can loan money for real estate, Gil, you know that," I said with a light laugh.

From his expression it was obvious that he hadn't known it, but naturally he was not prepared to admit to it.

"Sure," he said. "But why would a trucking company be interested?"

"Oh, I'm not showing this to Mullins Trucking," I said. "I'm approaching you, Gil Mullins, as a private businessperson."

Clearly, not many people, including Gil himself, had ever thought of the man as a private businessperson.

"I smell a scam," he said warily.

I shook my head. "This is completely legitimate," I assured him honestly. "You've got an excess of cash from Henry's buy into the company. I'd like to see you use a portion of it for a 110 percent mortgage loan on this house."

He looked puzzled. "110 percent? You seem to be asking more than the loan is worth."

"The house has been assessed higher than the asking price," I pointed out.

"Why?"

"The new light-rail transit has a proposed stop just three blocks away," I told him with the same optimistic enthusiasm I'd used on the appraiser. "We've already seen in Dallas and elsewhere how much that can mean to the nearby neighborhood."

The mass transit from the west side was still at least a decade away, and an awful lot could happen in that time.

Gil shrugged. "Great," he said. "It'll go up in value. But if the seller didn't ask for more money, why is the buyer? I've never heard of a 110 percent loan."

"They aren't that uncommon," I told him. "Admittedly they are more often used for refinancing loans used to upgrade or remodel a house."

"Is that what these people are doing? Expanding the house?"

"No, they aren't building on at this time," I said. "They need to get a couple of years of payments under their belt at least."

"Then what is this extra money? Down payment?"

"Partly," I admitted. "And to clear up some outstanding obligations."

Gil looked genuinely confused.

"Jane, what's the catch here?" he said. "Why don't you just go to a bank or a savings and loan?"

"Because they wouldn't give it to me," I told him honestly.

Carefully, and without any attempt at deceit, I explained the problem to him.

"The Guerras have an outstanding retail debt of six thousand dollars," I said. "They have been paying off a funeral at a high rate of interest. They are good debtors. They've never missed a payment. They've never been late. But in the world of banking, this doesn't work for them, it works against them. They still qualify for a home loan, but just barely."

"Close enough is close enough," Gil said.

"For you or me it would be," I agreed. "But making this monthly payment and their mortgage would have them walking a very fine line. If anything went wrong, a car breaks down, a child gets sick, or one of them is injured on the job, they'd have to default on one or the other."

Gil nodded as if he understood.

"By folding this funeral-home loan in with the mortgage, it's spread out over thirty years," I continued. "It's hardly noticeable in the monthly payment. It's a smart thing to do. It's a reasonable thing to do. But it is an unusual thing to do, and the regulations of banks and home mortgage companies make the unusual untenable."

"So you're trying to find somebody who will just loan this money on their own," he said.

"Yes, exactly."

I began to talk about the Guerra family, almost rambling. I talked about Mr. Guerra's work, his wife at the pizza place, his mother, his three children, his two nephews.

"Both he and his wife have perfect work records, both active in their church," I said. "They're active in the children's school. The boys play Youth League Soccer."

Gil didn't appear to be particularly impressed.

"Mr. Guerra has a personal reference from Les Weigan," I pointed out, rifling through the papers on the desk to show it to him.

I'd gotten the reference from Les's secretary, Linda. I showed up on a day when I knew Les was out of town and acted as if Les had forgotten to do it. Linda graciously wrote exactly what I dictated on Les's letterhead and signed it, as she did most of his letters.

Gil looked at it, at least.

"Still," he protested, "this is far from compelling."

"I think it could be very much so," I told him.

"If it's such a good idea, why don't you just loan them the money?"

It was a good question.

"I initially thought I would," I admitted. "But I just don't have the cash to do it. You mentioned the Barbara Jarman thing, so you must know I've lost my job. David gave me a good settlement, but the biggest portion of it is tied up in my house. I'd have to borrow money to make this loan. And I probably wouldn't have any more luck with the banks than the Guerras would."

"Give me one good reason why I should do this," he said.

"There are actually three reasons," I told him, glancing down at my notes.

"Okay."

"First," I said, "it is a really good thing to do." I hoped that the rationale that motivated me might appeal to Gil as well. "These people are very deserving. They work hard, they pay their bills. They are trying to build a better life for their children. They are the kind of people we should all be helping and encouraging."

Gil leaned back in his chair, crossed his arms and chuckled.

"That's not a reason, Jane," he said. "That's a soapbox."

I ignored his disparaging comment. "The second reason is that the Guerras are dependable and motivated to pay back the loan. The house itself is sufficient collateral for the loan, and the adjusted interest rate will insure you two percentage points above prime on your money for the next thirty years. It's a safe, steady return on your investment, insulated from the wild fluctuations that can infect stocks or commodities."

He nodded slowly. I could see that he was considering my words, trying to find an error in them. There wasn't one.

"And finally, you should make this loan because you know you need to get the money you made from your cousin, Henry, working for you. This loan is actually quite small. Even at 110 percent, it's less than sixty thousand, not much more than what you'd pay for a new car or a nice vacation. But it will buy you so much."

"Buy me so much what?" Gil asked the question directly.

"Independence," I answered. "I'm sure that both Henry and your wife have come up with a number of ways for you to invest this money. Henry probably wants you to pour a lot of it back into the company in some way. And Beverly would probably rather have it all in easily accessible money market funds. I suspect that even your father might have made some suggestions in his will if he'd thought about it. Wouldn't it be nice this time to rely upon your own judgment instead of theirs?"

I could see it in his eyes immediately. I had won. We both knew it. Altruism didn't interest him, and even a secure return on his money was pretty boring, but doing something on his own, one tiny step out from under the thumb of his wife and his father's handpicked successor, appealed to him totally and fundamentally.

At the end of our discussion we rose to our feet. We shook hands on the deal, transforming the nature of our unpleasant personal relationship for all time.

Because I was representing the buyer, I gave him Ann Rhoder Hines's phone number and asked that he contact her to set up the details.

He assured me that he would call her that very morning.

A few moments later when I walked out of the building, teetering painfully on the five-inch heels, I felt ten feet tall. I called Mrs. Guerra on my car phone, catching her right in the middle of the noon rush.

When I told her the news, she shouted for joy. Then I heard her hastily mumbled words of thanks to Saint Matthew.

I didn't begrudge sharing the praise for the day's

work with the most famous moneylender in history. Though I was fairly sure that such a holy, honorable soul hadn't felt the need to wear red shoes to make a deal.

Mrs. Guerra was too busy to stop and call her husband. She asked me to do it, so I got the satisfaction of announcing the good news twice.

I decided to celebrate, as I often had in the past after a successful sale, with a visit to Yesteryear Emporium. It had been months since I'd last visited my favorite antique store. I just wanted to walk around and look at the amazing collection. I have never understood what it is about antiques that has always drawn me.

I certainly never grew up in an atmosphere of fine old things. The house I'd shared with my mother was furnished from Montgomery Ward, with sturdy brown Naugahyde in the living room and chrome and Formica in the kitchen. Mama had very little sense of style in either home furnishings or personal fashion. I remember thinking as a girl that it was fortunate that she always wore nurses' uniforms, because the clothes she picked out for herself were hideous. Of course, I never told her that. I'm not sure I ever told her anything. In fact, I couldn't recall one significant conversation the two of us had ever had.

Anyway, I loved shopping for antiques. And even though I knew I wasn't going to buy anything, I looked forward eagerly to an afternoon of rifling through and seeing what was there.

I had already parked and gathered up my purse before I realized I was still wearing the red shoes and didn't have any others to put on. With a grimace, I decided to go in anyway.

The proprietor, my old school chum, was sitting behind the counter typing on his old Underwood.

"Hi!" I called out quickly, and hurried past.

"Janey!" Obviously excited to see me, and ignoring his cane, he sort of dragged himself to the counter.

"Hi," I repeated.

He was banging his fist hard against his thigh. "My leg's asleep," he explained. "It happens all the time. The circulation is not as good as it could be."

I smiled, a little nonplussed. There was nothing much to reply to that. I tried to move on past, but he seemed determined to talk with me.

"Haven't seen you in quite a while," he said. "But I've been hearing about you. Guess all that's kept you busy."

I was stunned. These days, comments about my marital status were a more common subject for discussion than the possibility of spring rains. But being reminded of my divorce by this man, in this store, was completely unexpected.

The guy just stood there, grinning at me. No consoling words about *how these things happen* or polite *I'm so sorry*. Scott, who had previously pushed me on the subject of trust, stood there smiling, as if taking potshots at my life was fair game.

I stared back at him, every bit of the annoyance I felt written upon my face. Eventually he grew uncomfortable.

He rubbed his hands together nervously. "Yes… well, I just wanted to let you know how proud I am of you. I'm sure it wasn't easy, but you did the right thing."

"As a matter of fact, I did," I said in my coldest, most haughty tone. "If it is any business of yours."

He hesitated. "Well, no, I guess it's not really any of my business," he said. "Except as a member of the community. I believe that this is the kind of thing in which everybody in the community has a stake."

I was incredulous. "Everybody in the community has a stake in my divorce!"

His eyebrows shot up. "You're getting a divorce?"

"Got one, past tense," I said.

"Oh…I'm…I'm so sorry," he said.

Now I was completely confused. "What were we talking about?"

"When?"

"Just now."

"The Hattenbacher House," he said.

"Oh, of course, the Hattenbacher House." I shook my head. "I wasn't thinking. When you said you knew I'd been busy, well, I thought—"

"No, I would never," he said. "I mean I…I don't even…well, gossip from the country club set rarely gets mentioned among the people I hang out with."

"No, of course not," I said.

The stupidity of my jump to this conclusion was so obviously ridiculous that I began laughing. Once I started, I couldn't stop.

He eyed me curiously.

"I thought you were proud of me for getting a divorce," I managed to get out between uncontrollable giggles.

He was grinning at me again, the laugh lines on his face rippled all the way to his temples. "Should I be?"

"Yeah, maybe so," I said, gathering some composure. "You must think I'm a complete idiot."

"No, I think I'm the one who's an idiot," he said. "I just assumed that you knew about my interest in the project. I wrote a letter to the editor."

"Letter to the editor? Scott Robbins. Of course, *you're* Scott Robbins."

"Yes, I'm aware of that."

"I knew that I knew that name, but I couldn't place you."

He nodded with feigned gravity. "Sheesh, Janey, are you trying to destroy my ego. Just like the days back in junior high, no matter what I did, I couldn't get your attention."

I was sure he meant that as a joke and I took it exactly that way.

"Well, thank you for the letter and the kind things you said about me," I said. "It was very welcome after the pummeling I took from the paper."

"All I did was point out the truth," he said. "That's my job."

"Your job?"

"Well, I guess it's not a job in that sense," he said. "It's more like a calling."

"I heard that you regularly write letters to the editor."

He shrugged. "I write to them, and newsmagazines and elected officials and corporate executives. Anywhere that I think I need to say something."

I nodded, as if I understood, but in fact I didn't. My feet were throbbing with pain. I raised my right foot, which was taking the worst of the abuse, and rotated my ankle for a moment to take the pressure off.

"Those are really great shoes," Scott said.

I flushed with embarrassment. The sexy red sandals were not meant to lure the unsuspecting. I felt exposed, as if the wind had just caught my skirt and I wasn't wearing underwear. I was desperate to cover up, but there was no way to do so.

"They are killing me," I said honestly. "These have got to be the most uncomfortable shoes on planet Earth."

He chuckled.

"Come sit down," he said. "Here, come sit down."

He moved to the edge of the high counter and motioned me to come around behind where he had his little office area. He moved awkwardly and with a visible limp.

"Is your leg still asleep?"

He glanced up at me, his expression surprised.

"No," he answered after a moment's hesitation. "It's just like that."

"Motorcycle accident?" I asked.

He gave me a long look, his eyes narrowing speculatively. "You remember me on my little Honda scooter?"

"Yeah," I said, somewhat amazed at myself. "I guess I do."

"That was a very long time ago," he said.

I agreed.

Scott hadn't answered, but I'd already forgotten about my question.

Beside his typewriter desk and chair, he had a beautifully rugged mission-style sofa. It looked to me as if it might have been a genuine Stickley. Even if it was not, it was a gorgeous, well-preserved piece of furniture from the era and in very good shape except for its dirty upholstery.

"This is great!" I said, running my hand appreciatively along solid, unpretentious wood railing.

"Yeah," he agreed. "I liked the look of it on sight. My dad had it sitting in a locked off room by itself upstairs. I figured he didn't put it out on the floor 'cause he figured he'd never sell it with that stain on the cushion."

I glanced over at him, looking for a teasing glint in his eye. I didn't see one.

"You are kidding, right?"

He wasn't. I could hardly believe it.

"If this is what it looks like to me," I told him, "then your father had it locked up because it's the most valuable piece in this building. The stain, the stain is nothing. This is the original upholstery. You can have it cleaned and restored for less than a hundred dollars. It's easily worth fifty times that much."

"Wow!"

I seated myself on the wonderful piece of furniture, sighing with pleasure at the perfect comfort it offered. I glanced over at Scott. He was watching me.

"What kind of antique dealer doesn't know the value of his inventory?" I asked him.

He shrugged. "The kind who inherits a junk store from his father," he replied.

His eyes were the most amazing blue. True blue, I thought. I wasn't sure if that was a real color, but it was certainly apt. There was no deception or wariness in his gaze. It was as if he had seen the world, knew it intimately and remained fearless.

I asked a few questions about the store. He answered me forthrightly, honest about his ignorance of the business.

"Don't you have any appraisal lists? Reference books?" I asked. "How do you set an asking price?"

He shrugged. "If I've bought it, I charge a little more than I paid. Of course, there are a lot of items that were purchased as part of whole households, and then stuff that's been sitting around here for years. Mostly I'm just guessing on that."

I groaned and shook my head.

"You just don't give a lot of thought to what's going on in this store at all," I accused.

He shrugged. "When I'm writing about something, I get so into it that it's really hard for me to pay attention to anything else."

"So what are you writing?"

"I told you," he said. "I write letters."

"We all write letters," I pointed out. "What is it that you're into writing so much that you don't notice your customers. A spy thriller? A treatise on western philosophy? A history of baseball cards? Come on, confess."

He shook his head. "I write letters," he said. "I see things that cry out for change and I write to whomever I think might be able to do something about it."

"Really? How long have you been doing that?"

He looked momentarily chagrinned. "About twenty years, I guess."

I whistled and we both laughed.

"Has anything you've written ever changed anything?" I asked.

"I don't know," he answered. "I don't know what would have happened if I hadn't written."

"That's fair," I agreed. "You know, this is a very unusual hobby."

"Maybe it's not a hobby, maybe it's a curse," he replied. "I certainly spend plenty of my time cursing at that old Underwood."

I glanced over at the typewriter he indicated. It was surrounded by little balls of crumpled-up paper.

"How did you get started doing this?" I asked.

He avoided the question. "Janey, that is a long and very boring tale," he stated. "I'd much rather hear about you."

"What about me?"

"Anything about you," he said. "Tell me about your divorce."

"My divorce? Why would you want to hear about that?"

He leaned forward in his chair as if eager to listen.

"It's obviously on your mind," he said. "You think that even your antique dealer is talking about it."

I giggled again and shook my head. "There is really nothing to say," I told him. "My husband left me for another woman, they are having a new baby very shortly and I...I'm moving on."

Scott nodded slowly. "Been there, done that, got the T-shirt," he said.

"Your wife left you?"

"Not for another woman," he answered teasing. "Worse."

"Worse?"

"She left me for a dentist."

We both laughed.

"You don't sound too broken up about it."

"It was almost fifteen years ago," he said. "They have four kids and she's kind of fat now."

"Oh, well, that's okay then."

"Yeah, I'd hate for her to be a hottie when I've turned into a gray old bachelor."

"You still look pretty fine to me," I said honestly, before having the time to think through the implications of such a statement.

He grinned, obviously delighted. "Why, thank you, Janey," he said. "You're blushing."

"I'm not."

"You are," he insisted. "Almost as bright as your shoes."

My shoes! I realized I was sitting there, legs crossed on his couch with the killer shoes right in his line of vision. I put my feet on the floor.

"Sorry," I said.

"For what? Giving me a compliment? Blushing?"

"No, for the shoes."

He looked puzzled.

Briefly I explained about Gil and the Guerras.

Scott found the whole story amusing.

"So, you wore these sexy, power shoes to give you the confidence necessary to talk some guy into a great real estate deal."

"Yeah, basically," I said.

"And you won," he said.

"It wasn't about winning," I clarified. "The Guerras are a very safe bet for Gil to make. They are not at all likely to default. They have faithfully made monthly payments to that funeral home. And what would happen if they didn't? Would the undertaker go out and dig the man up? That debt should have worked to prove what desirable borrowers they are. But because of the way the rules are set up, it worked against them, making them look less than able to buy."

"Maybe the rules need changing," he said.

"They are set up to winnow out those people who owe huge sums on credit cards," I told him. "That's not a bad idea—for the banks or for the folks with out-of-control spending. But not everybody's situation fits so easily within the rules."

"So you found a way around them," he said.

I nodded. "Let's just say I gave them the red shoe treatment."

Scott laughed.

"They work every time," I said, indicating my footwear.

He shook his head. "I think it's less likely that these shoes are the ruby slippers and more likely that you, Janey Domschke, had the power within you all the time."

"You make me sound diabolical."

"The flip side of that is saintly," he said. "What you did was close the deal and you did it on your own, without props."

I held my foot up in the air, showing off both the red sandals and a good bit of leg.

"How can you say these aren't magic?" I teased.

He smiled, warm enough to raise sea levels. "They certainly send *my* thoughts into the realm of fantasy," he answered.

I realized I was flirting. It had been so long since I'd

done so, I had forgotten that it was even in my reper-
toire. And the minute I saw what I was doing, I lost the
ability to do it.

I was a single woman, alone in the company of a
man, albeit one who was not my type, but an attractive
man nonetheless. Only moments before, those facts
had been innocuous. Now they were downright intimidating.

I put my foot back on the floor and nervously made
sure that my skirt was pulled down over my knees. My
heart was racing.

Glancing in his direction, I saw that he was watching
me. There was no menace in that true blue gaze, just curiosity and expectation.

To my surprise and great relief, he deftly changed
the subject.

"So how did you get involved with the Hattenbacher
House?" he asked me.

Business. I could talk business. I felt myself relaxing
into the conversation.

"I was the Realtor for the place," I said. "I found the
developer, investors, got the area rezoned. Then I met
Miss Heloise."

"She was against it?"

"She had no idea," I answered. "Her daughter-in-
law had told her they were going to sell it. She'd agreed
to give the place up, to go to a senior-care facility. She
had no idea, until I told her, that we were going to level
the place."

"It was a really good thing you did," he said. "Being
honest with her."

I was tempted to explain to him about the accident,
about Chester, about my vow that night. I wanted him
to understand that I wasn't naturally a good person,
that I didn't do good things. But I held back. I had been

flirting with the man. The memory of that still made me uneasy. I was careful about revealing too much.

"You know how I love antiques," I said. "That house is just one giant, perfect-condition antique. And when I heard about the history…" I shook my head. "Tearing it down for condos would have been like painting a yellow happy face on the Mona Lisa."

"Apparently the Jarman family didn't feel the same way," he said.

"Not exactly," I replied. "I still hear quiet whispers that they might sue me for breach of contract, or get the real estate board to revoke my broker's license."

"Do you think either of those things will happen?"

"It's possible, I suppose. But I don't really think so," I said. "Either way, I'm lying low. Miss Heloise asked me if I wanted to head up the foundation. I said no."

"You weren't interested?"

"I wasn't uninterested," I admitted. "But I just thought it would be more fuel to antagonize the family."

"And you didn't want to do that," he said.

"I thought it might be dangerous to do that," I said. "Not just for me. They are still Miss Heloise's family and they are still not to be trusted."

He nodded. "And she doesn't want to alienate them, I'm sure."

"She doesn't. The day she moved to the senior home, Barb came to see her and asked if she could have a couple of mementos from the house."

"Oh no."

"Oh yes," I answered. "Miss Heloise thought it would be wonderful to keep something special in the family."

"Nobody went with them."

I shook my head. "They brought a moving van, right

in the middle of the day, as if they had nothing in the world to be ashamed of."

"They cleaned the place out?"

"No, fortunately they didn't have time," I said. "One of the neighbors called me. I got the police over there to stall them while I found a judge willing to order a *cease and desist.*"

"That's good," he said.

I nodded. "But they did get a lot of stuff," I said. "It will be just one more challenge for the foundation to get donations of appropriate replacement pieces."

"Oh, but, Janey, I know you'll be up to the challenge," he said.

# 15

The drive out to Bluebonnet Manor Assisted Living came alive with the bright colors of wildflowers and the lush green of spring grass. I headed out there early one morning under a clear blue sky. When I pulled off onto the exit ramp, I lowered the top on the Z3. It was only a quarter mile farther, but I wanted to feel a little bit of the warmth of sunshine on my face.

A car dealership had opened on the feeder road directly beside the freeway, cutting off Chester's view of the road. If the place had been there the night of the accident, I would have died.

Strangely, thoughts like that no longer had the ability to send shivers up my spine. I no longer thought that my being saved was an unfathomable quirk of fate. I'd somehow come to the realization that there was a purpose for my being alive. I wasn't certain what that purpose was, but I was determined to seek it out and try to fulfil it.

I pulled into my usual spot in the parking lot and headed inside. In the weeks following the amputation of his lower leg, Chester appeared to be not much changed. There had been no talk of an artificial limb, rehab, or walking again.

I understood that patients often became depressed and therefore reluctant to pursue that direction. But, I'd always thought that health-care workers were the cheerleaders for getting on with your life, learning to live with what you have. The people on the staff acted as if they were perfectly content to allow Chester to just lie in his bed for the rest of his life.

I didn't understand it. And I really didn't like it.

I began to insist that Chester be gotten up into his chair. If I went to visit and he was in bed, I immediately tracked down his nurse's aide to get him up.

He let me do that. He let me grouse for him, nag for him, complain for him. But he was not at all interested in any discussion with me concerning his recent surgery, the state of his health or the quality of his care.

"In the nursing home we get to talk about our aches and pains all the time," he told me. "When you're here for a visit, I want to talk about something else."

I tried to abide by his wishes. Though I continued to worry about him. The stump, just below his knee, didn't seem to be healing up very fast and I was worried that he was perhaps not eating all that well. Maybe he needed vitamins.

Fortunately, one evening I left rather late and spotted a charge nurse whom I'd never seen before.

I went up and introduced myself and chatted for a few minutes. It was her first day on the job. She was in her mid-twenties, not all that much older than Brynn, bright and inquisitive, a very recent graduate of State University.

Uncharacteristically honest, I admitted it to be my alma mater as well.

"Were you in one of the sororities?" she asked me.

I shook my head. "No, I lived quietly on the second floor of Alma Willard," I said.

"You're kidding!" Anje said. "I lived in Thatcher, but I had a friend who was in Willard. I studied in their Quiet Salon all the time."

She updated me about the place, and I shared an historic anecdote or two. It had been a lifetime since I had even spoken about the four years that I'd lived there. The two of us became fast friends in five minutes.

"Listen, Anje," I said finally. "I'm worried about Chester Durbin. I like Bluebonnet a lot, but I'm not sure that he's really getting the best care here. Could you take a quick look at his chart? I'm thinking that a fresh set of eyes might see something."

I assumed that being brand new, she would have no vested interest in protecting her predecessors. That she would, at least, be able to give me some idea of how things were going with him, and she might just immediately see what more could be done.

"Anything in particular that you're concerned about?" she asked me.

"Honestly, I'm worried about his nutrition," I told her, not mentioning my own role in food consumption. I was still bringing him a Snickers at every visit. "He seems to have a pretty good appetite, but I'm not sure that he's getting any stronger."

Young Nurse Anje was already reaching for his chart when she asked, "He's your dad, right?"

"I'm his niece," I lied without hesitation. I was at least that, I assured myself.

"Let's see," she said, opening up the notebook that held almost a ream of paper, thick as the local phone book. She began riffling through the array of multicolored sheets and grafts, handwritten notes and test reports.

"Oh wow," she commented after a couple of minutes, but continued to read without elaborating.

Across the lobby I spotted a couple of nurse's aides, whom I recognized, holding an impromptu confab. If either of them walked over to Anje's desk and caught her revealing Chester's medical information to me, I'd be *so* busted.

Intentionally I moved a little to the left so that I was

standing between them and Anje. If they glanced in this direction I would be blocking their view of her looking through the chart. Hopefully, it would appear as if I was merely innocently wasting the young woman's time.

"Actually, Jane, it looks like the staff has been keeping very close track of him," she told me finally. "See these summary sheets." She showed me a thick section of handwritten tables. "These are really rigorously detailed," she said. "His diet is very regimented. And they've been keeping daily intake and output along with the blood monitoring since the day of his original admission."

I nodded. That certainly sounded good.

"The staff has really been doing everything possible to keep him within normal range. And he's been completely cooperative. I don't find any reports of noncompliance. And you can imagine how rare that is!"

"Um," I responded noncommittally.

Anje lowered her voice to a conspiratorial whisper. "Some of these people, you just can't turn your back on them for a minute, they are always sneaking something."

I had no idea what she was talking about.

"Still," she said sympathetically, "he *has* become very brittle over the last year, but that's probably expected with his age and deterioration."

*Brittle* seemed a strange choice of word. I assumed she'd misspoken. She probably meant to say Chester was frail or weak. Both things were very true.

I glanced nervously over my shoulder. The two nurse's aides had disappeared down the hall.

"You are right, of course, Anje," I said. "It just seems as if Chester's knee isn't healing very fast since the amputation."

She nodded and shrugged. "His circulation is terrible, of course. That is absolutely to be expected."

I didn't really know anything about old people, but I suppose I had heard that they often had trouble with circulation.

"Besides his internist, there are two specialists on consult," she said. "Try not to worry, Jane. Your family has done everything possible to see he gets the best care."

I left that night feeling somewhat better and having a little more respect for Chester's nephew. I continued to see Anje from time to time when she was on duty. Apparently no one had ever told her that I wasn't Chester's niece, and when she saw me, she always volunteered rather benign information on how he was doing.

This particular Monday, as I made my way through the lobby and past the nurses' station and down the hall to Chester's room, I didn't see her.

"Is anybody home," I called out as I walked in.

The good news, Chester was sitting up in his wheelchair staring out the window. The bad news, he was thin and pale and gaunt.

He turned to smile at me. "You are here bright and early this morning," he said.

"Early enough to catch you by surprise?" I asked.

"Well, you might have, but I saw you driving up in that fancy car of yours."

I walked up and stood beside him. From the window I could see my convertible. The luxury two-seater looked incongruous among the minivans and sensible sedans in the nursing-home parking lot.

"It is a pretty fancy little car," I admitted. "David bought it for me, of course. But it costs a fortune to maintain."

Chester nodded.

"I like those little Volkswagens they sell down the

hill there," he said, pointing to the dealership that now blocked his view. "If I could drive, I think I'd buy myself one of those."

I smiled. I suppose we're never too old for new-car fever.

"How long has it been since you've driven?" I asked him.

He laughed and shook his head. "I couldn't tell you," he said. "I can't even remember how long it's been since I've *ridden* in a car. The danged nursing home transport puts me in the back and strapped down to a gurney."

He laughed as if the image of himself, helpless and tied down in an ambulance-type vehicle, was funny. It wasn't. But I laughed along with him. It just seemed like the thing to do.

"So, have you heard from Brynn?" he asked me.

I shook my head. "No, she still won't take my calls. I don't really want to talk about it."

He nodded, understanding. "Then sit down and we'll talk about something else," he said.

I settled in. By now Chester knew all about my life. We discussed the people that were near and dear to me. The charities with which I had contact. My faltering real estate career. And my ongoing efforts to do good.

"Did you know the Special Olympics has a golf team?" I asked him.

"No, I don't suppose I did," he said.

"They are trying to teach the athletes leisure sports that they can participate in for a lifetime, rather than just team sports or track-and-field activities."

"That makes sense," he said.

"Locally they've got a men's golf team that's doing very well," I said. "But they haven't done anything about the women."

"Jane, I thought you hated golf," Chester said.

"Oh, I do," I told him. "But I've figured out that I don't have to actually *do* all the good that needs to be done. My friend, Teddy, is the new president of the Junior League. I talked her into including a Special Olympics women's golf team in their list of civic service options."

Chester frowned. "I thought you told me that 80 percent of the Junior League membership's main reason for participating was social chumming."

I shrugged. "That's what the interest surveys indicate," I said. "And that was me, exactly."

"But you are still hoping that they will voluntarily choose to take this on?"

"Every member has to do a certain number of hours of community work," I said. "I'm thinking that there are women who would look at this and think, 'Hey, this is great. I can get in my charity hours and play golf at the same time.'"

"But are those the kind of people who should be working with mentally handicapped golfers?" he asked.

"Maybe," I said. "What I'm thinking is that if *I* could change my priorities, perhaps other women will want to as well. I am definitely not the kind of person that you would count on to be out there trying to do good. But that might be our problem, the world's problem, all these millennia we've only expected doing good of the people we would expect it of. If we start expecting it of everyone, maybe we won't get it from everyone, but we'll get it from more people than we do now."

Chester considered my words slowly, thoughtfully.

"You don't think so?" I asked.

"Maybe," he said. "But what about the young golfers with all their hopes up? What happens if all the Junior Leaguers who thought it would be easy and find out that it's not, just quit. Won't those girls be disappointed?"

My bright and sunny optimism turned to dismay.

"I hadn't thought about that," I admitted. "That would be awful!"

Chester nodded.

"It could be a terrible thing," he agreed. "Or it could be just like you planned. Someone, given the opportunity, rises to the occasion."

"Can I risk that?" I asked.

"Can you?" he threw the question back.

"Chester, you've been doing this a lot longer than me. Tell me what you think."

He smiled like the wise old sage I believed him to be. "You can't do a bait and switch, luring people into opportunities where success or failure is totally dependant upon the charitability of their nature. You've got to lessen the chance that they drop the ball by giving them a better idea of what they are getting into."

"How would I do that?"

"Get the players from the men's team to talk to the group, perhaps," he said. "Or let the Junior Leaguers go and watch the partners interacting."

"It will seem like too much trouble to a lot of them," I said.

Chester agreed. "It will *be* too much for a lot of them," he said. "But maybe not for all of them."

"Maybe."

"You've just got to do the best you can, Jane," he told me. "And then you've got to trust that things will work out. They won't always work out the way that you'd like. But they will always work out how they are supposed to."

I left Chester a little before noon, remembering to give him his Snickers bar.

"Thank you, Jane," he said a bit more seriously than

the gift warranted. "I'm going to put this away and save it for later."

"You had better, mister," I teased threateningly. "I don't want you ruining your lunch."

As I stopped at the traffic light across from the new car dealership, I glanced at the Volkswagens for sale. Chester had said he'd buy one if he could still drive. I shook my head. Only a guy like Chester would prefer a Volkswagen over the Z3. I looked over the array of shiny colors and styles. They were kind of cute.

I double-checked my cell phone. It hadn't rung, but I made certain there were no messages either. Brynn still hadn't called. I held the cell phone in my hand thoughtfully. Two buttons to push, that's all that it required. My Brynn was always only two buttons away. I could call her again. I resisted the action and stuffed the phone back in my purse.

I worried about her. I had spent most of my life swooping in to help her. When she tottered on toddler feet, I'd held my hands behind her to catch her when she'd fall. When she was a schoolgirl in navy blue wool, I had taken charge, smoothed the way and been a constant presence. In the social world I'd chosen her clothes, her activities, even her friends.

I had done it because I loved her. Would still do it because I love her. But she'd told me the truth. Help, unrequested, is intrusion. It had taken me a long time to realize that. All she wanted from me was a chance to make her own choices. But what if her choices were bad? The question haunted me.

Behind me someone honked. The light was green. I headed back in toward town. It was only eleven, but I was actually hungry already. Probably the result of having had only a cup of yogurt on shredded wheat for breakfast.

I spotted a roadside fruit stand just off the express-way. A handpainted sign announced Peaches and my mouth watered appropriately. I made my way to the place, buying a hefty bushel before I remembered that I had no family to share them with, no dinner party to plan.

The huge basket barely fit on the floorboard of the passenger's side. I picked up a ripe, plump peach, wiped it on my slacks in lieu of washing and ate it. The fruit was so sweet and juicy, the taste so nostalgic, it was almost a melancholy enjoyment. My life was good, I decided. My life was very good.

I stopped by Hattenbacher House. I was deliberately trying to stay away. But by now I loved the old place and could hardly resist a visit, even when a phone call would do.

I turned into the driveway and pulled up to park all the way in the back. Julia Prentice, the woman Miss Heloise had hired to run the foundation, had set up an office in the three rooms of the servants' apartment attached to the garage. It was furnished with metal filing cabinets and garage-sale rummage. I worried about the woman's taste, but from what I'd seen, she did appear to be quite knowledgeable about the organization and management of a nonprofit group.

Her greeting was bright enough as I stepped across the threshold, but I was too experienced in the world of female smiles to be fooled into thinking it was totally sincere.

"What a surprise!" she said. "I wish you had called to let me know you were coming."

"I can only stay a minute," I said, hoping to reassure her.

I was aware that Julia didn't like me too much. Or perhaps she just didn't trust me completely. I don't know if she was aware that Miss Heloise had first offered her position to me. But she was aware of my part in saving the house. And she knew that Miss Heloise liked me. But from what I could tell, Miss Heloise gave everyone the benefit of the doubt.

Whatever the issue might have been, Julia was always perfectly polite and appropriately grateful for anything and everything I did to help.

"I've been calling potential antique donors," I told her. "I can't say that I've been all that successful. Most of the people I know also know Barb Jarman. It's much easier for them to refuse me than to offend her."

Julia nodded as if she understood. I was pretty sure that she didn't. "I've picked out a couple of nice pieces of my own that I thought might work well here," I told her.

"Well, of course we'd love to have them," she said, then added, "If they are truly suitable."

I refused to be insulted by the little dig. I *wanted* her to look critically at the gifts she was offered. The last thing Hattenbacher House needed was flea-market goods donated for museum write-offs.

"I've got a William & Mary lowboy that I think would work in that iris bedroom," I told her. "And a tilt top to replace the tea table in the front parlor."

"Oh, that sounds fine," she said.

"I'll try to get them delivered over here next week," I told her. "Just whenever it's convenient for you."

"Let me check," she said, opening up her Day-Timer to the following week.

I stood waiting as she casually perused her schedule. It looked to me, from half a room away and upside down, that her week was practically blank. Still, she leisurely looked through it.

"I have a luncheon scheduled on Tuesday to talk with the Master Gardeners Club about the grounds," she said finally.

"Oh, great," I said. "It would be wonderful if they would take it up as a project."

"Yes, that's what I told Miss Heloise," she informed me.

That comment was obviously meant to put me in my place, somehow. It didn't. It couldn't. It was an almost amazing discovery. When I have no ulterior motives, I am especially difficult to neutralize.

"She is such a wonderful lady," I said. "We are so lucky to have her. And we are so lucky to have you here looking out for her house and the best interests of all of us."

The woman was speechless. I could see she was looking for disingenuousness or trickery. She couldn't find any because there was none. She returned to our former subject.

"Other than Tuesday, then," she said, "I will be here to take delivery of the furniture."

"Okay, I'll call you."

"Good."

We stood together quietly, a little disconcerted, having run out of things to say. I suppose she was hoping I would leave. I was hoping she would offer to let me look around the house. I lingered. The uneasiness grew longer.

Julia finally broke the silence.

"I heard a very interesting and auspicious rumor this morning," she said.

"Oh?"

"I believe that some of the pieces Barb Jarman took from the house are going to be put up for auction."

"That's great!"

My very positive reaction was apparently appreciated. The woman was almost preening in self-congratulation.

"I've already contacted the heritage council for

funds," she told me. "When they come up for bid we can snap them right up."

I refused to allow my excitement at hearing this news to be in any way diminished by the knowledge that, in every way that was just and fair, the museum already owned all those pieces. Maybe Barbara Jarman's heart could only be soothed by cold hard cash. Maybe she would have the sense to make peace with Miss Heloise and knit the family back together.

"Julia, this is tremendous news," I agreed. "I'm sure you would have been able to find beautiful furnishings for the house. But the more original pieces we have the better."

Julia nodded. "I did get one donation this week that I'm personally very proud of."

"Who from?"

"The guy wants to remain anonymous."

"Oh yeah?"

"He contacted me wanting to make a donation," she said.

"That's wonderful."

She grabbed up her keys. "Come have a look," she said.

Together we left her office and traversed the width of the old-fashioned garden with its poppies, hydrangea bushes and gladiolus. Workmen at the back of the house were taking down shutters and scraping paint from the windowsills.

Julia led me in through the back door. The house looked too clean to be lived in. Already it had lost some of the feel of Miss Heloise's home and had developed that unmistakable aura of historical monument. In all honesty, I regretted the loss.

"We're going to have these floors redone," Julia told me. "And we're getting an estimate from an architectural conservator about restoring the kitchen to its 1888 appearance. It's really the only room that's had a lot of modern renovation."

We made our way into the dark-paneled library where the last Hattenbacher governor had retired to civilian life. His portrait now hung over this fireplace, it having been determined that the portrait of his wife had originally been displayed in the front parlor. The masculinity of the room lingered with ancient pipe smoke and snifters of rum.

Sitting in that room, in the most prominent place, below the window, was a Craftsman mission-style sofa. My jaw dropped open. Without question I was absolutely certain that it was one that I had quite recently sat upon behind the counter of the Yesteryear Emporium.

"Is this not absolutely perfect for this room?" Julia asked me, clearly delighted.

"Yes," I agreed. "It is perfect."

"This is the original upholstery, it's just been cleaned," she said. "And the donor has had it authenticated as a genuine Stickley."

"I thought it was Stickley," I said. "I'm glad that it's been proven so."

"I have to confess, I was taken aback at my own powers of persuasion," Julia admitted. "Once I saw it, I was very willing to accept it on loan. When the man just gave it to us outright, I almost wanted to argue with him."

I found myself wanting to argue with him as well. It was the most valuable antique that he owned. And he had given it away.

# 16

⟶ ⟵

I left Hattenbacher House a few moments later, still shaking my head over Scott's generous gift to the place. As I climbed into the Z3, I glanced over at the bushel of fruit on my floorboard. I'd been so hungry just an hour ago, but I'd never be able to eat all those peaches.

Loretta's safe house would be the best place to leave them, I decided. I buckled my seat belt, started up the car and drove over there. My thoughts drifted to Brynn. I checked for messages from her. Still none. I didn't have an inkling as to what I should do, but could I really do nothing?

Help, unrequested, is intrusion, I reminded myself. I was trying to make that my mantra, but I was no longer sure if I really believed it.

I left my car on the street in front of the safe house and carried the bushel basket to the front door. The smell of peaches reminded me of the hot summer days of my childhood. I remembered one afternoon eating peaches. In the little piece of shade at the side of our house where the TV antenna was set in the ground, I had munched on fruit and minded my own business.

My mom in her strapless one-piece swimsuit was lying out in the backyard trying to get a tan. She'd laid a rain umbrella at the top of her bath towel to provide shade on her face and the book she was reading. She never wanted to be bothered when she was reading. I suppose, if the truth were told, she never wanted to be bothered.

I was happily getting juice all over my cotton crop top when I saw the snake. It came slithering out of the grass, undoubtedly wanting to share the sunshine with my mother. I was afraid of critters; bugs, snakes, lizards, even frogs were not among the things that I considered as friends.

"Mom," I said nervously.

She ignored me.

"Mom," I tried again.

Still she didn't look up. The silent, black reptile was crawling right up beside her.

"Mom!" My plea was more desperate.

"Leave me alone!" she snapped.

I pointed to the grass beside her. "There's a snake."

She screamed and she jumped. I couldn't say which she did first.

Grabbing up the umbrella, she began trying to kill the snake with it. The creature was desperate to get away, but Mom wasn't about to let him go. Somehow she managed to get the point of the umbrella pierced through the width of its long body.

She held the snake up. It must have been three feet long. It was still wiggling.

"It's only a rat snake," she informed me. "Wouldn't do any harm."

It was as if my fear was a weakness she didn't share. As if she'd forgotten how she'd jumped and screamed.

She threw both snake and umbrella over the fence into the alley.

Mom never thanked me for warning her. But she did gather up her towel and her book and go inside.

I shook my head at the unexpected memory. It was strange how unexpectedly some things came to mind.

I rang the doorbell of the safe house. I waited patiently for quite a while. Nobody came. Somehow, however, I sensed that the place was not deserted. I rang again. I could feel eyes on me from the peephole.

"It's me, Jane Lofton," I said loudly through the door. "I've brought peaches."

It was a long moment before I heard the dead bolt turn. The door opened slightly, the chain still on. A familiar-looking face peered out at me suspiciously.

"What do you want?" she asked.

"Hi, I'm Jane," I said. "I bought these peaches and I can't possibly eat all of them, so I thought I would bring them to you."

The woman was hesitant.

"You're Shanekwa," I said. "I remember you from decorating the Christmas tree."

For an instant she seemed frightened that I knew her name, but as recognition dawned on her, her mouth curved into a welcoming smile.

"You're the job-talking lady who grew up in Sunnyside," she said.

I hadn't really thought of myself that way, but I supposed it was true. She closed the door to unlatch the chain. Then I was inside handing the fruit to her.

"I just wasn't thinking," I explained about the purchase. "The peaches looked so good and I bought a whole bushel before I remembered I'm living by myself now."

Shanekwa nodded, understanding. "That happens to me sometimes, too," she said. "I bought barbecue potato chips once and got them here before I remembered that I don't like them and the baby won't eat them. My man, Ellis, he'd eat a big bag of them by himself just watching a cop show."

I followed her through the house to the kitchen.

"I'm sorry I was so nervous about letting you in," she said. "I get a little scared when I'm here by myself."

"You're here all alone?"

"Yeah, everybody's at work or in school," she said. "I can't go to my job. Ellis found me there, now I can't go back."

"Oh, I'm sorry."

She shrugged. "I've got to find me another job. I was doing short-order at the lunch counter in the bus station. Ellis found me there. He found me at my apartment too. That's why we're moved back in here. It's like having a bloodhound on your trail. I can't go anyplace that man don't find me."

I didn't know what to say. Apparently nothing was required.

"You want some coffee?" she asked me. "I got some made."

"Yes, that would be very nice."

Shanekwa didn't like being alone in the house. And I had no place to be. It was a small thing, but I could be there for her, I decided.

She got a couple of cups from the cabinet and we sat down at the table. We were a little uncomfortable at first. I wouldn't say that we immediately discovered we had a lot in common. But we managed a few minutes of polite dialogue.

"I could make these peaches into some fine pies," she told me. "My mama used to say that I was the best pie baker in town. Maybe that's what I'll do this afternoon."

"I could help," I said. "I could peel."

It's surprising how close two strangers can get while working together in a kitchen. Within an hour, I learned all about Shanekwa's young son, Jarone, and the boy's vicious, abusive father. She had loved Ellis for a while, but those feelings had long ago been eclipsed by pure fear. The fact that she continued to live her life, to get out of bed every morning and get on with it every day, drew my utmost respect.

Conversation, of course, is a two-way street, and before I knew it, I was confessing my own troubles, which Shanekwa took as seriously as her own.

"Your daughter and I are the same age," she told me. "So I think I know how she feels. We're grown-up women on our own now. We don't need Mama telling us what to do."

"So you think I should keep out of it?"

"No, you can't do that either," she said. "When you love somebody and you see them messing up, you gotta speak out."

"So which is it?" I asked. "Give advice or keep my thoughts to myself."

Shanekwa laughed. "I think you've got to do both."

"Oh, that ought to be easy," I said sarcastically.

"I don't think anything about being a parent is easy," she said. "What you got to find is a balance. You've got wisdom that ought to be shared, but you can't be shoveling it at her night and day. You've got to trust her to find her own way in the world."

"I want to trust her," I said. "Why is it so scary?"

"Because plenty of things can go wrong," Shanekwa answered. "And believe me, I know what I'm talking about."

"Sometimes we can make a wrong turn," I said.

Sighing heavily, she shook her head. "I sure did," she admitted. "And I should have known better. Mama warned me. She told me to stay away from Ellis. She said he had a mean streak. She said if he ever raised his hand to me, I should run like hell and never look back."

"That's just what you've done," I said.

"Finally!" she said. "The first time Ellis slapped me, I knew he was just like my mama told me. Oh, he said he was sorry. He said it wouldn't happen again. I knew he was lying. I stayed with him though, taking it, for years before I got smart enough to do just like Mama'd told me."

"But you have done it," I said. "And if your mama knows, I'd bet she is very proud."

Shanekwa smiled at me. A big, broad smile that belied all the sorrow that had been hard earned with this wisdom.

She rolled out enough pie dough to cover four and twenty blackbirds.

"Do you know what the secret is to a great peach pie?" she asked me.

"What?"

She laughed, teasing. "There is no secret at all to peach pie. Everybody makes a good one," she said.

Ten hours later, dressed in my pink cotton cow-jumped-over-the-moon nightshirt, watching late-night reruns of "Big Cats" on *Animal Planet*, I took my first bite of her pie and knew the woman was a liar. Nobody, anywhere, in the whole wide world, had ever made such a pie. For a moment I couldn't quite believe it. The crust was so delicate and light it almost dissolved in my mouth. The peaches were sweet and still firm, the filling was a complement to them, not just a syrup for them. It was, in fact, a perfectly unforgettable pie.

I sighed with pleasure, made rapturous noises and licked my lips. It was unbelievable. I cut my bites in half and then quarters, trying to savor each little bit.

"Shanekwa," I announced to the empty room, "you are a creative genius."

It was really amazing when I thought about it. Here was this young woman, who'd lived a very difficult and often unhappy life. She hadn't finished high school. She was raising a child alone. And she had this terrible criminal following her around trying to mess up everything that ever went right.

But none of that made the slightest difference in the taste of her pie. She had a special knack, a God-given talent or she'd perfected a skill. Whatever the origin, the result was exceptional.

I scraped the last of pie up with my fork, tempted to lick the plate. This was, without doubt, the best pie I'd eaten anywhere, the best dessert I'd eaten anywhere.

"They'd charge fifteen dollars a slice for it at Le Parapluie," I said aloud.

My own words couldn't have been more portentous if they had been spoken by the Oracle of Delphi. Like a flash I was out of bed.

I glanced at the clock—it was a quarter to eleven.

"They should still be there," I said to myself. "If you hurry, they'll still be there."

I could not explain then, nor can I now, the urgency that I felt. I raced to the closet and grabbed up the first thing I saw, a pair of Brynn's old blue jeans that were sitting on the top of a pile of clothes destined for the Salvation Army Thrift Store. I pulled them on over the tail of my nightshirt and stepped into a pair of slides.

In the kitchen I covered the pie with aluminum foil, and headed out the door. At the last second I grabbed a jacket. It wasn't cold enough to actually need it, but at least it would disguise the fact that I was braless and wearing my pj's.

I carefully set the pie on the floorboard of the Z3 before roaring out into the street. At the traffic light at the cross-street, I got a quick glimpse of myself in the rearview mirror. My hair was wild.

The light turned green and I turned left while digging through my purse. I came up with a scrunchy and used the next intersection to pull my hair back into a ponytail.

Two minutes later I was pounding on the metal door at the back of Le Parapluie. The front of the restaurant was already locked up and dark. But, by the number of cars still parked behind the building, I was pretty sure there were still employees inside.

A huge man, who looked more like a bouncer than a restaurant employee, answered my knock.

"Sorry, lady, we're closed."

"Is Frederic still here?" I asked him.

He looked me over, a bit surprised.

"Yeah, sure…ah…come on in."

He held the door open and I stepped inside.

Activity was everywhere. A few surreptitious glances were cast in my direction. But basically these guys, and from what I could see it was all guys, were trying to get the place cleaned up and go home.

"Frederic's in the front. I'll get him for you," the big man told me. "Just stay here and…and don't let any-one run into you."

I decided that the phrasing "Don't let anyone run into you" was the more polite version of *Stay out of the way!* I followed that directive.

The place gleamed with stainless steel, the floors were spotless and the residual odors of the best food in town were masked with the scent of cleaning products. It was noisy. The dishwasher was operating, as was the trash compactor. The guys had to holler at each other over the din.

Standing just inside the doorway, wearing my cow-jumped-over-the-moon nightshirt and holding my alu-minum foil–covered pie tin, I felt like an idiot. This cer-tainly could have waited until tomorrow. But some-how, it couldn't have.

A minute later Frederic came around the corner. The instant he spotted me, his expression darkened with concern.

"My God, Jane," he yelled out. "Are you all right? Have you been in an accident?"

I realized I must look worse than I thought. Or perhaps, he, like most of the world, had simply never seen me in designer-free duds, ponytailed and without makeup.

"I've brought a pie I want you to sample," I said.

"What?"

I tried again, this time louder. "I've brought you a pie!"

The dishwasher finished its cycle just before the last word, which came out excessively loud in the contrasting silence. Several of the fellows turned to look. I ignored them.

"Taste this," I said simply, pulling back the foil that covered the pie.

He looked momentarily puzzled and then amused. "Jane, please don't tell me you've taken up baking?"

"Not likely," I answered. "Just taste it."

Frederic gave me a rather long-suffering look, but pulled a fork from a nearby drawer and used it to cut off a small sliver of the peach pie. He put it in his mouth with all the hopeful enthusiasm that one might have displayed for taking poison.

As soon as the pie hit his palate, he closed his eyes and moaned. First it was in pleasure and then immediately followed by dismay.

"Oh damn," he complained. "Did you get this at Newman's? Is this something his new pastry chef has come up with?"

"I never go to Newman's," I assured him. "They overcook the vegetables."

"So who does this baker work for?"

"The woman who made this pie doesn't have a job," I told him. "And she could sure use one."

"She's not a professional chef?"

"She's been working as a cook," I told him, deciding it might be better not to mention either the term *short-order* or the phrase *lunch counter at the bus station*.

"So what happened?" he asked. "Anyone with this much talent wouldn't be let go unless she was very undependable, or hit the chef over the head with something."

"Oh, she wasn't fired. She left on her own."

"Did she not like the place? Or was she looking for more money?"

"Neither." I hesitated and then decided that I had to trust Frederic with the truth. "Her ex-boyfriend is abusive. If he finds her at work he causes trouble for her."

Frederic raised a speculative eyebrow. He took another bite of the peach pie, savoring it.

"Well, Jane," he said, "I think this woman's troubles are over."

My mouth actually dropped open. I couldn't imagine that it would be this easy.

"Mario!" Frederic called out.

The huge man who'd let me in appeared from an inner office.

"You need something?" he asked Frederic.

"Taste this pie," Frederic said.

The big man looked at Frederic, then me. With a shrug, he enthusiastically cut himself a more generous slice than his boss's. He held it in his hand and took a bite out of the narrow end.

"This is really good," Mario announced with his mouth still full.

"The woman who baked this is coming to work for us tomorrow," Frederic said.

"That's great!" The big man was nodding.

"Her name's…" He turned to look at me.

"Shanekwa," I answered. "I…I don't know her last name."

"Her name's Shanekwa," he said to Mario. "We'll find out her last name tomorrow. She has a problem with a jerk that follows her around and causes her to lose jobs. I don't want her to lose this one."

The big man nodded as he swallowed a bite and was poised to take another one. "Don't worry," he told both of us. "I'll keep an eye out for her."

"Thank you," I said to him. "And thank you, Frederic. I promise to keep coming here for the rest of my life, and I'll always order dessert."

"I'm counting on that," he told me.

When I got back to my car, I called Loretta on my mobile. She was ecstatic with the news.

"This will be great for her," Loretta said. "She's a really good worker and they've liked her every place she's worked."

"She'll be back in the kitchen," I said. "So it won't be like the bus station where anybody might spot her."

Loretta laughed. "I sincerely doubt that Ellis and his cronies frequent that side of town."

"I know she needs a place to live," I told her. "I've got small guest quarters over my garage that are empty. It's not much, just three rooms, but it has a separate entrance and it's somewhere for her and her son to stay until she gets on her feet."

"The place she gave up was tiny," Loretta said. "And she can get everything she owns in a duffel bag and a couple of boxes."

"We can get some secondhand furnishings," I said. "We can fix it up really nice."

"Jane, you are a wonder," Loretta said. "I can hardly believe that you managed this."

"Believe me, it was easy," I assured her. "As soon as Frederic tasted that pie, he would have crawled over hot coals to get her to come to work for him."

"You have to tell her yourself," Loretta insisted.

Shanekwa was upstairs. I stayed on the line while someone went up to get her.

"Hi!" She greeted me like I was a friend. "Did you talk to Brynn? What did she say?"

"I got her voice mail," I answered. "I'm going to try again tomorrow. But that's not what I'm calling about."

I made it brief, but I covered everything.

She was a little bit stunned at the news. "They just want me to make pies?" she asked.

"I think you'll have to work that out with Frederic," I said. "But he hired you just on the basis of that peach pie."

There was silence on the other end of the line. I began telling her about the restaurant.

"It is absolutely my favorite. Some people say Newman's is the best in town, but I've always liked Le Parapluie best."

I talked about Frederic and working at the citywide Thanksgiving dinner.

"He's a fair, generous man who doesn't suffer from any of that excessive ego chefs are famous for. He says you've got talent and he appreciates that."

I explained about the little guest quarters over my garage.

"It's small, but it's really all brand new. I've never even furnished it, the space has just been used for storage."

When I ran out of things to say, I began to realize that she was just too quiet on the other end.

"Shanekwa, is something wrong?"

She made some kind of noise. Some kind of unexpected noise. "Are you crying?" I realized it just before I said it.

I was astounded and appalled. Was this another one of my doing-good attempts that wasn't good at all? Was my unwanted help just another intrusion.

"Shanekwa, I'm sorry. Don't cry. You don't have to take this job if you don't want it."

Her reply was a hiccup.

"It's not the kind of work you've done before, if you don't want to do it, then you shouldn't."

She couldn't speak.

"I know it's a different part of town than you're familiar with, but I think you'd like it. I'm sure we could get a great preschool situation for your son. Close to both your home and your job."

Still she said nothing.

"Or if the guest quarters are too small for you and your little boy, you can stay in the house with me," I said. "I thought that after being in the safe house, you'd want the privacy of your own place."

"You…you…" she managed to choke out.

"What?"

"You are so…so nice to me."

I answered without thinking. "Shanekwa, you were nice to me."

"I gave you a pie," she said. Her words brought on a fresh flood of tears.

"It was a wonderful pie," I told her when she regained some composure. "And you gave me some great advice about my daughter."

"That was nothing."

"It was something to me," I said. "Anyway, I didn't talk to Frederic to pay you back. I talked to him because your mama used to say you were the best pie baker in town. You deserve a chance to prove it."

# 17

I was so excited, so wound up after I got off the phone
I just couldn't see myself going home and getting into
bed. I thought about trying to call Brynn once more, but
it was one-thirty in the morning in Boston. If she wasn't
in bed, I didn't want to know about it.

The back parking lot was clearing out and I decided I
couldn't just sit there. I began driving aimlessly up and
down the streets. I felt the same sense of triumph, flush
of success, that I used to feel when closing on a big
money deal.

And just like on those days, I sort of naturally directed my car to the Yesteryear Emporium. Of course,
the store would be closed and of course I would drive
right by. But it didn't exactly happen that way.

Certainly the building was dark, but right near the
front door, in the area where Scott had his desk, a light
was burning. I pulled into one of the many empty parking places on the street. It was probably just a security
light, I told myself. I'd just peek in and see if he was
there and if he was, I'd see whether he looked really
busy or not.

When I got to the window, I realized that peeking in
wasn't going to be the casual glance that I intended.
He'd put up a paneled barrier between himself and the
street that required someone to be at least seven feet tall
to look in. There didn't seem to be any movement on

the other side of the panel, but somehow that wasn't enough to discourage me.

I looked around for something to stand on. There was nothing readily available. Then I examined the brick on the front of the building. The gaps in the mortar were pretty deep, especially on the corner. As a kid, I'd climbed up the sides of buildings using those gaps. I slipped out of my slides and carefully set my right foot about four bricks up and got handholds a little higher. I pulled myself up, putting my left foot into the brick as well, and gazed over the top of the obstruction.

Scott Robbins was sitting motionless staring at his ancient Underwood typewriter. He was a nice-looking guy. Not in the way that most of the men I knew were attractive. He was slightly unkempt and definitely unfashionable. But I found him attractive despite that.

He glanced up and caught sight of me and actually jumped. His unexpected move startled me and I almost lost my footing, but managed to keep my place.

Scott was chuckling then and shaking his head.

"What are you doing?" he asked me, the sound muffled through the window.

"I'm the human fly," I called back.

I puffed up my cheeks and pressed my face against the glass, distorting it. Eyes crossed. Nose squashed.

He was still shaking his head as he walked around the long counter toward the building's entrance. His limp was more pronounced than usual and he was leaning heavily on his cane.

I hopped down from my perch, retrieved my shoes and met him at the front door.

"You are an absolutely crazy person," he said.

"Yeah, and your point is...?"

"Come inside before my neighbors start calling the police," he said.

I glanced up and down the deserted street. "You have neighbors?"

He shrugged. "There's a flophouse in the next block. And I think there might be a guy sleeping in a box in the alley."

I nodded. "Well, at least it's good to know you're not alone in this part of town."

It was curious why he didn't ask me what I was doing there. Which was fortunate, because I hadn't thought of any plausible excuse. He led me around the counter to his little office area, now furnished with a 1970s vintage Early American sofa upholstered in orange flowers.

"Lovely," I said facetiously.

"If you tell me that's a valuable antique, I'm hanging up my gloves."

"I'm sure it has sentimental value," I told him.

"Not much," he said. "I found a chair that I wanted, and part of the price of it was taking this thing with me."

"At least it's found a home," I said, making myself comfortable on it.

"Yeah, and it kind of fits me, don't you think?" he said. "We're both worn, quirky and unfashionable."

He was grinning at me, daring me to agree. He seated himself in his typing chair, hanging his cane upon the armrest.

"Well, I do have to admit that giving away a museum-quality antique is pretty quirky," I told him. "You know the foundation would have been happy to let you loan it to them. That's what people do. They loan their best to museums."

"I didn't want to loan it to them," he said. "I wanted Hattenbacher House to have it."

"It's not the way it's done, Scott," I explained. "Rich people rarely give their art or antiques to museums. Either the museum buys it from them, or they loan it. Loaning is actually fabulous for the owner. They can take it back or sell it anytime. They don't have to be responsible for damage or security and they get a nice tax deduction for charity."

"Believe me," he said, "I don't need a tax deduction. I wanted to give it to them."

"Why?"

"Why what?" he asked me. "I know what kind of sacrifice you made to keep that house from becoming condos. Why did you throw away all the money?"

"The money was nothing compared to the real value of that place," I answered. "I couldn't have lived with myself if I had profited from its destruction."

"That's the same kind of motivation that got me to give away that sofa," Scott said. "That, and I was hoping to really impress you."

The last was surely a joke, I thought. When I looked at him, however, I couldn't really tell if he was being charming or simply sincere.

"Did it impress you?" he asked.

"Well…well, yes…of course," I stammered.

"Mission accomplished."

He was looking at me in a very strange way. It wasn't exactly sexual, but the fact that sex even came to my mind was pretty amazing. Scott just kept staring, as if he couldn't take his eyes off me. It was in some way flattering, but it was also a little disconcerting. Uncomfortable, off balance, I said the first thing that came into my head.

"So, what's the deal with your leg?"

He seemed momentarily startled, but regained his composure quickly.

"It has its good days and bad," he said. "This is one of the latter."

"How did you get hurt?"

"I damaged the nerves," he said vaguely. "And I've got some scar tissue from that."

He didn't actually answer my question, but I wasn't crass enough to press further. I observed his desk. It was messy, books and reports were spread everywhere. A piece of paper was still in the Underwood, but I could see that he'd already typed out *Sincerely yours*.

I gestured toward it. "Luckily, I caught you just as you were finishing up."

"Finally," he admitted. "I've been at it all day."

He turned in his chair, gathered up several pages and removed the paper from the typewriter, adding it to the bottom of the stack. Turning back to me, he held it out in my direction.

"Have a look," he said.

I did, though I did not read it word for word. It was well written, intellectual, thought-provoking. It was twelve pages of graphs, statistics and explanation. I managed to get through the first couple of paragraphs. "What is this?" I asked him.

"It's about the dangers of free trade," he said. "Everyone knows it opens up markets and creates jobs in the third world. But without constraints, corporations can go country shopping for the lowest wage earners and the least restrictive environmental regulations."

I nodded slowly. *Everyone* might know about free trade, but I didn't. I'd spent the last couple of decades lunching and shopping. Well, not entirely. But beyond my little world, I really hadn't ventured very far. To me the economy was stock prices, real estate values and prime lending rates. He'd written about third world labor practices and greenhouse gases.

My own ignorance was an embarrassment to me. I'd been the smartest girl in Sunnyside Junior High. I'd gotten a scholarship to a prestigious prep school. And had made the dean's list at State. I had been a very bright young woman. I'd parlayed that promise into…into a very false start.

There was no address heading and the salutation was blank.

"Who is this letter for? It's a little long for the newspaper," I pointed out.

"The *Courier* would never print something like this," he said. "As far as they are concerned, if it didn't happen in Mervin County, it just didn't happen."

"Are you suggesting that our local newspaper suffers from provincialism?" I asked, feigning shock.

"Of course not," he replied. "International events are always covered in great detail if they involve some kind of ball or stick."

"Who are you going to send this to?"

He shrugged and shook his head. "I honestly don't know," he admitted. "I'd like to send it to every world leader, U.S. senator and press organization. I can't do that, so…so I'll think of someone. I always do."

I continued to look through the carefully worded, exhaustingly thorough missive.

"It's pretty impressive," I told him honestly. "You do this kind of thing all the time, don't you?"

He nodded soberly.

"When did you start?"

"This one? About two days ago."

"No, when did you start this letter-writing avocation."

"Oh, I don't know, years ago, I guess."

His answer was deliberately casual. He was not being completely honest, I was certain of it.

"On what particular occasion years ago?" I asked with great specificity.

He laughed then.

"You're not particularly good at dissembling," I informed him.

Scott apparently knew that already. He raised his hands, conceding without argument.

"You want a beer?" he asked. "Soda? I could probably come up with a glass of wine."

"No, thank you."

"Water?"

"When did you start writing letters?" I asked again.

He sighed with resignation, giving up the effort to ignore the question.

"When I was in the hospital," he said. "I got shot up in Vietnam. That's what's wrong with my leg. I took some shrapnel, then I developed a blood clot. I had five surgeries, including two skin grafts."

"Oh no," I said. "I thought maybe you'd been in some kind of accident, but I never thought that."

"Actually, my recovery is considered a medical success," he said. "I'm walking around, living a normal life. Really lucky."

"Thank God."

"Yeah," he agreed. "I was in the hospital for several months. I didn't have any family to visit me. No girlfriend. All in all, it was pretty boring. I didn't have much to do except read. And most of what they had to read was the newspaper."

His tone was so very matter-of-fact, it was almost chilling in the fear and loneliness that it didn't mention.

"What was most interesting to me, naturally, was the war," he said. "I was a kid really, barely nineteen. I didn't know very much about anything, but I'd just spent eight months in the middle of that war. I knew what was happening there."

Vietnam had hardly made a blip on my personal radar screen. There was certainly plenty of talk about it at school, but it had never touched me personally. David had had some kind of deferment.

"I realized they were getting a lot of things wrong," Scott continued. "At first I thought it was just the *Stars and Stripes*, but then I started reading other papers, national newspapers, and I was disappointed in them, too. It was as if they were missing things, important things, that were obvious to me."

He laughed and shook his head. "You know where I come from, Janey," he said. "I'd never even imagined that a newspaper might be wrong about something. I started watching the TV news. They weren't doing any better. I didn't blame them or believe there was any kind of conspiracy. I just thought they weren't seeing things from my perspective."

"And you wanted to help them," I said.

"Yeah," he said. "One morning I was railing about an article in the *L.A. Times* and one of the other guys on the ward told me to let the guy know what an idiot he was."

"So you did."

"I was far more polite than that," he assured me. "But I did get myself a pen and some paper and quickly wrote the guy a letter. I didn't really explain things very much. I expected him to call me. I stuck close to the phone for three whole days. I thought I'd be able to tell him directly why he was getting it wrong. I was so innocent of the way things worked. I didn't know that papers don't respond to letters, they print them."

"They printed your letter."

He rolled his eyes. "I'd just whipped it off. It was full of bad grammar and misspellings. I wrote it just like I would have said it. I think I even used the phrase *sock it to me*."

"Oh no," I moaned sympathetically.

"I didn't give any reasons for what I thought," he

said. "I didn't list any of the facts that backed up my opinion. I sounded bigheaded, bullshitting and brain dead."

I giggled. I couldn't help myself.

"Immediately," he said, "I wrote another letter, a better letter. That one never got printed, of course. It's one of life's truths that if you write something that's truly insightful and accurate, it never gets published. But whenever you make errors, factual or clerical, they always get into print."

His exasperation was leavened with humor.

"Anyway, that's my story," Scott explained. "The war was nothing like I thought it would be. It was also nothing like what I saw on TV and read in the newspapers. I thought people deserved to know the truth. I began writing letters that, I think, tell the truth. And I've been doing it ever since."

"These letters must take a lot of your time," I said. "How often do you write them?"

"It depends on what's happening, what I'm thinking about and how difficult the subject happens to be," he answered. "Usually I'll write a couple of things a week, but there have been times when I've written about three different topics in one day."

I was astounded. "That's like a full-time job."

"Why do you think I'm up writing at midnight? The research alone can sometimes take weeks."

I was trying hard to understand but I didn't.

"You don't get paid for this, right?"

"Not everything that's important to do is a paid position," he said.

"I'm not arguing that," I assured him. "But you could do this same sort of thing and get paid for it. "Why don't you?" I asked.

"There's not a lot of demand for professional letter

writers," he said with a grin. "Though I admit I haven't checked for it on GettaJob.com."

I ignored his teasing. "You would be doing basically this same kind of work if you were a journalist."

"I thought about that," he admitted. "In fact, that was one of my original high-school ambitions. I dreamed of being a politician or a journalist." He raised his eyebrows expressively. "We can only thank God that all our dreams don't come true."

"It's not too late," I said. "You could still do it."

"I no longer want to do it," he said. "Anytime you get paid for an opinion, the value of that opinion has to be called into question."

"What do you mean?"

"All the news organizations are corporations," he said. "Even if journalists are supposed to be independent, corporate structure is not. Newsrooms assign stories. Editorial boards take positions. And all writers have editors. The only way to be totally free to speak your own mind is to do it of your own volition, without compensation."

I had never considered that, but what Scott said made sense.

"And then," he added, "there's that weird human thing."

"What weird human thing?"

"If it was my job, then it would be a job. I'd be writing because I have to not because I want to. It would never be the same."

There was some truth to that, I supposed.

"Besides," he said, "I already have a job. I own my own business." He spread his arms to indicate his surroundings. I found that the least believable of all his excuses.

"I think I've mentioned this before, Scott, but in case

you've forgotten, read my lips, *you don't know anything about antiques*," I said.

He laughed. "I guess it's more like the news business than I thought."

"What do you mean?"

"Complete ignorance is no deterrent to maintaining a long-term enterprise," he joked.

I enjoyed his humor, but was completely serious about his store. "I can't imagine how anyone can operate a business for more than half his life and still not know anything about it," I said.

"It's a struggle," he admitted, tongue-in-cheek. "But somehow I've managed."

"I'd think some of the basic knowledge would have rubbed off from your father."

He shook his head. "I didn't want anything to do with my father's avocation," he said. "My mother didn't want me involved either. She made sure I had plenty of other activities to be doing when Dad needed me."

"She had something against antiques."

"She hated junk," he said. "She still does. I think if she hadn't been afraid of jail, she would have burned this building down rather than see me working in it. She's remarried, lives in Waco with her new husband. Their house is as sparse and clean as an operating room."

"All right," I said. "She hated the business, but you must not have or you wouldn't still be in it. Yet you've virtually tried to let the place run itself."

He shrugged. "I admit that I've not been as interested or involved as I should have been," he said. "I'm just not that intrigued by old furniture and dishes."

"Antiques are like tangible chunks of history," I told him. "When we touch them, it's like we're touching the past."

He smiled. "You humble me, Janey," he said.

"I'd rather inspire you," I told him. "If you had half the passion for this store that you have for these letters, this could be a magical place."

Scott's eyes widened, "Magical," he repeated. "I like that."

"Well, it's true," I told him. "There is incredible stuff in here that is pretty much buried beneath the junk. If it was taken care of and presented attractively, it could go flying out these doors at top dollar."

"I'm sure you're right," he said. "I wish you'd known my father. You two would have had a lot in common. He was interested in everything. There was nothing so lowly that he didn't appreciate its potential."

"But you don't," I said.

Scott shook his head. "I guess I've inherited my mother's disdain for the stuff."

"Your mother would have burned the place down," I pointed out. "You've spent twenty-five years running the place."

"It's my legacy," he said.

I had the strange feeling that he was hiding something. But I couldn't imagine what it might be and decided that it was just late and I had a suspicious nature.

"So how do you keep up your inventory," I asked him.

"I do my best," he assured me. "Lots of people knew my father. I still have people contact me wanting to make a deal to buy everything left in an estate. Almost always there is at least some real quality piece that makes it worth my while. It's easier for the family. And for me, if it goes up for bid it will cost more. Of course, I go to all the big sales and auctions, like all the other dealers."

"If you don't know antiques, how do you know what to buy or how much to pay for them?"

"I suppose I don't, really," he said. "That's probably why I don't do as well there. Basically, I think you could boil down my entire business strategy to—Scott tries to get things that look presentable, as cheap as possible, and sell them for a bit more."

"From what I've seen," I told him, "that system isn't working all that well. I don't know how you've managed to make a profit."

"Oh, the business doesn't make a profit," he said. "On good years, I come out even."

"How do you live?"

"Cheaply," he answered with a chuckle. "I own the building outright, and the taxes in this area aren't very high. I make about enough money in the store to keep the lights on. And I get a small disability pension that I stretch to cover everything else."

I shook my head. "That's ridiculous, you know," I told him. "This is the best antique store in the city. You should be making money. I'm not saying you'd get rich, but with halfway decent management, you should be able to make a comfortable living."

"I know you're right," he said. "Dad always did fairly well—and that's when this merchandise was politely called secondhand. I've always been so distracted with my writing, I've just never been able to work up enough interest in the store to really do it right."

"Then why don't you sell out?" I asked him. "Let someone who would really love this business have it."

"I...I can't do that," he said. His words were hesitant but certain. "My dad left me this business. He'd want me to keep it."

That sounded foolish to me, but I didn't say so.

"What about hiring a manager," I said. "Someone who would know something about the value of the inventory that you have, and who would be smarter about what new pieces to buy."

"I can't afford to hire anyone," he said.

"Get someone to work on commission," I told him. "You wouldn't have to pay a salary, just a portion of whatever was sold."

"Where could I find someone who has the knowledge that I'd need and would still be willing to work for just commission?"

It was the question that I'd been waiting for. I smiled at him broadly.

"I'll do it," I told him.

"What?"

"Scott," I said, "this is my favorite store in the whole world. When things are going well for me, when I'm feeling good about myself, I always gravitate to this place. I could run it for you. Just getting it organized and getting everything priced right would be a labor of love."

"You're not serious?"

"I am serious." I tried another tack. If common sense wouldn't win him over, I was certain that sympathy would. "Scott, I lost my real estate job. It would really be a great new start for me, if you'd just give me a chance."

Finally he had to agree. In the face of such critical logic and abject begging, what else could the man do?

Taking me on as the manager of the store was a brilliant idea for both of us. It gave me an opportunity to see if I could actually make a go of working with something that I really loved. And it gave Scott a lot more time to devote to his unusual pursuit.

I was so excited about getting started that it was all I could do to remain on the sofa and not start digging through the shop in the middle of the night.

I convinced him to show me his account books. As I

expected, they were a disaster. He'd continued the record keeping in the same way his father had done it. I told him he was lucky he *hadn't* been making money. His books would have instigated a nervous breakdown in every accountant in the city.

We talked late into the night, drifting from the business to the personal and back to the business once more. We found it so easy to talk to each other. I knew very little about the things that interested him, and he knew nothing about what was important to me. Yet, it was almost as if our differences melded together.

He listened to my stories of the country club with all the rapt attention of an anthropologist learning about the habits of a curious and distant tribe.

I found his descriptions of all the angry and disparate political factions in Europe sounded very much like a poorly planned civic-appreciation dinner I had once attended, where nonmembers had been accidently invited to the club.

It was very late when I finally decided to go home, promising to return for my first day of work in a few short hours.

"Come in to work when you want to and stay as long as you want to," he said. "I think that's what working on commission is supposed to mean. I won't expect you here eight hours a day."

I secretly hoped that he wouldn't get impatient if I worked ten.

He insisted on walking me to the car. It felt nice, sort of sweet, to be out in the warm breeze of a spring night with an interesting, attractive man. Scott put his hand on the car's door handle and then hesitated.

"Janey," he said, "I've got to ask you something."

"What?"

"The other day when you were here you had on those red shoes, remember?"

"Of course."

"You explained that you wore those red shoes to make yourself feel powerful, confident."

"Yes," I said. "I explained that to you."

"Okay," Scott said. "What I want to know is—what is this pajama top with the little cows and moons supposed to do?"

# 18

I hardly slept all night, I was so excited and happy and hopeful. I couldn't believe that I was going to have a new job. I hurried from my bed earlier than usual, pumped up, eager, almost giddy in anticipation.

I took a long hot shower. Letting the water wash over me felt like such decadent luxury. I was thrilled by my new friendship with Scott. Maybe I was a little embarrassed about being with him at the store all that time without remembering how I looked, but I was honestly sort of proud. There had been a time in my life when, if my clothes weren't perfect, I would have gone home. He'd compared the red shoes to the cow-jumped-over-the-moon pj's. That fellow needed to get out more. I started laughing, really laughing, leaning against the wall of the shower, laughing. It was a good thing I lived alone. If David were still here, he would think I'd lost my mind. Inexplicably, that sent me off on another giggling fit.

Clean and revived, I chose clothing that I thought would be appropriate. I decided that, ultimately, I wanted to dress well for retail, to give the store a sense of style and elegance that could command higher prices. But until I had the place in order, jeans and a T-shirt were much more appropriate attire. Of course, I rolled the sleeves up and tied a coordinating scarf around my neck, in case I actually did encounter some customers.

I was trying to drag my hair into a reasonable facsimile of a *do* when the phone rang.

"Hello."

It was Loretta. Shanekwa was just getting her son onto the day-care bus, and then she and Loretta would be going over to Le Parapluie a little later.

"I had hoped to be here after her meeting with Frederic," I said. "To show her the guest quarters, help her get settled. I thought we could go shopping for furniture and curtains and...well...everything. But I just got a new job and I'm anxious to get started this morning. Can I leave the key somewhere and you two can let yourselves in?"

Loretta eagerly agreed to that.

"This actually works out better," she told me. "In fact, I was calling you to suggest that you make yourself scarce for the next couple of days."

"Really? Why?"

"It's very easy to be dependent on other people," Loretta said. "Much easier than fending for yourself. If Shanekwa is going to make it out in the world without Ellis, she'll have to do it on her own. You've done a lot for her. Now it's important to step back and let her do things for herself."

That was valuable advice, I thought.

I agreed to leave the key for the guest quarters under the doormat by the garage-stairs entrance. And I promised Loretta that I would not be too available for the next week or so, and that I would give Shanekwa at least two days before I offered to do anything else for her. That seemed like a worthwhile pledge to make.

Before leaving the house I went into the kitchen, poured myself a last cup of coffee and made a phone call.

"Buddy Feinstein's office," a cheery little voice answered.

"Good morning, Sissy," I said, greeting Buddy's young wife. "This is Jane Lofton. How is the baby?"

We chatted pleasantly for a few moments before she put me through to her husband. As always, his obvious delight in hearing from me was tempered by knowing that I must have a reason to call.

"It's Brynn," I told him. "She's going to spend the summer in Europe. She won't say who she's going with. I suspect it might be her therapist."

Buddy listened quietly as I brought him up to speed on all that had happened: Brynn's insistence that her life was none of my business, David's unwillingness to get involved, and my own ambivalence about how to stop her from making what I feared was a big mistake.

"What do you think?" I asked him finally.

"I don't know what to think," he said. "The whole thing just doesn't seem credible to me."

"What do you mean?"

"Taking a patient, any patient, for a personal vacation with you is way off the scale of reasonable action," he said. "If the patient is nineteen and there are hints of an intimate relationship, that is unethical, and completely inappropriate on his part. He has the responsibility to keep the relationship therapeutic. If she accompanies him to Italy for any other reason than to check her into a clinic, and that is questionable, it could cost him his license. "

"Brynn's not going to be his patient anymore," I told him. "I think she's planning to stop therapy at the end of this semester."

"That doesn't make any difference," Buddy said. "Most states have a waiting period of at least six months before doctor and patient are ethically allowed to have any type of personal relationship. Did you say this guy came highly recommended?"

"Yes, he's apparently very well known and has a fabulous reputation."

"Then he is sure to know the consequences of something like this," Buddy said. "It's hard to imagine that the man would risk his career."

"You mean, he'd be either completely crazy or madly in love," I said. "It could be one of those," Buddy agreed. "Or…"

"Or what?"

"Or maybe it isn't happening," he said.

"You think she's making it up?"

"She never actually admitted that she was going with him, did she?" he pointed out. "You accused her and she simply refused to deny it."

"You think I jumped to the wrong conclusion?"

"I think so," Buddy told me. "Terrible, unethical things do sometimes happen in therapy. However, this just doesn't quite have a ring of truth."

"Why would she let me believe something like this?" I asked him.

"Well," he said, "there are a number of reasons, bad and not so bad."

I swallowed bravely. "Give me the bad first," I said.

"The worst case is that she doesn't know that it's made up. In a transference way, Brynn might sexualize the relationship with her therapist, especially given the recent entry into her life of her father's new family."

"But wouldn't Dr. Reiser see what is happening?" I asked.

"He would as soon as she lets him," Buddy said. "But she may be attempting to sabotage her therapy and force the doctor to reject her the way she thinks everyone else has."

"That sounds very serious," I said.

"Yes, if that's the case, she is really troubled, and is dealing with the attachment, anguish-ridden, borderline personality disorder that attempts to cling and drive people away at the same time, *I hate you, don't leave me!* This type person exists in chaos and lies, a very painful style of life."

"Oh my God," I moaned into the telephone.

"But that's the worst case, Jane," Buddy hurried to insist. "There are other things much more likely."

"Such as?"

"Such as, she made up the story to get her parents' attention at a time when they seem to finally be a little more focused on their own lives," he said. "In that case, she knows exactly what she is doing. She's a smart young woman pulling your chain and enjoying having you react as you always do."

"How do I always react?"

"You tell me."

"I get in there and change things to what they ought to be."

"But this time you won't be able to," Buddy said. "She's nineteen now. This time you are going to have to let her make her own decision."

"What if she screws up?"

"Then she screws up," Buddy said. "We all do now and again."

I took a deep breath. I felt as if an elephant was lying on my chest.

"Give it up, Jane," Buddy said. "The days of controlling Brynn's life are over. Now you have to love her and support her in whatever decision she makes."

When I arrived on the first day of my new job, Scott, who already had the place open, greeted me at the door, looking neater and better dressed than I'd ever remembered. Perhaps I had simply never seen him early in the morning.

"I was afraid that in the clear light of dawn you might have reconsidered taking on the job," he said.

"Oh no," I assured him. "This is something I'm really excited about."

"Then let me give you a tour of the place."

As he showed me around, it was clear that I knew the store nearly as well as he did. I certainly knew the inventory better—at least the top layer of it. There was so much. And it was piled so deep, neither of us had any clear inkling of what might be there.

I was determined to see that change.

It was past lunchtime before we decided on a break. He walked to the deli three blocks down and brought back hot pastrami sandwiches with chips and giant dill pickles.

I rolled my eyes at the fabulously tasty but high-fat lunch.

"I admire a man who watches his cholesterol," I teased.

He nodded. "You forgot to put that in the employment contract," he said. "Rabbit food only. That's a tough go for us meat-and-potato guys, but I'm a man who is ready to make concessions."

"Concessions? Really?"

"Yep, popcorn, hot dogs, Junior Mints. Whatever kind of concessions you want."

It was like that with him, stupid jokes and wordplay. We brought out the silliness in each other. Of course, neither of us was truly all puns and games, but I did really enjoy myself with him, even when we were serious. For all the disinterest he claimed in antiques, he listened intently when I talked about them. And my total lack of knowledge about what was going on in the world didn't preclude my being fascinated by the subjects he chose to write about.

As the days passed, I became a fixture at the Yesteryear Emporium. I worked long hours and often sat on that awful orange flowered sofa talking with Scott late into the night.

I got acquainted with all the regular customers. Most seemed very much accustomed to fending for themselves, but delighted that somebody was at the store now who could talk about the merchandise.

I learned as much from them as they ever did from me. I knew an impressive amount about period furniture, glass and art. But tools, farm machinery and baseball cards were a whole new world for me. I made trips to the library, read everything I could get my hands on and made copious notes for myself on what to look for at sales and auctions.

I made my first big sale the second week that I'd worked there. I'd made several prior to that, but they were with regulars—they were sales that Scott probably would have made without me. This one was a tourist who caught sight of a 1920s doll carriage that I'd put in the window and had come in just to see it. Once I chatted with her, showed her around and promised to ship whatever she bought to her home in Florida, she went on an antique-shopping spree. That merchandise would have never left the door without me.

I celebrated my success by purchasing a gift for my boss.

"What is it?" he asked.

"You can't tell until you open it," I said. "That's actually the purpose of the wrapping."

He made a face and began tearing at the paper.

A few moments later he unearthed his new laptop from its protective Styrofoam.

"You bought me a computer?" He seemed stunned. "It's for keeping the store accounts?"

"No, it's not for the store accounts," I told him impatiently. "It's for you. I'm selling that Underwood to the next person who walks through that door."

He glanced at his old typewriter and then back at me.

"I've got one word for you, Robbins," I said. "E-mail."

"E-mail," he repeated.

"And this," I said, handing him a little booklet I'd got at the library. It contained Web addresses of newspapers, wire services, government agencies and top five hundred corporations. "And when you don't know where to send it…" I turned to the back page where I'd printed in big bold letters: president@whitehouse.gov.

He looked at me as if I were a genius.

I didn't allow Yesteryear Emporium to take over my life. I continued to do my volunteer work. It was important to me and to those who had come to depend upon my time. Scott never asked about my comings and goings. He took it as natural that I had other obligations, other interests. They were none of his concern and he obviously knew that.

He had other interests of his own as well. I was surprised to learn he was a big fan of the Texas troubadours and old-time western music. He went to Pioneer Hall nearly every Thursday night to hear musicians imitating the style of the Light Crust Doughboys or singing the tunes of Townes Van Zandt.

We discovered that we both liked Native American arts and handicrafts. He invited me to attend a museum opening of an exhibit of Hopi kachina dolls.

Scott and I were business partners. And we were also friends. We were becoming very close yet, we weren't really close at all. It was as if there were things he wasn't saying to me, and there were things I certainly wasn't saying to him.

But I was saying a few things to Brynn. I had mailed her passport to her with a long, well-thought-out note that I'd first run past Scott for his opinion.

I still didn't know for certain if the invitation from Dr. Reiser was bogus or not. So, my message stated unequivocally all my reasons for not wanting her to "personalize" her relationship with him. But I also pointed out that she was an adult woman now, very much in charge of her own life and that I would always love her and be proud of her, even if she didn't always make choices with which I agreed.

I mailed it and waited. Considering normal postal delivery, Brynn responded almost immediately.

"So you're going to let me go?" she said incredulously, in lieu of any greeting.

I framed my answer carefully. "I'm not *letting* you do anything," I said. "You are an adult person and you have to follow the dictates of your own conscience. It's not my life, Brynn, as you've told me so many times. It's yours."

The conversation was short. As if she didn't quite know how to proceed now that she had won.

I got off the phone and anxiously awaited a second call, perhaps confessing that there had never been an invitation in the offing, or maybe just telling me that she'd decided not to go. A full week went by without hearing anything at all. When she finally did get in touch with me it was as if she needed further clarification. "No questions asked?"

"If that's the way you want it."

"So you're letting me go to Italy," Brynn said. "So does that mean you'll be giving me money?"

I hesitated, quickly trying to think through the answer. I was pretty certain this was a test, an attempt to discern how deep my commitment to her freedom was. If I said that as an adult on her own she wasn't taking my money, that would be controlling again. I had to find a way to give the control to her without making her feel abandoned.

"No," I said finally. "I wouldn't like the idea of you being in Europe without funds. I'll talk to your father. We'll keep cash in your account. Just be sure and take your ATM card."

I had made a decision to trust her. For good or not so good, I'd finally given her her freedom and now I had to live with it. It wasn't easy.

# 19

On a bright and sunny Monday in May, Mikki gave birth to a healthy seven-pound-three-ounce boy. David called me, sounding upbeat but a lot like David.

"I double-bogied the ninth hole on the Sunday dawn patrol. It must have been sympathetic labor."

I laughed appropriately. He filled me in on all the details. The emergency cell-phone call on the eleventh green. The mad rush to the hospital, fearing that the baby would be born on the floorboard of the Volvo. The following twenty-two-hour marathon wait in the labor room. W.D.'s helpful advice to the expectant mother about getting on with it and giving birth. Edith, nearly tearing her hair out with anxiety, finally telling her husband to simply "Shut the hell up!"

Edith raising her voice and actually cursing at W.D. was so out of character, that everybody in the room must have been stunned.

"What did your father do?"

David chuckled. "We didn't hear another peep out of him until the baby was born."

"Unbelievable."

"I swear," David told me, "it was as if Mom morphed into General Patton. The minute she took charge of the situation, Mikki started pushing the baby down into the birth canal. They moved us into delivery within fifteen minutes."

David made it sound like so much fun and such a family occasion that I actually felt a little left out.

The little fellow was given the very large name of Wentworth David Lofton IV.

"Mikki thinks we should call him Worth," he told me.

It seemed logical to me. David's grandfather's name was shortened into Went, his father was W.D. and he was David. Worth was about all that was left.

"I think that would be fine," I assured him.

"It's kind of a pretentious name. Don't you think it sounds too…I don't know…too economic?"

I laughed. "Well, maybe it is a bit," I said. "But better to call him something economic than to take to calling him Booger or Diaperbutt."

David chuckled.

"I like you, Jane," he said. "You know, I think I like you more now than I ever did."

Strangely, I felt the same way. I realized at that moment that I liked my life a lot. And David's small part of it was just exactly enough.

"How's Mikki?" I asked him. "Did she have a tough time?"

"Oh my God, it was hideous," he answered. "I thought the labor room was the very worst. When she wasn't screaming, she was moaning or crying. But then we get into delivery and there was blood and mucus and gook everywhere. It was disgusting."

"It's always like that," I said.

"Well, I was just grateful to have Beau Tatum as her doctor. If he hadn't kept talking, keeping my mind on golf the whole time, I probably would have thrown up or fainted."

"Well," I said, "at least now you know where babies come from."

"I liked it better with Brynn," he said. "I just showed

up at the hospital. She was all pretty and sleeping in a little pink blanket and you were sitting up in bed with your hair brushed out and your makeup repaired."

"You remember that?"

"Of course I remember," he said. "It was one of the most important days of my life."

I smiled into the phone. It felt good hearing him say that. I don't think he'd ever mentioned it before. That's one of the downsides of being married. Those things that are so important to say often go without being said.

"I'm not sorry that you and I didn't have more children," I told him sincerely. "But I am glad that you are lucky enough to have more with Mikki."

"Why, thanks, Jane," he said. "Mikki tells me she wants a whole houseful of kids. I'm not sure how good an idea that is, but I guess we'll work it out."

"So what did Brynn have to say about Worth?" I asked him. "Is she anxious to get down here to see him? Has she given up on Italy to volunteer for babysitting?"

He hesitated.

"I called you first, Jane," he said. "I was kind of hoping you would call and break the news to her."

My disappointment was like a blow to the stomach.

"Oh, David, no," I said. "You should tell her."

"I know I *should*." His tone was whining. "She hasn't been all that pleased about this baby idea," he said. "In fact, she's been downright hostile to Mikki."

"You have to expect that, David," I told him. "Changes you and I make in our lives affect her, too."

"I know," he said. "I just thought she'd get over it by now."

Brynn had managed to hold a grudge against me since the onset of puberty, but I decided not to point that out.

"Let's give her time to sort out her own life, David,"
I said. "Love her, include her in your new family and
give her time."

He heaved a big sigh. "Yeah, I know you're right,"
he said. "I want to invite her to spend time with us, but
Mikki's worried about all that negativity around the
baby."

I didn't want to see Brynn cut off from her father.
"Mikki is wrong on that score," I told him. "Once
Brynn sees little Worth, I promise you, she won't be
able to resist him."

David laughed. "That would be hard to do," he admitted.

"But you have to be the one to call your daughter," I
insisted.

"Jane, please."

His words were unapologetically pleading. I was
very tempted to do as he asked. I resisted.

"Brynn deserves to hear from you," I said. "If I call
her, she'll feel more left out of your life than she does
now. Call her, David. Just give her the details and then
talk golf like you always do. It will be easier than you
think. I'll talk to her later, but she needs to hear the
news from you."

Reluctantly he agreed, and I got off the phone
quickly before his courage failed him. It was not my responsibility to make sure that Brynn and David maintained their relationship, but it was a good thing to do
and I was in the business of doing good these days.

I called Scott and told him about the baby and that I
was going to take the day off in celebration. In fact, I
wanted to spend the morning with Chester.

I talked to Chester about Scott all the time, but I'd
never actually mentioned the man to Scott. Somehow it
didn't come up. I suppose because I hadn't told him
anything about my vow, my new focus, my scorekeep-

ing. It wasn't just because I thought it made me sound sort of crazy. Scott was sort of crazy himself and I knew he wouldn't pass judgment like my in-laws, or suggest therapy like David did. I think I kept my secret because I didn't want him to know the truth about me. That I was really a narrow, selfish person. All the things he liked about me were the new things—the new me, and I wanted all the old things, the old Jane Lofton, to simply disappear. But that doesn't happen.

I told Chester about how I felt. He was sitting up, but not in his lounger. He was in a very uncomfortable-looking wheelchair. His one leg was awkwardly elevated.

"You can't make the past not exist," he told me. "Are you sure you would really want to?"

"No," I admitted. "There are things I don't want to lose. David and I were talking this morning about when Brynn was born. I had a lot of happiness in my marriage. There were lots of good times, many things I never want to forget. But I was so single-focused, uncaring, self-absorbed—I was completely wrapped up in becoming part of a world that doesn't even hold my interest anymore."

"I guess most of us have found ourselves in that position a time or two," he agreed.

"Scott has such respect for me and he likes me, too. I guess I just wish I was the person he thinks I am."

"Maybe you are," Chester said.

I wanted to believe him, but I couldn't quite manage it.

"You've changed your life completely before," he said. "You walked away from the world you grew up in, from everything that was familiar to you."

"But that was easy," I told him. "I walked away, but somebody else tore it up. My friends were scattered, my mother died and there was not one street, building, house or tree to remind me of what had been."

"That was easier?" Chester sounded as if he didn't believe it. "Sometimes memories are far stronger than any tangible evidence."

I didn't argue. It was hard to compare yesterday with today. And had I really left all my days at Sunnyside behind me? In some ways they were always with me.

"I wish I could make some sort of symbolic break," I told him. "Find a way to demonstrate that I've changed."

"You demonstrate that every day," Chester assured me. "If you need a symbol, I'm sure you'll find one."

He was right, of course. And it was less than a hour later, sitting in my own kitchen, fixing myself a tuna sandwich, when I recognized it.

I called Scott to find out how his day was going.

"I've been up to my ears in energy policy all morning and I'm about to run off all your new customers," he said. "You'd better come racing in like the cavalry, Janey Domschke, and save this business."

The minute I heard it, I knew.

"The human contact will do you good," I told him. I've got one more errand to run. I need to go downtown to the clerk of courts office to file a petition."

"What are you doing now? Getting signatures to have antiques declared a protected species?"

I laughed. "Not anything quite so dramatic or globally charged," I told him. "I'm getting my name changed."

Just saying it aloud made me feel better. Jane Lofton was no longer the kind of woman I wanted to be. It would be good to put her and her life behind me, at least in name only.

I gathered up my driver's license, social security card, birth certificate and divorce decree and was thirty seconds from the front door when the telephone rang. I almost let the voice mail pick it up, but at the last second I checked the caller ID. It was Brynn's college.

"Hello," I answered, dropping my purse to grab up the receiver at the last minute.

"Mrs. Lofton, please." The voice at the other end of the line was middle-aged, female and very formal.

"This is Jane Lofton."

"Good afternoon, I'm Genevieve Pipington, coordinator of the Simmons Summer Overseas Program."

She hesitated as if that should mean something to me. It didn't.

"Yes?" I inquired finally.

"I have received Brynn's application," she said. "And I commend you for filling it out and getting it back to us so quickly. We hardly ever accept applications this late in the year. But for Brynn, of course, we would love to make an exception."

I didn't remember filling out anything, but I kept that to myself.

"I do have a couple of questions," Ms. Pipington continued. "That is, naturally, if you have a moment. Brynn has told us how very busy you are these days and has asked me not to bother you."

"Believe me," I told her, "it is no bother. What questions do you have?"

"I understand that both you and your husband will be out of the country yourself all summer," she said.

I made sort of a noncommittal murmur.

"However, we have our policies and we absolutely must have some emergency contact person," she said. "Listing her friend Hailey will simply not do. If Brynn has no other family, could we perhaps list Hailey's parents? I would really prefer that over listing another student."

For a moment it was as if I was in a fog, possibly the

result of too much stimulation and too little sleep. Fortunately I was able to get a grip, and quickly. I had not made inroads into local society without recognizing the earmarks of a genuine connive. The apple, apparently, hadn't really fallen all that far from the tree.

"Ms. Pipington, I'm so glad you called," I said effusively. "Honestly, I was going to call you myself just this morning."

"Really?"

"Yes, as it turns out, I will not be leaving the country for the summer," I said. "I've undertaken some new management responsibilities at an adorable little antique store and I am going to stay right here in the city."

"Well, that's fine then," the woman said. "I'll just change the emergency contact to this number."

"Yes, and," I continued, "I'm beginning to rethink this trip. I'm not sure that Brynn needs to go overseas this summer. I'm thinking that maybe she should come home and stay with me."

"Oh." She sounded particularly sad. "I am terribly disappointed to hear that. I just adore Brynn. She's so bright and funny and has such a natural sensitivity and understanding about art. I was so thrilled when she changed her mind unexpectedly and decided to go. I was so looking forward to showing her Florence."

"You are going on the trip?"

"Oh yes, I do these every year," she said. "Dr. Sally Milton and I have been shepherding young women through the finest art in Italy for the last nine years."

"Just the two of you, with all these girls?" I asked.

"Nine serious students of art," she said. "Believe me, we haven't had a moment's problem with any of them."

I sat there for a long moment, thoughtful. Then decisive.

"Would you hold on a moment, please?" I asked.

I set the phone down and hurried into the privacy of the kitchen, digging into my purse for my mobile. I quickly pulled up the directory screen and scanned down to Dr. Reiser's name. I hit talk.

It took a moment to connect, and my thoughts were racing, but my attitude was hopeful. A nasally female with a Boston "r" answered the call.

"Hertzhog and Reiser Family Counseling."

"Yes, I'm calling to inquire about who will be taking Dr. Reiser's calls this summer while he's on vacation," I said.

"Dr. Hertzhog will be taking emergencies," she said.

"What about regular weekly visits?"

I could hear her mouse clicking as she checked the appointment screens.

"I believe all of his regular appointments have been rescheduled," she said. "What is your name and I'll check on yours."

I ignored the question.

"He can reschedule after being on vacation for three months?"

"Three months?" Her voice was incredulous. "He'll only be on vacation the first and second week of July."

"How can he go to Italy in that amount of time?" I asked.

"Italy?" The woman's voice was incredulous. "He's going fly-fishing in British Columbia."

"Oh well, never mind," I said, and hung up before she had a chance to ask any more questions.

I raced back to the phone in the bedroom.

"Ms. Pipington, I'm so sorry to have kept you waiting," I said. "I've checked with my husband and we've decided that it would be perfectly wonderful for Brynn to go with you to Italy this summer."

"Marvelous," she said. "I think it will be a memorable, broadening experience for her."

"I think so, too," I said.

I sat there for a long moment, sorting through my thoughts. Chester must be right. Brynn was a lot more like me than I thought.

I laughed out loud.

In the following weeks, as spring heated up to summer, my newly resolved motherhood crisis, fabulous job and new/former name had me so cheered up and optimistic about life, I just had to share it.

Chester had mentioned on my last visit that he very much wanted to meet Scott. I considered inviting Scott to go to the nursing home with me, then real inspiration dawned on me. One summer Sunday I decided to skip church and called Scott just after breakfast.

"You want to go for a drive with me this morning?"

"Ah, yeah," Scott said, still kind of yawning. "Where?"

"Oh just around, we'll take a picnic."

"Sure, okay," he answered, perking up.

I made all the appropriate calls. Fixed some salad and sandwiches and pulled up in front of the store about ten o'clock.

I beeped my horn instead of going inside. Scott came out to meet me, wide-eyed.

"New car?" he asked, as he opened the passenger door.

I nodded. "Bought it this morning. Do you like it?"

"It's…it's cute."

"Faint praise," I claimed.

"It's *your* car," he said. "Do you like it?"

"I do," I told him.

"I'm surprised you didn't get a convertible," he said.

"I would have," I told him. "But the Beetle doesn't come in that model. Two or three years, the dealer told me."

"That's a disappointment," he said.

"Yeah, but the sunroof is nice," I admitted. "I think I actually like it better than the Z3."

"I hope you got a good trade-in," he said. "You could get three of these for the price of that BMW."

"Who would want three of these?" I asked, teasing.

We drove out to Bluebonnet Manor Assisted Living.

"Got to pick up another passenger," I told him.

Scott seemed amenable to that.

And Chester was thrilled to be getting out for the day.

The nursing staff was far less so.

"Just keep a close watch on him," Anje told me. "Don't bump him into anything. If he gets a cut or scrape, I want to know about it."

"Of course," I told her.

"If he starts getting overtired, he might appear either jittery or faint," she said.

I nodded appropriately, but secretly I figured that if Chester got overtired, he'd just tell me so.

"He has to be back here in time for his two o'clock needle," she told me.

I nodded, assuming she referred to those shots he often had. B12, Chester had told me.

"Neither I nor the doctor think this is a great idea," she told me. "But Chester's so happy about it, we just couldn't disappoint him."

I was glad.

I introduced my two favorite guys to each other and, because Chester didn't weigh much, Scott, with his heavily muscled arms, was easily able to scoop him out of the wheelchair and into the back seat.

"I knew this little Volkswagen bug was made for me," he joked. "There's only room in the back seat for one leg."

We all laughed. Scott caught my eye. I could tell that

he, like me, was impressed with the guy's wonderful heart.

"It looks like we've only got two good legs between the both of us," Scott told him. "I hope Janey doesn't have a sack race planned for this picnic."

With the sunroof open and Patsy Cline on the CD player, we drove out to Lago Vista Park. We found a wonderfully secluded table that looked out over the city and was cooled by the feathery shade of an ancient mesquite.

Chester breathed in the fresh air and gazed off into the distance as if he could actually see what was there.

I unpacked the lunch while he and Scott got acquainted. Amazingly, Chester remembered many of Scott's letters that had been in the paper. Including one he'd written over five years earlier on euthanasia.

"I can't believe you remember that," Scott told him. "That seems like a lifetime ago."

Chester shrugged. "When a man says something that you totally agree with, you remember it."

"You flatter me," Scott said.

Chester shook his head. "No," he answered. "I admire you."

The meal was leisurely and interesting. I was delighted at how well my two men friends got along. And even more pleased at how well Chester fit into the pattern of philosophy and funniness that characterized conversation between Scott and I.

The food disappeared and I poured more iced tea.

"And now, gentlemen," I announced. "Can anyone guess what we have for dessert?"

"I hope it's some of that wonderful pie your friend makes," Scott said.

"Wrong," I said, and made a sound like a game-show buzzer.

"Chester, your turn."

He shook his head.

"Tah-dah!" I said, pulling three Snickers bars out of the bottom of the basket. "This is Chester's favorite," I told Scott as I passed them around.

Scott and I both immediately tore into the candy wrapper and began consuming our sweet chocolate treat. I glanced over to see Chester just looking at his.

"Don't tell me," I said. "You're going to save it for later."

Chester looked sheepish. "I'm stuffed," he said. "That sandwich, the salad, the fruit."

I laughed. "Scott," I said, "this guy tells me he loves these Snickers. I've been bringing them to him every week for the last six months, and I have yet to see him take one bite."

Scott chuckled with me. "Give the guy a break, Janey," he said. "Maybe he likes them so much, he wants to savor them in private."

"That's it exactly," Chester said, though he was still acting a little ill at ease.

I thought it a bit weird, that instead of just putting the candy bar in his pocket, he carefully folded it into a napkin first. When he caught me observing him, he made an excuse.

"Don't want it to melt and get on my shirt," he said.

That seemed unlikely but I didn't want to make a case out of it.

The moment passed and the conversation moved on. I talked about Brynn's cryptic messages from Europe. She wanted to share her good time, but provide as little actual information as possible.

Chester told a funny story about one of his former neighbors who pretended, for fifteen years, that she had a dog.

We all laughed together and traded stories of silly things we had done.

Scott bragged to Chester about all the changes I'd made in the store. He talked about his new computer, the miracle of e-mail and the luxury of spellcheck and cut and paste.

Chester listened with as much attention as if he were thinking of getting a laptop of his own. But being Chester, he did come out with the question that was on his mind.

"Why are you running this antique business?" he asked. "Before Jane stepped in, you could hardly keep it in the black. What is that all about?"

I had wondered that myself, I'd even asked Scott about it more than once. I couldn't remember if I'd mentioned it to Chester, or if the situation simply appeared as curious to him as it did to me.

Scott hesitated a long moment. I thought he might be thinking up an excuse not to answer, or giving Chester time to back off and say it wasn't any of our business. Neither happened.

"I made a promise," Scott told him.

His words hung out there on the breeze, almost floating in the quiet of the summer afternoon.

Scott glanced in my direction a bit uncertainly. I knew this was something he wouldn't normally share. And he was afraid of what sharing it now might mean. Could he trust me with the truth?

"I guess Jane told you that my father was a junkman," he began.

Chester nodded. "I remember that store," he said. "Never went in there myself and I don't recall ever meeting your father, but I remember walking by." Chester laughed. "The place was bulging at the seams with just about everything imaginable."

Scott smiled, pleased. "He did seem to have everything," he agreed. "And the old man could lay his hands on any piece of it in five minutes."

"That's why he never bothered to keep good records," I said.

Scott agreed. "Before antiquing was fashionable, my dad took up collecting odds and ends. He bought junky old cars and equipment, used furniture, other people's castoffs. He was convinced that the things people had used, or the things that still could be used, shouldn't just be filling up garbage dumps. Whenever I read an article about the virtues of recycling, I am reminded of Dad and think that maybe he was ahead of his time."

"That happens," Chester said. "So your father must have loved his business."

"Oh, he did," Scott answered. "My mother hated it. She thought it was low-class. She thought Dad was low-class. He kept the garage full of stuff for years. When we moved out of Sunnyside to the suburbs she wouldn't allow him to bring any of his treasures. That's when he bought the building downtown. She absolutely forbade him to bring any of his 'trash' into *her* new house."

Scott made a face, indicating that that edict hadn't gone over so well in his childhood home.

"She was equally stern," he continued, "about not wanting me in the store. I think my father knew that the junk he bought would be worth something someday, but I think, as he grew older, he worried that the value of his collection might not be appreciated in his lifetime. He tried to push me into becoming a part of the business."

"How did you feel about that?" Chester asked.

Scott laughed. "I was a super-cool dude with long hair and a hot bike. I was not the least bit interested in old washtubs and kerosene lamps." He glanced over in my direction. "That was before I learned that touching them was touching history."

I was heartened that he'd remembered my words.

"What interested me was ideas," Scott said. "I wanted to live in the world of ideas. I didn't know for certain what I wanted to do with my life. But I felt very sure that it *did* involve college and it *didn't* involve the junk business."

"I'm sure your father wasn't very happy to hear that," Chester said.

"I put off telling him," Scott admitted. "When the time finally came, it wasn't easy. Dad and I really had it out. We said terrible things to each other."

He rubbed his temples as if it hurt him just to remember.

"The argument went on for weeks," he said. "My mom got into it, too. She was on my side, of course, but that just made it worse. They'd been having trouble for a long time, but she picked this fight to finally tell him she wanted a divorce. He moved into the store, and they both hired pit-bull lawyers."

"Oh, Scott, I'm so sorry," I told him.

Chester concurred.

"It was awful," Scott said. "And it just made Dad dig in his heels even more. He refused to pay for college. He said I could work in his business, or I could just forget that I was his son."

My heart ached for Scott as he said these words.

"Maybe Dad knew he wasn't well," he said. "Or maybe he never thought I'd really go against him. But I did. I volunteered for the draft. I figured I'd do my two years and use the G.I. Bill to go to college. I was on my own at last and I was glad to get away from them both."

"Understandably," I said, sympathizing.

"I got a note from Dad at boot camp," he said. "He said he was sorry about how things had worked out. He said he was proud of me and he wished me well."

"That was good," I said.

Scott nodded. "He asked me to come see him before I shipped out." He shook his head. "I spent my furlough traveling around the country, enjoying myself. I hardly gave the old man a thought."

The guilt was evident in his voice.

"It's the way we are when we're young," Chester told him. "We can't see any farther down the road than the end of our nose. Don't beat yourself up about it, we are all like that."

Scott thanked him for the reassurance.

"So you went to Vietnam," I said.

He shrugged. "I went where they told me to go. I did what they told me to do," he said. "I was a pretty good soldier, I guess, for about eight months."

He glanced toward me with a big grin.

"The definition of a good soldier," he told me by way of explanation, "is that you don't get yourself or anyone else killed."

Chester liked that. He chuckled a little bit.

Scott talked about the war as if it were basically one long unpleasant walk through the jungle, punctuated by boring days in camp. He found the world in Vietnam to be very different from anything he'd ever experienced. He made a few friends. He decided that he didn't like military life.

"Then one morning we were out on patrol," he said. "It started raining, nothing ever happened when it was raining, so we started back to rejoin our group. We were on what was thought to be a safe road. A jeep passed us. It was right it front of me, no farther away than you are."

Scott's eyes took on a faraway look, as if he could gaze off into the distance and see it again just as it had looked then.

"I'm still not sure what happened," he said. "The jeep ran into a trip wire or the road was mined or a grenade landed under the gas tank. Suddenly everything around me exploded and I was blown up into the air."

Scott dragged a handkerchief out of his pocket and wiped the sweat that had suddenly dampened his forehead.

"When I hit the ground, I landed away from the road," he said. "My weapon was gone. There were shots being fired from two directions and I was in the middle."

His tone was matter-of-fact but it came out of his mouth at a volume barely above a whisper.

"I tried to get deeper in the grass," he told us. "That's when I realized I was hit. Any little movement felt like hot knives being stabbed into me."

I noticed that Scott had begun to rub his bad leg.

He paused. The quiet settled all around us. I caught Chester's eye. It was as if we both knew it was not the time to press.

A moment later Scott seemed to realize he was no longer speaking. He cleared his throat, sat up a little straighter and spoke once more.

"The firing was so heavy at first that I kept my head down. When it started to lighten up, I was grateful, until I realized why," he said. "My unit was moving back, away from me. I wasn't in any shape to go with them. If I called out, I wasn't sure they could get to me, and if they couldn't, Charlie would sure know my location."

Scott took a deep breath and shook his head.

"I had no choice but to lie there in the grass, pretend I was dead and hope that nobody came up close to check," he said.

Scott glanced in my direction. It was difficult for him sharing this, but he was determined to do so.

"I don't know how long I was there," he said. "Nearly thirty-six hours, someone estimated later. I was losing a lot of blood, so I went in and out of consciousness. I thought about my dad and about the junk business and how hard I'd fought to get away from it. Dying in that grass suddenly seemed so much worse than working in the store."

He became uncomfortable as he tried to explain.

"God and heaven and all that sort of thing seemed really close to me out there," he said. "So I prayed. I said, 'Please get me home.' I didn't ask to be whole. I didn't ask to be happy. I just pleaded for that one thing, 'If you'll just get me home,' I promised, 'I'll stay and run that store for the rest of my life.'"

Scott hesitated, glancing up at Chester. "And I have."

The silence at the table lingered. The summer breeze was the only sound in our ears, that and the distant cry of a mockingbird. The three of us sat, sharing that table and something just as tangible.

Unexpectedly, Chester burst into laughter.

"What do you know, Jane," he said to me. "Scott Robbins is one of us."

# 20

➤ ◄

Anje had taken charge of Chester the minute we'd driven up to the doorway. We weren't late, but she acted as if we were, fussing over Chester, who looked as happy and flushed with health as I had ever seen him.

"Thanks, Chester," I told him, preempting any gratitude that he might have wished to express. "I had a wonderful Sunday with you."

He laughed. "Don't you forget it," he said. "It was one of the best days of my life. It was the two of you that made it so."

We were shooed away and he was taken to his room. Scott and I got back into the Beetle and headed downtown.

At the red light on the intersection, I pointed to the infamous spot on the divided highway. "That's where I had my accident."

Chester and I had both revealed our own personal vows and the stories behind them.

Scott glanced at the place and then back toward the Assisted Living Center. He didn't say a word, but I knew what he was thinking.

"It's amazing that Chester saw me," I said. "Even more so when you think of him getting down here to save me and having the foresight to bring that butcher knife."

Scott nodded. "That's the way I feel about the patrol

that had somehow missed the road and was wandering through the grass to stumble over me thirty-six hours after I was hit."

The light changed and I turned onto the expressway.

"Do you think it was...like God?" I asked.

He gave me a faint little smile. "I've never said that aloud."

"But do you think it?"

"Yeah," he said. "I think it was God in the jungle. I think it was God getting Chester to that car. And I think it was God bringing you into my little store."

"Maybe it wasn't God back in the old days when I got such a thrill out of cheating you."

He laughed and he reached over and laid his hand atop mine on the gearshift.

"Well, you know, Janey, I've been thinking about *all my worldly goods to thee endow*," he teased. "Perhaps I can see about getting that made retroactive."

It was a little joke, of course. A silly, intimate little girlfriend/boyfriend–type joke. Somehow it kind of thrilled me all over.

When I pulled into my parking spot in front of the store, he asked me to come in with him. It seemed very natural to do so.

We walked right past the counter area where our tête-à-têtes were commonly held, to the mezzanine stairs. Holding my hand in his own, we hurried up the oak steps. He didn't bother to unhook the flimsy cord that held up the Private Keep Out sign. He just climbed right over it and helped me to do the same.

I just went rather naturally into his arms. I don't know how long it had been since I had been kissed; really, sweet, soul-searching, heights-reaching kissed. Maybe I never had been, or perhaps I had just forgotten what it was like. But at that moment, it was everything.

We continued up the stairs once more, only to stop at

the landing and kiss again. This time our knees turned to jelly and we ended up sitting on the stairs, necking, only ten steps from his doorway.

Like a couple of hormone-driven teenagers, we were eager and hesitant. Both of us aroused, neither of us in our right minds.

Scott pulled away from me. Sweat was beaded up on his forehead and he was breathing heavily.

"Okay, Janey," he said. "This is your call. Do we go upstairs and have sex or do we go downstairs and pretend this never happened?"

"Let's go upstairs and have sex," I answered. "We can go downstairs and pretend that it never happened later."

He laughed. He slid one arm around my back and another behind my knees and lifted me up into his lap.

"I'd like to carry you to my bed," he told me, "but I don't think my leg could stand it."

"Save your strength," I told him. "You're going to need it when we get there."

We continued to kiss and grope and tease each other on the stairs. I loved sitting in his lap, feeling the hardness in the front of his trousers pressing urgently against my tush. I was eager to get a look at him naked. But he was in a better position to undo buttons and drag down zippers. By the time we made it across the threshold of his apartment, his shirt was hanging open and I was stripped down to diaphanous blue panties.

We made it to his bed eventually and were squirming passionately when I mentioned the word *condom*. It had the effect often seen in the great newspaper movies of the 1930s, where the editor, upon hearing the hero's latest communiqué yells out, "Stop the presses!"

He searched fruitlessly in the drawer beside the bed. Then he checked out the shelves in the bathroom. While I found the interruption of our romantic moment somewhat irksome, it was also endearing and reassuring.

"Found 'em," Scott said, hurrying back to bed, where he tossed the small box of Magnums.

"Did you check the expiration date?" I asked him.

He nodded. "We still have time," he said. "But I do think we ought to hurry."

I laughed. And he laughed.

We went into each other's arms once more, but it was without the mindless rush. We took our time, enjoying the moment, reveling in the experience.

I admit, it had been a while since I'd had sex. It wouldn't have taken all that much to impress me. Scott managed it. It had obviously been a while for him as well.

We were good together, neither of us really unsure about ourselves, both of us willing to take some chances. There is always excitement in newness, but especially so when trust and respect are already firmly established.

Afterward, exhausted, we lay in each other's arms. I wanted to talk to him, I wanted to luxuriate in the warmth of it all.

"That was great," I told him for starters as I snuggled up close.

A moment later I was sound asleep.

When I awakened, it was very dark. Across the room a match sparked into life. In its faint glow, I watched Scott light a kerosene lamp.

"Don't tell me," I said as he carried the light to the beside table. "You haven't paid your electric bill."

He sat down on the edge of the bed next to me.

"I've got two bare bulbs overhead," he told me. "Bright and harsh. I thought I might look better dimmer."

"Dim guys are my specialty," I assured him.

He leaned down and kissed me.

"The Janey Domschke I knew at Sunnyside wasn't particularly interested in guys at all, especially not dim ones."

"That Janey was only fifteen years old," I said.

"Ah yes," he said. "Innocent and virginal, young Janey had not yet discovered the sins of the flesh. And how good she was at them."

"I don't actually recall you being Mr. Conquest," I pointed out.

He shrugged. "I was slow getting off the mark," he admitted. "But I'm a real player now. Luring women up to my badly lit mezzanine apartment and driving them with crazy insatiable lust as I search for protective latex."

"Insatiable?"

"Or maybe insensible?"

"More like incensed."

"You're thinking of that Strawberry Alarm Clock song, you know, about mad-candy disease, 'incensed peppermint.'"

I groaned as if in pain, and then simultaneously, we broke into song.

*"Who cares what games we choose? Little to win but nothin' to lose."*

Scott's expression was stern. "Janey," he said, "you're gorgeous, but you can't sing."

I smiled. "What a lovely compliment," I said. "I'll be sure to pass it on to my plastic surgeon."

"He probably can't sing either."

"Stop, you're killing me."

"What a way to die!"

It was three-thirty in the morning. We were both wide awake. So we made sandwiches, took showers—one together and two separately—and we had more sex.

The dawn was seeping in through the windows when I thought about going home.

"What's your hurry?" he asked as he came up behind me, wrapping his arms around my waist.

In truth, there was none.

I was reluctant for the idyll to end. He seemed to feel the same way. I think we both worried that once we stepped back into the real world, into our real lives, what we'd shared together would all slip away like a pleasant dream that had you smiling when you awakened, but that you were never quite able to recall to mind.

So I didn't go home. I put on yesterday's picnic clothes, used his comb and toothbrush and wore only the lipstick, powder and blush that I carried in my purse.

He fixed a breakfast fit for ranch hands: sausage, eggs and toast. We ate at his little table next to the window with the street view. We decided we were a perfect division of the newspaper. I got the Metro and Style. He took the front section and Sports. But neither of us read much. We kept getting distracted by things we wanted to say, thoughts we wanted to share.

We opened the store promptly at nine. Scott wanted to write a letter about political favoritism in the presidency.

"I read the president said he considered loyalty to be the most important trait he looked for in the people around him," Scott told me.

"It's a good quality," I agreed.

"Yeah, it sounded okay to me, too," he said. "Then it stopped me in my tracks. That kind of committed single focus can be scary. I mean, Hitler's supporters were absolutely committed and faithful."

"So you're going to compare the president with Hitler?"

He shook his head rapidly. "Far too incendiary and
not anywhere near fair," he said. "I guess you could
say I'm writing about loyalty versus leadership. A truly
forward-looking leader ought to seek out independent
thinkers, not try to stifle their influence."

As the sun came pouring in through the front windows, Scott pursued the clear expression of his
thoughts and I sorted through boxes of costume jewelry.

We had a broad range of morning shoppers. Traffic
in the store was up, and I took some personal pride in
that. It was amazing what a generous amount of
friendly, personal service could do for a business.

I sold some badly weathered and damaged picture
frames to a young artist from the college, who said he'd
heard about us from a friend who'd purchased a broken mirror the week before.

The fellow's girlfriend, who was probably about
eighteen but looked twelve, went crazy over my quilt
display. She couldn't actually afford to buy any of
them, but I gladly spent forty-five minutes telling her
what I knew about the styles and patterns.

Ramon Glasse, an interior decorator whom I had
known for years, dropped in. His eyes lit up at the sight
of me, and we hugged like old friends.

"So you have bought yourself this store," he said.
"It's a very good one. Lots of quality inventory and
priced very cheap."

"Not as cheap as it used to be," I warned him. "And
I haven't bought the place. I just work here."

The expression on his face changed immediately. He
was embarrassed for me to be caught employed.

I diffused any further sympathy by suggesting that
the management was instigating new store policies and

we would be willing to offer him a small professional discount on items he purchased for his clients in return for helping us establish our name. Ramon was completely amenable to that.

"I heard about your divorce," he said, tutting sympathetically.

"I suppose it is still prime gossip at the club," I said.

"Up until a week ago," he told me. "Now the gossips have a new, more luscious tidbit."

"Oh?"

"Gil Mullins has left his wife," Ramon said emphatically.

"You're kidding?"

"I never kid," he assured me. "And the woman he left her for is an absolute nobody."

"Young bimbo?"

"If only!" Ramon said. "That would be understandable. This woman is dumpy, middle-aged and wears knockoffs."

"Who is she?"

"Some real estate woman," he said. "You probably know her. Ann…what is it they call her?…Ann Roller Hind."

"Ann Rhoder Hines!"

"Yes, that's her! You do know her. Enough said then."

He left laughing, happy and carrying a set of ceramic chickens that were kitchen canisters. The rooster was for flour, the hen sugar and the two little chicks, one brown and one yellow, were tea and coffee. I had unearthed them in a back room. And they were, in my opinion, four of the ugliest examples of arts and crafts on earth. But they were just the kind of eclectic fribble that Ramon would convince his customers they couldn't live without. I made him pay through the nose for them.

We had a lull about one-thirty and I raced up to the mezzanine and threw together a salad from what flotsam I could find in Scott's refrigerator. We shared it together behind the counter as Scott read the first draft of what he'd written from the screen of his laptop.

The man truly had a fine way with words. When he finished I gave him a well-deserved round of applause.

"You like it?" he asked.

"It's great," I said.

"It's too long," he said. "I need to whittle it down quite a bit. Keep all the meaning and cut out the wordiness."

"Don't you dare cut out that part about virtue," I told him. "That was absolutely quotable. Let's hear it again."

He scanned through the document until he found the line I meant.

"If Goldwater were commenting on the policies of *this* Oval Office, he might remark that virtue taken to its extreme is as dangerous to our liberty as any vice."

"Wow," I said.

"Wow?"

"Yes, wow, and that's my final word on the subject," I told him.

He chuckled. "I'd better get back to work," he said. "I want to try and get this finished today. The more timely it is, the better chance it has for getting in the paper."

"For the local paper?"

He nodded. "Well, yeah. That's where I've printed all of my stuff before."

"I don't think you should send it to them," I told him.

"You don't?"

"Why start locally?" I said. "It's a national issue, send it out nationally. What are the top newspapers in the country, the *New York Times, Washington Post, L.A. Times?* Send it there first."

"Why would the *New York Times* print a letter from me?"

"Scott, it's a global village, right?" I told him. "The world is their readership. And it's exactly what you say here. If they are good leaders, then they'll want to fill their newspaper with independent thinkers."

He went back to his laptop as soon as we finished eating and I continued combing through rhinestones and paste. I had a couple of interesting afternoon customers, and made a few good sales.

About three-thirty I found a brilliantly colored Morpho brooch. These pretty pieces from the 1920s used South American butterfly wings as part of the decoration, but they did not necessarily sell at high prices. But I felt the value of them could only go up. After admiring it thoroughly, I placed it in the padded case I'd marked as Not for Retail and returned to my labors.

It was after six when Scott came back to find me.

"How's it going?"

"Found a few pieces with genuine gems," I told him, indicating the little box I'd set aside.

"Valuable?"

"Moderately," I told him. "And even a lot of the inexpensively produced items are unique enough to command some good prices."

"I'm glad you're going through those boxes," he said. "I always knew it was a bad idea to have that much stuff just packed away."

"You know, Scott, we might think about setting up a special jewelry section here in the store."

"You think we could sell anything here?" he asked. "We haven't had many people interested in it in the past."

"Because the people who would buy this kind of thing never made it to our door," I said, "we probably need to heighten our profile."

"You have an idea for doing that?"

"I'm thinking we could put some of the stock on consignment with jewelers around town," I told him. "I could make sure Yesteryear Emporium was listed as the origin of the pieces. That would get our name in front of those people who might be our potential customers."

When I glanced up at him, he was smiling at me.

"What?"

"Janey, you are undoubtedly the best thing that has happened to this store in a very long time."

I laughed. "The feeling is mutual," I told him.

He leaned against a support pillar, arms folded across his chest.

"You may be the best thing that has happened to me, as well," he said.

That statement was considerably more serious.

"That feeling is also mutual."

We just looked at each other. Our relationship was so new, we were both still too surprised by it to make the effort to link it to definition.

He stepped forward and bent down to touch my lips with his own.

"Thanks for being here, Janey Domschke," he said.

"I can assure you," I teased politely, "that it's my pleasure."

Scott tweaked my nose in retaliation.

"Have you got time to proofread my final version?" he asked.

"I will make time."

He snapped his fingers. "Make time?" he said. "Didn't we do that yesterday."

I groaned with complaint. We made our way hand in

hand to our little semiprivate hideaway behind the counter.

His finished letter was, in my humble and perhaps moderately biased opinion, a masterpiece.

I helped him find the appropriate Web sites on the Internet and showed him how to paste them into e-mail addresses.

"And in just a few keystrokes," I said, doing a fair imitation of a newsreel narrator, "we send the words of Scott Robbins hurtling headlong into the digital universe of twenty-first-century technology."

"It's so easy," he said. "I should have been doing this years ago."

"You certainly should have," I agreed. "But when the good comes, it's never too late."

"That's a pretty quotable line you've got yourself," he said.

"Yeah, but it's not mine," I admitted. "Better cc a copy of that to the White House. Wouldn't want them to say they didn't get a chance to look at it before it went to print."

We closed the doors at 8:00 p.m. and went upstairs intending to make dinner. We made love instead and lay together afterward, so satisfied.

"I just can't quite believe you're here with me, Janey," Scott whispered. "I want to say…to say something special, but it seems too early."

"It is too early," I agreed.

"But I feel it," he told me. "I feel it intensely."

It felt so wonderful being there in his arms. I wasn't sure that I really deserved it.

"Scott, I'm not really the person you think I am," I told him.

"What do you mean?"

"You think I'm a good person," I said. "But I'm not. Before the accident, I didn't even try to be."

He opened his mouth, probably to contradict me, but I didn't give him the chance.

"I wasn't evil," I assured him. "I did the right things. I went to church, gave to charity, didn't make judgments based on race, creed, color or national origin. But I never really gave a damn about other people or their problems."

"You were busy," he said. "You had your career and your family."

That sounded like a plausible excuse, but I didn't want to make excuses with Scott.

"Those things were always secondary with me," I admitted. "My husband was a means to an end. My daughter was an obligation to my husband. All I wanted was to be wealthy and well thought of. Those were my two main pursuits, and beyond that, nothing else much mattered."

"Maybe that's the way you saw things," Scott said. "But David was obviously quite satisfied with you as a wife, he stayed married to you for twenty years. And Brynn, for all her adolescent issues, sounds no worse off emotionally than many other young women of her age."

"Those things worked out in spite of me," I told him. "Not because of me. I could have done better. I should have done better."

"We can all say that when we look back at the past, Janey," he said. "Don't beat yourself up about it. Besides, it sounds to me like Sunnyside syndrome."

"Sunnyside syndrome?"

"That's what I call it," he said. "I don't think it's made the list of recognized psychological disorders, but it's nonetheless pretty common."

"What are you talking about?" I said.

"Do you ever see anyone from our old neighborhood?" he asked me.

"No," I said. "I think you're about the only person I've ever run into."

"You should see some of them again. It would be an eye-opener for you," he said.

"We were all scattered," I pointed out. "Who knows where anybody is."

"I sometimes see guys I knew," he told me. "They come by here, remember the store and drop in. They all have the same problem that you have, that I have."

"What is that?"

"We're not sure where we come from," he said.

"I don't understand."

"Our roots are torn up, Janey," he said. "Maybe the adage is true that you can never go home again, but what if your home ceases to exist? You try, we try, to fit in somewhere else, with people who have pasts and histories. We never quite manage it and that makes us try harder and harder."

I frowned. I wasn't sure if he was completely right, but what he said did ring true somehow.

"It makes sense that the struggle to fit in somewhere, to have a place that's yours, could impact your real life and obscure the things that are really important to you," he said.

"Lots of people live their whole lives continents away from where they grew up," I pointed out.

"But those people know the places they lived are still there," he said. "When we don't have any tangible evidence of where we came from or who we were, our memory comes into question and we begin to think our view of it is unlikely."

"Having no place to be from was perfect for me," I insisted. "I've been able to live for years just pretending that whole part of my life just never existed."

"But doing that leaves holes in you, Janey," he said. "And those holes are like wounds that don't heal."

"That don't ever heal?" I asked him.

"Maybe they can," he said. "Maybe I can heal them. After all, I can verify that it was really you living in that little house on Coral Street with your mother."

"Coral Street," I said aloud. "You remember that? The whole street was just obliterated. I'd forgotten the name. I remembered the house, but I couldn't remember the street—114 Coral Street."

Hearing the address from my own lips sounded funny and I laughed.

Scott smiled with me.

"Not everyone from Sunnyside tried to fit into the country club like you," he said. "But all of us have been trying to fit in somewhere."

"You think so?"

"I know so," he said. "Maybe we should plan a reunion, have all the Sunnyside people come in, and do some kind of psychological survey on everybody."

"Maybe we could get Dr. Reiser to do it. I think I probably still owe him an apology."

"You certainly do," he teased. Then more seriously, he said, "When you separate people from their past it's going to have an impact."

"So you would have written a letter to the editor about allowing that expressway to cut right through our lives?" I asked.

He shrugged. "I don't know if I would have been against it," he admitted. "The city had to grow and it had to connect the suburbs to the downtown to keep it from drying up completely. But I think we always have to anticipate the fact that there are always unexpected consequences in everything we do, no matter how valuable or compelling the reason for doing them."

I thought about that for a long moment, then nodded.

"Like Chester in assisted living," I said.

Scott just looked at me, so I explained.

"It was a necessity. He really couldn't take care of himself. And selling his house and his things was probably reasonable. His nephew lives far away and there was no one to take care of everything, and no one anticipated him ever getting well or going home," I said. "It was probably the right thing to do for him, but he's getting sicker and sicker. And maybe that's an unanticipated consequence of believing that the next big thing that he is going to do is die."

Scott nodded. "But it doesn't have to be that way," he said.

"No, of course it doesn't," I agreed. "Think of Miss Heloise, she certainly doesn't feel that way."

"Maybe that's because she believes the house she lived in goes on," he said. "It's a kind of immortality that makes living more full of promise."

"I think you're right," I told him. "I think that really might be it."

"Why don't you try introducing Chester to Miss Heloise," he said. "Those two might really enjoy each other's company."

I propped myself up on my elbow and nodded down to him. "You know, I thought of that months ago," I told him. "But I just let it go. It seemed kind of silly to set up a blind date with two nursing-home residents."

"I guess it wouldn't be typical," he said. "But that doesn't mean it wouldn't be good."

"Maybe we could do another picnic," I said. "And we'd take both of them."

"That's going to be one crowded Volkswagen," he said.

"We'll look like clowns getting out of a car at the circus."

"It could be good for Chester to meet somebody,"

Scott agreed. "And it might be fun for Miss Heloise, too."

"You sound like you are about ready to play match-maker yourself," I said.

Scott laughed. "That's what happens when you fall in love, you get so schmaltzy you want to fix everybody up."

I let the "in love" comment go without reaction.

"Have you got anything to eat in this place?" I asked.

Scott cooked up some spicy okra in tomato sauce that he poured over instant couscous. It wasn't Le Para-pluie, but it wasn't bad for a quick dinner for two peo-ple who seemed to be spending a lot of time working up an appetite.

After dinner we snuggled together on his living-room couch and watched Jay Leno, laughing even when the jokes weren't all that funny.

"Can you believe that we've been together for thirty-six hours," I said.

Scott looked at his watch. "Actually thirty-seven hours, eleven minutes and twenty-four seconds, but who's counting? Twenty-six, twenty-seven, twenty-eight."

I playfully elbowed him.

"It's just amazing to me that I'm still here," I admit-ted. "That I haven't felt strange and put upon and pres-sured like it's all too much. I feel comfortable here. I feel comfortable with you."

"You don't crowd my space either, Janey," he said. "Being with you is…well, it's like being alone, only bet-ter."

We kissed and giggled like kids, and kissed some more.

At the commercial break, the hospital walkathon was highlighted. A popular local deejay was doing the voice-over about how the money raised would be used for a Special Therapies wing of the new cancer center. There were shots of smiling children who were obviously sick, a young woman wearing a turban, posing for the camera with her happy family all around her, a woman with a weathered old face, lined with experience.

"Your help brings hope," was the oft-repeated phrase.

The next shot was completely different, obviously an add-on to the previously produced message. It was set outside on a sunny parking lot. The long-haired, tattooed deejay looked very pleased with himself as he sat in a blue Z3 convertible.

"Look at me, dude," the deejay said. "I'm helping in the fight against these deadly diseases and have a chance to win this way-phat ride. You can too. Participate in the We-Can-Do-It Walkathon and buy a chance to win this nearly new and very hottie, hot, hot BMW. I want it, I want it."

"God, Janey," Scott said. "That looks just like your car."

I hesitated just a second too long before I responded.

"Ah, yeah, it does, doesn't it."

Scott leaned forward and looked me straight in the eye.

"You gave them your car?" he asked, incredulous.

"Hey, you gave away a genuine Stickley," I pointed out. "And now I have a car I like just as well."

"And I got a couch I…well, I've got another couch anyway," he said.

# 21

It was Wednesday before I finally left Scott's place to go home. If I'd had any clean clothes there, I might have stayed even longer. I walked through my house with no sense of being home. The place was roomy, beautifully decorated and expensive. Not any more welcoming than a movie or a TV version of what an upper-class American life might look like. Ours had always been more soap opera than sitcom. I didn't miss it. And my house was no longer where I really wanted to be.

Dutifully I sorted through the mail. It was mostly bills, but I did find a postcard from Brynn. It showed a lovely Tuscan landscape. I flipped it over and found she'd attempted to counteract the sweetness of the photograph with a happy face and a flippant message.

"Having a wonderful time," it read. "Good thing you're not here."

I burst out laughing.

The doorbell rang. I was still smiling when I answered it.

"Shanekwa," I said, delighted to see her. "Good morning. And, Jarone, how are you, sir?"

The little guy grinned at me.

"Juss fine," he said in his lispy singsong voice.

"Come in," I told his mother. "I don't know if I've got coffee. But if I do, it'll just take a second to brew some up."

"Thanks," she said, "but I can't stay. I promised to

get into work early today and I still have to get him to the day-care center. I just wanted to drop this off."

She handed me a check. I looked at it. I looked at her. "What's this?"

"I know we didn't talk about me paying rent," she said. "But I'm on my feet now. I *can* pay it. You don't know how good it feels to be able to say that. I'm looking for a place and this is what I'll have to pay for anything around here. I thought I'd start paying it to you, that way I'll be in the habit by the time I find a place of my own."

I hardly knew how to respond. My first thought was that I shouldn't take it. If Shanekwa wanted to move into a real apartment there would be two months' rent and deposits to pay. She was going to need this money. Then as I looked into her young, determined face, I smiled.

"Thank you," I told her. "If I can do anything to help, let me know."

"I will," she assured me.

We shared a hug, and Jarone let me kiss him on the forehead. I watched them walking all the way down the block.

Maybe they wouldn't have to move away, I thought. Maybe they could rent my house. I glanced down at the check and shook my head. Shanekwa would never be able to afford to rent a five-bedroom Italianate in Cambridge Heights. Nobody would. I was back to that.

Undoubtedly, I should sell the house. It was a drain on my income and I didn't even really like the place anymore. I would prefer to keep it if it could make me an income, but I couldn't figure how I would manage that. What kind of business venture could effectively utilize a huge, completely furnished house? The kind of people who could afford to rent it wouldn't want to rent. What I needed was a group of people who didn't have high incomes and were willing to live together. I couldn't imagine where I might find folks like that.

I took a long soak in the tub and thought about Scott. There was a phone right next to the tub and I was sorely tempted just to call and hear the sound of his voice. Out of sheer strength of will, I managed to resist. I needed to prove that I still had a life separate from his. That I wasn't so infatuated with the man that I couldn't enjoy a morning alone.

The truth was, I already missed him.

I got out of the tub, got dressed and groomed and began packing. I'd filled two suitcases, a huge portmanteau and a rolling carry-on before it occurred to me that arriving at his doorstep, or mezzanine in this case, with a month's worth of clothes might be a bit threatening. Scott had at no time ever asked me to move in with him. He did say he loved having me there. And he'd told me that he was happier with me than he could ever remember being in his whole life. But that was far from saying, "Let's live happily ever after." And I wasn' even sure if that was what I wanted either. I wanted to be with him. But did I want to be married? What if I re verted to being the old Jane Lofton? Would Scott end up being David?

Thinking about it made me crazy. I threw one suit case and the carry-on into my trunk and drove out to Bluebonnet Manor Assisted Living. Chester might no know what I should do, but he'd let me talk it out— we'd brainstorm and I'd have a far better idea of wher I stood.

I was so lucky to have that man.

When that thought hit me, I found it humorou enough to laugh out loud. Without Chester I woul have died in the auto crash. But his value to me as savior was now outweighed by being my confidan counselor and friend.

The air was very humid and the sky was gray, but I opened the sunroof nonetheless. I just enjoyed driving like that.

I ruminated on my relationship with Scott, wondered about Brynn and reminded myself about things I wanted to do at the store. I was feeling a bit less anxious as I pulled into the nursing-home parking lot. Rain was still threatening, but it held off.

I made my way through the glassed-in entry and the wide, nicely furnished foyer. The desk in the reception area was deserted as usual.

In the living room the usual wheelchairs were parked in front of the blaring television set. And the occupants didn't seem to be paying much attention to the screaming accusations thrown among the guests of a tabloid talk show.

On the surrounding couches people who were by now familiar to me sat quietly, some watched TV and some ignored it. The woman I referred to as Big-Haired Blanche was talking nonstop to nobody in particular. As usual her clothes were fashionable and expensive, her hair and makeup the envy of evangelists' wives everywhere.

"Good morning," I called out as I walked by.

"Good morning," a number of people responded.

I'd grown accustomed to this place, these people. It was a part of my life, and I decided that despite the strange smells and somewhat dreary atmosphere, I had come to relish my visits here.

I was halfway down the hall when Anje stepped out of Chester's room. I was already smiling at her when she looked up. As soon as she saw me, her expression changed.

"Jane!" She said my name as if my presence startled her.

She hurried to my side and took my hands in her own.

"What is it?" I asked.

"I tried to call you," she told me. "For some reason your name and number weren't listed in his records. I even asked his nephew in California, but he didn't know it. He wasn't familiar with your side of the family at all."

"You called Chester's nephew?" I was horrified. This immediate reaction was based on the fear that I would be found out. That I would get into some kind of trouble for pretending to be one of Chester's relatives. Self-preservation quickly subsided as niggling fear overrode it. "You called Chester's nephew," I repeated. This time it was a statement.

"We had to call somebody," Anje said.

The question why suddenly loomed large before me. I didn't get a chance to voice it.

"I am so sorry," she said.

I pushed past her into his room.

"He's not there," she called after me.

It was true. The room was exactly as it always was, his books and papers stacked in familiar chaos. Too much furniture crowded into far too little space. The accumulation of almost eight decades boiled down to space eight feet by ten.

The bed was empty. Its brown plastic mattress bare, the sheets and blankets gone.

I turned to Anje standing in the doorway.

"Where have you taken him?"

"Serenity Mission," she answered.

The name was unfamiliar to me. "Is that a hospital?"

Her brow furrowed. "It's a funeral home," Anje said. "Chester passed away last night. I am so very sorry."

Her announcement startled me completely.

"No, no. That can't be true," I told her. "It's impossible."

Anje was shaking her head.

"It's always hard to accept," she said.

"He was fine on Sunday," I insisted.

"Well, he wasn't *fine*," she corrected me. "But he was doing pretty well. I'm so glad you took him for that outing. He was so pleased and he had so much fun."

"Was it the picnic? Did he catch cold or get too much sun?"

"No, of course not," Anje assured me. "Don't even start that, Jane. Of course, it wasn't your fault. You know how sick he was."

I hadn't. I was sure that I hadn't.

"He was getting better," I argued. "He was feeling stronger."

Anje shook her head. She obviously didn't agree.

"He'd been going downhill for a long time and you knew it," she insisted.

On some level I had known. She was right about that. I knew he was old. I knew he was sick. I knew that he would die. But I hadn't expected it to be soon. I hadn't expected it to be now.

"It's so sudden," I said. "It's not supposed to be like this. Sunday he's fine and Wednesday he's dead."

"Sometimes that's exactly the way," she said. "We're honestly not sure what happened. He'd been under really good control for months. And then last night, unexpectedly, we lost him."

"Was it the breathing problems?" I asked her.

Anje looked surprised. "What breathing problems?"

I didn't bother to answer. "Then what was it? Heart attack?"

"No, of course not," she said, and then quickly backtracked. "Or maybe it was, ultimately. Renal failure, cerebral edema, respiratory distress, the whole body malfunctions in ketoacidosis and hyperglycemic shock."

My hands were trembling. I clasped them together to make them stop.

"Just tell me what happened," I insisted.

"I'm not sure we know," Anje said. "In the evening his levels were well within acceptable range, everything seemed normal. But when the nurse came in for his 2:00 a.m. needle he'd gone into crisis. His glucose was through the roof. I don't remember the number, I'll check the chart, but it was over three thousand."

She said the number as if it had tremendous importance. I had no idea.

"The poor old guy," Anje continued. "He just wasn't strong enough to hang in there until we could get him hydrated and stabilized. His blood must have been as thick as syrup in his veins."

As I listened to her, my brain didn't seem to be functioning correctly. It was like some fouled-up computer system. I kept feeding in the correct data but it was giving me nothing but error messages.

"He had diabetes." I stated the obvious.

She nodded. "We know it'll get you eventually," she said. "Chester lived a lot longer than most."

Had he? He was only seventy-eight.

"I honestly think he'd lost heart," Anje said. "Don't you?"

I nodded vaguely. "Yes," I said. "He seemed depressed since he lost his leg."

"They were going to start dialysis this week," she said.

"Dialysis?"

"He didn't tell you?" Anje tutted and shook her head. "I'm not surprised," she admitted. "He didn't seem too upset about the prospect of another amputation, but he really didn't like the idea of being hooked up to that machine twice a week. He'd held the doctor off for months."

"They were going to take off his other leg?"

"Probably," she said. "I suppose they were hoping to get him stronger before doing surgery."

"I just can't believe it," I said. "I didn't realize he was in such trouble."

Anje shrugged. "His diabetes was so brittle," she said. "Blindness, kidney failure, circulation problems, wounds that don't heal. It's all textbook. He knew what he was facing from the time he was in his twenties."

I just stared at her. I had no idea what to say.

Anje picked up a book on his table, looked at the title and set it down again.

"His nephew said they wouldn't be able to come out here for the funeral," she told me. "He had me call Molly...Molly somebody, she's a niece, I guess. She can't come either, but she's making the arrangements for the service and burial. I told her I was sure you'd be by. She said if you wanted his personal things, that would be fine."

I nodded. "Okay."

We both just stood there. Uncomfortable.

"I really am very sorry," Anje repeated.

"Thanks," I said. "Could I have a moment alone?"

"Sure," she said, very willing, even anxious, to leave me with my grief. "Take your time."

I gave her a brave little smile that was totally forced.

She shut the door behind her. Tears clogged my throat. My knees were shaky. I sank into Chester's recliner and the silence of his room. The scent of him still clung to the furniture. I ran my hand along the arm of the chair where I'd seen his own fingers so often lay idle.

Chester was dead. I had no trouble accepting that. I had loved him and now he was gone. The pain and emptiness in my heart couldn't be caused by anything less. But what was impossible for me to grasp at that moment was the truth, staring at me so starkly. I had not known Chester at all.

I began to dissect the past in a new light. Stories and events in retrospect took on meaning that would have been so obvious to me if I'd been searching for clues. I remembered once more the strength of his grip as he'd pulled me out of my car. I had allowed that image of my rescuer to blind me to everything I had heard and seen thereafter. It was as if I had defined Chester by my own need for him and never allowed myself to see him as he really was.

I stifled a moan and bit back tears.

I had been in this very place once before. Not this room, not this time, but this very place in the depth of the soul. This regretful, sorrowful abyss of unwanted solitude.

Vividly I was reminded of the last time I'd faced the death of someone I'd loved. I hadn't known Mama either. I hadn't known she was sick. I hadn't known what she'd gone through. There was nothing about her needs or desires or fears that I was privy to. All I knew of her was her life as my mother. I had been a very greedy, selfish, uninterested young woman. The price I'd paid for that was never knowing my mother at all.

But my relationship with Chester was different. We had things in common. We'd understood each other. He knew I was trying to be a better person. He tried to help me. Why would he have kept the truth from me? Not because I wouldn't have listened or wouldn't have cared. He knew that I would. Why had he been unwilling to share what was happening in his life?

Almost like a vision, I recalled the sight of his face tilted away from me, uneasily, hiding something he didn't want me to see. The sound of his voice came as clearly as if he were speaking once more that phrase I'd heard so many times.

*I'll save this for later, when I can really enjoy it.*

"Oh no!" I said aloud, and got to my feet.

I walked to the little chest beside the bed where Chester always hid the gifts I brought him. I opened the drawer and looked inside. The huge pile of green- and red-candy wrappers was right on top. He'd made no attempt to hide what he'd done. He knew I would find them. At last, he'd wanted me to know.

The scent of sweet chocolate filled the air. He had saved every Snickers bar and enjoyed them all that one last night.

# 22

$A$s I stood shaking hands on the front porch of my house, the hot sun of an August afternoon wilted me. The man beside me, Edmund Crowley, executive director of Friends Resource, didn't seem to even notice the heat. He was as excited as a kid at Christmas.

"It's a great opportunity for us," he said. "It's a great opportunity for our clients. And I have every reason to believe that it will be a financially prosperous venture for you as well, Ms. Domschke."

"Yes, I think so," I told him.

The sound of an approaching automobile caught our attention and we both turned to see an aging Toyota sedan pull into the driveway. Shanekwa was behind the wheel.

As she got out of the car, she was grinning broadly.

"We couldn't miss the opening," she called out.

Mario, the huge bouncer-looking assistant chef at Le Parapluie, emerged from the passenger side of the vehicle.

"And what's a welcome celebration without something to eat," he added.

"You didn't have to do that," I said, surprised and delighted.

"Frederic bought all the food," he said. "Shanekwa and I just donated our labor."

"That was very kind," I said. "And terrific of you two."

He glanced over at Shanekwa, who was retrieving a sandwich tray from the back seat.

"I'll get that, honey," Mario told her. "Go on inside to the air-conditioning."

"I'll carry this one," she told him. "But I'll leave the rest to you."

"I can help," Mr. Crowley volunteered and headed to the car.

"How's your love life?" I asked Shanekwa as we greeted each other with a kiss on the cheek.

The young woman blushed.

"Oh, I guess about like yours," she answered, a teasing glint in her eyes.

"Glad to hear it," I told her. "He seems like a good guy."

Shanekwa nodded. "Just when I'd been thinking there weren't any left."

Mario brushed past us, his arms loaded down. "Are you leaving, Jane?"

"Yeah, I need to get back to the store."

Shanekwa gave me a look indicating she didn't quite believe me. I let Mr. Crowley get by us and safely into the house before I explained myself.

"When I'm around, Mr. Crowley focuses totally on me," I told her. "I want today to be completely about the kids, I mean the *clients*."

She nodded slowly, giving me an admiring look. "How is it that you always seem to know the good thing to do?" she asked me.

Her words elicited a big laugh.

"I only wish I did, Shanekwa," I said. "Most of the time I'm as clueless as everybody else."

From the kitchen, Mario called out, "Honey, get in here with those sandwiches before you all melt."

I winked at her. "See you soon," I promised.

She went inside and I headed toward my car. I

opened the driver's-side door and slid inside. The interior of the Beetle was hot enough to roast a pig. I opened the sunroof, to let the worst of the heat out, and turned on the air-conditioning, optimistic that it might be almost comfortable by the time I reached my destination.

I had just backed into the street when a white Lexus SUV which I immediately recognized as Mikki's pulled up in front of me. For a moment I was puzzled. I couldn't imagine what David's new wife might be doing here. Then as I glanced at the woman behind the wheel, my curiosity dissolved into full-tilt thrilled!

I shut off my engine so quickly the little Volkswagen jumped at the clutch. A second later I was out of the door.

"Brynn! You're home," I said, hurrying to her side.

My daughter hugged me with surprising enthusiasm.

"Hi, Mom," she said. "You look great."

She was looking very chic and very grown-up, herself. So I returned the compliment.

"When did you get back?" I asked. "Why didn't you call me?"

"I flew in yesterday," she answered. "And I tried to call. They said our number here has been disconnected. Did you, like, forget to pay the bill? And I've left a half-dozen voice mails on your cell phone."

I was immediately contrite. "Oh, I'm sorry. The mobile is probably at the store somewhere. I can't remember to keep it charged up, so I never bother to carry it."

She nodded as if she understood. But she was looking at me as if she clearly did not.

"How was Italy?" I asked, changing the subject.

"Incredible," she said, her expression youthfully rapturous. "You should go, Mom. Europe changes your whole perspective."

"Really?"

"You see all the stuff that really seems to matter. Your clothes, your clique, even your parents' cash, it's just more smack. It's meaningless," she said.

"Meaningless?"

"Yeah, or maybe that *is* the meaning," she said. "It's so like existential, you know."

I wasn't sure that I did. But I liked the sound of what she was saying.

"The kids I met, we would sit in the piazzas half the night, all of us students, from all over the world," she said. "We'd drink espresso and talk philosophy."

"Well, that certainly sounds...ah...fun," I said.

"We were foreigners, all just foreigners," she explained. "There's tremendous equality in that. Losing the boundaries of culture and class. It's just so freeing."

She looked up at me, smiling. I got a flashback of the bright inquisitive child who had somehow disappeared into my daughter's adolescence.

"It was the first time in my life," she continued, "that I felt like I was more than just your daughter. I was me, Brynn Lofton, citizen of Planet Earth."

"So you had a good time?"

"Yeah, I had a great time," she admitted. "But I've ruled out art history as a major. I like it, but I wouldn't want to make it my life's work."

"Art history?" I said. "I didn't know you were even thinking about that."

"I went to Italy with my art studies class," Brynn admitted. "The stuff about Dr. Reiser, that was just talk-smack. It sounded so ripe! I'm sorry if it worried you."

She said that with the nonchalance of a someone who has never lived through the torture of worrying about another person. I forgave her that and let it go. Life has a way of teaching those lessons all on its own.

"Brynn," I said carefully, "nothing you do as a person, no choice that you make, no matter how much I might disagree with it, could ever devalue who you are in my eyes or cause me to love you less."

She stared at me with a creased forehead, allowing my words to sink in.

"Sure, Mom," she said as easily as if the fact had never been in doubt.

Somehow that made me feel exhilarated.

"So what's going on with you?" she asked me. "Dad says you've, like, got a boyfriend and that's why you're never at home."

"I do have a gentleman friend," I admitted. "Actually, I've moved in with him."

Her mouth dropped open. "Mom, that is so *not* you," she insisted.

"It's me now," I said.

"It's not that old guy?" Brynn asked. "You're not living with that man from the nursing home?"

My heart momentarily caught in my throat.

"Chester? No, it's not Chester," I said. "He passed away while you were in Italy."

Her teasing grin immediately disappeared.

"Oh gee, Mom, I'm sorry," she said. "I know he was a special friend to you." She hesitated, not sure exactly what to say. "He was, like, really old, right?"

I took a breath and managed a half smile. "Yes, he was old," I said.

At that moment a green minibus with Friends Resource painted on the side pulled up in front of the house. I waved to the familiar faces inside the vehicle as it turned into the driveway.

"They're coming here?" Brynn asked.

I nodded.

The door to the bus opened and a young man with Down's syndrome stepped out excitedly. He was pulling along with him a wide-eyed and giggling young woman who appeared handicapped as well. Within the next couple of minutes a half-dozen other mentally challenged adults emerged. They had different reactions. One woman appeared timid, almost fearful. Another jumped up and down, full of exuberant energy shouting, "We're home! We're home!" The rest were somewhere in between.

Four men, four women, the driver of the bus and a Friends Resource staff member were all greeted at the door by Edmund Crowley, Mario and Shanekwa.

"What is going on here, Mother?" Brynn asked. "Is this your latest do-gooding charity project? Afternoon tea with the handicapped?"

"No," I told her. "This is a business venture. These people are my new tenants."

"What?" Brynn's expression was horrified.

"I was trying to figure out a way to make money on the house without selling it," I explained. "Then I read about what a shortage there is of group homes for mentally challenged adults. These people have supervision, steady employment and a genuine desire to be a part of the neighborhood. The opportunities to live on their own are so few, that a well-managed group home is likely to have occupancy at one hundred percent for the next twenty years or more."

"So you're renting our home to make money," she said.

"I'm leasing a house that I got in my divorce settlement to a non-profit foundation that provides group home facilities to mentally challenged clients," I said.

My daughter's strange expression gave me pause.

"Oh, Brynn," I said. "I didn't think. Did you love this house? I should have asked. Do you feel like I jerked your home out from under you?"

She looked as if that was exactly how she felt. But she waved my words away.

"No, it's okay, Mom," she said. "It's really okay. If we're not going to live here, then it's silly to keep this house empty. You did the right thing."

Brynn was so vulnerable and yet she was so brave. Her parents' marriage had disappeared while she wasn't looking and now her home, the symbol of family life, had been swept away without a thought for her feelings.

"You're a very good daughter, Brynn," I told her. "You're very good to try to understand me."

Our gazes locked for a long moment, then one side of her mouth curved into a wry grin.

"Mom, you are too weird," she said with conviction.

"Believe me, you are not the only person who thinks so," I admitted, laughing. "Would you like to go get some lunch?"

"Only if it includes a frozen margarita," she answered.

"I think we can manage that," I told her.

"That's the only bad thing about Italy," Brynn told me. "No Mexican food."

"Have you got your phone? I'd like to call Scott and get him to meet us there."

"He's, like, your boyfriend, right?"

"Yes," I answered simply.

Brynn considered that for a moment.

"Okay," she said finally. "It'll give me a chance to check the guy out. See if he's really like a total waste or whatever."

"Yeah," I said. "Whatever."

"Let's take your car," she said.

I was surprised and it must have showed.

"Mikki's mega-transport is way lofty," she said. "But yeek of the universe, Mom, it has a car seat in the back. That's a natural guy repellent."

"Little Worth has to sit somewhere," I told her.

"You mean Lofton IV," she said. "That's what I call him."

"Sounds more like a space mission than a baby," I pointed out.

"Yeah, well, let's take this Beetle-thing; it's like…sort of cool."

She was right. It was sort of cool. We were in agreement on that.


Dear Chester,

Today is the two-year anniversary of my car accident on the interstate. I know I thanked you at the time, but I never actually expressed my gratitude in writing, and Buddy Feinstein thought that doing so now might bring some kind of closure.

I remember you with lots of love, a blossoming understanding and moments of regret. I wonder if things might have turned out differently if I had never befriended you at all? I've thought about that—I've thought about it a lot.

If I'd taken my chance at a new life, with the same selfish entitlement that was so typical of me, then you might never have been given the means to end your own life. Today you might still be lying in that bed in Bluebonnet Assisted Living. Growing weaker and maybe blind, but you could be breathing and talking and living among us here—if I hadn't become your friend.

Would that have actually been a good thing?

It wouldn't have been for me. Without you as my mentor and confidant, I would never have been able to keep my promise to do good. And working to fulfill that vow has changed everything in my life.

Just exactly as it was meant to.

Brynn and I have found some peace together, though I'm not taking it for granted. The road to mother/

daughter understanding is a long one and we're working on a couple of generations of bad track record.

Scott and I continue to grow closer. The "M" word has yet to be spoken, but it would be a natural progression from where we are right now. Though it will surely mean change. I'm not afraid of the future—perhaps because I'm too busy living in the present.

My journal entries went into the trash a long time ago. I don't give myself point scores for deeds anymore. I found that over time I was having to subtract almost as often as I was adding. The math just got too much for me and I gave it up.

I am convinced that there is justification for all things and the logic to the universe is benevolent rather than benign. Whether that is God or just the result of God, I have no idea. All I know for certain is that when I prayed for help, you were sent to my rescue. I am alive and that is not happenstance or inconsequential. My life has purpose and meaning beyond my intentions. The full scope of that, I can never fully know.

I suppose that is about all I have to tell you. Though I think I could talk with you for hours if you were here. Say "hi" to my mother if you see her, and tell her that I am doing good.

Jan

# Ask Anyone

## Sherryl Woods

**Something new is developing in Trinity Harbor...**

Jenna Pennington is a desperate woman...and she will do anything to catch the attention of Bobby Spencer. Bobby is the owner of the riverfront property in Trinity Harbor, and Jenna knows she's the perfect person for the job to redevelop it. She just has to convince Bobby.

The last thing Bobby wants in his life is a sexy, single mom who's driven to succeed. The last thing Jenna needs is another emotional roller-coaster ride. But in Trinity Harbor, love has a way of defying expectations.

**"Sherryl Woods gives her characters depth, intensity and the right amount of humor."**
**—*Romantic Times***

On sale mid-March 2002 wherever paperbacks are sold!

MIRA

MSHW90

NEW YORK TIMES BESTSELLING AUTHOR

# SANDRA BROWN

## HONOR BOUND

Aislinn Andrews didn't know if escaped convict Lucas Greywolf
was a troublemaker who aroused dissidence among Arizona's
Native Americans...or a hero who'd gone to prison for a crime he
didn't really commit. It didn't really matter now, since he'd taken
her hostage. Lucas was going home to the reservation of his birth,
honor-bound to pay his last respects to his dying grandfather. And
Aislinn was his ticket home....

In this classic romance, Sandra Brown explores the myriad emotions
that drive men and women to cross the boundaries of fear,
uncertainty, even hate, to explore the uncharted territory of love.

**"A tour de force reading experience...
explosive, fast-paced and sensational."**
**—Romantic Times**

Available the first week of March 2002
wherever paperbacks are sold!

MIRA®

MSB890